SURRENDER

She didn't want this, she didn't. But his mouth worked magic. How could the cold, controlled duke taste so sweet? How could his lips brush such a gentle feeling into hers? And his tongue was the best kind of temptation, a fleeting glimpse of heaven that retreated just when she wanted more. Emma followed that hot pleasure and felt his hands grasp her shoulders. He eased her an inch away.

"Completely inappropriate . . ." He tasted her bottom lip, then her top one, and rewarded her sigh with a much deeper kiss than the first. This kiss pushed aside tender thoughts, and Emma felt pulled down, sinking into heat. *My first kiss,* she thought, which was ridiculous. She'd been kissed before, and not just once. But this . . . this was *intimacy.* An introduction to that other world. The world she'd watched and wondered about, the world of pleasure and secrets and wickedness.

"You . . ." Somerhart whispered. He kissed the corner of her mouth, her jaw. "It's you. Driving me mad." His teeth nipped the edge of her jaw before he tasted his way to the skin beneath her ear. He opened his lips over that spot and Emma shivered . . .

Books by Victoria Dahl

TO TEMPT A SCOTSMAN

A RAKE'S GUIDE TO PLEASURE

Published by Kensington Publishing Corporation

A Rake's Guide To Pleasure

VICTORIA DAHL

ZEBRA BOOKS
Kensington Publishing Corp.

www.kensingtonbooks.com

ZEBRA BOOKS are published by

Kensington Publishing Corp.
850 Third Avenue
New York, NY 10022

All Kensington titles, imprints, and distributed lines are available at special quantity discounts for bulk purchases for sales
promotion, premiums, fund-raising, educational, or institu-
tional use.

Special book excerpts or customized printings can also be created to fit specific needs. For details, write or phone the office
of the Kensington Special Sales Manager: Attn. Special Sales
Department. Kensington Publishing Corp., 850 Third Avenue,
New York, NY 10022. Phone: 1-800-221-2647.

Zebra and the Z logo Reg. U.S. Pat. & TM Off.

ISBN-13: 978-1-4201-0016-7
ISBN-10: 1-4201-0016-5

First Printing: August 2008
10 9 8 7 6 5 4 3 2 1

Printed in the United States of America

For my husband, Bill,
who believed in my dreams from the moment we met.
Thank you for being my hero.

Acknowledgments

First, thank you so much to my readers for helping to make this dream come true. The letters I've received mean the world to me.

Thank you to my lovely agent, Amy, for always being supportive, and my wonderful editor, John, for taking a chance on me.

And to my family . . . I could not dream up a more supportive family than the one I have. Thank you to my boys, who hand out bookmarks to surprised customers at the bookstore. (And sometimes try to charge for them!) To my husband, who says that each book is my best ever, and means it. And to my mom, for being so proud.

The romance community is a nurturing one, so I couldn't possibly thank everyone who's contributed to my success, but there are two people I cannot miss. Thank you to Eloisa James for being an inspiration. And thank you to Connie Brockway for being always generous. Also, my continued gratitude to all the writers on all the loops who know so much more than I.

Every writer needs mental support, some of us daily. Thank you, Jennifer, for being my critique partner and my voice of reason.

Chapter 1

December 1844, outside London

The storm had passed only hours before, blanketing the countryside in half a foot of snow. Moonlight and torch flame glittered and sparked off the icy garden, and the sight called to Emma Jensen through the hard cold of the window. Nature had reclaimed the tamed bower, swept in and buried the pathways, softened the stark angle of hedges cut to precise corners. This garden, painstakingly shaped by man, now lay hidden under gentle hills and deep drifts of snow, and Emma wondered how it would feel to be so effortlessly smothered. So still.

Her deep sigh fogged the glass and blanked the stark scene. Straightening, she glanced back to the bright whirl of the ballroom. Boredom had set in, and when she grew bored her mind turned to useless melancholy. Her life was not so bad, after all, or someday wouldn't be.

"Lady Denmore!"

Emma angled her chin, set a smile on her face, and turned toward the half-drunk voice.

"Lady Denmore, your presence is greatly desired in the hall."

"Why, Mr. Jones, whatever for?" Emma forced the words to come light and pretty.

"Matherton and Osbourne have arranged a race and they wish you to start it."

A distraction. Good. Emma smiled more genuinely and took the arm the thin young man offered, leaving behind the cold escape of her daydream.

Giggles and loud voices filled the cavernous front hall of Wembley House. All heads were turned toward the sweeping staircase and the impossible sight at the top. There, perched atop the landing, were Lords Matherton and Osbourne, peers of the Realm, each crouching down to sit on what looked to be huge silver platters. The men, once seated, began to slide gingerly over the Persian runner, easing themselves closer to the edge of the top stair.

"This is a race?" Emma laughed, but she didn't let her amusement distract from a quick study of the men. "Fifty pounds on Osbourne."

The noise around her paused, as if the whole room drew a breath, then exploded in a flurry of betting. Emma took the bottom step with a smile, meaning to climb to the top to start the race, but a loud shout stopped her.

"Ho there! The starter can't bet on the race!"

Emma only shrugged and stepped aside with a flourish of her hand, letting another woman take the starter's position, a woman not so cursed with the need to gamble on the outcome of every contest.

A moment passed, then a handkerchief dropped and the men burst from the landing, gaslight glinting off silver as the trays tilted and shot down the stairs with surprising speed. Emma gasped—everyone gasped—and the crowd parted in the face of imminent danger.

She almost closed her eyes, afraid to see the crash that surely awaited both men, but she did have fifty quid riding on this, so she watched the men fly down, watched as Osbourne's greater weight proved its advantage. She nodded in satisfaction as Osbourne shot past her perch, then grimaced as he crashed with drama, a cacophony of metal and wall and groaning man.

The crowd dispersed almost immediately, back to their drinks and gossip, and Emma wound her way between the guests, working toward Osbourne to see how he'd fared. Matherton, she saw, had already righted himself and stood laughing with his friends.

"Osbourne," she called past a small crowd of attendees, "are you injured?"

"Just my elbow," he wheezed.

"Oh, Lord Osbourne," Emma sighed at the sight of his flushed face. "Tell me you haven't broken it?"

"No, no. Just banged it up a bit."

"Thank God. Lady Osbourne would have my head if I'd encouraged your injuring yourself."

"Mine as well."

"Come, my lord, let's see if there is ice—"

"Henry!"

"Oh, no," the earl breathed.

"Oh, no," Emma echoed. "Well . . . if Lady Osbourne is coming to help, I'll just leave you to her care."

"But—"

"Henry! Have you lost your mind?"

Emma ducked away, not willing to be caught between a tipsy old man and his loving, outraged wife.

Mr. Jones caught her arm and presented her winnings with a grin. Seventy pounds. Not as much as she'd hoped for. Her reputation for good hunches had begun to cut into her profits, as people often bet *with* her instead of *on* the wager. Luckily, the tables still proved profitable.

Tucking the bills into her glove, Emma craned her neck, looking past the soggy smile of Mr. Jones for Matherton. She spotted him moving away, toward the card room, waving

friendly acknowledgments to those he passed. Emma followed, though she was waylaid for a moment by an agitated
Lady Matherton who was sure her Persian carpet must have
been damaged. After much patting of hands and sympathetic
murmurs, Emma edged away from her hostess and moved
swiftly toward the card room.

She couldn't help but smile when she spied the familiar
shock of white hair glowing in the dim light at the end of
the hallway. Lord Matherton would play the wounded party
well. No doubt he planned to accuse her of treachery and betrayal for placing her bet with Osbourne. Perhaps she would
let him win a round of piquet to help heal his wounded pride.

Emma drew a breath, meaning to call out to him, but just
as her lips parted, he stepped aside and revealed the face of
the man he spoke with. Emma froze. Someone plowed into
her back.

"Oh, my dear girl. I'm so sorry."

Emma steadied herself against the wall as the man tried
to help her stand upright. But she didn't take her eyes off the
black-haired stranger just ahead. "No need to apologize, sir.
'Twas my fault, after all."

"Still, I should have been watching."

"No, I'm sorry. I shouldn't have stopped like that." She finally glanced to her collider. "Admiral Hartford, that man
looks familiar—the one with Matherton—but I can't place
him."

"Oh." The admiral's eyes widened, then slid back to her
with a sympathetic smile. "That, my dear, is the Duke of
Somerhart. A committed bachelor, I'm afraid."

"Somerhart," she murmured, feeling the name on her lips.
"Oh, yes, of course. Somerhart. Thank you, Admiral."

Emma spun on her heel and retreated, hurrying back to
the front hall, then around a corner to the ladies' retiring
room. She darted into a corner that had been curtained off
and sat down hard on the padded chair.

A *duke*? She would never have believed it.

Had he seen her? And if he had, would he know her?

"Of course not," Emma breathed. It was ridiculous to think so. She'd only met the man once and that had been . . . what? A decade before? Yes, she'd been nine at the time. He couldn't know her. He'd probably forgotten her that very evening.

Still, the whole of her plan rested on this charade, this lie of being the widow of the tenth Baron Denmore, and if Duke Somerhart did remember her then the game would be up, for she could not have been married to her own great-uncle.

She'd planned on at least another two months before doubts began to surface. There were few fashionable members of society from their county, and none who'd arrive before the Season. She needed just a few more weeks . . .

Emma sat up straight and looked into the wall mirror. No, the duke would not know her. Her brown hair had been dark blond then, and she had certainly filled out in important places. Also, she was not wearing a white nightgown and braids. She was unrecognizable.

He, on the other hand, had been etched into her mind the first moment she'd seen him, stepping from his shadowed space on the wall.

"Hello, pet," he'd called, as she snuck down the wide hallway, trying desperately to get a peek at one of her father's strange new parties.

By God, he'd scared the devil out of her, his voice like a ghost's, floating from the dark. Then he'd come into the light and Emma had gasped.

"What are you about so late?" he asked, voice soft and low. Emma thought he might be an angel. He was far prettier than any of her father's other friends. But did angels wear red waistcoats and smoke cigarillos? "You should be in bed, kitten."

"I . . . I wanted to see the dancing. I can hear the music from my bed."

His eyes, pale sky blue, swept over her, from her braided hair to her bare toes, and his beautiful face turned sad. "This is no place for you. You shouldn't come down to your papa's parties, all right? Best to stay in your room."

"Oh," she breathed, amazed at the kindness of that voice. He was an angel, the most beautiful creature she'd ever seen. Emma eased one foot back, meaning to turn toward the servants' stairs, but his eyes stopped her, blue warmth closing her throat with something hopeful.

She drew a breath. "But . . ." When she leaned forward a little, his mouth quirked up into a smile, but the smile blurred when her eyes pricked with tears. "But someone has come to my room."

"What?" She'd thought him enormously tall, but he drew himself up taller. His pretty mouth hardened and thinned. "What do you mean?"

Emma took that step back. "I don't . . . My, my room. Someone came in last night. While I was sleeping. I don't want to stay there." Her cheeks flushed hot at the burn in his gaze. "He kissed me."

Something hard and terrible stole over his face. Emma cringed and meant to spin around, but his mouth gentled with a twitch and he reached out one hand to curl her fingers into his.

"I'm sorry." He crouched down and offered a small smile. "You are certainly pretty enough to want to kiss, but only a husband should do that, you understand?"

"Yes, sir."

"And no one has hurt you?"

Emma shook her head.

"All right. Is there a lock on your door? Yes? You go back to your room then, and lock the door. Then put a chair under the handle. Do you know what I mean?"

A nod this time.

"Do that whenever your papa has a party. And do not try to spy again, pet, all right?"

"Yes." And she had fled. And though she hadn't ceased her spying, she'd nursed an infatuation for that nameless man for nigh on four years. Then she'd forgotten him. Until now.

A duke. A rather notorious duke at that. Not known for his kindness. And still the handsomest man she'd ever seen.

Well, there was no choice; she could not accomplish her goal by sneaking nervously about for the next few weeks. If her plans were in danger, she needed to know now. So Emma forced herself to her feet and went to meet her old protector.

"Ah, the traitorous Lady Denmore!" Lord Matherton boomed, eliciting a husky laugh from a woman somewhere behind Hart's back.

Hart turned toward her and let his eyebrows rise in surprise as he looked her over. It wasn't often one met new women at a ton gathering, and certainly not lovely young matrons.

"I can't think what you mean, sir," she laughed, her hazel eyes sparkling. She glanced at Hart, then away just as quickly.

"How could you do it, Lady Denmore? Put money on another man?"

She reached a gloved hand out and touched Matherton's sleeve. "I am deeply wounded, my lord. Surely you can see that I had complete confidence in you. I thought only to salvage Osbourne's pride, fully expecting you to trounce him."

Matherton snorted. "You, madam, would do the country a great service if you were to offer yourself as a diplomat.

Words flow so prettily from your mouth that it matters not in the least if they are true."

She laughed again, and Hart took in the sound with pleasure. What a bedroom voice she had, soft and rich. It didn't quite match the rest of her. She was pretty in a mild way, certainly not exotic.

"Lady Denmore, may I present the Duke of Somerhart? Your Grace, this lovely woman is Baroness Denmore."

He watched her curtsy, her dark lilac skirts crumpling a bit. Those hazel eyes crinkled in a smile as he took her hand.

"Lady Denmore. A pleasure. And no 'Your Graces' if you please. Just Somerhart."

"You do not employ your title, sir?" she teased.

"Oh, I make full use of it. To the extent that I command how others may address me."

"Ah. A man heady with his own power."

Hart smiled, watched her full lips curve in answer, and wondered quickly if her husband were in attendance. If not . . .

"Madam," Matherton interrupted, eyes darting toward the open doorway to his left. "I believe my table awaits me. May I leave you in Somerhart's care?"

"Certainly. I will, however, be in to take your money soon."

Hart smiled at Matherton's sigh, happy to be left alone with this appealing woman. "Shall I escort you to your husband?" he drawled.

"Ah. I am a widow, Somerhart. The *Dowager* Baroness Denmore."

Hart blinked, surprised by both the information and his faux pas. "My apologies." This girl was a *widow*? She looked no older than his baby sister. "And my condolences for your loss." His mind began to tick through the history of the Denmore line.

Baron Denmore. He had known the ninth Baron Denmore, that lecherous, perverted drunk, but he'd died years ago. Hart had no idea who'd inherited the title. No one of his circle, certainly. A servant passed, and he plucked two glasses of champagne from the tray.

"Have you been in London long?"

Her pink mouth smiled at the glass he urged into her hand. "No. Not long."

"And will you be staying with us through the Season?"

She glanced up at the word "us," a flash of surprise lighting her eyes. She recognized his flirtation. Good. He did not like obvious women. He was a man of subtle tastes and subtle actions, or he was now at any rate.

"For a little while, certainly," she murmured before raising the glass to her lips.

Hart's eyes widened as he watched her, this modest young woman, drain a full glass of champagne and pop it back into his hand.

"Thank you. A pleasure."

And then she spun away and disappeared into the card room, leaving behind the faint scent of citrus and one startled duke.

Chapter 2

Crystals glinted in her hair, caught by the flickering gaslight as she glanced at her cards. Hart glanced too. "Split," she murmured, and placed another bet.

She was good at the game, Vingt-et-un, had been winning steadily since she'd sat down a quarter hour before, but she seemed distracted now . . . bored, glancing toward the players at the loo table even as she played her hand.

"What do you know about this Lady Denmore?" Hart asked of the man next to him.

Lord Marsh chuckled. "Ah, she's a tempting bit, isn't she? Married to an old man for a year and now she's free to pursue more interesting interests."

"An old man?"

"Yes, Baron Denmore must have been seventy at least, a recluse, and she no more than nineteen when they married. She'd never even been presented."

Hart's mind turned over the possibilities. "And who introduced her to London?"

"Ha! No one. She arrived in *October,* of all times, and still in mourning. The Mathertons were practically the only people left in town. And the Osbournes, of course. She's rather become their pet."

Hart watched her collect her winnings and rise. She made her way immediately to the loo table, inviting several of the men already playing to wince.

"She's an accomplished player, I gather?"

"Mm. That coward Brasher is already fleeing the table. See the men tremble at her feet."

Hart allowed himself a small smile. The men were, indeed, unhappy to see her. Lady Denmore, on the other hand, was all gracious good humor. "She seems a woman who enjoys taking risks."

"Indeed." Marsh grinned. "And I am hoping that will translate to other habits as well. Did you get a good look at that mouth?"

Hart pressed his lips together. He knew his own reputation with women, but it was just as well known that he preferred privacy above all else. He disdained to speak of women like whores on the bartering block, just as he expected not to be evaluated like a stallion on parade.

"Well, old man," Marsh continued, oblivious to Hart's anger, "I do believe I'll join the play. Perhaps I can divest her of her coin and move on to other trade."

Lord Marsh approached the table, and when Lady Denmore looked up, her eyes slid to meet Hart's. They widened as if the sight of him surprised her. Odd, considering he'd followed her into the room. She blinked, a strange flutter of her lashes, and turned away from him to glare at the cards she'd been dealt.

She reacted to him almost as if she knew him. Perhaps it was only his reputation that made her so nervous. She was a country miss, after all, despite that her voice gave one visions of tumbled sheets and sweat-damp hair.

A seventy-year-old husband. Hart shook his head and pushed away from the bookcase he'd leaned against. She stiffened when he passed her table on his way to the door, her awareness of him tempting him to stop and stand over her shoulder . . . but he walked on.

She was a bit young for him, perhaps. But he preferred widows, after all, and he was presently unattached. Still, well-bred, proper innocents rarely offered up much excitement in bed, unless one counted declarations of love as exciting. Hart did not. Not that he'd had much experience with innocents, but one did hear things.

He moved at a quick pace toward the ballroom, ignoring the dozens of people who tried to catch his eye as he passed. Being a duke was very much like being a prized stud, and as an eligible duke . . . He suppressed a cringe of disgust even as he spied his quarry at the edge of the dancing.

"Osbourne," he started, planting himself next to the old gentleman.

"Ah, Somerhart! On your way into town?"

"Yes. Lady Matherton was kind enough to offer a room so I wouldn't have to fight this damned snow."

"Well, thank God none of the new crop has arrived. If it were April you'd be awash in eager mamas."

"As you say. By the way, I made the acquaintance of your friend, Lady Denmore."

"Ah, where is Emma? In the card room, I suppose?"

Emma. "Yes. The men cower in fear."

"As they should. By God, she's livened things up for us this winter. Taught me a thing or two about whist, I can assure you. Do you play brag? Do not go betting your estate on a game with her. She will divest you of more than your pride."

Hart smiled at the man's hearty laughter. "I was not acquainted with her late husband, Denmore."

"I wasn't acquainted with Denmore either! When I knew him he was plain old Mr. Jensen. He never expected to inherit the title, you know. We ran about town together long ago. I hadn't seen him in . . ." Osbourne shrugged. "Must have been fifteen years now."

"Really? So you had never met Lady Denmore?"

"No, no. Denmore had become garden-mad in his old age. He had no time for hunting or balls. He had ceased to even write letters." Osbourne's bushy eyebrows lowered. "I cannot imagine his interest in a young girl like Emma, but duty comes along with the title, I suppose. Still, they must have got on well. She knew all the old stories about me—some I wish she hadn't, I can tell you that." His chuckle turned to a sigh. "She speaks of him with great affection."

"Of course."

Something of his doubt must have cooled Hart's voice, because Osbourne turned to glare at him. "I daresay she knew him even better than I, and she'd only spent a year or so in his house. She's a fine woman and she was clearly a fine wife. A bit wild for games of chance, but that's the extent of it. A good girl."

"I didn't mean to imply otherwise. She seems quite lovely."

"Hmph."

"How is your arm?"

"Damned thing aches like the devil, but I can't let on. Lady Osbourne is not pleased."

"Well, you seem to be good at charming her out of these piques."

Osbourne flashed a reprobate's smile. "That I am, young man. That I am."

Emma left the table abruptly, startling the other players. She still had twenty pounds in the pot, after all. But better twenty than two hundred. Her thoughts would not bend to her demands and kept careening away from the game to a certain black-haired gentleman.

Glancing about the hallway to be sure he'd gone, Emma hurried toward the music room. She hadn't been prepared for him, not up close. She knew now why she'd thought him an angel that night. He was beauty and power and mystery. Those ice-blue eyes framed by black lashes. That lush mouth and careful control. And he was tall, just as she'd remembered, tall and impossibly elegant.

He hadn't remembered her, and she should have felt relieved, not nervous. But he'd flirted with her. And she'd flirted back.

Unwise and reckless as ever. She thought she'd learned her lesson.

The music room was crowded with women, and Emma had to weave her way through the door. But the suffocating heat proved bearable when she heard the name she'd hoped to hear.

Somerhart. She felt an urgent need to know something about this man and, as luck would have it, the whole party seemed abuzz with excitement at the duke's appearance.

Emma had heard things about the famous duke. Winterhart, they called him. Or Hartless. But she'd never paid attention, not realizing she knew him. And now . . . now the things she heard were like a veil of sadness over the fantasy she'd once created.

Oh, she had woven quite a hero out of their brief meeting. Yes, he had been at her father's house, a place well known for its unsavory assemblies, but he had left after their encounter. Emma had hounded the housekeeper for information and learned little—just that a man had left Denmore that very night after having words with her father. So she had excused his presence there. He'd likely had no idea what kind of party it was and, upon learning, had confronted her father. Perhaps he'd even threatened violence before leaving in outraged shock.

It hadn't seemed a fantasy at all when she'd imagined it

ten years before. It had seemed definite. The actual scenario. He might have even thought of coming back to check on her, to save her from her life.

But . . . no. No, of course not. The man was pretty, but he was no angel and never had been. The easy gossip confirmed that. Emma plucked bits of it like low-hanging fruit as she strolled through the crowd. *Cold. Cruel. Ruthless.*

And lower voices whispered other words, tales of his past that did not match his present. Decadent and wicked. Shameless and insatiable.

He was no pillar of morality, no upstanding gentleman. It seemed he had attended many scandalous gatherings like that in his youth, though he was more circumspect now. Quieter about his pleasures, but still in pursuit of them. He was a reprobate, just like her father, so why had he bothered with defending a little girl?

"He must be *sans* lover," Emma heard Lady Sherbourne whisper to a friend. "He only ever makes an appearance to troll for a new bedmate." The woman spoke derisively, not noticing the way the other lady perked up at the words. "No doubt that Caroline White displeased him with her indiscreet prattle. You know why he despises indiscretion, of course."

The other woman nodded thoughtfully, then turned keen eyes on Lady Sherbourne. "Did you ever actually see the letters?"

Emma leaned closer to hear the friend's reply. Her efforts failed. She caught only the word "shameful."

Was he looking for a woman to warm his ducal bed? He had flirted with her, watched her. Emma felt a swarm of sparks float up from her belly, heating her chest and setting off a buzzing in her head.

The thought of his bed excited her, though she tried to feel nothing but disgust. She hated the burst of anticipation she suffered at the thought of danger, of risk. Her father's blood, she knew. And if she indulged it, she'd no doubt follow in his path—always compelled to search out that next adventure, that next conquest, till her soul suffocated beneath a sticky film of debauchery.

She would not accept her father's inheritance. She would not be a whore to pleasure.

Jaw set, she worked her way back through the crowd and toward the card room, ignoring more talk of Somerhart and titters about some scandalous sister of his.

She could not afford to become distracted. She had only weeks to finish her work and leave town. Right now she was risking little. The Osbournes had accepted her with unexpected warmth; their approval went a long way toward paving her way through society. But soon the ton would begin their slow return to town.

Someone from Cheshire would spy her. Someone in town would ask the right questions. And her game would be done.

Instead of walking toward the card room, Emma found herself standing again at the window that overlooked the garden. She stared out at the calmness of the frozen yard and told herself to be glad that Somerhart had not recognized her, thankful that he was nobody's angel.

Her deception could continue until the start of the Season. Then she could retreat with her winnings and never set foot in this impolite world of polite society again.

And if the Duke of Somerhart was a heartless bastard just like her father, Emma was better off. She had only one dream left, one fantasy, and it had nothing to do with a man coming to her rescue.

Hart strolled toward the breakfast room with unusual anticipation. He did not particularly enjoy dining with crowds. In fact, he always took his morning meal in his room at these gatherings, but he found himself eager to search out one of his fellow guests. He had small chance of catching her though; she'd turned in at midnight, for God's sake, before supper had even been served. It was late morning now, nearly eleven, and surely she'd been up for hours.

He spared a quick glance for a tall bank of windows to his left. Sunlight streamed through, belying the ice that frosted the panes. He'd seen her there, last night, fingertips pressed to the glass like a yearning. The tableau had captured him, intrigued him, and Hart had watched instead of approaching. And when Lady Denmore had turned back to the party, when she'd swept past the group of people that hid him from her view, he hadn't reached out to stop her. Her eyes had stilled him, startling in their distance. He doubted she would have seen him if he'd stepped into her path.

She had floated up those stairs and not shown her face again. Perhaps she had only been drunk. Perhaps she hadn't been lonely and lost.

Hart shook his head at the memory. Fanciful nonsense. The scent of coffee invaded his thoughts and led him to the breakfast room, to a table populated by people he'd spoken meaningless words to for years. Men who admired or envied his title. Women who sneered at or were aroused by his reputation. Prigs who would scorn his scandalous sister if she sat down among them. Strangers, acquaintances, false friends. And not an Emma among them.

"The snow's melting," a whiskered gentleman offered as Hart took a seat next to him.

"Admiral Hartford," he answered.

"The roads'll be muddy as all hell today. Are you shoving off?"

Shrugging, Hart considered. London was a mere half hour's ride away—perhaps an hour or two in this muck. Still, an easy escape from this unwanted company. Odd that he hadn't vaulted out the door at first light.

"The wife'll kick herself for not coming. My little Lizbeth is coming out this year, you know. Don't suppose you're finally looking for a bride?" The admiral nodded at Hart's flat look. "So I thought. Well, no harm trying."

"I suppose not. But I doubt I'd make an ideal husband for your little Lizbeth, Admiral."

The man nodded in answer, but his guilty squint made clear that a duke could be any kind of husband he wanted and still make a young woman's family happy. The girl herself . . . not a concern.

Hart drained his coffee, glanced at his untouched plate, and pushed away from the table with a "Good morning," to the assembled guests as he fled.

He should go. Leave for the blessed solitude of the Somerhart town house and be done with this foolish interest in a girl too young to be his kind of widow. The decision crystallized in his mind, prompting a quick turn toward the stairs. He'd leave; have his valet repack, and they'd be gone within the hour. Better yet, he'd borrow a horse from Matherton and the carriage could follow through the mud as best it could.

A raucous burst of laughter leaked through a back window and halted Hart on the third step. He frowned, narrowing his eyes at the alcove that had framed Lady Denmore last night. Laughter again, and shouts. Young bucks, no doubt, and no interest to him. But it sounded as if a crowd had gathered outside. And he'd yet to spot Lady Denmore. Refusing to think why it mattered, Hart spun and stalked to the window, to angle his head so close that the cold flowed down from the glass to cool his skin.

The sun blinded him, sparkling off the melting brilliance of snow and ice. A moment passed before shadows began to coalesce, then solidify. He spotted the source of the laughter just as another round of shouted glee erupted from the group.

Several women stood among the young men. Hart squinted, leaning closer to the glass, feeling more than foolish as he pressed his forehead to the shock of icy cold. The three women

were bundled against the wind, hidden beneath layers of wool
and fur. Still, one was obviously too short and he caught a
glimpse of pale blond hair peeking from beneath another's blue
cloak. But the third . . . ? It could be her.

The whole group stood angled away from him, facing a
large pond at the edge of the soggy gardens. Across the
frozen length, a smaller group had gathered, the men nudging one another, occasionally stepping forward to test the ice
with taps and stomps.

Even as Hart watched, that third woman turned her head
to laugh and roll her eyes and Hart straightened with a start.
It *was* Lady Denmore, her face bright against the hood of a
simple black cloak.

"Hm." Hart pulled a watch from his pocket and measured
his plan for escape against the impulse to say a pretty
farewell to Emma. She'd thrown off her hood by the time he
looked back to her, and the sun set her hair shining like an
autumn leaf.

A quick farewell then . . . if he could catch her. She'd already set off for the far side of the pond. The men on the
other side looked pleased with her approach. Hart turned
and headed toward the entry, hunting for the footman who'd
taken his coat the evening before.

"Lady Denmore!"

Emma laughed at the severity of the handsome young
man's posture. Mr. Jones nudged him, earning a hot look in
return.

"Mr. Cantry, you really musn't regard me as a matron
come to interrupt your play. I daresay you're my elder by
two or three years, aren't you?"

"Oh, I suppose." His muddy green eyes dipped to sweep
over her, as if he could see beyond the cloak to the blue dress
beneath, and under that even, to her bare skin. His eyes

brightened. "Yes, of course." The smile he offered this time held more than a hint of interest.

"Do you think this pond frozen enough to walk on?"

"I do." Cantry threw a scornful smirk over his shoulder. "These cowards here won't set foot on it."

"Really? It looks quite solid to me."

"But look, Lady Denmore, how dark it is in the center?" Jones insisted.

"Oh, surely only the depth of the water makes it so. Don't you think, Mr. Cantry?"

"I do."

Emma dimpled up at the blond man, tying him to her with a smile. "What do you say we show these men their mistake? A race perhaps?"

"A race?"

She grinned. The last gentleman—older than the others, if she wasn't mistaken—smothered a laugh behind a cough, his eyes sparkling at her, aware of her game. Emma nodded in recognition.

"My brother," Cantry mumbled, "Viscount Lancaster."

"Viscount. An honor."

"My pleasure, madam, I assure you." And it was, she could see by the way his gaze fell to her mouth. Men were such easy creatures.

"Well, let us teach this lord a lesson in assurance, shall we, Mr. Cantry?"

"Indeed," the younger brother growled.

"And a wager to make things interesting? The last to touch the other side of the pond forfeits . . . hmm. Shall we say fifty pounds?"

"Ah . . . Lady Denmore, surely you don't mean I should race against *you*? A lady?"

"Well, your pride is safe, sir, as I issued the challenge. Unless, of course, you fear I'll best you."

Cantry couldn't stifle a laugh at the idea.

"And you'd be doing a good deed by entertaining me."

"True." He was warming to the race. She watched his smile spread to wickedness. "Of course, I couldn't accept your money. But if you were to offer a token instead . . ."

"Ah. A kiss in lieu of fifty pounds?" She cast her eyes down for a moment, trying to look demure. "A kiss. All right. You have a bet, Mr. Cantry. A kiss if you win. Fifty pounds if I do."

Oh, the young man was pleased with his chances, though his brother, clearly the smarter of the two, stood shaking his head at Cantry's gullibility. Jones looked simply dismayed.

"It isn't safe," he protested.

"True," Viscount Lancaster agreed, smile fading.

"Nonsense, gentlemen. I am a country lass, after all, and well acquainted with such dangers. This pond is no more than four feet deep in the middle. Fear not." She picked her way down the sloping bank before they could protest further, and looked up in surprise when a strong hand clasped her elbow. "Thank you, Lord Lancaster. Would you take my cloak?"

"Certainly." He leaned close to untie the knot, speaking softly near her ear. "Perhaps this is not such a grand idea. I hear you enjoy a good wager, but when the ice breaks . . ."

"Pah." Emma let him sweep the cloak from her shoulders and tried not to shiver in the cold. She was saved from his concern by the appearance of his brother, flush-faced and already gloating.

"Lady Denmore, shall I give you a handicap? Say ten feet?"

"Hardly, Mr. Cantry."

Jones was convinced to start the race and they were off. Emma's half boots slid well across the ice, but Cantry's stride gave him the immediate advantage. The large group near the house began booing him, drawing a laugh from Emma despite her breathless pursuit.

Cantry had crossed nearly a third of the pond before he
began to slow. Even fifteen feet behind him, Emma could
hear the ominous groan of the ice. She slid faster.

"Wait," he called, barely moving now, his mouth an O of
alarm when she shot past him. He'd stopped, afraid to go farther. A sharp crack sounded beneath her. Emma slowed, sliding carefully now, edging closer to the bank as she approached
the midpoint of the pond, trying to keep her weight even on
each foot.

Cantry must have shifted or dared to take another step, for
a flurry of small pops crackled through the air. Even she was
startled by it, glancing back to be sure he hadn't plunged
through the ice. But he stood safe—stranded, but safe—and
his eyes widened at her smile.

"Don't go any farther," he called as she turned away and
inched ahead.

"You're far larger than I, Mr. Cantry. I do believe it will
hold my weight."

She'd passed the center of the pond now and relief loosened her limbs, but her next step proved her hope false, for
the ice caved beneath her boot and sucked her leg into freezing water. The force of the fall pitched her forward, her other
knee smashing to the ice with a muffled thud. Shouts floated
to her ears.

A writhing, stretching ache enveloped her foot and calf.
When they grew numb, the pain twisted its way to her knee,
then up to throb mercilessly in her hip. Emma bit back the
curses that flew to her lips and tried to smile toward the
nearest shout. It was Lord Lancaster, standing a dozen feet
away, shoes sunk in the soggy snow that lined the bank.

"Stay there, Lord Lancaster. The ice won't hold you and
if you rescue me you'll forfeit my win."

"Damn the stupid bet," he muttered but didn't approach.
He could not; the pond would never support him.

"I'm fine," she lied and shifted her weight to her gloved hands to try to pull her nerveless leg free.

"*What is going on here?*"

That voice stilled her attempts and whipped her head up in alarm. The Duke of Somerhart approached the pond, his striking face hardened by a frown. Emma glared.

"Bloody hell," she whispered and yanked with all her might. Her leg scraped free, but the sudden pull spilled her to the ice, slapping her face against the slick wet. "Hell, hell, hell."

Ice creaked and shifted beneath her like some beast she'd woken from slumber. She couldn't see Somerhart now, but she heard his vicious curse to her right and assumed he'd joined Lancaster.

"What the hell have you gotten yourself into?" he growled, as if he had some right to scold. Emma's anger gave her the will to rise to her hands and knees.

"Hold still. I'm coming out."

"No!" she shouted, piercing him with a glare, trying to ignore the way her heart lurched at his tall form. "I'll not forfeit my prize."

Somerhart muttered something that widened even Lancaster's eyes.

"I concede the win," Cantry cried from behind her.

The duke stepped onto the ice.

Emma inched forward, moving toward the solid white of firm ice that loomed ahead. A crack and a splash told her that the duke's foot had already breached the surface. She tried not to smirk at his growl.

"I may be a woman, gentlemen, but I do have some sense of honor. I won't concede now when I knew the ice was too thin to hold Mr. Cantry." She'd reached a thicker patch and pushed to her feet, hoping her sparking, tingling leg would hold her. A new pain joined the ache, sharper and more distracting. Emma took a tentative step. Then another. Within two minutes she'd reached the far bank and the gawking crowd that gathered there.

Several hands clapped her on the back in congratulations, though the two young matrons stood apart, mouths flat with disapproval. *Let them disapprove,* Emma told herself. *You are fifty pounds richer.* A sudden hush alerted her to the approach of the other men and gave her time to fix a smile to her mouth.

"Your Grace," she murmured when he loomed into view.

"Are you injured?"

"I am well, thank you."

"Lady Denmore," Lancaster interrupted, "your cloak."

"I wouldn't have expected you to encourage this, Lancaster."

The viscount swept the cloak over her shoulders, offering Emma a hidden grimace at Somerhart's chiding. She held back a nervous giggle when his twinkling brown eyes caught hers. "I wouldn't use the word 'encouraged.' The lady seemed determined."

"Determined," Somerhart growled. "Determined to make a fool of herself for a few quid."

Emma froze, her eyes locking with the duke's when Lancaster moved away. The murmur of the crowd died out as all heads turned toward Somerhart.

Blood rushed to Emma's face, but she forced her mouth into a laughing smile. He blinked and seemed to remember himself, for his face flushed too.

"And where are my winnings, gentlemen?"

Cantry rushed forward to thrust the coins into her hand. "I admire your bravery, madam," he offered with a pretty bow, though his lips were stretched thin with embarrassment.

Emma forced her neck to bend in an easy nod, then turned her shoulders slightly, angling away from Somerhart and his glinting blue eyes. "A fine bit of entertainment and noon has not yet struck. I thank you, Mr. Cantry, for accepting my silly proposal. A pleasure to have met you, Lord Lancaster."

Somerhart stepped close, his fingers wrapping around her elbow. "Let me escort you inside."

Emma gritted her teeth and felt her mask of gaiety slip. She couldn't help the sneer that stiffened her mouth when she looked at his hand, dark against her pale sleeve. His grip loosened in response, fell away. A murmur swept over the group.

"Viscount? I do believe my skirts are somewhat soggy. Will you see me to the hall?"

"I'd be honored," Lancaster drawled and gave her his arm.

Hart watched Lady Denmore walk away from him for the second time in as many days. The first time, of course, her hand hadn't been locked in a cozy clasp around Viscount Lancaster's arm. And Hart hadn't just insulted her in front of a large group of her peers.

"I say, Your Grace, that one's giving you a merry chase."

Setting his jaw, he turned his eyes to the young pup who'd spoken. "Pardon me?"

"Uh . . ." The boy's eyes fell to the snow at Hart's feet. "Nothing, sir."

He let his gaze sweep over the group of staring people, noticing the wide-eyed looks they exchanged, the tittering of the ladies. Wonderful. He'd given them a sensational story to tell over luncheon. And he'd been unconscionably rude to Emma. She hadn't shown a smidgen of hurt in her expression, but her face had burned a dull red, betraying the wound he'd inflicted.

And in playing the villain, he'd thrust Lancaster into the role of rescuer. Lancaster—that charming, golden-haired fortune hunter.

Hart hid his anger behind a cool glance of displeasure for the closest group of bucks. When he crossed his arms and glared, the boys took the hint and sidled away, back toward the house, trailing the rest of the group. The women had disappeared, no doubt eager to spill the details of Lady Denmore's undignified behavior and Somerhart's contempt. Hart simply stood in the cold, watching his breath condense into clouds under the bright sun.

By God, he'd felt an ax strike him over the head when he'd stepped into the gardens and spied Lady Denmore careering across the pond like some gleeful bedlamite. And when she'd fallen, when her face had melted from determination to pain, he'd felt such a sudden bolt of anger that he'd actually stumbled. Why he felt concern for the irresponsible chit, he couldn't imagine.

Giving his head a hard shake, Hart attempted to throw off his roiling thoughts as he swung about to return to the house—and his plans to leave. But his eye caught on something discordant . . . a strange shock of color. He blinked, narrowing his gaze to the trampled snow just a foot away. Four crimson spots flashed in the white. Even as he watched, the red began to fade, spreading to deep pink in the snow.

Blood. He was sure of it. He searched the ground for more evidence and found two more drops on the path Lady Denmore had taken toward the house. The woman had injured herself, likely she'd cut her leg open on that blasted ice. Christ.

Hart stalked to the door and back to the front hall where he spotted Lancaster walking away. Ignoring his spike of irritation, he bounded up the stairs and down the hallway to the guest chambers. A peek into one of the open rooms rewarded him with the startled gasp of a young maid.

"Would you be so kind as to direct me to Lady Denmore's room?"

"Uh . . ." Her eyes blinked rapidly, fluttering with fear. "Two doors down, sir. To the left."

"Please bring hot water and soap to her chambers."

The girl dropped a wobbling curtsy as Hart spun away to stalk down the hall and knock on the door.

"Come in," she called before his hand had fallen away. Hart pushed open the door. "If you—" The words ended on a sharp draw of air and her hands flew to flick her skirts down, but not before Hart spied the gash that ran from mid shin to her knee.

He looked to her red-stained boot and the crumpled ruin of a silk stocking puddled on the floor. "A maid is coming with water and soap."

She ground out, "Why are you here?"

"I saw blood. I wanted to be sure you were all right." Uninvited, Hart closed the door behind him and crossed to kneel by her leg.

She scooted it away from him. "As you can see, I'm fine."

"On the contrary, that looks rather nasty."

"Just a scrape. And your opinion doesn't signify."

He almost laughed at that. He was quite sure no one had ever said those words to him. Excepting his father, of course, but he was long dead. "It looked to be more than a scrape. It may need stitching."

"Unlikely. Please leave."

Hart shifted back a little, startled by the hardness of her words. Her hazel eyes met his in unflinching scorn. "I apologize, Lady Denmore, for my earlier words."

"Fine. Now go."

"I was taken aback when I saw you in danger—"

"I can't imagine what you mean, Your Grace. We do not know each other. And I sincerely have no wish to be chalked up as another of your paramours, so please leave my room."

"I see." Hart stood, the movement quickened by a rush of anger. "I'm sorry I bothered then."

"Sorry you bothered to check on my well-being? Only because I don't wish to be in your bed?"

He blinked, caught by her logic. "No, I—" Her smirk dissolved any awkwardness he might have felt. "Good day, Lady Denmore." The nod she gave was no more than a jerk of her head.

Hart stared down at her, perched so stiffly on the bed, her back straight as a column of iron. He looked to her hands, one clutching the bedspread, the other her skirt. The knuckles of both were livid white, pushing against the skin. And her jaw ticked forward and back, forward and back, shifting the tiniest fraction of an inch against clenched teeth.

Hart felt the shift in his own jaw and sighed. She may very well find him irritating, but the anger she showed had little to do with him and more to do with pain striking through her body. A tap at the door saved them from further sparring.

Opening the door to find the maid bobbing another curtsy, Hart fished a sovereign from his pocket and slipped it to her as he took the ewer of hot water and stack of towels.

"An inconvenience, I'm sure, but could I bother you for something more? We need clean linen and a salve if you've something good at hand."

"Of course, sir," she bubbled, bobbing again as he closed the door.

Lady Denmore glared. "I thought you were going."

He gave her a shrug and knelt at her feet again, like a supplicant to her sharp tongue. Before she could even open her mouth to protest—loudly if the set of her chin was any indication— Hart flipped her skirts up and settled them over her knee. The flat of his hand held them down despite her attempts to dislodge it.

"I believe I made clear that I would not invite you to toss up my skirts."

Hart looked down, away from the slits of her eyes, and grimaced at the bloody mess she'd made of her leg. A fine leg—slender and long.

"I will do that," she growled when he dipped a cloth into the hot water. "Ouch!"

"Sorry. This'll sting a bit."

"A bit!"

Her breath hissed sharply through her teeth when he dabbed at the blood again, drawing another wince from Hart. He nearly gave in to her demand to leave her alone when he saw the bright glint of tears in her eyes, nearly shoved the towel into her hand and fled the room, but he was no coward. Still, he was relieved when she closed those glittering eyes and eased herself back to lie on the bed.

Hart tried not to see the twist of her fists in her skirts as he did his best to manage the twin feats of cleaning the wound and not hurting her. Impossible.

"This will scar, I'm afraid."

She gave a huff that he took to be laughter. "Best to deposit me directly on the shelf then. I'm ruined."

Sassy chit. "You're right. No one will want you like this. You might consider locking yourself away in a tower." He'd cleaned the easiest parts first, and now found himself left with only the rawest area of the scrape. Her chest rose and fell in a quick, steady rhythm. Best to distract her from the next bit. "I seem to find myself surrounded lately by ruined women. I wonder why that is."

"Surely that's not one of the great mysteries of the world." She tensed when the hot towel touched her, but his sacrifice was well rewarded when she pressed on. "You're a rake."

"I disagree." When he dabbed at a particularly nasty spot, she gasped and twisted the yellow velvet of the bedcover. "Sorry."

"How . . . how can you disagree? You're a rogue. A connoisseur of women. And I understand you spent the better part of your youth perfecting your sense of taste."

"Taste, hmm?"

Her head popped up, eyes wide with shock at what she'd

said. "I didn't mean . . . I only meant that you spent a good
many years sampling . . . Ow! Good God, isn't it clean yet?
It's not as if I fell into a pig trough." Her face disappeared
again, though he could still make out the occasional growled
curse.

He finished, finally, and sat back to stare at the fresh
blood oozing from her shin. He hadn't been kidding about
the scar, though she hadn't seemed to care either way.
Strange girl.

"The maid's bringing bandages," he said and heard the
bedcover shush as she nodded. "It should be just a moment."

The pain of the wound must have worsened. She didn't
bother to pursue her assault on his character, she only lay
still and stiff on the bed. A strange awkwardness crept over
his skin as he sat and stared at the bare leg of a woman who
wanted nothing from him. Her pink toes curled into the
carpet, drawing his eye, and he noticed that her leg shook a
little, from pain or cold. He smoothed a hand down her
instep and curled his fingers around her toes. The icy cold
against his skin shocked him.

Not bothering to wonder what she'd think of it, Hart
raised her foot and unbuttoned his waistcoat to settle it
against his stomach. He pressed his palm close to warm
those shell pink toes. When they curled into the linen of his
shirt, awareness prickled down his belly, and her small sigh
affected him like a moan.

"Are you . . . ?" He cleared the unexpected huskiness
from his throat. "Are you being chased by creditors, Lady
Denmore?"

"Not that I know of. Is someone hanging outside my
window?" Her toes curled again. Hart stroked his palm over
the top of her foot and up her ankle, chasing goose flesh
ahead of his touch. There hadn't been goose flesh before.

He shook his head. "You seem in reckless need of a few
pounds. I thought perhaps your late husband left you wanting."

Another wave of chills. "I can't imagine what you mean."

"Really?"

"Not to mention that it's still none of your concern."

Hart smiled, intrigued by her refusal to concede anything to his title and wealth. Her body, however, was conceding something to his touch. He eased his thumb beneath the curve of her arch and worked small circles into her foot. Those pink toes curled obligingly and her knee bent a little, prompting Hart's brain to craft a series of fascinating images. The little widow bending her knee farther, tilting it to the side, so that he could see the soft white flesh of her inner thigh. Then she'd slide her foot across his belly until she could hook her ankle around his waist and tug him closer. His hips would fit perfectly in the cradle of those thighs, the skin so white, never once touched by the sun.

Hart sighed. He had a libertine's soul but the mind of a man yoked with responsibility and pride. If only he were twenty again, and unconcerned with the world and its fascination with his life. And though he had thought Lady Denmore subtle, she was not the least bit subtle. The very opposite of circumspect. She'd already goaded Hart into embarrassing them both.

He gave her foot one last lingering rub, then lowered it to the floor. "I will go check on that maid."

"Thank you," she said, sounding as if she choked on it. She rubbed the sole of her foot against the deep-piled rug before he turned away to yank open the door.

The maid was flying down the hall, hanks of blond hair escaping her cap. "Sorry, milord! I'm sorry. There was a—"

"Wonderful." He plucked the bandages and the little brown crock from her hands. "My thanks."

"Yes, sir," she gasped, and curtsied over and over until Hart closed the door.

He found Lady Denmore pushed up on her elbows, watching

with a smirk. "I do believe you're the queen in disguise. My, my. Such deference."

"You have no respect for your betters, Lady Denmore."

She laughed. Really laughed. That same husky sound he'd heard the night before. "So true," she chuckled. "None at all."

Women never laughed at him. Never. Hart found himself suddenly smiling. "You remind me of my sister."

Her amusement died in a fluttering blink of her eyes. "I'm not surprised."

"What do you mean?" He knelt before her again, and lifted the skirt she'd dropped over her leg. Dark stains of blood marred her petticoats. "You can't have met Alexandra."

"No. But I've heard that . . . she sounds quite . . . unconventional."

"Yes," he said carefully. He dipped a square of linen in the salve and dabbed the pale yellow muck against her leg. "She is that."

He listened for a pained gasp or at least a sigh, but instead, her muscles began to relax. "Oh, that's not too bad at all. Lovely, actually."

"Good."

"I'd imagine your sister has placed a daring wager or two in her life."

"Mmm." Hart picked up the length of linen and began to wrap it around her calf. He let his fingers brush the silk skin at the back of her knee. Impossibly soft. "My sister," he went on, "tends to wager more important things than coin. But that is neither here nor there. I've patched you up as best I can."

She flipped the skirt down before he'd even withdrawn his hands, but her modesty left Hart with the sight of his arms disappearing under her skirts. A far more intriguing image than the reality of her injured leg. He would have let his hands linger, but she kicked him.

"Well then." He stood with a nod. "Was it worth the fifty pounds?"

"Suffering your arrogance? Not really."

He sighed, surprised that his pique was mostly feigned. "Then I'll take pity on you and leave you to exercise that razor wit on an empty room, shall I?"

"Thank you, Your Grace."

Hart wanted to stay, which was ridiculous really, so he spun around and let himself out the door. She was decidedly unpleasant, so why did he find her sharp tongue entertaining? Perhaps the boredom of winter had finally overwhelmed him. Or the undying boredom of having too much. Too much money, too much power, too much say over who came to his bed and when. And far too much time spent alone.

Chapter 3

"Bess!" Emma shut her front door behind her as she heard Matherton's carriage pull away. Her back protested when she crouched down to pop the latch of her traveling chest. She'd stayed up too late the night before, and the long carriage ride from Matherton's Wembley estate had left her spine aching, but she had work to do.

Bess hurried in, wiping her hands on her dingy apron.

"Help me carry these back. I'll be leaving for Moulter's in less than a week. The dye will hardly be dry."

Emma scooped up as many dresses as she could hold. As she turned to move toward the kitchen, Bess held up a midnight blue dress.

"What of this one?"

"Too dark. Anyway, if we dye it one more time it will likely fall apart. If we can't rework it I'll trade it for another."

Bess nodded and followed behind with the rest of the dresses.

"I think if we change the bodice on that gray one, it will do. It's a fairly unnoticeable skirt, and the color is even less memorable."

"Yes, ma'am."

"Do we have more indigo? That turned out nicely."

"Yes, ma'am."

Emma hid a smile against the mound of silk and satin. Bess was hard-working, unassuming, and definitely not chatty. And she didn't care a whit that her employer was an impoverished fraud, she was simply glad to be away from her brute of a husband. She was the perfect housekeeper for a scoundrel.

Emma dropped the pile of dresses on the spotless kitchen table and watched Bess do the same. Then her housekeeper hurried to the stove to stoke the coals and start a large pot of water boiling. Emma began examining each garment. "I've only worn this once," she murmured and shifted a dark green dress to the side. "But Osbourne has admired the lilac dress twice now. It will take the indigo dye well."

"I'll take apart the gray one, ma'am, while we wait for the water."

"Thank you, Bess. Give me a moment to change into something more serviceable and I'll help. I can rip out seams, at least."

Bess was, thankfully, a serviceable seamstress, because Emma had never sewn a straight line in her life and couldn't afford to send the dresses out. It was all she could do to afford Bess, but this scheme would have been impossible without the woman's help. Emma felt selfishly thankful that Bess had finally decided to flee her husband just as the London coach passed by her tiny hamlet. As soon as the woman had boarded, eyes bruised black and mouth set in a determined line, Emma had started to plan. *There is a woman who needs a new life even more than I,* she'd thought. And so she had offered it, and Bess had quietly accepted.

"Long as you're not staying in London long. I was planning to pass through."

"No," Emma had agreed. "Just long enough."

They had only two months left before Emma lost her lease on the town house. She couldn't afford the jump in rent, and the Season didn't interest her anyway. Two more months to round out her coffers, then she'd leave forever.

She finished her sorting just as a tap sounded at the kitchen door.

"Let me," Emma said, as Bess began to set aside her work. She opened the door to find a scrawny boy waiting in the dank stairwell. "Yes?"

The boy looked her up and down with hostile confusion. "Who're you?"

"Pardon me? Can I help you with something?"

"Ye're the housekeeper?"

Emma rolled her eyes at his boldness. "What is it?"

"I got some information might be valuable to you."

"Really?" He didn't look particularly trustworthy. His layers of clothing were blackened with grime and his face had clearly not been washed in days.

"A man is asking after your mistress. Wants information 'bout who lives here and how long."

Emma tamped down her spark of alarm. This boy was likely as much a schemer as she, only he took his nonsense door to door. "Why should that concern me?"

He shrugged. "P'raps it don't."

Well, he was good. Not pushing too hard. His eyes suddenly glinted with wile. "You don't believe me. A'right. But he asked if you'd come six weeks ago. And you did."

Emma cocked her head. "True. But you'd know that, I suppose, if you lived nearby."

"I do." His chin inched up. "That corner one street over is mine. But I don't know if you come from Cheshire. Do ye?"

The blood fled her face and left her cheeks cool. The air flowing down the stairwell was suddenly too cold to bear.

The boy's eyes brightened another notch. "That's what he said. 'Find out if they're from Cheshire way.'"

Oh, God. Matthew. She'd worried he might try to follow.

He would ruin everything, given the chance. Emma forced herself to focus. "And what did you say to this man?"

"Well, I took his ha'pence. Told him I'd find out."

"Is that why you're here? To find out?"

"P'raps . . ." He smiled suddenly, revealing straight white teeth. "He didn't look entirely well-to-do. I thought I'd take my chances with your household. One ha'pence won't change my life, or the life o' me mum."

Emma nodded. He was honest about his scheming, at least. More than she could say for herself. "What is your name?"

"Stimp."

"Stimp?"

He shrugged away her question.

"All right, Stimp. A penny now and another penny after you talk to him again."

"A shilling. No charge for the return trip."

"A shilling?" She looked him up and down again. He had shoes anyway. Shoes polished to a fine shine that spoke of a wage. A boot black perhaps. He wasn't a beggar. "Fine. A shilling, but it will wait until you come back."

He grinned, revealing a plan to flee with her coin if she were dumb enough to hand it over. "Deal."

"Now tell me more about this man."

Emma smoothed a hand down her deep blue skirt. If there were ladies at this party who cared about such things, they likely thought her unfashionable, or at least too poor to afford more elaborate dresses. The truth was that she could not afford dresses at all, except to buy them secondhand, then alter and dye them until it seemed she owned a full wardrobe. It would not do to appear too desperate, after all, or her gambling would take on the taint of work instead of eccentricity.

"The lovely Lady Denmore," a man purred from close behind her.

Emma glanced over her shoulder to spy Lord Marsh leering down. She fought the urge to sigh in disgust. "Lord Marsh," she answered.

"I hoped you might make it to my little gathering."

"I'm pleased to be here. I understand the play is excellent at your tables."

"Indeed. I endeavor to please."

"Mm." She pretended not to notice his flirtation. She couldn't stand the way he licked his lips whenever he looked at her. He'd likely be terribly chapped by the end of the evening.

"Let me show you my home."

Unable to think of a polite way to extricate herself, Emma was forced to take his arm and follow him up to the first floor of his town house. Several gentlemen tipped their heads in her direction as they passed, but none stopped to introduce their companions. This party was less than respectable, and she'd never have been admitted if anyone knew the truth about her marital status. But widows could get away with more than virgins, and the presence of a few of the demimonde was hardly enough to shock her.

Still, her muscles tensed as Lord Marsh led her to the first room and stopped just inside. "Piquet," he said simply, and indeed, that's all it was.

It's just a gambling party. Nothing more. Nothing like her father's "gambling" parties, for instance, where you were as likely to see a man laying a woman on a table as you were to see him laying down cards.

"But piquet is not your game, is it?" Marsh asked.

"I play, but 'tis not my preference."

"Too simple, I'd imagine. You enjoy more stimulation."

Emma cut her eyes at him to let him know he'd gone too far, but he only smiled back unashamedly. "Come. The next room." And so they proceeded through six rooms, each one eliciting some barely veiled entendre from Lord Marsh until Emma didn't care if she offended him or not.

"Thank you for the tour, Lord Marsh. You may leave now."

Unfortunately the man remained unoffended. He waggled his fingers in farewell as she turned and headed for the second room she'd seen. A footman stood at attention with whisky and champagne. Emma chose a whisky and tossed it back as she observed the play.

No women sat at the table, though a few had gathered around, leaning against the shoulders of the players. Emma had seen a woman downstairs whom she recognized, but the females in this room were likely demireps or even common whores. Good. They'd keep the men distracted as Emma divested them of their coin.

"Lady Denmore?" a familiar voice growled as she took a step toward the nearest table.

Emma spun around to glare at the Duke of Somerhart. His sudden, unexpected presence flashed heat through her blood.

His blue eyes scorched her as they flicked down over her body. When he met her eyes again, he scowled. "What are you doing here?"

"Why, gambling, of course. What else do I do?"

"Nothing, as far as I can tell."

"Just right, Your Grace. A pleasure to see you again. So charming."

Except that he didn't need to be charming. When she started to turn away, Somerhart wrapped his hand around her elbow and sent more warmth gliding into her veins. Overbearing bastard. He could be as rude as he wanted, because his hands were hot and strong. She could still feel his thumb exploring the most sensitive parts of her foot, her ankle . . .

"Is there something wrong?" Emma snapped.

"Yes. I'm shocked to find you at this party."

"And yet you are here."

"*I* am not a very young woman from the country."

A laugh broke free from her irritation. Oh, yes, she was all bluebirds and innocence. "Somerhart, I am not a young miss, fresh off the estate. I'm a widow and free to do as I please. A fact I feel certain you've made note of."

"Pardon?"

"Widows. They are your companion of choice, are they not?"

His scowl turned into a sneer as he dropped her arm. "I cannot believe I thought you subtle."

"Subtle? Good God, Somerhart. How very misguided."

His anger kept him from stopping her this time, and Emma made her way to a vacated seat at the brag table. She hoped the man would leave before she started play, but she did not turn around. She wouldn't give him the satisfaction, nor the people in the room who were watching with happy interest.

And she would not let him chase her from her work again. She threw herself into the game and quickly accumulated three hundred pounds. She just as quickly lost it all. One of the men at the table laughed.

"Lady Denmore, you are reckless tonight."

"Yes," she snapped and placed a new bet. She could *feel* him there, a few feet behind her, glaring a hole into her neck. She wished her hair weren't up. Wished she hadn't worn a dress with such a low back. Wished the thought of him looking wasn't quite so thrilling.

Emma pushed the play harder, and the men happily obliged, sure that she was off her game. A collective groan went up as she turned her cards. "Reckless," she muttered, pulling the pile of coins toward her. Yes, she was reckless and unsubtle and a liar as well.

Two more months.

An hour later, she was up two hundred pounds and sick

of looking at the wench across from her, the one whose ample bosom couldn't quite stay contained. "Good night, gentlemen."

Unseen hands pulled her chair out, but she knew who it was. Somerhart hadn't budged since she'd begun play. She'd only been able to tolerate his presence by picturing him as one of the hangers on: forearm perched on the back of her chair, shirt unbuttoned to his breast bone, his fingertips trailing teasingly against her hairline as he awaited her pleasure. But he had done no such thing and looked as rigid and elegant as always when she turned to him. His eyes burned. Had he waited just to resume their argument?

Emma ignored his hand and walked from the room. "What is it that you want, Somerhart?" she tossed over her shoulder.

"To speak with you."

"Why? I seem to annoy and offend you with very little effort on my part."

"You do."

"So why seek me out? To suffer? I hadn't heard you were the type to enjoy paddles and degradation. And one would expect that to get out."

"Pardon?"

"Then again . . ." She kept walking, heading for the stairway. "You do insist on circumspect partners."

"You are utterly outrageous," he growled, managing to sound quite ominous, but Emma smiled down at the balustrade. He could act horrified, but the truth was that she entertained him.

"How old are you? Twenty? Twenty-one? And speaking to me of *paddles*?"

"Yes. Paddles. Shocking, as you've pointed out before."

He muttered something she couldn't make out, but it made her laugh all the same. From what she'd heard of the duke, he never muttered. Just as he never yelled. But in the three times she'd met him, he'd managed to do both.

"You say things just to surprise me," he said, as she stepped into the grand entry of the town house.

Emma rewarded him with a wide smile. "Why would I do that?"

"Because it amuses you."

"And you."

Somerhart frowned down at her, eyes narrowed. He stared until Emma felt her face grow pink. Not with embarrassment, but with pleasure at being the focus of this man's attention. His face was masculine despite its beauty, angles drawn out in strong jaw and high cheekbone. Emma couldn't help focusing on his wide, indulgent mouth. She thought of touching his jaw to see if the skin was smooth, or if it was roughened by the dusky hint of his dark beard.

"Where did you learn to play?" he asked, breaking the spell he'd woven.

Emma blinked and pulled her thoughts into strict compliance. "Lord Denmore loved games of chance. Nothing to do with the coin, I mean. He would play with pennies, with beans even. We spent hours playing every night. He said I had a gift."

"But you don't play because you have a gift. You don't play for beans. Or pennies."

"Mm," she hummed and glanced around for the footman. "My cloak, please. And a hack."

"I will drive you."

"There's no need. People would talk."

"People are talking already. The whole of London knows we are lovers."

Emma couldn't help her sharp breath. His voice had dropped to an unexpected timbre with those words. The sound of pleasure. Nothing at all like his normal, clipped tone.

"We are not lovers," she whispered. He took her plain cloak

and settled it over her shoulders. The backs of his fingers brushed again and again over her throat as he slowly tied the ribbons. He looked suddenly softer, more sensual. Like a libertine. She could see him as he must have been in his youth—hedonistic and hunting for pleasure in every dark corner. Shivers slid down her skin and squeezed her nipples into tightness.

"I am neither subtle nor circumspect," she reminded him.

"The talk has already started, Lady Denmore. It will continue whether we indulge ourselves or not. I created quite a scene at Matherton's, you'll recall."

"And here," Emma managed to say, though her lungs seemed to tremble.

"Yes. And here."

Emma was caught up in the moment, in *him,* and she could not afford to be. She could not take this man to her bed, despite what she wanted. And she definitely wanted. Him. Naked and aroused, letting her experiment with all her useless, unsavory knowledge. But perhaps he was too commanding to let her play by her rules. Perhaps he would insist she follow his.

She thrilled to the thought, and had to part her lips to draw enough air into her parched throat. Somerhart leaned closer.

"I have shocked you for once, Lady Denmore."

"You . . . you do not even like me."

"You are . . . intriguing."

"And I can suddenly see how such a rigid nobleman has managed to seduce half the women of the ton. I'll remind you that I do not wish to join their sordid ranks."

The sensuality cleared from his face, gone in the blink of an eye as he drew himself to a straight line. "Ah, yes. I'd forgotten your convenient modesty."

Emma gritted her teeth against his arrogance. Life was so easy for rich men. She was relieved her anger so easily replaced her arousal. "Yes," she spat. "I am quite picky. Often

I like my seductions to consist of more than 'Hallo there. Care to spread your knees for a duke?' Silly miss that I am."

Oh, she'd definitely caught him unawares again. A flush crept from under his cravat and stopped just under his ridiculously lovely cheekbones.

"Reconsidering your offer of the carriage, Your Grace?" Emma cooed.

"No," he snapped and tugged his coat sleeves into place as if they would dare to rise above his wrists. "Despite your vulgarity, the offer stands."

"How very tolerant of you."

Somerhart crossed the entry in three strides and jerked the door open before the footman could reach it. The poor servant looked as if he might drop into paroxysms of dismay. "Come," Somerhart ordered.

"I haven't accepted your offer," she replied. "My reputation is not something to be so lightly ruined."

"Oh, for God's sake. You are notorious, Lady Denmore. Already. A woman heralded for rampant gambling and undignified behavior, and you've only been in town for a month."

"True, but I have never taken a lover, Somerhart, and no one has ever accused me of such."

The tic in his jaw stilled, and his eyes slid slowly down her body, warming to that seductive glint she'd seen moments ago. *Never,* he was thinking, and she knew it. She was thinking the same thing. That if she agreed to this, he would be her first lover. This man, famous for his prowess. He *knew* things, she could see that in those glinting eyes. Things about women's bodies and their needs. *Her* body. *Her* needs.

His eyes passed from warmth to heat.

"You may escort me home," she said quickly, to try and quell the need rising up in her blood. "And that is all you may do."

"You sound very sure," he murmured, drawing even

closer. Emma could smell the starch of his linens, the subtle tang of soap. She slid her fingertips up his chest and let them rest against the muscles there, just for a moment. She felt his heart beating, sending blood to all that vital muscle, warming his skin . . . then she pushed him away with a shove that nearly toppled him.

"Really, Your Grace. Crooking your little finger again? At least buy me a bauble before you try to tup me in the carriage."

Somerhart looked as if he'd like to throw up his hands, but he was simply too dignified. He only jerked at his coat cuffs again and shot a glance toward the footman who was most assuredly looking elsewhere.

"Get in the damned coach." He jabbed a finger at the waiting carriage, and Emma obeyed, hiding a smile as she passed. "You are intolerable," he growled and followed her down the front steps. "A minx," he added for good measure.

And Emma couldn't help but laugh in agreement.

Hart knocked on the gleaming black side of the carriage, one foot still on the street. "Your direction," he snapped toward Lady Denmore's shadow as she arranged herself inside. There was a definite pause before she answered.

"Belgrave."

Hart did not sigh his impatience, because dukes did not do such a thing, but a very sighlike sound emerged from his lips. "*Where* in Belgrave?"

A longer pause. "Marlborough Road. Number Twenty-three."

He stared at the pale smudge of her face in the dim confines of the carriage. Marlborough Road. Not quite Belgrave then. More like Chelsea, or just at the edge of it. Hart had been telling himself quite forcefully that he needn't accompany her, that he should send her on her way and have his driver fetch him afterward.

If he left with her it would fuel the gossip about them to a fever pitch, add permanence to her fledging notoriety, and revive the old talk about him. Talk he'd been trying to forget for years. And Lady Denmore would either torture him further or tempt him into going forward with these impetuous thoughts of seduction.

But she lived in Chelsea, for God's sake. The edge of respectability. Not precisely a safe place to simply drop a woman at her doorstep and wish her well. It seemed he had no choice.

Hart gave the street and house number to his driver, then stepped up to his doom. The carriage rocked with his weight, reminding him that the sturdy boat of his life was about to be swallowed by rough waters. Breath escaped his lips in a definite, undeniable sigh.

As his eyes adjusted to the lamplight, he could make out her gloved hands folded against her black cloak, and the dark line of her eyebrows against pale skin. Those eyebrows arched with some scathing emotion.

Hart braced himself for an attack but none came, and he slowly settled into the strange feeling of being closed up with a woman he didn't know how to handle. She irritated him to no end and prodded the beast he'd kept contained for so long. It had once roamed free, and she *reminded* it, revived it to its former hunger.

Just the memory of her ankles aroused him, and those ankles were right there, resting mere inches from his own. Hart could reach down and ease her slippered foot up, rest it between his knees. He could explore the delicate puzzle of bone and muscle, then glide up until his hand rose over her firm, warm calf. She had strength in her legs, the muscles of a country girl who'd explored hills and marsh and forest. Her calf would be relaxed, but her thigh . . . Oh, her thigh would tense under his touch. Her muscles would clench and strain as he stroked. They would tremble. He wanted them to tremble.

His fingers curled into his palms.

This was not how he chose a mistress. Not anymore. He did not pick a woman because of her *ankles*. He chose women who were easy. Simple. Women who volunteered for seduction and wanted him enough to keep their mouths closed about it. Hart dictated the terms, and forced the woman to voice her agreement before he would arrange a meeting. It was all business until he got to the bedroom, and even then . . . even then he was composed and . . . and . . .

"You did surprise me," Lady Denmore said in a rush, as if she could not resist speaking.

Hart blinked and felt himself settle back into his body. His *new* body. The one that didn't explore sordid fantasies with every desirable woman. "Pardon?"

"Your suggestion that we indulge ourselves. It shocked me. Your reputation is . . ." She raised both hands slightly. "Confusing."

Hart leaned into the cushions at his back. He let his gaze fall to her skirts, thinking of those damned ankles again.

"You are a rake. You do not fall in love, do not even pretend affection toward your lovers. You simply engage in affairs. Everyone knows this. *I* know it. But . . ." Her hands rose again, hovered. "You were worse than a rake in your youth. A reprobate. You attended parties . . ." Her breath jumped in her throat.

Hart thought of Lady Denmore at one of those gatherings . . . but she would be with him, only with him.

"You were notorious, Somerhart, but you have changed. A circumspect duke with a heart of ice, a study in control. But still a rake. How can that be?"

His distraction vanished and Hart felt a brush of panic over his nerves. He didn't like this, didn't like her looking at him with such focus. "Your confusion is easily dispelled. I am not a rake."

"But you were."

"I never seduced virgins, never lied to get into a woman's bed. I—"

"You had Mrs. Charlotte Brown and her sister-in-law in your bed *at the same time*."

"I was hardly past my nineteenth birthday," he snapped, flushing almost immediately at the ridiculousness of his own words. He felt stupid. *She* made him feel stupid and he had sacrificed for years so he wouldn't have to face that feeling again. Her ankles could go to hell.

She wasn't even beautiful, merely pretty. Unremarkable except for those wicked eyes and that midnight voice. And the delicate pink toes and tensing thighs.

Lady Denmore made a thoughtful sound and pressed on. "There was—"

"Why did you accept my offer of a ride?" Hart ground out. "You clearly don't enjoy my company any more than you say I enjoy yours. Perhaps *you* are the glutton for punishment."

Her husky laugh enveloped him. "Perhaps I am. But you are an attractive man, Somerhart, and so very cool and arrogant. I admit I enjoy needling you. And I daresay you need it. No one else seems willing to try."

"No, they'd rather practice their sword thrusts from a distance."

Her head cocked infinitesimally and Hart tried to call the words back, but they were already free, revealing secret things about him.

"Is that what you like about me?" she asked. "That I tell you what I think? Everyone's afraid of you, you know. I assumed you preferred it that way. Every man in his place, every woman trembling at your feet."

"Yes."

"Well, I do not tremble."

I could make you tremble, he thought. When she froze, Hart realized he'd said the words aloud. He could hardly manage to summon up regret. He *could* make her tremble, and often.

"I'm sure . . ." She paused to swallow the rasp from her words. "I'm sure you could. I do not doubt you learned very useful things in your youth. But it's simply not possible."

All his frustrations coalesced with a wrenching jolt. Hart leaned forward and made her jump. "*Why?* Are you working toward some quiet, profitable marriage? Because you are already spectacularly unsuccessful at being a respectable widow."

Her mouth curved up.

"Any man who would accept your rampant gambling would accept a few indiscretions as well."

"Would he? How very generous of him."

"I don't understand you."

"Then we are both equally confused."

Hart laughed, not truly amused, but he could laugh or jump from the carriage or strangle her. So laugh he did. The coach leaned around a corner, and Hart snapped open the window coverings to see the neat row houses of Belgrave Square.

"I am sorry that I cannot accept an invitation to your bed, Duke. But I cannot."

"Why," Hart muttered, "do I feel the veriest idiot, attempting his first, bumbling seduction?"

"If you aren't forced to exercise a skill, finesse vanishes. No one has challenged you in years, I'd imagine."

Hart slid his gaze across the darkness to meet hers. "Is that what this is? A challenge?"

Her eyes widened in alarm. "No."

"Hmm." His muscles relaxed a bit. He leaned back into his seat and turned to the window.

"No," Lady Denmore repeated. "This is *not* a challenge. Pray don't launch a campaign."

"Don't be alarmed." Anticipation inched up his spine and spread pleasure over his skin. How long had it been since he'd felt that? "I am not an invading army."

"You could be," she insisted.

Hart smiled at the view. "The neighborhood is deteriorating. We must be drawing close to Marlborough Road."

Her exasperated huff filled the carriage and drew Hart's thoughts to gasps of pleasure. *A challenge.* He felt his skin draw tighter across his whole body, felt his blood expanding. "Yes," he said, as if she had spoken.

"I was not challenging you. My life is not a game, Your Grace, and I would not appreciate your treating it as such." Her voice shook a little, he noticed. *Trembled.*

Hart grinned into the night. "My sister would say I've been an arrogant ass, and I've found her to be frighteningly intelligent." He met Lady Denmore's wide-eyed gaze. "Like you."

She shook her head.

"Will you be attending Moulter's retreat?"

"No."

"Of course you will. Three days of deep-pocketed noblemen, half of whom wouldn't know a good hand if it introduced itself. I do believe I'll accept Moulter's invitation."

Her mouth had lost its will to smirk at him. Her lips pressed tight together. "I will not be your lover."

"Mm."

"Do what you wish. It will be in vain."

"I appreciate the warning, Lady Denmore."

She crossed her arms and fumed, pleasing Somerhart to no end. The woman was tempted, very tempted, and with very little help from Hart. He'd been rude and presumptuous, not the least bit seductive, and she was *tempted*. The last vestiges of Hart's perpetual boredom floated away like smoke.

When the carriage tilted around a corner, Hart put his hand to the seat and spread his fingers wide, thinking of Lady Denmore's thighs again. A dark shadow tore him from his pleasant thoughts, and Hart leaned closer to the glass to scowl at the distraction. A man stood on the corner, bundled against the cold. Only his eyes were visible above a thick, gray wrap, but those eyes watched closely as the lights of the carriage passed.

Thief, Hart thought, without much alarm. Both his driver and footman were well-armed against the city's dark-minded inhabitants. But alarm reared its ugly head when the coach pulled to a stop just a dozen yards from the corner.

"Thank you, I suppose," Lady Denmore murmured, confirming that they'd arrived at her home. The latch clicked open and the footman swung open the door. Hart didn't bother waiting for the step. He jumped from the carriage, surprising his servant and no doubt pleasing Lady Denmore with his rudeness. But he was rewarded with a brief glimpse of the man on the corner, who was quickly backing away into the shadows. Hart stared after him, wanting to give chase and knowing he must not.

"Whatever are you doing?" her voice purred from his side.

"A thief. He was right on your corner."

"How do you know it was a thief? Likely it was our local boot black. He lurks about at all hours."

"Is he six feet tall?"

"Oh. Still—"

"He was standing right here, not a dozen yards from your home. You must take care. He likely already noted that you travel alone."

"Yes, I . . ." She glanced around, eyes darting from shadow to shadow. Hart felt a sudden anger. She should not be living here like this, in an unfamiliar city in a neighborhood only pretending at gentility. She should be traveling with a groom, at least, and not returning to her home at all hours of the night.

"You—" He started, but she spun on her heel and hurried toward a narrow set of steps.

"Don't bother, Your Grace. I can hear the censure in that one word. I am not wealthy and I am not married, so whatever you are about to say is meaningless. This is the neighborhood I can afford, the life I can afford. Good evening."

She fished a key from her skirts as she mounted the stairs, and actually unlocked the door herself, not a servant in sight. Hart watched, stunned, as the simple gray door closed with a solid thump. And Lady Denmore was gone.

Hart wasn't sure how long he stood there, frowning, but his driver felt compelled to clear his throat.

"Right," Hart muttered, and made himself step toward the open carriage door. "Drive around the block a few times, Lark. And keep a sharp eye out. I want to be sure we've chased that ruffian away."

And he and Lady Denmore would speak at length about her situation when they met at Moulter's estate. After he'd charmed her drawers off.

Chapter 4

The note glowed against the dark, polished wood of the sitting room table. Emma did not know what to think of it, but she was grateful for the distraction. A ride around the park with the handsome Viscount Lancaster would ease her worries for a few moments. If she were lucky, it might even annoy Somerhart.

"If that Stimp comes around," Emma called, "please bid him return. I need to speak with him."

Bess grumbled a sound of assent from the hall, and Emma turned her attention back to the cloak she was mending. The cheap fur edging around the hood had begun to free itself in clumps and tufts, but Bess had found a finer strip of fur at a market stall. The stitching required not the least bit of finesse, so the task was perfect for Emma. But the work needed little thought even with her lack of experience, and her mind turned immediately back to the man lurking on the corner the other night and the danger he presented.

Stimp had claimed that her spy was an older man, and not a gentleman at all, but he'd also assured her that he'd convinced the man to leave.

But if the spy truly was older . . . Matthew was smart, his father was a magistrate, and he could as easily pay some

ruffian to look for her as come himself. She thought of
Matthew's delicate good looks, his slim, elegant body . . .
No, he would not hang about a London street corner, risking life and limb to ferret her out, not if a man could be
hired.

A hired man could be fooled or chased off, though this
one seemed determined to stay. Or maybe it was just as
Somerhart had said. A simple thief.

Emma sighed as she tied off the thread and held the wool
cloak up. It looked halfway decent, but the sight didn't raise
her mood. She was tired of this place, this cold house that
echoed its lack. Most of the rooms were empty and none of
them comfortably furnished. Perhaps she should have taken
a suite of rooms at a hotel, but the hotelier had sprung at the
opportunity to offer her the vacant home that would be
empty until March.

Somerhart thought her living on the edge of respectability, but he had no idea. She was nowhere near the edge, had
long ago fallen deep into the maw of indecency, had been
deep into it ever since her mother's death, so long ago. Their
ancestral home had become her father's personal play-
ground; the caregivers hired for Emma and her brother nothing more than her father's favorite whores. Her home had no
longer been a home, just as this place was no home, just
shelter from the elements. She wanted a home, *needed* a
home, and she was less than two thousand pounds from that
dream.

The Moulter party began in three days. Three days, and
Emma could almost feel the coins sliding through her fingers. But it wasn't just the coin causing her excitement.
Somerhart, that wretch, he had tapped directly into both her
weaknesses. Gambling and lust. He could not know, but he
did. Something about her advertised her wickedness to
Somerhart, and called to his own.

Since that night in the carriage, she had fantasized about

him. Imagined him doing things to her that she had seen men do to women. She had been raised in wickedness and now she wanted to experience it herself. But she couldn't.

She couldn't.

Emma shivered and spared a glance for the faint glow of the coal fire. She would be leaving within the half hour. There was no point wasting good coal on a soon-to-be-empty room, so Emma wrapped the cloak about her shoulders and settled back into the chair to try to warm up before Lord Lancaster arrived.

"And have you been staying out of mischief, Lady Denmore?"

She smiled at the sparkle in Lancaster's brown eyes. "I'm not sure how to answer that, sir. I suspect mischief is my greatest appeal."

"Not so," he protested, though he couldn't keep a straight face.

"I was surprised by your invitation."

"Unpleasantly?"

"No, not at all. Very pleasantly surprised. You were quite gallant on the day I took advantage of your brother."

"You deserved the advantage. My little brother is as arrogant as any other young man."

"And you are so very old."

He graced her with a wide smile. "I'm grown ancient under the weight of my familial responsibilities."

Emma nodded with real sympathy. "Yes. I hear you must take an heiress to wife."

Lancaster blinked several times before his laughter boomed out to bounce off the houses around them. The horses twitched their ears in simultaneous irritation. "'Tis true, though I hadn't realized it so well known." When his laughter faded, true weariness showed on his face. "My father died last year. I hadn't known until then . . ."

"I understand."

His mouth curved up on one side. "Do you? Well, let's not ruin the day with somber talk."

"It is a fine day."

"My dear Lady Denmore, you must be a fan of the frigid cold. I am quite the gentleman, taking you out for a winter drive." He laughed again, a wonderful laugh, and Emma realized she was truly enjoying herself, was truly relaxed. If she were an heiress looking for a husband, she would be ecstatic.

"You are not laboring under the belief that I have money, I hope."

"No." He shook his head and gave her the half smile again. "No. I daresay you haven't a cent. But I thought of taking you for a drive and the idea wouldn't leave my mind. I hope you don't mind my using your company for selfish enjoyment. I'm not free to court you and, frankly, I'm quite relieved that you exposed my problem so charmingly."

This time Emma's laugh echoed off the brick walls of the surrounding homes. Lancaster did not inspire her to fits of lust, but he was dangerous in other ways. He could steal her heart, could likely steal any woman's heart with no effort at all. He would have no trouble getting his heiress.

"You must have been quite young when you married," Lancaster commented. "You are twenty-one now?"

"Yes," she lied without a twinge of guilt. "Lord Denmore was a wonderful man. I was not opposed to the marriage."

"And you hope to marry again soon?"

"I do not."

He darted a surprised look in her direction, but whatever he wanted to ask he kept to himself. "Here," he murmured, and bent down to rummage beneath the seat. He straightened with a thick wool blanket, and when he laid it over her knees, Emma realized it had been resting atop a warming box.

"Oh," she sighed. "Oh, that is so, so lovely. Thank you."

"Hm. Well, I can't help but appreciate such a beautiful thank you." His eyes studied her, his gaze lingering on her mouth, and Emma felt warmth flood her cheeks. "I hope you won't mind my impertinence, but Somerhart is a very lucky man."

She blushed harder, though it seemed ridiculous. There was no reason to blush.

"You're quite sure your husband didn't leave you a secret inheritance? It'd be damned convenient."

And just like that, Emma's embarrassment dissolved and she was laughing again. She might never again take a carriage ride with such a handsome gentleman. She'd be wise to enjoy it.

The booming knock on her door startled Emma into a strangled gasp. It wasn't a polite knock, and it wasn't at the back door. A constable, was her first thought, and the only logical one she managed in the minute that followed.

Emma set aside her sewing and rubbed her cold hands against her skirts. The skirts themselves were dark brown and merely serviceable, and it occurred to her that she was dressed quite appropriately for a morning trip to jail.

Just as she was pushing stiffly to her feet, the pounding started again and at the edges of her graying vision, she caught sight of Bess rushing down the stairs to the door. Emma edged toward the doorway of the parlor to watch her housekeeper open the front door and make a ponderous curtsy.

"Is your mistress at home?" a familiar voice growled. *Somerhart.* Emma's knees nearly gave up their fight to hold her weight.

Bess murmured something and began to close the door, but Somerhart's hand jumped suddenly into view. "It's barely noon," he explained, as he pushed the door open and stepped over the threshold. His gaze traveled past the hall and caught her. "Ah, Lady Denmore. A moment of your time?"

"Fine," she muttered, trying to be angry at his impertinence, but far too relieved to do more than pretend. She backed up to the settee and let her knees give way.

When Somerhart entered, he made a show of glancing about as he strolled toward Emma. His study stopped with her brown wool dress. "I see no signs of hidden wealth, so I can only imagine that Lancaster doesn't have marriage on his mind."

"What?" Emma finally felt the dumbness of her relief burn away.

"Several people stopped me at my club last night, apparently hoping for a delicious reaction to the news that you've taken up riding with Lord Lancaster."

"Oh? And did you deign to whet their appetites?"

"Of course not. But they hardly needed it. You offer ample encouragement on your own."

"Good reason to sever our fantastical relationship, Your Grace."

"Mmm." He sat next to her without invitation and crossed his ankle over his knee. "You've insisted that you have no interest in taking a lover. So what are you about with Lancaster?"

"That's none of your concern."

"None of my—"

"What are you doing here? As you said, it's barely noon. This is completely inappropriate."

"Ha!" The man's absolutely luscious mouth softened into amusement. He chuckled, then the deep rumble bloomed into a real laugh. "Inappropriate? This from a woman who participates in footraces?" He rubbed a hand over his eyes and laughed harder. "Inappropriate to visit before three. In my jealousy, I stormed over here *before three*. Good God, I've gone mad."

He looked nothing like a duke in that moment. With no hat to protect him from the wet day, his black hair was damp and ruffled. His blue eyes blazed with anger and amusement, shielding her from none of his emotions. Emma tried to cover her smile with a discreet hand, but in holding back a laugh, she gave a very indelicate snort.

Somerhart pulled his chin in. "Are you laughing at me?"

"I'm sure . . . I wouldn't . . . Yes! Did you say 'jealousy'?"

"I did, so laugh away. I insist."

So Emma laughed, half at Somerhart, and half with the remnants of her relief. When she stopped laughing, she found Somerhart regarding her with a secret kind of smile. It twisted her throat into knots and she found she couldn't manage a witty comment. Still, she opened her mouth and waited for her breath to come back, but she waited in vain. Before she was over that beautiful smile, Somerhart pressed it to her parted lips. His smile was warm and tender and silky soft. But his tongue, when it touched hers, was even better . . . hot and slow and rich as velvet.

She didn't want this, she didn't. But his mouth worked magic. How could the cold, controlled duke taste so sweet? How could his lips brush such a gentle feeling into hers? And his tongue was the best kind of temptation, a fleeting glimpse of heaven that retreated just when she wanted more. Emma followed that hot pleasure and felt his hands grasp her shoulders. He eased her an inch away.

"Completely inappropriate . . ." He tasted her bottom lip, then her top one, and rewarded her sigh with a much deeper kiss than the first. This kiss pushed aside tender thoughts, and Emma felt pulled down, sinking into heat. *My first kiss,* she thought, which was ridiculous. She'd been kissed before, and not just once. But this . . . this was *intimacy*. An introduction to that other world. The world she'd watched and wondered about, the world of pleasure and secrets and wickedness.

"You . . ." Somerhart whispered. He kissed the corner of her mouth, her jaw. "It's you. Driving me mad." His teeth nipped the edge of her jaw before he tasted his way to the skin beneath her ear. He opened his lips over that spot and Emma shivered.

"I left my house furious."

"Why?" she managed.

"You know why." He touched his tongue to her . . . *Fire.* Hating herself for doing it, Emma arched her neck.

"But on the drive over . . ." He drew a fiery path up to her earlobe. "I realized . . ." Every word whispered a cool secret against wet skin. "I'd promised to be charming."

She would have shaken her head, but he caught her earlobe between his teeth, trapping her.

"Oh," Emma sighed, then moaned something less intelligible when he began to suck.

Several parts of her body came to strict attention at the sensation. Nibbling, sucking . . . His tongue worked against the sensitive flesh, and Emma thought she could swoon given a few more minutes to enjoy.

She dug her fingers into the shoulders of his coat just before he let her ear go with a tiny, wet *pop*. "Am I?" he asked.

"Mm?"

"Am I being charming, Lady Denmore?"

"No." The word betrayed itself, all dusk and softness.

His chuckle was so close she could feel it marching through her bones. "Little liar," he whispered and nipped her ear again.

Her brain muttered a protest, but Emma's body glowed with joy and triumph. She wanted this, wanted more than this, because she *knew*. She knew what he meant by these kisses, knew that he could use these delicate skills on more important places. More *needful* places.

Yes! Her body sang as he licked lower, down the column of her throat to the high collar of her gown where he gave one final, lingering kiss.

"Now we will have something besides your ride with Lancaster to think about."

Emma was still blinking when he rose and tugged his coat into place.

"I've used up all my charm for the morning. I'll see you in two days." His words thrummed with hot warning and seemed to echo through the room long after the man closed the door behind him.

Hart didn't know what to think of himself anymore. Had no idea, in fact. He felt young again. Young and hot and reckless. And the feelings were memories, aching with pleasure, but straining all over with a sense of doom.

Heartache had followed these feelings last time. Heartache and humiliation and fury and shame. He'd thought he'd learned his lesson, but apparently his libertine's soul had only retreated. It had regrouped, reformed, and now loomed over him, too heavy and insistent to resist.

Lady Denmore was a woman to be thoroughly enjoyed, and Hart meant to have her in every way she'd allow. He wanted to indulge again, *live* again.

When he came to himself, he was standing at the bottom of her front steps, blinking. He found his driver very carefully staring at a spot beyond his ducal head. Attentive, but not aware. Seeing, but not noticing. The perfect servant.

"I'll walk a moment," Hart said, thinking of the thief he'd spotted. "Wait here." Her neighborhood was attractive by day, even a cloudy, cold day like this one, but the facades were simple, and the windows more likely to be curtained in bright, flowered fabrics than stately silk. The area felt solidly prosperous, but not genuinely rich. Still, Hart wasn't sure that Lady Denmore fell into either of these categories.

Her entry and parlor had been shabby at best, and rather bare. After seeing them, Hart couldn't quite fathom why she wasn't trolling for a rich husband. Or perhaps she was. Perhaps she'd challenged him more purposefully than she'd let on.

Scowling at the thought, Hart turned the corner the thief had snuck past. There was nothing and no one there, of course.

The possibility of Lady Denmore being a scheming, deceptive jezebel presented a problem, because Hart had suspected her of being scheming and deceptive from the moment he'd heard about her young marriage and unusual arrival in London. It hadn't affected his attraction in the least. In fact, he suspected it was part of the appeal.

He knew from experience that scandalous women were just as daring in private as they were in public. Lady Denmore took risks, she thrived on danger, she enjoyed confrontation. And the woman could turn a controlled duke into a sensualist with nothing more than a sigh. This was her gift. And Hart's weakness.

But he dreamed of being transformed. Just for a few nights. Just enough decadent pleasure to see him through another ten years of responsibility. It would be worth it . . . if he could avoid a trap. God, it would be worth it.

His role as duke was stifling, but he had taken it on with only a small amount of resentment. He'd had no choice after all, and he wasn't a child to whine and stomp his feet. As to any misgivings or rebellion . . . well, his father had shown him the value of discretion and respectability before he'd died, a lesson he'd imparted with his usual brutal efficiency. Easier to mold a man if you pounded him into mush first.

And after his father had died, Hart had been left with duties to master, a sister to raise, social obligations to finesse, not to mention his commitments in the House of Lords and the constant, exhausting watch against mamas on the lucrative husband hunt.

So his vague sense of misery had been easy to ignore, but something had changed. He'd grown older, or more miserable, or maybe it was simple solitude. His sister was no longer a joyful child, waiting for his return from London. She wasn't even a worrisome adolescent, sure to cause him trouble. She was a woman, married now, and far away.

Hart was alone, isolated by his elevation, and no one seemed to understand anything about him, no one except a very suspicious young widow from the wilds of Cheshire.

He stepped toward the shadow of an alleyway, and glanced down the gray length. A boy stood at the other end. He watched Hart without fear and didn't move when Hart stepped onto the wet stones. Instead, he crossed his arms and raised his chin a little higher.

He was too small to be the thief from the other night, but that didn't mean he wasn't some sort of criminal.

"You need sumpin'?" a wary voice demanded when Hart continued to approach.

"Maybe." He stopped about ten feet from the child. "Why?"

"I don't hire myself out if that's what ye're after."

"Good God, no." He was sure he'd never been accused of the like. Hart shook his head. "Who do you work for?"

The chin rose again. "No one."

Hart glanced behind to be sure no one was sneaking up to crack open his skull. "Well, you're clearly selling something. What is it then?"

"You're clearly buying. What is it?"

An involuntary laugh choked Hart for a moment. Perhaps this boy had been trained by Lady Denmore in obstinance. "I need information," he finally conceded. The stubborn face brightened.

"Why, that's my specialty, guv."

"Mm." Hart studied him, all bright eyes and scrawny limbs. His gloves were shiny with black grime and his coat was smeared with it. The local coal picker? The boot black she had spoken of?

Well, he likely couldn't do much harm. "I saw a thief the other night, near Lady Denmore's door. Do you know who she is?"

"Course."

"Do you know who the thief was?"

A quick shake of his head.

"Well, I'd like to find out. I want to know if he comes back and what he's about. How much?"

The bright eyes narrowed. "A quid."

"A quid." Hart looked him up and down again before he dug into his pocket for two coins. "I may be fine and shiny, boy, but I'm no fool. A quid is far too much." The child's mouth fell open when Hart opened his hand. "Two quid, but that buys your dedication. I expect absolute loyalty, you understand? Will two pounds buy that?"

"Yes, sir."

"You're not to work for that thief or anyone else. If you see him again, you send a message. I want to encourage him to move on. At the least, find out who he is, who's working the area. Do you think you can do that?"

"I can."

"Well, then." Hart handed over the coins. "I'm Somerhart."

"Stimp," the boy replied, either some sort of agreement or his name. Hard to say.

"I'll be back tomorrow, but I'm on Grosvenor Street if you need me this evening."

"Right. Best get to work then, sir." The boy was walking away, one coin caught tight between his teeth, before Hart could say a word.

* * *

The pungent fragrance of incense hung over Matthew Bromley's head, then it wound around him, offering a strange, exciting mix of comfort and guilt. He bowed his head and prayed along with the rest of the small congregation, but long after they'd all risen and filed out, he stayed.

God would bring her back to him. If he prayed hard enough, sacrificed enough, she would be returned. He did not want her for selfish reasons, after all. The woman had led him astray, and Matthew meant to see both their souls saved from eternal damnation. Marriage, piety, grace; what more noble wish for a man?

There is a stain on your soul, Reverend Whittier had said, and Matthew had wept to hear the truth spoken aloud. He wanted to be clean again, clean of the lust and fornication she'd wrapped him in. He hadn't realized the danger at the time, had been blind to her deception. He'd thought it all to do with love, and hadn't once thought of the devil. Not until he'd confessed to Reverend Whittier and seen her for what she truly was.

Even with her gone it wasn't better. Every night she came to him in shameful dreams. Every night she coaxed his body to lust. He woke each morning with the proof of his sin like a brand on his flesh.

He could not simply forget her. In order to save himself, he had to save her. She would be his wife or they were both doomed. As soon as they married he would be redeemed, and he could begin his work for the Lord. He would start with her jezebel soul and temptress body.

"God will lead me to her. Soon," he murmured as he rose from his aching knees. "And I will save her from herself."

Emma arrived at Moulter's estate at six o'clock and was dressed and ready for the party by eight. By nine she was glowing from the effects of good cards and even better champagne. Everyone around her was beginning to glow, actually, though she doubted they were drinking for the same reasons she was. Probably not one of them was attempting to drown their anxiety over Somerhart's coming seduction.

Her stomach fluttered again, and Emma took another sip. Not too much more though. She'd had trouble stifling a groan at the sight of her first bad hand.

He hadn't put in an appearance, might not even be here yet, but she knew where his room was because the maid had mentioned it quite casually as she'd unpacked Emma's clothes. Somerhart's door was directly across from Emma's, a careful arrangement undoubtedly arranged by an attentive and helpful host. A duke's mistress must be accommodated, after all.

She had no idea how she would avoid the man if he was sleeping only a few feet away from her.

Emma shook her head and placed a few coins in the pile. His presence wasn't the true problem; her own temptation was the danger. The *knowledge* that he was near would be far more vexing than his physical proximity.

A murmur of surprise took the whole table when Emma laid down her hand. They hadn't expected her to win, and she couldn't blame them. Her worry over Somerhart had translated as displeasure with her cards. But she couldn't rely on that kind of luck for long. She needed to concentrate. The duke was a distraction she could not afford.

Emma cleared her mind and raised her stake in the game, which was all the incentive fate needed to intervene. The next three hands went to a young lord she'd never met before, and nearly flattened her pile of coins. But Emma persevered. By the time she looked up an hour later, she was flush with coin again, and not thinking about the Duke of Somerhart.

Which was, of course, when he chose to invade her world.

Her little jump of surprise at seeing him standing at the table made the other players laugh. Knowing, indulgent smiles were exchanged among the men. Even the great duke arched an eyebrow in amusement.

"Lady Denmore," he said, with a dignified nod.

"Your Grace," she growled in answer.

The laughter swelled again, though it stopped in an instant when Somerhart aimed a frown at the nearest gentlemen. *Puppets,* Emma thought. No wonder he was bored.

"I'm sure these gentlemen would appreciate if I offered to escort you to the dining room. They look quite pale with impoverishment, yet none will risk disgrace by calling a retreat."

"You flatter me," Emma said, though she made quick work of sneaking her feet back into her heeled slippers.

"Enjoy your refreshment," one of the men said, and the rest collapsed into renewed laughter. "Yes, do," another called.

Emma offered each man a smile as she gathered up her winnings. Somerhart circled to her chair and she was sure she could feel his body heat as he stood behind her. A flush overcame her, adding credence to everything the other guests assumed.

Hasty with self-consciousness, she tugged her reticule onto her wrist and stood in a rush, shoulder brushing along his hip. Her hand found its natural place on his arm. A faint clink sounded as her bag hit his belly.

"Ouch. I feel rather like I'm courting a pirate."

Emma let him sweep her away from the table, but she refused to laugh. "I will not be your lover," she murmured as they moved toward the door.

"I sense that only one of us is allowed to be polite at any given time. True?"

One side of her mouth refused to obey and curled up. "Perhaps."

"Well, it is my turn, I suppose. Would you like a glass of champagne?"

"Yes," she answered too quickly, but her fingers were beginning to tremble against his sleeve. She'd been thinking about him incessantly since he'd kissed her. She felt written in those thoughts, every wicked fantasy revealed on her skin. Seeing him—his lips and eyes, the flash of his teeth when he smiled—reminded her of what he'd done and what she wanted him to do.

She had to keep from snatching the glass from his hand when he finally found a servant with champagne. As it was, she couldn't bear to sip it demurely, but turned away and drank it down in three great swallows. When she turned back, Somerhart said nothing, merely removed the empty flute from her hand and handed her his own.

"You've worked up a well-deserved thirst, Lady Denmore. You must be hungry as well."

"Yes. No." She took a sip from his glass and put her hand to her throat instead of pressing it to his chest, his flat stomach. "I cannot do this." Her heart beat too hard, fueling the insane fight that had broken out inside her. Lust and . . . *fear*. She wasn't used to it, didn't know how to appease it. She was afraid of him, and so very, very afraid of herself.

"Lady Denmore . . ." Somerhart's hand took her elbow and pulled her toward a deep-set window that looked out over blackness. "Tell me what is wrong."

"You are what's wrong."

"I'm merely attempting to feed you."

"Nonsense. You are trying to seduce me, and I've explained before—"

"Yes, you have explained." He closed the curtains and guided her down to the window seat; his shoulders seemed impossibly wide, looming above her. "You were quite impertinent, rude, and arrogant in your position. Which is why I'm surprised to find that you've turned suddenly cowardly."

"I have. I'm afraid. Of *you*. Please leave me be."

His hand nudged her chin up, and Emma glared at his silhouette.

"Afraid," he huffed. "And I am the Queen. Or near enough," he added, reminding her of one of her many insults. "You don't look afraid, Lady Denmore. You look anxious and even a bit angry." His fingers lingered under her chin, stroking tiny waves of heat into her skin.

"I am angry. You will not leave me be."

"I am not planning to pounce upon you in a darkened hallway. You are very much in control of your own fate. So why so much upset?"

She shook her head and took a gulp of his drink.

"Has anyone ever told you that you drink like an alewife, Lady Denmore?"

"No, no one. I believe 'like a sailor' is the preferred comparison."

"Ha! Hoyden." He shook his head at her. "Move over."

She scooted an inch to the left and he took the seat beside her. There wasn't nearly enough room. His body pressed against hers in mirror image. His arm against her arm, his hip against hers. If she leaned over, her head would rest perfectly on his shoulder. If she looked up, his lips would find her kiss.

"How old were you when you married?"

"Nineteen," Emma said without having to think about it.

"And were you happy with the arrangement?"

"Mm. I wasn't displeased. Lord Denmore was a lovely man, and my family had declined in the world."

"So you were a local miss who caught the eye of an older gentleman."

"Yes."

"A squire's daughter perhaps?"

"I didn't grow up in a tavern if that's what you're asking."

His shoulder nudged hers. "No, you're well-mannered enough, at least with others."

Emma smiled and took a slightly smaller drink.

"Do you miss him?" Somerhart asked, his deep voice quiet.

She was shocked by the gentle question. No one had asked if she missed him. Everyone assumed she was delighted to have thrown off the bonds of a marriage of calculation, and she supposed she might have been. Except that Lord Denmore had been her uncle and he had loved her. He'd taken care of her and shown her a real home for a brief, shining moment in her life.

"I do," she finally answered, horrified when her voice broke over the last word. She coughed to clear the tears away. "He died in a fire, you know. He wasn't ill; it wasn't expected."

"I'm sorry."

Emma nodded, and drank the rest of his champagne with ruthless efficiency. "So you see, Somerhart, I am a hopeless gambler and an impolite drinker, but I am also a respectable country widow. Boring and not fit to act out a scandal with a duke."

"Hm."

She knew she should stand up. Just two steps and she would be free of the intimate darkness of the window seat. And it *was* intimate, despite the occasional voices that passed their nest. She felt sheltered here, warm and safe. Cradled in the strength of the very beast who meant to eat her up. Somehow the danger made her feel even more languid, helpless to resist the sweetness of the moment.

Somerhart shifted, his shoulders turning toward her while she waited for his touch.

"I can barely see you in the dark," he said, "but your voice is its own seduction, Lady Denmore." And then he stood and stepped past the curtained alcove, out into the light. "Shall we go to dinner?"

"Dinner?" she mumbled. "Now?"

He flashed a smile. "Is there someplace else you'd rather go? *Now?*"

Yes. "No!" she snapped and managed to stand without the slightest hint of a sway.

"Dinner, then." He offered his arm.

Emma gritted her teeth. "Stop being charming and circumspect, Somerhart. It doesn't suit you."

"Liar."

Emma took his arm, but she had the distinct feeling that he was leading her not to dinner, but to her destruction.

Chapter 5

Nothing. Not even a kiss. All that anxiety and suspense and Somerhart hadn't even accidentally brushed his knuckles over her bosom. Emma smoothed her own hand over her nightgown, over the hard jut of her nipple, the curve of her breast, then down to her belly and lower, until she pressed her palm to the soft mound of her sex.

Somerhart would touch her there, if she let him. And she wanted to let him. If she didn't have this secret to keep, she would cross the hall to the door of his room. She'd heard him go in an hour before, had heard his valet leave ten minutes later. She'd expected a knock then . . . a servant with a carefully worded note or, more likely, Somerhart himself, half undressed and dark-eyed with expectation.

She shivered at the thought, pressed her palm harder to her own heat.

She'd steeled herself against him, she'd been ready. But the minutes had ticked by, and with no one to argue against, her resistance had simply trickled away, unneeded and certainly unwanted. Or perhaps this was part of his plan as well. To make her so angry that she would storm his room and demand an accounting.

Emma sighed and let her hand fall away from her body.

She was alone as she'd always been, and it would not do to forget it.

Snow blew against her window, a speckling of icy drops, and Emma was drawn toward it. Lights from the rooms below shone across frosted grass. A tree branch sparkled with a thick layer of clear ice. Nothing moved but what the wind blew. Another empty night, and she was tempted again.

She wanted to run down the stairs in her bare feet and sneak out a side door. She wanted that blast of impossible cold, the stinging of her skin. She could walk for miles, she thought, before her body froze into crystals and was picked apart by a gust of wind, scattered into the world like magic. The little pieces of her would float forever, the whole sky would be her home. Everywhere. Nowhere.

A sound in the hallway pulled her away from the winter se-duction. Her heart leapt. Emma held her breath and waited, waited . . . but it was nothing and no one.

What if she did cross the hall? What if she simply slipped into his bed and gave into both their desires? When he dis-covered her secret, she could tell him the truth. It would be such a relief.

He'd been kind tonight, his arrogance a volatile genie that appeared only when someone else approached. His every smile and attempt at humor had called to mind that night when he'd reached out his protection to a young girl, if just for a moment.

So if she told him the truth, would he reach out for her again?

Emma's heart began to thud. He'd been so gentle . . . asking questions about her life, escorting her from table to table to wait patiently while she played. Then he'd walked her up the stairs, pressed a lingering kiss to her hand, and watched her walk to her doorway, hot eyes burning into her back.

He hadn't treated her as a challenge. He'd been . . . *charming.*

And now she sat alone in her room, wondering if Somerhart would rescue her from her life.

Her thumping heart picked up speed as the thought swung through her, battering her insides. Somerhart coming to her rescue. That had been her long ago childhood fantasy, the hope of her little girl's soul.

He had seemed so gallant, so *good,* and she had wished and prayed for his return. Even months and years later, when her body had begun to mature, when the sights and sounds of her father's gatherings had begun to arouse instead of frighten . . . Oh, she'd still waited for rescue then, with thoughts of a wedding and his marriage bed.

But then her father had died, dragging her little brother to the grave with him, and Emma had known there was no hope of rescue. Or she'd *thought* she'd known, but the leap of her heart was recognizable. Stupid, reckless hope.

"No," Emma said aloud. Her heart beat faster, harder. *"No."* There was no salvation waiting around the corner. There would be no rescue. She could not afford to dream of fairy tales.

Oh, she had no doubt that he would *help* her. Men were always willing to help young women who had fallen on hard times. She'd met many of those women in her father's home.

And how easy it was to imagine being Somerhart's lover, being kept by him in a beautiful home. She could live a glorious, disreputable life, bright with laughter and wicked nights. She could set aside all these dark worries and live like a woman.

But a lover wasn't a wife, and the march of years would find her with a new protector and another and then, perhaps, a handful of less affluent gentlemen. And soon enough, she'd be older, less desirable, a doxy trotted into country parties to take on any guest who cared to bend her over the nearest chair.

No, she had no illusions about what life held for an impoverished young gentlewoman. Whore or wife, and she would be damned if she'd become her mother. Whore or wife. Emma chose neither.

She blew out the lamp and snapped back the layers of bedclothes.

Somerhart was trying to seduce her and, oh, he was good. Better than she'd thought he could be. But his charm was a delicate thing. Emma would break it like glass and watch the pieces fall.

There were no dreams of the Duke of Somerhart that night. Instead she dreamed of Will, her brother. His warm hands always creased with dirt. His infectious, chortling laugh. His stubborn jaw. She dreamed of him hugging her tight, wrapping his small legs around her waist as he clutched her neck. Even after he'd grown too old for clinging, he'd still held on that way after a bad dream.

Oh, God . . . his tangled brown curls and bright hazel eyes. His angry pout.

She could not reconcile it. Could not. How his little body—always hot and grimy from running, jumping, climbing, always restless—how could it get so cold? His pink cheeks turned to wax. The sweet, sticky fingers stiffened to wood.

It had seemed to her as if that body had not had anything to do with Will. And, God, she'd been so sure that a mistake had been made. It hadn't been him, not Will.

And yet it had.

Emma woke with deep red crescents gouged into her palms. Her pillowcase was stiff with salt, but her throat burned with fury and renewed determination.

She was not weak enough to need rescue. She would rescue herself.

Chapter 6

Unbelievable. He'd been looking for the woman all morning and now this.

He'd spent the previous evening on his best behavior, doing his best to relax her stiffened back to a more sultry line, and he'd had a surprisingly nice time. He'd enjoyed watching her eyes lose their suspicion of him, watching her cheeks glow with laughter. He'd even enjoyed the thought of her wondering why he had stopped his pursuit. But he'd still spent the night with thoughts of her body instead of the real thing. And now this.

She had eaten little the night before. Hart had expected to pile her plate high with breakfast this morning and tease her about it while she ate. But he'd lingered in the breakfast room for over an hour, conscious all the time of what he was doing, and she'd never come down. A maid had returned from her room with a little shake of her capped head, so Hart knew she wasn't there. And it was too damned cold for a ride.

It had been a short-lived mystery though. Hart had found Lady Denmore just where he should have looked first . . . in one of the gaming rooms. He had forgotten for a moment that she wasn't a respectable young widow at all. He was reminded now, and beginning to think that she wasn't out to trick one unlucky man into turning over his fortune . . . she wanted the fortunes of many.

"Ho!" several of the young men cried at once. "Another drink!"

"Lady Denmore," one gentleman chuckled as the woman in question turned a wine bottle up to her lips, "you are a regular bounder." Hart glared from the doorway, trying to place the young pup's name.

"That's another twenty-five pounds, gentlemen." She gestured to a pile of paper and coins. "In you go."

The men paid up, and then one of them retrieved a heavy leather ball from the corner as Lady Denmore reset five wine bottles in a triangular pattern on the floor. Hart felt fury rise up through his chest at the two players lounging against the fireplace, eyes roving over her backside as she worked. They spoke in quiet whispers to each other, then toasted their opinions and drank.

The young man with the ball—Mr. Richard Jones, Hart's brain finally supplied—asked for luck, and Lady Denmore complied by pressing a kiss to the brown leather. All the men in the room watched her mouth as it lingered over the skin.

"Now that's good luck," someone murmured, and then the ball was rolling across the carpet. Three of the empty bottles fell before it, but they toppled into each other and two of them broke with a crack. The room cheered, everyone drank, and Richard Jones tossed several coins into the middle pile.

"Time to play for the pot," she called with a gesture toward the middle of the table. "Most bottles knocked over wins, but if you break one, you're out. Agreed?"

The men were still in evening wear. They'd clearly not been to bed yet. Emma stood out like a rose in a field of rocks. She wore a simple morning gown of dusky pink muslin that dipped in a low scoop over her bosom. Little white blooms were woven into her braided chignon. She looked fresh and lovely as a flower, and just as likely to be plucked.

The two men near the fireplace—Lord Marsh and some portly fellow—moved in for this final round of play. They were heavy with drink and exhaustion, and crowded too close to Lady Denmore. Not that she seemed to mind. She smiled and sipped from her wine. Marsh leaned over her, eyes devouring her pale skin as he whispered into her ear. She blushed and laughed and shook her head, but her eyes were on the man pitching the ball. One of the bottles cracked open and Emma's smile stretched wider. That was when Marsh's hand touched her hip.

The door hit the wall with a loud bang that snapped everyone in the room to attention. Marsh swayed, blinking owlishly, but when his eyes found Somerhart standing in the doorway, he swayed well away from Lady Denmore and her enticing hips.

"Your Grace," the lady murmured, and all the men in the room followed suit. "Are you up for a rousing game of pins this fine morning?"

He didn't bother answering. Her eyes glinted her lack of goodwill. She wasn't surprised to see him.

"Carry on, gentlemen," Lady Denmore laughed in the face of his silence. "We've a match to finish." The men didn't move. "My turn then?"

She fetched a new bottle from the rows near the wall and replaced the broken one. She repositioned all of them into another neat triangle before she fetched the ball and walked jauntily back to the table. "Good luck?" she suggested, but no one complied. The men's eyes darted toward Somerhart.

Nothing untoward had happened as far as Hart could tell, but all of them had been thinking about it. Their guilty eyes spoke volumes.

Lady Denmore shrugged and held the ball up to her own mouth for a kiss. Her lips brushed slowly over the stitching and, one by one, the men's eyes shifted back to her. Hart felt his face stiffening. He couldn't quite tell what his expression was, but he knew it was unpleasant. She was deliberately dancing along the edge of scandal, creating an aura of wickedness that would fuel the talk about her into fire. And she was dragging Hart deep into the flames. He should never have set foot in the room. He should have turned his back on her and walked away.

The bottles clinked. Four fell to the carpet without damage.

"Four!" she cried and Richard Jones offered halfhearted congratulations.

"Who will challenge me?" Her lips curved into an enticing, flirtatious smile. "No one? Mr. Jones?"

He looked around at the others before he shook his blond head and bowed in her direction. "Your match, Lady Denmore."

"I think," Somerhart growled, "it's past time you men found your beds for the morning."

"Just so," Marsh agreed, with an overloud laugh that the other men echoed as they each collected their winnings. The largest pile remained when the group quit the room. Someone closed the door.

Lady Denmore calmly went to collect the empty bottles of wine. After she'd placed them back into the line against the wall, she began to fold up the edges of the thick rough-spun cloth that had been laid out for the game. Broken glass shifted and clinked.

Somerhart forced his jaw to unclench. "Will you do anything for money?"

Her mouth held its impersonal smile as she continued her work.

"Because you seem quite hungry for coin. And I have a lot of it."

She gave a nod and dusted off her hands. "And?"

"And if you will do anything for it, you should simply tell me. I'm sure we could come to an arrangement."

Her smile widened until her teeth showed, but the woman refused to look at him. She stared down at the mess she'd made. "Do you think I find it charming to be called a whore, Your Grace?"

Goddamn it. Somerhart looked around, but there was no wall close enough to punch. "I waited for you at breakfast," he growled instead. "I did not expect to find you hidden away with a group of young bucks making a spectacle of yourself."

"No? Well, I think I've told you before that you are quite naive when it comes to my behavior."

"I am not naive, damn it. I am disgusted. You will drag me down with you."

"Oh, my. I suggest you remove yourself from my presence then. There will only be more of this. Gambling. Flirting. Wine before luncheon. Keeping company with rakes and fortune hunters. Why, I wouldn't be surprised if I were utterly disgraced long before the Season even begins. And I *will* drag you down with me, Your Grace. I promise you that."

She finally met his gaze, and her hazel eyes flashed scorn. That smile, that damned smile, mocked him in every way.

"You were a very different person yesterday," he said.

"As were you. Charming. And kind."

Somerhart winced and shook his head. "Is that what this was? A lesson?"

"Not for you, Your Grace. For me."

"How so?" he asked her, but his stomach felt hollowed out.

"Yesterday you meant to be charming and you were. But charm is not character, and I will not be seduced by pretense."

"No? What will you be seduced by then? Youth? Drunkenness? A ridiculous game?"

"Coin?" she suggested.

Her smirk coaxed fury into his blood. That little smirk of self-righteousness. He hadn't seen it for a long while, but it had graced the faces of many of his peers ten years before. "I don't need coin to have you," he snapped. "You can claim modesty, or whatever the hell reason you want, but we both know I don't need coin. You want this, Lady Denmore, just as much as I do."

Blood rushed to her face. She started to speak, but Hart cut the air with his hand. "You may mock all you like, but your words are nothing more than a shield, and a paltry one at that."

"Wanting something doesn't make it—"

"Oh, but it does for someone like you. You are not in the business of restraining yourself. You do what you like, and you will do this too."

"I won't." Her jaw trembled, but there were no tears in her eyes.

Hart moved toward her and watched her back away. Her hips hit the carved edge of the heavy mahogany table; several coins slid from her pile and clanked into each other.

"Why do all this?" He eased closer. Her fingers gripped the wood. "Just for money? Why not simply marry?"

"I-I won't marry." Her knuckles turned white as her lips flushed a deeper shade of pink.

"Why not? You already married for money once, though it doesn't seemed to have helped much. Or did you lose his fortune at the tables?"

She shook her head. He'd reached her full skirts now; the pretty fabric pressed against his black trousers. Hart stood stock-still and looked her over. She looked so clean and fresh, completely out of place in this room that smelled of whisky and stale cigars. She looked like morning, like innocence stolen from a garden and set down in hell. He was over-whelmed with the urge to make her match her surroundings.

"Lady Denmore," he whispered, listening to the way her

breath rushed from her throat. Her breasts pressed high with every pant. She wasn't frightened. She was aroused, nearly as much as he, thrilled with the heat of his anger.

"Lift your skirts," Hart rasped.

"What? No. I—"

"Do as I say. Lift your skirts."

She shook her head again, but she could hardly breathe now, her panting was shallow and far too fast.

"Your dress," he ordered, and her hands sank slowly to the soft muslin at her thighs. She grasped the fabric and pulled her skirt up to her calves, and Hart's cock swelled to a glorious ache. Blood rushed low to bring all his nerves to screaming life.

"More."

She jumped a little at the harsh word, but her hands obeyed. She lifted the skirt higher, then shifted her grip to pull it higher still. Hart saw the plain tops of her pink stockings, and then the smooth skin at the inside of her knees. Then her thighs. By the time he saw the lace edge of her drawers, Hart's legs were weak.

He reached for her waist and lifted her gently onto the table.

"I won't be your lover," she protested, but her hands clutched the lapels of his gray jacket.

"Oh, I'd never take you here, like this." He curled one hand around the back of her cool neck and pulled her closer. "Actually, I would. But not the first time. The first time I won't risk being interrupted. Spread your knees," he added, deliberately echoing her own scornful words.

She spread her knees wider and Hart moved between them.

"Somerhart . . ."

"Call me Hart. And I . . ." He lowered his mouth to hers. "I will call you Emma." Her mouth opened, her tongue licked out to meet his. Lust burned through him, sensitizing his skin. He kissed her deep and hard until her knees clutched at his hips. She kissed him even harder, worked her hands under his coat to dig her nails into his ribs.

The woman was fighting a rough battle with herself and knew that she would lose. Hart recognized denial. He'd lived with it for a decade, and he could just as easily recognize the fissures and cracks of weakness in her will. He was here, after all, despite his bitter words about scandal and pride. He'd fought himself and lost, and he'd be damned if he'd grant any mercy now.

He took a handful of her skirts in his hand and pulled them higher. When he touched her thigh, she was already trembling, shaking in anticipation of his touch. Hart let his fingers spread, let them experience the texture he'd wondered at. Oh, yes, her muscles were tight beneath that soft skin, straining. He bit her bottom lip gently before he broke the kiss.

"Tell me what you want." He stroked higher, ran his thumb back and forth at the edge of her drawers.

"No," she sighed.

He slipped his hand beneath the warm fabric and rubbed over the softest skin he'd ever felt . . . surely the softest. His fingers brushed damp curls. Emma gasped.

"Tell me."

"No."

"I'll not have you accuse me of heartless seduction when you want this as much as I. You're already slick, aren't you? Wet and beautiful. Wanting."

She was shaking her head, eyes clenched shut, when Hart went to his knees. He kissed the inside of her thigh, dragged his mouth up the tense line of muscle and tendon until she sobbed. "I thought about this last night. Dreamed of your taste, of you pressing yourself to my mouth. I pleasured myself to this fantasy. Tell me, Emma."

"Oh, God."

He nibbled higher.

Emma sobbed, "Oh, please."

"Please, what?"

"Please. Touch me. *There."*

His hands shook against her skin, a separate trembling from her own. He breathed out hard and watched her jump at the sensation. "You've said you won't be my lover."

"I won't. *Just touch me,* you bastard."

Hart chuckled. "Cheeky wench." He pressed an open-mouthed kiss to the fabric and found it damp and fragrant. Emma cried out as if he'd done much more. He reached for her drawers and untied the waist, pulled them down, pressed her knees together and pulled them off completely. When he pushed her legs open again, he was treated to the sight of her sex, pink and wet. All for him. A shudder of need raced through him.

"Please," Emma whispered, but he needed no further encouragement, and doubted he would have stopped for anything. He smoothed his palms up her white thighs, until they met at her sex. He feathered both thumbs up and down, up and down, over plumpness and heat and dark, dark curls. She rocked back, balanced on her elbows, back arching with shock.

God, he wanted to drive deep into her right now. Take her here, on the table, spend himself into the core of her. But he wouldn't. Not yet. He'd meant what he said about being interrupted, and yet . . .

The idea that the door could open at any moment, that anyone could walk in and find him cradled between her legs . . . Hart's mind raced with arousal as his blood pumped harder, faster.

His fingers spread her open for his mouth.

The barest touch of his tongue and she was panting, "Yes, yes."

He explored gently at first, taking in her intoxicating scent, the delicate texture of her need. Her taste flooded his tongue and made him want more. He probed into her, then deeper when she groaned her approval. But when he worked his way up to that tight bud of her clitoris, Emma cried out, a deep groan that couldn't quite be contained by her clenched teeth. He lapped at that spot again, and smiled when her fingers curled cruelly into his hair.

"Yes," she moaned. "There."

As if he couldn't tell. Hart chuckled against her flesh and rewarded her demands with a firmer touch. She shuddered and pushed herself higher against his mouth.

"Hart." Her voice was a high, breathless keen. "I've wanted this . . ."

God, he'd wanted this too. This and so much more. Almost from the moment they'd been introduced. He slipped one finger inside her. She bucked beneath him, trying to hold back a scream. Her flesh clutched at him, and, oh if it were his cock . . . pushing in, finding its way into that tightness. He suckled at her little bud, felt her muscles tightening, felt his need spiraling higher.

Hart looked up, expecting to find her blind, reaching for her peak, but he was shocked to meet her gaze. She was watching him, any trace of hesitance long dissolved in pleasure. Her eyes were narrowed, glinting. Her lips parted before her breath, but they curled up at the corners, hinting at satisfaction and demand. She didn't look away from his gaze. Instead, her eyes narrowed even further and glittered with wickedness.

That kind of boldness deserved a reward. Hart closed his lips around her, suckling, and slid another finger into her body. Emma threw her head back with a grimace and a scream. She tried to back away, but it was too late. Her hips jerked and strained. Hart's name was torn from her throat in a hoarse scream.

He let her go when her hips finally fell back to the table,

then he laid his cheek against her hot thigh and tried to calm himself down. Not easy given the view, but he tried. That glance into her eyes . . .

He'd recognized her. They were kindred spirits. Depraved and wicked and trying to deny it to the world. But she'd *liked* it. She'd liked being ordered about, liked being set on a table and devoured like a candied treat. The danger and the depravity. Whatever reason she had for denying herself, it had nothing to do with what she wanted. And Hart understood that completely.

His understanding helped him gather the will to raise his hands to her crumpled skirts and ease the fabric down her thighs. A quick check of the floor and he had her pale pink drawers in hand.

Emma snapped from her daze. She sat forward and slid to the ground so quickly that Hart was forced to scoot back. He fell to his backside, suddenly struck with the image of how he must look: sprawled on the floor with a cockstand, a pair of pink drawers in his fist. Utterly ridiculous. Corrupt. Depraved. Hart couldn't help but grin.

His lover didn't seem to appreciate his good humor. She glared at him, clearly wishing she could roast him with her eyes, then swooped down and snatched the delicate garment from his fingers, muttering something under her breath. Hart heard the word "obnoxious" quite clearly.

She looked fetchingly enraged as she turned her back and stepped into her underclothes. "You tremble quite keenly, my dearest Emma."

"Are you trying to tempt me to murder?"

"No, but something just as impulsive."

"Maiming?"

"Hmm. No, not that. One more guess."

"You." She spun about and speared him with a glare. "You needn't be so ridiculously jolly. Not only is it completely

absurd on your ducal countenance, but your happiness is premature. I will not be your lover. Your work was in vain."

"Well, not for you, I hope. It seemed quite fruitful."

She wrinkled her nose in disgust. "What is the matter with you? You're positively . . ." She waved a hand in a tight circle. "This isn't amusing."

"No." Hart shook his head and finally bothered with pushing up to his feet. "It's not amusing. It's delightful." He pulled her into his arms before she could shout whatever she meant to shout. The sound died against his lips. He kissed her soundly, and when he let her go, she blinked hard and touched her fingers to her lips.

"I won't be your lover," she whispered.

Hart inclined his head. "I believe that you could resist me, Emma, but I don't believe you can resist your own nature."

Her pink cheeks paled considerably at that.

"I assume you haven't dined this morning. May I escort you to the breakfast room?"

Emma shook her head. She turned purposefully away to see to her winnings, then brushed past him without a word. He followed her toward the door, but as her hand reached for the knob, the door opened on a silent rush of air.

"Oh!" a startled maid gasped and dropped into a curtsy so quickly that she almost fell. "Your pardon, ma'am! Sir!"

"For God's sake," Emma muttered, and the girl backed away. But Emma wasn't glaring at the maid, she was glaring at the doorknob and then at Hart. "Do not ever accuse me of indiscretion again, Somerhart. You've surpassed me."

"So I have," he chuckled, feeling lighter than he had in years.

The thick carpet muffled any satisfaction Emma could have taken from stomping back and forth across the floor of her room. Her pacing sounded peaceful instead of agitated, and she longed to smash something against the wall just for the racket it would make. And every frustrating step was a reminder of the new sensitivity between her legs, the aching satisfaction that had turned her insides to liquid.

Good God, she wanted more. More, more, more, which was exactly what she'd always feared. He'd awakened the wickedness lurking just beneath the surface of her skin. She wanted to have him again, *now*. Then stay in his bed, languid and nude, awaiting his return from dinner. Give him anything he demanded. Sleep with him, wake with him. She wanted to luxuriate in her body with his.

Emma pressed a hand to her hot forehead and squeezed her eyes shut. She needed to regain her control, what little there had been of it. But she'd never dreamed that his touch could be so much more magical than her own. And his *mouth* . . .

"Oh, God, his mouth," she groaned.

She should leave. She should. Run away before sunset and fly back to her cold little town house in London. But gentlemen were losing money at this party as quickly as she'd lost her willpower. She'd won nearly three hundred pounds in two days. She couldn't walk away from that kind of profit. It was only one more day. Surely she could persevere.

But she'd thought herself hardened against him this morning, and arrogance had gotten the better of her. The enjoyment of driving him mad, flirting with those men, needling him with her insolence. And, oh, he'd been so angry, and she'd loved that too, his blazing eyes and rough demands.

She'd never responded so to other men's more gentle seductions. How could Hart know that? What other lady would melt with lust when ordered to raise her skirts? Emma shuddered to think what she would have done if he'd pushed her further. Thrown her careful plans to the wind, at the least, and that only the start of her descent.

If she'd ever doubted that her father's tainted blood flowed in her veins, she had her proof.

Her only consolation was the very stricture of the lies she'd told. Her deception would force her to leave London before a life of sin became normal. As long as she could keep from his bed until the ton returned to the city for parliament, she'd have no choice but to leave, to disappear, before anyone from Cheshire appeared to question her story. But maybe . . . in the meantime . . . if she could just get him to touch her a little more.

Madness, her mind hissed and she knew it was true. Madness, not to mention idiocy. And she wouldn't do it. She wouldn't.

But that happy lust in his smile as they'd quit the gaming room . . . it would haunt her every waking moment, and likely every sleeping moment as well. Because if he looked like that after giving her pleasure, she couldn't imagine his happiness when he found his as well.

She could not afford to find out.

Chapter 7

Her opponent, Lord Chestershire, aimed his small eyes in her direction and sneered with triumph. Marsh was there as well, licking his lips at her. Emma wished that Somerhart would make himself useful and lurk behind her chair again, but he had wandered off an hour before.

Marsh leaned close and spoke to her breasts. "It appears your luck has taken a sad turn, Lady Denmore. May I offer the comfort of my arm for a stroll about the room?"

Idiotic cur. Even Chestershire slanted the man an incredulous look. If there had remained any doubt among society that Somerhart was her lover, it had disappeared over dinner. They'd been seated at nearly opposite ends of the table, but the distance hadn't stopped Somerhart from staking his claim. He'd aimed several smoldering looks in her direction, not to mention the occasional wicked smile. Some of the guests had stared at her in openmouthed wonder. Winterhart was not known for displays of affection.

But Lord Marsh was apparently not averse to making open advances to a duke's mistress. Perhaps he just considered it another gamble. And he was right about one thing; Emma's luck hadn't held. She'd lost exactly one hundred and eighteen quid in the past hour. Marsh might as well have been poking at a badger with a sharp stick.

"Well?" he drawled, face angling closer to her cleavage. "Are you available for a bit of . . . exercise?"

"Lord Marsh . . ." She spoke through clenched teeth, though she smiled for the audience. "Kindly remove your face from my bodice."

He drew back and shot her an arrogant look. "You were not so cold this morning."

The conversation at the table stopped at his overloud words. Emma's jaw creaked. "I was on a winning streak this morning, Marsh. I could afford to be indulgent with lesser players. Excuse me, gentlemen."

"Fool," she heard Chestershire whisper as she walked away. "You could at least be quiet about it." Marsh was still protesting when Emma quit the room.

The tension in her shoulders had built up to a steady, sharp ache over the day. Not only did she have to deal with her unrelenting thoughts about Somerhart and temptation, but her fellow guests had begun to treat her differently. At luncheon, the few other ladies attending had ceased to speak whenever she drew near. They'd smiled benignly, so it wasn't that she'd fallen completely out of favor, just that their conversations were either about her or Somerhart or both.

Since dinnertime, the men had begun acting strangely too, sneaking sideways looks when she passed. Emma was growing worried that someone had espied them in the card room this morning. But no, she told herself, there wasn't enough tittering.

Her annoyance edging to anger, Emma swore off the tables for an hour and headed for the conservatory. It opened onto the music room, where delicate piano playing signaled the presence of ladies. Real ladies. Emma stole through the sweet green leaves of orange trees and orchids. The curtained glass doors of the music room were closed, so she eased the latch up and let the door fall open an inch. Music chimed into the air, followed quickly by the chatter of female voices.

There weren't many women in attendance at Moulter's retreat: most were wives of some of the older gentlemen, though there were also two well-to-do widows and a dowager countess. The countess was quite fond of piquet. And gossip, it seemed. Her voice rang out above the others.

"I can't begin to imagine what it is about her."

A gruff male voice interrupted. "Just what I've been wondering all evening."

"Well," the dowager countess pushed on, "there must be something, though she seems exceedingly average. He's been the Duke of Winterhart for over a decade, now suddenly he's thawing as quickly as snow in spring rain."

Another woman cleared her throat. "Not entirely. I commented on the uncommon blue of his eyes and he brushed a piece of lint from his coat and walked away without a word!"

The countess descended into gales of laughter. Emma was sure she could actually hear the other woman seething.

"It was quite rude," she bit out.

"Oh, my poor Lady Worster! I *am* sorry!" Despite her apologies, the countess continued to laugh for several more seconds. "I once heard the duke comment that if there were one lady in the country who hadn't mentioned the color of his eyes, he'd pluck them out and hand them to her."

"Such rudeness should not be tolerated!"

"Ah, but it will be. Did you hear he's acquired another railroad? Is that three now?"

The man cleared his throat. "Well, there must be something about her. The duke seems almost, dare I say, human?"

The dowager snorted. "Ha! He used to be quite human back when I was Countess Shrewsbury. Or perhaps not human, but more of a satyr!"

An ancient female voice cracked with laughter. "Yes, goat hooves and all. That letter . . . my word."

"The letter! Did you see it?"

"Oh, I did."

Emma leaned closer, lip caught between her teeth. The letter. She'd heard whispers about it, unsatisfying snippets of information. It was the stuff of legend, this missive Somerhart had penned to his lover.

She was sure the story must be exaggerated, despite that the occasional speaker claimed to have seen the actual note. The man was Winterhart, after all. Notoriously icy and controlled. And even though she'd recently seen him in his old incarnation, Emma found it hard to believe that words like *lush* and *thrust* and *worshipped thighs* had ever fallen from his pen. Surely he'd never woven lust into poetry. Even after the morning's debacle she could not believe that the man had ever proposed marriage to a woman ten years his senior who'd played mistress to half a dozen of his peers.

Despite Emma's best efforts, the rumors of his past proved hard to confirm. The voices on the other side of the conservatory door grew hushed as they always did. No one wanted to risk the duke's displeasure. He'd made his ruthlessness quite clear over the past decade.

He kept no one close. No one. But even a nodding acquaintance with Somerhart was better than the alternative: frozen disregard, perhaps even outright hostility. Not to mention the occasional infliction of cruelty. Somerhart had purchased more than a few gentlemen's debts when he'd heard particularly nasty comments made about his scandalous sister. The debts had been called in, and whatever terms the gentlemen managed to negotiate had changed their faces in some permanent, inscrutable way. One simply did not cross the duke . . . unless one had nothing and no one to lose.

Emma leaned her head against the white-painted doorjamb.

Eavesdropping had proven useless, but she did not want to leave, didn't want to resume the night's performance. The confidence and dry amusement, the tolerance for arched eyebrows and moistened lips. And now this other ruse—this pretense of being Somerhart's lover. Or worse . . .

Emma pressed her fingers to her eyes as if the pressure would counter the aching tension behind them.

It wasn't the pretense of being his lover that proved so distressing, it was the struggle with herself. The struggle against what she wanted so badly. Something lush and fiery. Thrusting and secret and sacred. Something wrong and unbearably beautiful.

And suddenly Emma could see the impossible: Hart whispering words that could never, never have passed his lips.

But hadn't he already done impossible things? They'd lit his eyes with joy. Ordering her to lift her skirts and spread her legs. Kissing, sucking, risking everything to chance. Oh, he'd enjoyed that, reveled in it nearly as much as she had. He was wicked and cold. Debauched and impenetrable. Sensual and utterly removed. Like opposite halves of two different men.

Lost in thought, Emma breathed deeply of the brightly scented trees and the heavy weight of fragrant blooms. Only a scattering of the sconces were lit, and heavy curtains shielded the room from the cold night. The space felt veiled and protected. A magical solitude. The air shifted like warm liquid against her skin every time she moved and she felt protected even by that. The world was removed from her, not part of her, and for once she was glad to be isolated from every other soul.

This place felt like summer, like a still, sweltering night, and Emma wanted to curl up on a bed of grass and stay here forever. If she couldn't have secret thrusting, she could have some damned peace.

Someone new must have sat down to the piano, because

the music swelled to richness, and the last of the tension fell from Emma's shoulders in a great wave. When she closed her eyes, she was gone. Elsewhere. Beside the pond in her uncle's yard, curled into the long grass with a book. Or perhaps farther away, at that oceanside cottage with her mother, safe and happy as they were whenever they went away. But that comforting scene—snug next to her mother, the gentle touch stroking her hair—was fraught with foreboding, a fog of horrid knowledge of what lay ahead, so Emma scrambled back from it.

Her eyes popped open and *he* was standing there, arms crossed, watching her. "Hart," she whispered, not knowing if she was happy to see him.

His elegant head tilted slightly to the side. "Emma," he answered. Her name must have felt right to his tongue, because his mouth eased into a half smile. But the smile flitted away, to be replaced by a vague frown. "Are you well?"

Emma let her head fall back to rest against the wall and nodded.

His hard, cold eyes studied her, a close perusal that seemed not to satisfy his thoughts. "I'm intruding?"

Was he? "No, I—" The music ended on a series of faint notes that reminded Emma of her original purpose. She reached over and eased the French door closed before someone overheard them. When she looked back to Hart, his blue eyes glinted with amusement.

"Eavesdropping, Lady Denmore?"

She shrugged and pushed away from the wall, let her eyes fall to the sturdy glass in his right hand. "That's for me, I hope."

He finally gave her a real smile. "You are shameless."

"Mm. And thirsty."

He handed over the snifter of brandy and Emma saw to its quick demise. Hart plucked the empty glass from her fingers and set it on a low table. "What are you hiding from, Emma?"

"I played badly tonight." She wandered past him, trailing her fingers over glossy leaves.

"I don't mean tonight. I mean every night."

Despite the shock that hit her at his words, Emma smiled. "Don't be dramatic, Somerhart. I'm not hiding any more than you are." She shot him a pointed look, and he arched an eyebrow in acknowledgment.

"All right then. What are you hiding from tonight? Or did you sneak in here only to spy on the other guests?"

"Possibly."

"Because I assume if you wanted to enjoy the music, you could simply retire to the appropriately named room."

"Perhaps." She was unable to contain her smile, though she tried to keep her head angled toward the plants instead of the insufferable man.

"Did you hear anything interesting?"

"Mm. Some passable Haydn, a touch of Bach."

"And?"

Emma sighed and sat heavily on a stone bench. "I had no idea you enjoyed gossip so much."

He didn't relent. "I had no idea that *you* did, Emma."

She couldn't help but look up at her name, such an intimacy, and he had every right to use it now.

"What is wrong?" he pushed.

She gave in with a sigh. "People are treating me strangely—"

"Poorly?" he interrupted.

Emma shook her head. "Not at all. Only . . . they seem curious."

"Curious."

Emma met his gaze and held it. "About the woman who could thaw the great Duke of Winterhart."

The skin around his eyes tightened. "I see."

"They seem to find me singularly unremarkable and can't imagine that I could inspire you to such . . . indiscretion."

His jaw shifted forward a fraction of an inch, but he said nothing.

"You clearly can't stand the idea of people discussing you. So why are you doing this? And for no reason, I'll remind you, since I won't give in."

Though his jaw jumped with tension, Somerhart shrugged and let his arms fall to his sides. "It seems this morning that I enjoyed myself far too much to care that people may talk."

"It can't happen again." Her words conveyed a strength she didn't feel, and he must've known it for his teeth flashed in a quick, wicked smile. Emma steeled herself, knowing he was about to press his seduction, knowing she must tap some heretofore unfound resolve.

But he surprised her. Instead of sliding into the seat beside her, Somerhart took the bench across the narrow aisle. The man seemed content to talk. Again.

"Do you have family?"

"No. Will you tell me about your sister?"

He grunted and crossed his ankles. "What do you wish to know?"

"Is she truly scandalous?"

"Oh, yes. Truly."

Emma smiled at the affection in his voice. "Yet you seem to love her."

"Of course. She is my sister. Why don't you wish to marry?"

Emma had been relaxing, but now she scowled. "You should be careful of your choice of topic, sir. The wrong lady would assume you were leading toward negotiation."

"Pardon?" His eyes flared with horror and Emma choked on her laughter, relieved she wasn't some young maid with dreams of marrying the handsome duke.

"This is twice now you've asked why I won't marry. Are you quite interested?"

"Good God, I'm usually more careful. Your bad influence again, I'm sure."

"*Me?*"

"Your recklessness is catching."

His gaze fell to her mouth as she chuckled. "You think it reckless to consider marriage?"

"I'm a bachelor duke. It's reckless to even be this near an unmarried woman. Many of them have hidden tentacles, you know."

"Quite hunted, are you?"

"Quite."

"Then what are you thinking, Hart? I'm the worst possible choice of lover. Unmarried, poor, clearly grasping for wealth and attention. And then there is the notoriety! For God's sake, employ your ducal brains."

Her speech had no effect, or rather it coaxed a wide grin from his lush mouth. "You are a harsh mistress."

"I'm no mistress at all."

"You will be."

"Hardly."

The grin faded to something secret and sly. "Must I order you to lift your skirts again? Or perhaps something more wicked this time?"

More wicked? Good Lord. All the moisture in her mouth dried to sand. "No," she started to say, but her voice was swallowed by his.

"You are quite naughty, aren't you, Emma?" She'd thought herself safe because of his distance, but he was too dangerous for safety at any length. "That picture of you hasn't left my mind for a moment. Would you obey any command, I wonder?"

"No."

"What if I ordered you to your knees, Emma? Right here?"

His words exploded through her. She had to open her mouth to draw even the smallest breath. Images played behind her eyes. Those things she'd seen and never done. A man's head thrown back, fingers tangled in a woman's long hair. A woman on her knees, mouth opening. Lust spun tight deep inside her.

Hart leaned forward, forearms braced on his thighs. "Would you, Emma?"

She shook her head as her nipples peaked. His eyelids dropped until he showed nothing more than glittering slits of bright blue. "I think you would."

"No." But she could almost *feel* it. His hand fisted in her hair as she did his bidding. Pleasure racking his body, shaking his muscles to steel. Oh . . .

"No." She pushed to her feet, tried to lock her liquid knees. Hart stared up at her with sleepy eyes. "I did not come to London to take a lover," she insisted.

"Regardless, you have."

"No."

He leaned back and searched her face with an insolent gaze. "You want me to take control." His own words made him smile as the blood drained from her face. "That's it, isn't it? You want me to tell you what to do, so you'll have no choice but to give in and enjoy it."

"I want you to leave me alone!"

"This morning you wanted me right . . ." His gaze dipped low, his cheeks flushed. "*There.* You demanded it."

"I . . . don't . . ."

"Don't what?" The sharp look had faded to unfocused softness, a haze of blue desire. His left hand rose to stroke down the front of her skirt. A feather touch that whispered over the navy satin. "You smell like . . . *heat,* Emma. Like someplace I want to be."

"Oh." She wanted to give him that, give him everything. Oh, God, she *wanted.* "I can't! You don't understand!" With an awkward lurch, Emma broke free of his mesmerizing nearness. He rose slowly, shaking off the spell he'd woven around both of them.

"What are you looking for?"

Emma backed away, but he stalked forward, keeping her within reach. She was conscious of his long-fingered hands and the warmth they contained.

"A challenge?" He nodded in answer to his own question. "A challenge. Am I making this too easy for you, a woman who needs risk?"

"No, I don't want—"

"Fine. I won't come to you tonight. I'm not a supplicant, nor will I ever be. But a challenge? I can be that. I'd love to be that."

Her back hit the wall. She was only six inches from the closed door, but Hart reached her before she could catch hold of the doorknob. His palm hit the wall above her head. He loomed above, his clean scent sneaking into her soul.

Emma's breasts strained the seams of her bodice with every rapid breath.

"You take control, Emma," he whispered. The words tickled her ear, he spoke them so close. Shivers raced down her neck, down her chest and her belly. "Take control of me. Come to me." Her neck arched, wanting his mouth to bite her. "If you do, Emma, I *may* give you what you want. Or I may offer more than you can handle.

"Risk. That's what you like, isn't it? So play with fire. Play with me."

She was shaking, trembling, just as he'd wanted. His breath grew warmer, closer, till his lips *must* touch her and still they didn't. His mouth hovered just over the skin of her temple, and then he sighed out a secret wish.

"Order me to my knees, Emma."

She sobbed and grabbed blindly for the doorknob. When she slipped under his arm, Hart let her go without a word.

Cheers erupted from the small crowd around her, and Emma made herself smile. She'd tried to relax into the chair, recapture her careless persona, but her body was rebelling. Every few minutes she'd find herself perched on the edge of the cushion, back straight and screaming of tension.

It didn't help that she'd just bet on a third game of billiards. She had no idea how to play, and so she was forced to watch and depend on others for her luck. She hated depending on others.

Shifting in her seat, Emma ran a hand over the hard line of her corset. The motion drew the attention of at least one pair of eyes. The nape of her neck burned with awareness.

Emma scowled. She wouldn't turn around to look, but he was there. Lounging against the wall, receiving obsequious admiration from the people who hovered near. And keeping himself in her thoughts.

Retiring to bed would be worse, of course. And there was nothing else to bloody well do, because one billiard game had tumbled into a full damned tournament among the male guests. Most of them, anyway. Somerhart was far too dignified to participate. *Dignified. Ha.*

Order me to my knees. He'd purposefully titillated her. Aroused her. Stuck himself like a burr beneath her skullcap.

Lord Marsh, who'd already been knocked out of play, sidled closer to her chair and laid an arm across the high back. "Lady Denmore, I congratulate you. Your luck has improved."

"Mr. Jones is offering tips."

"Helpful pup, that one."

Emma stared silently at the players. Her limbs ached with the desire to leap up and try her hand at the game. It didn't look all that difficult, but she knew it must take subtle skill. It couldn't possibly be as simple as it seemed.

"Lady Denmore . . ." Marsh angled his head closer, though he avoided the appearance of intimacy by keeping his eyes on the billiard table. "I think it only fair to warn you—you being new to our society—that Somerhart is not known for his—"

A bowing footman intruded and Marsh straightened away from her. Emma didn't care. She didn't need additional warnings. She could barely heed her own.

"My lady," the footman said, offering a letter on a silver tray. Emma glanced around before she realized he spoke to her.

"Me?" How odd. It certainly wasn't a proposal of assignation, which might be expected from one of several different gentlemen here; the scrawled writing indicated it had come from London.

She stared at it, a bit dumbfounded, as the servant retreated. There was no one outside these walls who'd write her letters. Too uncertain to open it in front of others, Emma rose and made for the door.

She wondered if Somerhart followed her, and the idea pushed her faster but also sent an unwelcome thrill down her spine. Insidious plague of a man.

Emma ducked around the corner of the massive front staircase and took a deep breath of lemon-scented air. Her childhood home had smelled of lemon polish too, before her mother's death. Afterward, it had smelled mostly of stale tobacco.

The unmarked seal gave way with a sharp crack. Emma recognized the choppy writing and uncertain spelling with a glance. Bess.

Her pulse quickened, then flooded to a drumbeat as she deciphered the message. *A thief. A broken window. Nothing missing.* Nothing missing. An extremely inefficient thief then. Or no thief at all.

Matthew, damn him for a determined pest. It had to be him, or some lackey of his, trying to find proof of her identity.

What could she do? Nothing from here, certainly. She had to return to London and try to fight him, but with what?

Her heart boomed against her throat, choking her. She only needed a few more weeks. If she could bribe him or convince him that she'd return to Cheshire and consider marriage . . .

Or maybe it was time to give up. If she were arrested, all her money would be eaten up in bribes and solicitor's fees. But she didn't have enough yet. What would've been the point of all this, of risking everything, if she left in the same position she'd been in before? A thousand pounds would support her a few good years, but she had no skill, no income, and absolutely no intention of depending on another.

She needed the rest of the money.

Emma folded the note into a tight square and snuck around the corner and up the main stairs. Mr. Jones would collect her money and hold it for her until she could retrieve it. She trusted him, though youth and kindness aside, she wouldn't trust him more than that. If he found out the truth about her, he'd react with as much viciousness as any of them. Outrage at being tricked. Anger. Punishment. They'd want to put her in her place. She had no intention of being near when the truth came out.

Packing would take no more than an hour. Then she'd get as much sleep as she could manage before dawn.

Chapter 8

Never before had Emma realized how variable time could be. How a minute could vanish in a blink. How one night could drag on for an impossible eternity.

Anxiety and fear sank their twin jaws into her belly over and over again as the night's hours stood still. She felt shaky and exhausted and wide awake. She wasn't sure if she should be relieved that dawn was only a few hours off or upset that she couldn't even hope for more than four hours of sleep now.

She just wanted the fear to stop. The fear fed doubt, and doubt was a gambler's worst foe.

Trapped in the solitude of her room, Emma alternated between tossing and turning in her twisted sheets, and pacing from one corner of the chamber to another, doubt dogging her every step.

She should not have left London. She should never have come to London in the first place. What if she lost everything, including her freedom? So many doubts . . .

Emma paced faster, wishing she could take action, do something.

So many regrets . . .

Perhaps she should have stayed in Cheshire and made the

best of it. But Matthew had refused to accept rejection. He'd grown more aggressive, more obnoxious. And even months after her uncle's death, she'd still been racked with guilt every time she'd passed the ashes of his home. If she hadn't snuck out that night, if she'd been there to save him when the fire had started . . .

When she rubbed a hand over her face, Emma wasn't surprised to find tears. Because her uncle's death wasn't her greatest regret. Not by far. She'd failed her brother in the same way. Worse, she'd known of the danger, known her father was drunk, and still she'd let him take Will riding. She could live with the mistakes she'd made with her own life, but not those she'd made with others'. Will. His body so cold. Stiff with death.

"Oh, God. Please," she prayed, or tried to. "Please." The pressure in her chest failed to ease. Guilt wound through her like a snake tightening its hold. Emma stumbled to the window and pried open the sash.

Freezing air burst in, swimming over her exposed skin. The wind pressed her nightgown to her body and coated her in damp cold. Emma gulped at the sharp, fresh air as if she'd been drowning. She drank it deep in desperate gasps. Within seconds she was shivering, but she could feel the serpent loosen its hold on her soul.

She slowed her breath and leaned her weight against the windowsill.

She needed a distraction, that was all. Something to consume her thoughts. If she could get through this night, she could fix things in London or at least plot her quiet escape from the city. She just needed to get through this one night. Just as she'd gotten through others.

Emma leaned forward until even her shoulders passed the edge of the glass. She hung her head and let the night air caress the nape of her neck. She didn't know why the cold soothed her, didn't know why she found winter so fascinating and tempting. She only knew that the rest of her life was smothering her, squeezing all the blood and air from her body. But out here she could breathe.

And, strange as it was, she could breathe with Hart. Even though they were constantly sparring, even though he pushed her toward what she couldn't have.

Order me to my knees.

Emma sighed out a long, long breath, then drew air into her lungs as slowly as she could.

She couldn't risk it. The situation was too precarious. She couldn't go to his room and let him touch her. Her will was gossamer thin, worn down by desperation and vulnerability. But Hart was exactly the magnitude of distraction she needed. Totally overwhelming. All encompassing. Her solution and her problem.

Hart.

It would be madness to let him near tonight. Utter madness.

His room was silent and too dark. The cooler air of the hallway drew a warm, spicy scent from his chambers and swept it over Emma's face. She shivered and slid one bare foot from the hall rug onto the wood floor at the threshold of his room.

As she stepped farther in, her eyes began to adjust to the faint light of the night candle left burning on his bedside table. His short hair smudged black against the pillowcase. One bare arm was flung wide and, as she followed the curve of muscle up, her eyes found a bare shoulder that curved to an angle of naked chest.

The bedclothes cut across that delicious view and made her want to strip him bare for her basest pleasures.

Her skin tightened and tingled with the thrill of her risk and daring. She was sneaking into a man's room, a man she'd fantasized about for years. His skin glowed richly in the candlelight, and though his face was turned away, Emma could see the perfect edge of his jaw and the corner of that succulent mouth.

By God, she wanted to touch him so badly, wanted to explore the texture of every part of him, but that wasn't what she'd come for. Her will simply couldn't withstand such overwhelming temptation. If she felt him under her hands, she'd want to feel him above her, around her, inside her.

Breath shuddered past her lips at the thought. Emma closed the door behind her and leaned her liquid body against it.

The line of his face changed as the flame wavered. She could read a frown in the tense line of his jaw. His long fingers spasmed. Emma watched them, remembering . . .

Her lips felt numb when she licked them. "Don't—" she started, but the word came out a whisper. Emma swallowed and tried again. *"Don't get out of bed."*

Hart jerked to awareness, startling her into a gasp. He was sitting up and facing her before she'd seen him move.

"Who's there?" he barked.

"Me," Emma answered. "It's me."

His wariness melted into confusion, but only for a moment. Then a feral smile appeared, flashing white in the dimness. "Emma." A leg snuck from under the sheets as he started to rise.

"Stop!"

He froze.

"Don't get up."

He glanced down to his legs and back up to her. "Shall I don a dressing robe?"

"No. Just stay there."

Confusion again. Hart rubbed a hand over his sleep-heavy eyes. "You're planning to join me? Consider yourself invited."

She could only shake her head, saving all her courage for her next request.

Somerhart's mouth sank into a scowl. "I don't know what you're about, Emma, but it's the middle of the night and you're in my room—"

"Take off the bedclothes," she said in a rush.

"I . . . Pardon?" He blinked. Twice.

Emma raised her chin. She hid her shaking hands and tried to make her voice as steady as possible. "I wish to see you naked. Push the coverlet aside."

He stared blankly for a moment, then emotions began to pass over his face like clouds: shock, curiosity, and then, finally, something fierce and hot and infinitely dangerous. "You're taking up my challenge, Emma?"

She curled her fingers tight and pushed herself straighter against the door. "Take off the bedclothes, now." She didn't want him thinking, didn't need his cutting commentary right now.

Her gamble paid off. After a long, arched look, Hart chose to comply. He held her gaze and reached down to the quilted green silk that hid his body.

Her eyes must be adjusting, because she could see the shape of him now, beneath the covers. And then he slowly swept them aside.

Emma held her breath at the sight of his nudity. His wide chest, the dusting of dark hair that trailed down over a hard, muscled belly and lower, to the thatch of black hair that surrounded his sex.

Her heart drowned out any other sound, but Emma was sure that she sighed. His body faced her, shoulders propped high by one elbow, and she had an unobstructed view of his thick erection. Even as she watched, it grew heavier, larger, as if it relished an audience. Emma watched until it grew so firm that it stood only slightly away from his stomach.

It looked made for her to wrap her hands around. Her

belly melted into a knot of warm tension at the thought. Her hands clenched and unclenched, crumpling the delicate wool of her nightgown.

"Well?" he growled. "Do I please you?"

Oh, yes. Yes, he pleased her very much and he would do much more than *please* if she'd let him.

"Touch yourself," she ordered before she could give in and cross the room.

"What?"

"Touch yourself. I want to watch you . . . pleasure yourself." Her whole body clenched at her own words.

Shock again on his beautiful face, and then Hart's eyes narrowed, his brow fell. "No."

"Yes."

He gave one curt laugh. "No."

She swept her gaze down and watched his cock jump as if she'd touched him. "I want to see you, Hart. I want to *watch.* Now do it."

He started to push up, started to swing his feet to the floor, and Emma reached for the door handle. "If you touch the floor, I'll leave. Lie down."

His scowl didn't budge, but he fell back to his elbow.

"Good," Emma sighed, the sudden burst of alarm spiraling back down to aching anticipation. She watched him, waiting . . . waiting for him to rebel or acquiesce.

His hand twitched against his side. Emma licked her lips. "Touch yourself," she repeated, more a whisper than an order, but he finally obeyed. His fingers, dark against his belly, slid down and curved around the dusky skin of his shaft.

She nearly whimpered at the sight. Nervous with heady, sexual power, Emma glanced up to his face. His cheekbones were flushed and stark, his eyes glittered.

"Did you really think of me the other night? When you did this?"

"Yes." His voice rumbled through her, shooting sparks along the way.

"Show me."

His hand was still for an impossibly long moment. Then his fist tightened. He stroked.

The knees that had previously supported her trembled away to mist, and she had to press her back more firmly to the door. He gave her nothing more in the meantime. His face was carved into lines of anger and tension. And lust.

"More," she ordered, and his whole body shuddered. But he obliged. He fell to his back and stroked again, working his flesh in a slow, steady motion. Emma's body glowed— a dull aurora of power and joy that pulsed brighter with every movement of Hart's arm.

But her feelings fascinated her almost as much as his actions. Her sex beat like a sharp, beautiful pulse. Her face burned with heat. Her limbs felt numb and insubstantial, as if she'd burned into nothingness.

And Hart . . . Oh, he was breathtaking. A long line of tensing muscles and sweat-touched skin. His shaft was thick and so very hard, straining against his tight grip. She wanted to *feel*. To stroke lightly, trace with her fingertip, squeeze him in her fist. She wanted to work him, see if she could find a rhythm that would make him gasp for mercy. As much as she'd seen in her short life, she'd never actually *touched,* but she couldn't go to him.

Instead, Emma placed a cupped hand to the throbbing between her legs. The slightest pressure of the heel of her palm made her gasp.

Hart's head snapped toward her. His eyes opened, blank with pleasure. But his gaze sharpened as it swept over her body, lingering on her indiscreet hand. She pressed her fingers harder and Hart's free hand clutched at the sheet next to his hip. His teeth showed in a grimace of lust, his movement quickened.

She explored him with her eyes instead of her hands, drinking in the absolute wickedness of this night. She wanted to remember this forever. Wanted to think about this when she lay in bed with only her own hands for comfort. And, oh, he'd think of this too. She knew he would, and that made her satisfaction so much keener.

The muscled line of his thighs shifted. His taut belly sucked in and his chest rose and fell in a faster rhythm. Emma looked to his face, to his mouth drawn tight with pleasure. His eyes glittered with something close to rage.

"Watch me," he snarled, and Emma looked back to his stroking hand. She pressed her palm closer and her jaw shook. Her heart kept time with the rhythm he set, speeding up to meet his movements as they quickened. His free hand tightened around the silk.

"Emma," he whispered, *"yes."* And then he shuddered to his climax while Emma watched. And, oh, God, she wanted to feel him them, find out everything she'd never know. Was it hot? Slick? What would he taste like if she took him into her mouth right now, if she drank him up? Would he rise again if she went to him and crawled over him as she wanted?

His deep, desperate breaths began to slow, and this would be over soon, and Emma didn't want it to—

"Get out," he gasped.

She shook her head. She wasn't ready to leave and he couldn't mean that. He couldn't. So she stood, trying not to move, trying to *stay.* But his breathing was almost normal now, and his limbs growing limp with relaxation. His eyes opened, bright blue against flushed cheeks.

The eyes narrowed. His mouth curled in a snarl. "Get the hell out of my room. *Now.*"

And Emma fled, slamming the door behind her.

Chapter 9

The bedcovers were a warm weight against his body, holding in heat and an unusual lethargy. Hart felt as if he'd sunk deep into the feathered mattress and he wasn't the least bit interested in climbing out. He threw an arm over his eyes to hold off the morning and floated slowly back into a heavy sleep of satisfaction.

A few minutes passed, perhaps an hour, and he blinked awake again. Before he'd even had time to stretch his limbs, memory returned and, with it, anger. His muscles froze to stone.

What the hell had he allowed to happen? What the hell had he *done*?

Hart's body responded to that question by swelling with a renewed arousal that only further infuriated him. How quickly he'd been pulled back into the depths of his unnatural lusts. How easy to transform from the self-controlled duke into the debased rake. For God's sake, if she started spreading tales of his little show . . .

Hart sat up and reached over to jerk the bellpull, but he'd only brushed it with his fingers when his valet tapped at the door.

"Enter!" Hart shouted. His blood was rolling too quickly

through his veins and pushing heat into his face. He wanted to take back the night or at least turn it into something else. Something *he* controlled, despite his challenge to Emma. Somehow this seemed so much worse than being caught ravishing a woman in the card room. To be snickered at. To be turned into a freak . . .

His head spun as Wellford brought tea and toast into the room. "I'll need hot water for washing," Hart barked.

Wellford murmured, "Immediately, sir," as he bowed back out the door. He did not say, "Of course, sir. I bring you hot water every single morning, even when you haven't debased yourself for a woman."

Hart gulped the scalding tea. As the liquid burned down his throat, his brain slowly began to right itself. He wasn't a foolish young man anymore. He may have indulged his baser needs last night, but there was no evidence, no proof in his own handwriting to titillate his peers. At worst, a story might circulate and then he'd make that woman pay.

He finished his cold toast, and Wellford returned with a steaming ewer of water. Wellford set out towels and soap next to the basin, then shaving powder and a razor. "Shall I return in a moment to shave you, sir?"

"Yes," he answered, but he was thinking of the woman across the hall, wondering if she were still abed. It didn't matter. He'd track her down and make himself clear. She had more to lose in this affair than he did. Risking exposure was one thing, and he could decide what he'd risk. But to let her have control—that had been a mistake.

A half hour later he was feeling more himself and almost entirely unashamed as he shot his crisp white cuffs and rolled the tension from his neck. "Would you send a message to Lady Denmore's room, Wellford? Inquire if she requires an escort to breakfast."

Wellford disappeared with his usual grace. Hart's brain began to buzz again, but this wasn't anxiety, it was anticipation.

Of seeing her again and what the day would bring. Would she be cool this morning, or still trembling with need? Would she make him laugh or yell? And tonight . . . How would their game play out? Whose room would be invaded? How far would it go?

He was in control again. He could handle this situation. He could handle her.

"Sir?"

"Mm."

"It seems Lady Denmore has departed, sir."

"All right." She'd damn well better be in the breakfast room this morning. If he caught her in . . .

Wellford's throat had caught a particularly large and unmanageable frog.

"Yes, Wellford?"

"According to the chambermaid, Lady Denmore left this morning around eight. Lord Moulter was kind enough to lend his coach."

Hart froze in the act of tucking an extra handkerchief into his coat pocket. "Pardon?"

"I believe she has returned to London, Your Grace."

Hart's fantasy of control vanished with a little *pop* that stung more than just his pride. Oh, yes, he would make that woman pay.

Hart looked away from the distant sight of Emma's front steps and glared down at Stimp. "Her home was broken into almost two days ago. Why the hell didn't you send word?"

"I'm not exactly part of the household, guv. The housekeeper didn't tell me 'til last night. Then I had to find a man to write the note for me and a rider to carry it. I must've missed you."

"You are supposed to be *watching* the house."

"Well, it's a big house, isn't it? And a long night as well."

"Do you know who it was, this supposed thief?"

The boy broke into a smile wide enough to reveal one missing tooth. "I don't know his name, but I know where he's sleeping."

Hart's mood immediately improved and he responded with a predatory smile. "Even better. Lead the way."

"It's blocks away. Call for your damned carriage. 'At's what it's for."

Sparing a haughty glare for the little urchin, Hart raised a hand. As the sound of horseshoes against stone drew closer, Stimp's eyes grew brighter. He struggled to remain expressionlessly unimpressed, but he was only a child after all. His big brown eyes glimmered with joy, and Hart had to hold back a snort. The boy fought hard for his dignity, and Hart would let him have it.

"In," he ordered as the wheels slowed to a halt. The boy jumped in, agile as a cat. "Push up that little hatch there and tell the driver where to go."

Stimp needed no further prompting. He took over directing the carriage, opened all the windows and settled into the cushions, lap blanket pulled high against the breeze he'd created.

He shouted instructions several times. The carriage turned left and right and right again, then seemed to go through the same motions once more. Hart was certain the journey was rather longer than strictly required.

"What do you know?" he asked Stimp.

"Whoever he is, he's a stranger 'round here. A big fellow. Closemouthed but not good at keeping hid."

"The same man who paid you for information last month?"

"The same. And he come back last night too, dumb as you please. I chased him off and followed him. Wasn't sure you'd want the constables involved."

Hart shrugged, unsure himself.

"He went straight to a tavern, drunk himself into a mean

stupor, and he's been snoring it off at this lodging 'ouse ever since."

Hart tugged his watch free. "It's three in the afternoon."

"He drank 'til seven this morning."

He was impressed with the lad's fortitude. "You must be tired, Stimp."

The little shoulders shrugged, though his eyes shown with pleasure again. "Spying ain't exactly hauling coal." The boy's eyebrow rose in a startlingly accurate impression of Hart's favorite expression. "It's practically gentlemen's work, isn't it, guv?"

Hart found himself holding back another smile. No wonder the street rat reminded him of Lady Denmore. Insolent to the core. "I'm not entirely sure I trust you, Stimp."

The boy's laughter rang like a bell as they finally jerked to a stop.

When Hart stepped down, he found himself at the doorway of a rambling three-story structure that seemed to stretch on for the entire block. Stimp darted past him and through the propped-open door. Sparks began to race over Hart's skin as he followed through narrow halls. The air was just as cold as it had been outside, but it was thicker here, tainted with bodies and old, bad cooking. He took care not to brush against the mottled gray walls.

What the hell did this man living in cold and filth have to do with Emma? His anger was sharpened and magnified by his doubts about her. This man was no ordinary thief. There was something else going on, something to do with gambling, he didn't doubt. Idiot woman.

He ran up the stairs after Stimp, around a corner and into an even darker hallway. Stimp slid to a stop in front of a battered brown door. Hart waited for the boy's nod before he smashed the door open with the flat of his hand.

Two men looked up from sleeping pads and caught sight of Hart's face. They'd scrambled up and out the door within three heartbeats, abandoning the third man curled into the corner.

Hart picked his way through a maze of stained, rumpled blankets and nudged the man with his boot.

"That's 'im," Stimp offered as Hart nudged again, much harder this time. The man stirred and gin fumes wafted up like pungent smoke.

"Christ."

"If he's from the country, he's likely not used to that brew."

Grimacing at the idea, Hart leaned down and grabbed a fistful of the man's shirt. Whatever stained it was dry at least.

A good shake roused the drunk bastard, but his eyelids fluttered closed as soon as Hart stopped shaking.

"Wake up, you thieving wretch."

"Ernnh," was the only reply.

"Damn it." He yanked the man to his feet, rather unsuccessfully. "Either stand or I'll drag you down the stairs." He had to get the man out into the fresh air. Hell, he had to get himself out into the fresh air, the combination of gin and stale sweat and God knew what else was making his eyes water.

He dragged the man across the room and down the hall, thankful when he woke enough to slide his feet beneath him to bear some of the weight.

"Stairs," Hart warned before he pulled him, thunking, down the steps.

The loud groan of protest was easily ignored, but the big hands that came up to clutch Hart's wrists were more intrusive. Not only were they sticky, they were strong as hell. He tossed the man out the front door and wiped his arm against his jacket.

By the time he made it into the open air that smelled of

coal smoke instead of gin and onions, Stimp was standing guard, arms crossed and eyes glaring at passersby.

Hart paused to consider how best to wake the drunkard. A bucket of cold, foul water over the head? A boot to the ribs? The appeal of giving the man a good thrashing proved tempting, but Hart reconsidered even as he drew his foot back. The man knew Emma somehow from somewhere. He might not reveal their secrets, but she would.

"Help me get him into the carriage."

Stimp's eyebrows neared his hairline. "He's likely to cast up his accounts all over your finery if you bounce him around in there."

"We'll put him on the floor and pray for the best."

Stimp shrugged his opinion and helped wrestle the man's large body through the narrow opening. They had him halfway in when the driver jumped down and offered his shoulder as effective leverage.

The driver dusted off his shoulder. "Perhaps you'd prefer to ride above, Your Grace."

"Perhaps I would. Stimp?" But Stimp declined, unwilling to give up what might be his last carriage ride.

They were back at Emma's street and pulling into the alley within minutes, the driver having taken a more direct route. Stimp jumped from the coach with a pointed frown.

"Go and fetch Lady Denmore, Stimp."

The boy made sure to toss a scowl over his shoulder as he skulked toward her back door. Hart followed at a distance, keeping close to the damp brick wall. He heard Stimp walk down the steps, heard the door open.

"Yer mistress," Stimp said. Footsteps rushed across a stone floor and the door opened again.

"Where have you been? I sent word hours ago. I need your help."

Hart swallowed the fury that rose at the sound of her voice. She'd abandoned him without a word. Like a rented mount.

Stimp was making his excuses when she interrupted. "That man you claimed to have run off has returned. Had you noticed?"

"Aye."

Her impatience vibrated through the atmosphere. "Oh, you had? Because the very man I hired you to watch out for has likely broken into my home. You were supposed to be keeping an eye out, but you've only come around once in three days. Did he pay you off?"

"Who?"

"The man who broke into my home!"

"Well, I took his ha'pence that first day, but I already told you about that."

"Stimp, listen." She sounded frightened now. Desperate. "If you can't find out who he is and what he wants, I at least need him gone. This is important. Is there some way he can be gotten rid of?"

Hart blinked and stepped back, shocked at her viciousness.

"Well . . ." Stimp tapped his foot. "I'm sure I know one or two who might be willing to open the man's throat, but it'll cost more than—"

"No! Good God, what kind of child are you? I don't want the man murdered! I just need him run off. For good this time."

Hart felt muscles he'd never recognized relax at her words. The woman was wily and deceptive, but she'd never struck him as violent.

"What if I were to catch 'im for you," Stimp went on, seemingly unfazed by the exchange. "For, say, a half crown? Would that suit yer—"

"Enough," Hart said, and crossed the half-dozen feet to her stairway.

Emma yelped when she spied him, though she clapped a hand over her mouth to try to stop it. But she couldn't hide the fear that blazed to life in those hazel eyes. Stark alarm was followed quickly by bright, scrambling thoughts.

"What are you doing here?" she asked from behind her fingers, but then she lowered her hand and stepped out from the doorway. "I am not receiving visitors, Your Grace. Please send a note next time."

"First of all . . ." He had to unlock his jaw if he wanted to continue. His teeth were beginning to ache. He just felt so . . . *outraged*. Yes, outraged. Used, even. And expecting to be betrayed.

"First of all, if I sent a note, you would never admit to receiving visitors, correct? Second, I am not here to pay a social call, or not a pleasant one at any rate."

She clearly did not know what to think. Her eyes darted from him to Stimp, then back. "If this is about Moulter's . . ." She blushed. Actually blushed. "I apologize for not leaving word. I simply did not have time."

"Liar. You knew that night that you were leaving in the morning. Let's not pretend you were anything but dishonest."

Her eyes flicked to the boy again. "Regardless—"

"Yes," Hart sneered. "*Regardless.* It has nothing to do with that night except as it pertains to the news you received in that note."

"There was—" She broke off and studied him, trying to read his hand and not succeeding in the least. "There was a personal issue. Now if you will excuse me."

"Lark!" Hart shouted over his shoulder.

A lot of thumping and grunting preceded his driver's appearance, but Hart kept his eyes on Emma, measuring her smallest reaction. She looked worried and scared, but he didn't sense even a hint of recognition on her part. Then again, the woman was a consummate gambler, which meant she was a consummate liar.

"Your thief," he said simply when Lark dropped the man on the ground next to Hart.

"Is he . . .?" She swallowed. Hart watched hope and dismay, disgust and anxiety, shudder over her face. One emotion replaced the other in a dizzying show. "He's dead?" she finally asked.

"No, simply drunk. Do you recognize him?"

She stepped up two stairs and craned her neck. Her hands held her skirts in a death grip. "No."

"Well then, let's find out what he was looking for, shall we?"

Hart crouched beside the now snoring man. "Wait!" she cried, just as his palm cracked against the stubble-rough cheek. The man grunted and stirred, but nothing more.

"Wake up," Hart growled and slapped him again.

"Sir," Lark said as he appeared at Hart's side with a bucket filled with murky water.

"Perfect." Hart's murmur was overtaken by Emma's renewed command to wait. She flew up the stairs, close enough when Hart dumped the bucket that drops of dark water soaked into her gray skirts. She jumped back as the drunk finally sputtered to life. The man roared, spitting water, flinging it wide as he threw his arms out.

Hart resolved to take a bath within the hour as he dug his fingers into the man's dripping hair and yanked.

"What is your name?"

The man grunted and swung, earning himself a hard kick to the thigh. He yelped as Hart snarled, "Your name."

"Arse."

"Your name is Arse?"

"No, you're an arse. Now let me go before I tear your arm off, you rump eater."

Hart held up a hand to stop Lark's approach. He let go of the man's hair and smiled when his skull hit the ground with a meaty thump. The bastard was still reaching for his head when Hart carefully placed a boot over his throat and let some of his weight bear down.

The brown eyes began to bulge almost immediately. The

hands flew from his bruised head to Hart's ankle, but Hart pressed harder. "Remove your hands from my person or I'll be sure to lose my balance and crush your worthless throat."

The hands shook, but they rose an inch above the shiny black leather of Hart's boot. Hart eased up and let the man wheeze out a few breaths.

"Now I'm sure you are lying there thinking that in this enlightened age, in this modern city, a man cannot simply kill you in an alley in broad daylight and get away with it. But let me introduce myself, Mr. Arse. I am His Grace, the eighth Duke of Somerhart. I could kill you in front of the House of Lords and they would all swear they'd seen nothing. And if they didn't, I could buy the judge presiding over the case and walk away a free man. So do not doubt that if you don't give me what I want, I will kill you and never spare your sorry life another thought.

"If you refuse to cooperate, Lark here"— the man's eyes rolled toward the driver—"will drop your body in the Thames while I attend the theatre this evening. Am I making myself clear?"

The man's face had faded to white, but it quickly began to turn a dull green. He stretched up his chin so that he could nod past Hart's boot.

Thinking of the wounded attitude his valet would assume at having to clean vomit from his master's boots, Hart slowly slid his foot down to the ground.

"And watch your language. There is a lady present."

Hart was thankful when the man's color returned to a more normal shade of unhealthy white. Then the brown eyes rolled again, and his gaze caught on Emma who had retreated to the bottom of the stairs. The white face tensed, and Hart could trace the rush of his blood as a flush rose up to the man's greasy hairline. His mouth twisted in a sneer of hatred as he pointed a finger at Emma.

"You," he spat, malice rolling off him in gin-scented waves.

Emma backed farther away, but she was caught like a cornered fox by the closed back door. "No," she whispered, and Hart felt betrayal looming close.

"Whore," the man spat, but worse than his vitriol was Hart's gaze. He studied her like a falcon would study a mouse. Emma had not imagined her unmasking would happen in front of him, had never planned for it. How was she to vanish if a sharp-eyed bird of prey stood between her and freedom?

"Whore," the man repeated, his hatred pushing her heart to an even higher gallop. Hart kicked him without looking away from her.

"You do not know him?" he repeated, and Emma shook her head.

He finally turned away from her and, in the same motion, swooped down to slap the man's square face. Emma's ears rang with the startling sound.

"I told you to watch your tongue. Now what is your name?"

"Burl." The man's lip curled in rebellion.

"Burl what?"

"Burl Smythe."

"And what is your interest in Lady Denmore?"

Smythe's mouth grimaced, his eyes darkened with violence. "*Lady?* Is that what she calls herself?"

Hart kicked his thigh again and muttered a few curses under his breath. She could tell he was reminding the man to curb his tongue, but Emma couldn't quite hear it. She was waiting, waiting. She probably should have run. If she could make it past the carriage, they might lose track of her, spend precious time figuring out which direction she'd turned. But then what? She wouldn't have even the money she'd brought to London with her. She'd be destitute. Ruined.

So Emma just stared at this stranger who was about to destroy the world she'd worked so hard to weave together.

"She's a jezebel," Smythe was saying. "A whore leading other women down the path of evil. She's a deceiver. Satan masquerading as a highborn lady."

Some part of her brain insisted that this made no sense. Why would this hired spy hold such contempt for her? Why was he so angry? But the rest of her mind was buzzing, buzzing, drowning out everything but his hateful words and the incessant pounding of her panicked heart.

Emma breathed in deep and heard herself moan as she exhaled.

"She says she doesn't know you, Mr. Smythe."

"Lies! Lies on top of lies!"

Hart's eagle eyes swung toward her and paused there for a moment. His gaze narrowed. "You know what he speaks of."

"I don't," she whispered, pressing harder against the door. Maybe she could go through the door and escape out the front, maybe she could grab her winnings from Moulter's as she fled.

Hart aimed that piercing gaze back at Smythe. He said, "Perhaps you could be more clear in your grievances," and then the world opened up behind Emma.

The solid door vanished and she was falling into fear and uncertainty and wondering if she'd fainted. But her flailing hand caught smooth wood and her back bumped against something warm. "Ma'am?" Bess murmured close to her ear. She helped Emma right herself just as Smythe began to roar with fury.

"Lizzy," he shouted. "Lizzy!"

The solidness that had been Bess trembled against Emma's back, turning into something weaker. "Oh," Bess sobbed. "Oh, no. Oh, God above, save me."

"Lizzy!" he roared again and lurched to his feet. He lunged toward them, throwing himself down the stairs. Both Hart and the driver sprang forward to catch him. He hitched back, but then his jacket slid from his shoulders and he pulled his arms free, leaving the two men to stumble back, hands clutching brown wool.

"Burl, no. *Please,*" Bess cried out, but her words pushed fire into his eyes.

"Faithless whore," he growled.

Stimp flew at him and was brushed aside as easily as a fly.

The man loomed huge, fists rising. Bess backed away, retreating into the house, and Emma fell to the floor, landing hard. She didn't have time to register the pain that shot up her back; an angry bull was charging straight for her.

She scooted backward and almost managed to dodge the rock-hard fist that swung toward her. The blow caught the top of her head and knocked her into the wall, but he didn't stop moving. He pushed right past her and snagged Bess's dress as she tried to escape around the corner into the kitchen.

Bess was pulled off balance and swayed right into his punch. Bone cracked. Blood spurted from her nose. Emma screamed in horror. She tried to push to her feet, but when a shadow crossed her vision, Emma ducked and flung her arms over her throbbing head.

"I've got him," Hart grunted. "Emma, are you all right? Emma?"

She looked up what seemed to be an impossibly long distance and caught sight of Hart's worried face as he pulled Smythe out by his neck.

"Fine," she murmured as she tried to catch up to the meaning of what had happened. "Bess?" She searched out the huddled form pressed into a far corner. "Bess?"

A meaty thump sounded from the alley and then Somerhart

walked back in. He started to reach for Emma, but she shook her head. "I'm fine."

He nodded and stepped past. "Mrs. Lizzy?"

"It's Bess," the woman sobbed in a wet voice. "It's Bess now."

"All right, Bess. I'm going to call for a doctor."

"Don't bother. Please. It's just a broken nose. I've had them before."

"I don't think—"

"No," she insisted, though her voice was still muffled by blood and grief and the hands pressed to her face. "No, don't. Please, sir."

He looked to Emma. "I'll take care of her," she said.

"Bess," he said softly. "Is that man your husband?"

She began to cry in earnest. "I'm sorry to have caused trouble. I didn't think he'd find me here."

"Did you run from him?"

Emma still wasn't sure of her steadiness, so she crawled across the few feet of floor that separated them and curled her arms around Bess's rounded back. "It's all right. Shh."

"I'm sorry, ma'am. I'll go. Just don't send me with him. He'll kill me. He will."

Helpless, Emma looked up to Hart's face. He looked carved from granite, hard and cold.

"Do you have children?" he asked.

Bess shook her head, blood trickled from between her fingers. "None. He beat them all out of me."

"Christ." His cool facade cracked then, revealing the cruelty she'd heard tales of. "You're determined to be free of him, then?"

"Yes."

"Then he's bound for a dozen years in Her Majesty's Navy. Will that suit?"

"Y-yes."

"Lark," he ordered. "Head for the docks. Stimp will help you find a likely taker, I'm sure."

A few moments later, the crunch of carriage wheels echoed against the walls of the alleyway.

The threat was gone, and it had had nothing to do with Emma. She held Bess while she cried and wished that she could cry too.

Chapter 10

"She'll be all right," Emma whispered as she closed Bess's door and faced Hart. His brow was pulled into a dark frown, his eyes as sharp as ever.

"And you, Emma?"

"I'm fine," she insisted, though she raised a hand to the crown of her head. Hart reached for her and his hands cradled her face, fingers spread to ease into her hair. He pressed a soft kiss to her head, a lingering touch of his lips. A strange sensation overcame her at this tenderness, a feeling like melted wax flowing down through her body.

"I'm sorry," he whispered, brushing a hand over her head as if searching for bumps or bruises. "I'm sorry I didn't stop him, sorry I brought him here."

Emma wasn't sure she could speak. She shook her head and drew a shallow breath. "It wasn't . . . You needn't apologize, Hart." His fingers trailed over her temples, gentle and perfect. Her eyes closed as she murmured, "It wasn't your concern."

The soft stroking stopped. His hands stiffened. "Not my concern? Your life? Your safety?"

Oh, she did not want to do this now. She wanted to keep her eyes closed and keep his hands moving, but the hands had stopped; the strange warmth was beginning to fade. Emma sighed and opened her eyes as Hart's arms fell back to his sides.

"No," she said simply. "It's not your concern."

"I disagree."

"You often do." She suddenly found it impossible to believe he'd touched her so tenderly not seconds before. His eyes glinted ice and judgment.

"Who did you think he was, Emma?"

"Who?"

"Burl Smythe," he bit out. "Who did you think he was?"

She wasn't in a frightened state anymore, and if he thought he could corner her into a confession, he was sadly mistaken. Emma gave him innocent eyes. "I thought he was the thief. Then I thought he was a madman after my person. Or some dockworker with no position and a vengeance against his betters."

"Liar," Hart said very clearly.

"You do love to insult me."

"I saw your face," he insisted. His features grew harder still. Not only did he not believe her, he resented her self-defense.

Emma steeled her heart and moved toward the kitchen. She strolled past him, offering an arched brow and a pout. "I was terrified, Somerhart. I feared for my life. Are you determined to sit in judgment of my reactions? '*This* was not genuine enough. *That* was condemning.'?"

"You say that you—"

Emma spun around, stopping his path through the narrow kitchen. "Why don't *you* explain something to *me,* Somerhart? How is it that you know Stimp, hmm?"

Silence.

"Spying on me, Your Grace? Paying local children to watch my home? Or perhaps he follows me around and reports back to you on who I've been with, who I've talked to?"

"Don't be ridiculous."

Emma turned and continued into the hallway that led to the larder and then on to the stairs that climbed to the front door. "You have no right to spy on me. You have no claim and no cause."

"I was concerned."

She glanced over her shoulder to see him below her, following up the stairs. "Oh, I don't think so. I think you are suspicious. You were betrayed by a woman in your past. A lover. A scandalous woman."

"That's nothing to—"

"But I am not your lover, Somerhart, and you've no right to treat me so poorly. What is it, exactly, that you suspect?"

They'd both reached the landing at the front door. Emma felt Hart's hands close around her upper arms. He pulled her back against him, her back to his chest, and his mouth pressed just behind her ear.

"You are my lover, Emma, and well you know it."

"No."

"I've brought you to climax. And you've brought me as well. Remember?"

Remember? My God, she couldn't stop remembering. His beautiful naked body in the soft candlelight. She shivered under his grip and fought the need to press her hips back against him.

"We are lovers, Emma, but if you require formal consummation, allow me to provide it." His mouth opened against her skin, his teeth grazed her, scraping more shivers down her flesh. Sensation flowed like water, dipping between her breasts, spreading over her belly.

Her nipples tightened as his hot mouth pressed harder. His tongue flicked up to her earlobe as she became aware of the hard length of his arousal snug against her back. Oh, she wanted it, wanted everything. No one would interrupt. She could take him upstairs right now and truly become his lover. But she had just avoided disaster, and though the relief had made her giddy and reckless, it made no sense to take any more unnecessary risk.

Emma shook her head. "Tell me about the woman."

That stilled his mouth. His fingers tightened to vises on her arms, then abruptly released her. "Who?"

"I've heard the rumors."

"Oh, really?" The words snapped out like cracking ice. "Which rumors are those?"

Emma lifted her chin. "You know."

"I'm sure I don't."

"The rumors that you fell in love with a demirep. Someone else's mistress. You asked for her hand. Begged her. There were letters . . ."

"Ah, *those* rumors." His bark of laughter was hard enough to make Emma jump. "That story is a decade old and I'm sure it has only gotten more sordid with each telling. And, by the way, my dear, I don't take kindly to the telling of it."

She swung toward him and met his gaze. Cruelty again. Ah well, she had certainly distracted him from his seduction. "I see," she said carefully.

"And those old stories have nothing to do with our affair."

"That is patently untrue. You control your world, Somerhart, and now you consider me part of it. You issue demands, dictate rules. You have been paying that child to spy on me. Why, I cannot imagine, but your real fear . . . your real fear is that a woman will make a fool of you. Again."

His sculpted lips disappeared into a tight white line. "Watch your mouth, Lady Denmore."

"You have controlled every one of your partners in the past decade, Somerhart, but you cannot control me. I will not be intimidated. You have nothing to take from me and nothing to threaten me with."

"Nothing but your secrets."

She'd been expecting this and was very careful not to let

her fear show. "I have no secrets. No more than the next woman, anyway."

"If I dug into your past—"

"Why would you? Why even think it? You are a duke. Rich and powerful. I am no threat to your life, your position. Look into my past if you feel the need. But my life is mine, just as private and valuable as yours is to you. If you really wish to investigate me, do so. But don't bother calling on me to apologize for your unfounded suspicions, for I'll have nothing to say to you ever again."

"Unfounded," he scoffed.

"I am not pursuing you!" Emma cried. "I have resisted you at every turn! And still you come skulking about here with your questions as if I were applying for the exalted position of the duke's whore. My God, you are proud. Horribly arrogant."

Somerhart rocked back on his heels and pierced her with a hostile glare. "Is that what last night was about? My pride? Bringing me low?"

Emma inhaled so quickly that she felt momentarily dizzy. She watched past blurry eyes as Hart crossed his arms over his chest. She managed to take another breath. "W-what?"

"You meant to knock me off my arrogant pedestal."

"I . . . *No.*" She was so shocked by his words—a confession, really, of vulnerability—that she didn't care that she'd been trying to drive him out the door. "Yes, you are proud. Of course you are. And I wanted to see that. Your body, so proud and strong. I wouldn't . . . I just wanted to see what I couldn't have. I cannot act on it, but I wanted . . ."

His crossed arms relaxed and fell to his sides. Emma shook her head and looked away from him, down to her scuffed shoes that had once been pale ivory and butter-soft. Now they were as worn and hardened as she felt.

She started when his fingers brushed her hair. "You look so young all of a sudden, saying those lovely things to me."

No, she wasn't young. She was as old as the earth, and determined to be just as unknowable.

"Why are you so resolved not to have me, Emma?" The pads of his fingers were touching her again, spreading that warmth over her cheek, her chin. She jerked away.

"We cannot manage a quarter hour together without arguing. We more often exchange barbs than compliments. So why are you so determined to be had?"

His lips quirked into a half smile. "There is passion between us. Irrational passion. If we'd only acknowledge it, I daresay we wouldn't argue half as much."

"If we didn't see each other, we wouldn't argue at all."

His smile didn't budge. "Speaking of arguments, you start one every time I ask you about your stubborn position. Had you noticed that? And I would truly like to know what ridiculous idea you have stuck in your head. You say you will not take a lover, but it's clearly nothing to do with morals. Or your reputation. Both are tattered or at least worn to a sheen."

"How dare—"

"And you've said several times that you won't marry, so it's nothing to do with some future, honorable gentleman. And you want this, want it enough to do wicked things with me in public places. Perhaps I am dim-witted—no, don't say anything—but I cannot fathom your reasoning."

Emma refused to answer. She strolled toward the small front window and stared blindly out.

"I'll have an answer," Hart insisted. "And I don't think it's arrogance to say you cannot resist me forever. You want this. You want me. And I won't go away until you tell me."

No, she could not resist forever. She was hardly resisting at all anymore, vaguely hoping that he would overwhelm her and she would mindlessly give in. Emma pressed her hand to the cold glass. Perhaps she should tell him that she had the pox. That would cool his blood. But, no, her cheeks were reddening at the mere thought. She wasn't quite that desperate yet, though she might be in the future.

Then the perfect answer occurred to her. Unconventional as he was, he was still the young man who'd come to her rescue as a child. The man who'd raised his younger sister. Despite his cold veneer, he wouldn't find a heartless, selfish woman attractive.

"My mother was ruined by childbirth," she whispered. The words fogged the glass.

"What?"

Emma whirled toward him and made her mouth smirk. "My mother. She ruined herself having children for my father. Only two, mind you, but both were a tragedy. The first one ruined her looks, as my father pointed out often enough. She grew fat, you see. But it was the second that did her in. It took her almost a year to die, and I wished every day that she had died during the birth. She was made useless and ugly and sick. A foul embarrassment to the family. So I do not wish to risk having children, Your Grace, and therefore I will not engage in intercourse with you or anyone else."

His face was wiped blank with shock. "There are ways to—but you were married."

Emma lunged in with the final blow. "Well, I did my best, you understand, between prayer and resistance. I was determined not to become a fat matron saddled with a passel of sniveling brats." She smiled brightly. As she watched, his eyes grew incrementally more distant.

"You are young. You—"

"Yes, I am. And I mean to make the most of it."

"By living as a nun?"

"As you've pointed out, I'm hardly living as a nun."

His body grew stiffer and straighter as each second passed. "There are many ways to prevent conception."

"None of them reliable enough for me. It is not that I

want to wait to have children, Somerhart. I do not ever want them. Apparently you are willing to take the occasional risk. I am not."

"I would support—"

"Oh, and would you carry the child for me as well? Grow fat and bloated? Would you go through the blood and pain and gore of childbirth? Turn your chest into a pair of swollen cow's teats? Become a slave to every clinging need of an idiot child?" She forced a little shudder. "No, thank you."

"I see," he said simply. He studied her again, as he had so many times before. Studied her and found her wanting if the downward curve of his mouth was any indication. He gave her a slow nod. "Well, thank you for the explanation. You must be tired after your disturbing morning. I'll honor my promise and leave you to rest."

"Thank you, Your Grace."

His carriage had not returned, but she did not inquire how he would travel. She couldn't speak. The door opened and closed in a rush of freezing air, cooling the tears that only now pooled in her eyes.

She'd spoken the truth—almost—and the pain of that truth held her rooted to the spot. She stood there, dumb and silent and staring at a small rip in the wallpaper against the far wall.

No, she did not want children. She could not bear the thought of it. Not because her mother had grown fat; Emma suspected she'd done that purposefully to avoid her husband's desires. It wasn't even her mother's slow descent into death after Will's birth.

Emma did not want a husband, and so it had always been easy to dismiss the thought of children. But when she'd spoken the words aloud, the truth of it had stabbed through her heart. She had already had a child. Will. She had loved him and raised him. Seen to his needs. She'd comforted him after his nightmares, and held his little body when he'd hurt.

She'd taken him everywhere with her, even taught him to read when his nanny had been occupied in the baron's bedroom. And then he'd died.

One moment he'd been her whole world, and the next he'd been lowered into a dank, muddy hole and covered up with dirt. The world had moved on, and she'd been left standing there, staring at turned earth.

She had loved one child, and that had been enough pain to last two lifetimes.

Emma made her feet move back to the stairway. She trudged slowly up to the second floor, shuffled into her bedroom and climbed beneath the cold sheets. She was too tired to prepare dinner, and she knew that Bess was just as heartsick as she.

The sky outside slowly darkened, and Emma closed her swollen eyes.

"She is gone. You will have to forget her."

Matthew glared at his father. "How can you say that?"

His father threw up his hands with a grimace. "How can I say it? She is gone, Matthew. Now I agreed she was a fine match when she was here, but the girl is clearly determined not to marry. She turned down your every offer, and then she ran off. Use your head for something more than prayer."

Matthew shot to his feet and slammed his hands down on the table. "*How dare you.* I am obligated to honor you as my father, but I will not tolerate you mocking the church."

"Our church is the Church of England, and that vicar is nothing but a Romanist."

"Reverend Whittier is a great man! He and others like him are determined to bring the church back to God. He is helping the church find its soul, just as he is helping me find mine."

His father ran a hand through his thin white hair. "Your

soul is right here and there is nothing wrong with it. And there is nothing wrong with the church. Those men you speak of will soon be driven out of it like the vermin they are. And if you continue your plan to join their ranks, you will be driven away too."

"You know nothing about it," Matthew spat.

"The church has made its position clear about your Romanists and their papist rituals."

"I will not listen to this. As soon as I'm married, Father Whittier will sponsor my admission to the clergy. I will heal people's souls. I will help lead the church back to its spirit. But I cannot do that if my own soul is shadowed with sin and wanton lust."

His father only shook his head. It was a conversation they'd had many times. Matthew stared at the old man's cottony puffs of hair and his pink skin. He was weak; he'd always been too kind, too forgiving. Always given into his wife's stronger personality. Matthew said a quick prayer of thanks that he'd inherited his mother's spine.

"You promised that I could marry her. Promised you would help."

"I thought she wanted the same. She—"

"She made her choice when she led me astray. She toyed with my heart and sullied my soul and now she will reap her harvest. I will marry her, Father. I must."

The old man's head dropped into his hands. "You have no idea where she is. You've done nothing for the past months but travel half the country looking for her. I refuse to support you any longer. I cannot afford it."

Frustration urged him to rail and fume, but Matthew managed to hold onto logic. When the time came, his father would do as he asked; he was sure of it. So he tempered his voice when he spoke. "I understand, Father, but I am praying for an answer every day. If God brings me information about her, will you offer me one last chance?"

His father said nothing for a long time. His shoulders dropped.

"I love her," Matthew whispered.

Finally, his father nodded. "If you find her, I will send you to see her, but I will do nothing to force her back. You understand?"

Satisfaction burned through him. Yes, he understood, but it didn't matter. He would need no help forcing her back. Matthew smiled down at his father's bowed head. "Of course. Thank you, Father." And he headed back to the church to pray harder.

Chapter 11

The sun was warm against her back, nearly as warm as the heat of Lancaster's arm beneath her hand. She smiled toward the bright, shifting light of the Thames and slowed her pace a little. Their walk was coming to an end and she didn't quite want it to stop. Lancaster was charming and handsome. A friend, it seemed, since he wasn't a suitor. And the day felt like spring.

She felt a prickling of alarm at the idea and pushed it away. She had a month, nearly, before the crowds began their return to London, and her assets grew daily. A few members of Parliament had begun to trickle back to town, but they left their families in the country until March. The men wanted entertainment, and gambling was the order of the day. Whoring too, she supposed, but the gambling was all that interested her.

And for the moment, winter was gone, and all the dark thoughts that came along with it. The day reminded her of afternoons in her uncle's kitchen garden, or mornings collecting warm eggs from the henhouse, the smooth, perfect curve of heat in her palm.

A gull flew past, only feet away, and Emma thought of her

mother exclaiming with delight at the sight of every seal or pelican as they'd walked along the seashore.

"What are you thinking of, Lady Denmore?"

Emma smiled up at her companion. "I was thinking of being a child, walking with my mother along the beach."

"Ah. I have never been to Brighton."

"Neither have I, actually! We preferred Scarborough. She did not go to be seen, you understand. She wanted peace." Peace. Just what Emma wanted for herself.

"Well, you certainly looked peaceful thinking about it."

"It is my favorite place in the world," she said, before she thought better of it. When she disappeared, she needed to disappear completely. She saw that Lancaster was about to speak and rushed to change the subject. "I was shocked that there would be yachting so early in the year. The water must be frigid."

"As long as there's no ice, it is always the right time for a race, I gather. There are people to place bets"—he shot her a sardonic look—"and so there are people willing to race."

"Some men are easily persuaded."

"Ha! When you are doing the persuading, I'm sure that is true of all of us."

Emma tapped his arm and laughed, but his words reminded her of Somerhart and how she'd finally persuaded him away. Three weeks had passed without a word. Oh, she spied him at a few parties, but he'd spared her nothing more than a nod and a look. He hadn't made his way to her, and she hadn't dared approach him after she'd finally gotten him to keep his distance. It had been necessary. Painful, but necessary.

Lancaster interrupted her thoughts. "Lord Osbourne tells me that your luck has only improved in the past month. He is quite proud of your skills."

Emma laughed past her twinge of guilt. The Osbournes had welcomed her as if she were a long-lost niece. They had been quite close to her uncle in their youth, and they delighted in hearing stories of him and his garden battles, but they were even happier to pass on tales of their collective youth. They'd be hurt by her elaborate deception, perhaps humiliated.

"Lord Osbourne," she said sincerely, "is the soul of kindness."

"He also mentioned that Somerhart has been conspicuously absent from most gatherings you attend."

She glanced up to find Lancaster watching her, a sardonic smile tilting up his mouth. He was an attractive man, he made her laugh, and she would undoubtedly have been flattered by his attentions if she weren't so conscious of her lies. He was more open than Somerhart, and so she felt constantly guilty. But she needed her falsehoods. If the rumors persisted that the duke was already done with her, she would be fighting off men like Lord Marsh every night.

"I rather think that Somerhart was conspicuously *present* a few weeks ago. He has only fallen back into old habits. I'm sure you know he prefers less public company."

Lancaster nodded his understanding. "So he does."

"Did you know his sister?" Emma asked, almost surprised at her own words.

"Lady Alexandra? Yes, I did. She was smart and impetuous. Entertaining. You remind me a little of her, actually. Though she was . . ."

"Younger?"

"Younger, definitely. But I was going to say more reckless. You are more calculating in your risks."

Emma had been wondering about her, about this girl that Hart apparently loved so much even though she courted scandal and rumor at every turn. He had tolerated it, defended her. He hated notoriety, but he loved his notorious sister. He despised scandal, yet he pursued Emma. Or had pursued her.

They'd returned back to the yacht club where their walk

had started, but instead of releasing her, Lancaster put his hand over hers. "My carriage is here. I hope you'll allow me to escort you home."

"Thank you, Lancaster."

He waved to his man. "I was thrilled to see you here. We don't often run in the same circles. We are clearly handling our impoverishment in different ways. A good thing, since I have neither your luck nor skill at the tables."

Emma stepped into his landau. He took the seat opposite.

"You've had no luck with heiresses?"

"Not yet. But the Season should solve that problem."

Emma cocked her head and studied the sudden tension around his eyes. "You are so troubled by it. Are you one of those who despises the cits and their vulgar money?"

Lancaster sighed and smiled, his brown eyes shining with wry humor. "No, it's not that. It is just stubbornness, I suppose, mixed with a splash of romanticism and perhaps a touch of pride."

"A touch?"

"No more, I assure you." His laughter faded and, facing him like this, the sun at her back, Emma saw true weariness in his eyes and not a little sadness. He shook his head. "He kept us all in the dark, you know." His voice had turned quiet and serious. "My mother . . . my brother and sister, they all refuse to see the truth of it. But I cannot help but see it. The creditors will not stop showing me."

His sad smile touched her heart. Emma reached out and took one of his hands in hers. "There are just as many lovely girls among the cits as there are among the ton. More even."

"Of course."

"You will find someone who will make you forget that she brings twenty thousand a year."

Lancaster laughed again, his normal, open laugh, and Emma smiled and squeezed his hand.

"I do wish your husband had left you some money. Have you not managed to earn your fortune yet?"

"I'm sorry."

"Well, you should be. The perfect woman right before me and not a shilling to her name."

"Perfectly scandalous, at any rate." Emma was still smiling as they turned onto her street. The smile froze when she caught sight of a man's profile in the distance, delicate and pale. He stood almost a block away and the brim of his hat threw a shadow over his face, but she felt a jolt of recognition. Her gut tightened with fear.

"Lady Denmore?" Lancaster turned to look over his shoulder. "What is wrong?"

"Nothing," she murmured as the figure turned and walked in the opposite direction. She recognized that walk, she was almost certain of it. Almost. "Nothing," she said again, more strongly.

"I'm not convinced. You must tell me if something is wrong. Ever."

Emma forced herself to meet his eyes and smile. "Someone walked over my grave. That is all."

He glanced over his shoulder again, clearly doubtful. But the carriage had pulled to a halt, and he could do nothing but descend and offer her a hand.

"It has been a lovely afternoon," Emma murmured.

"A beautiful afternoon," Lancaster agreed. He looked as if he wanted to say more, but Emma gently extracted her hand from his and moved up the stairs. She managed to say a happy farewell, but her face fell as she closed the door behind her.

She waited for the sound of Lancaster's carriage moving away before she shouted, "Bess, I need your cloak. Hurry!"

With the hood of Bess's brown cloak pulled low over her face, she could pass anyone without being recognized. It couldn't have been Matthew. It was nothing, just as Burl Smythe had been nothing, and she would not live in fear for days because of some stranger's profile. She would search the street and shops and find the man and put her worry to rest within the quarter hour.

She heard a noise from the first story and rushed up the stairs. "Bess, I need—"

Bess emerged from the parlor and held up a hand. "You've a visitor, ma'am. I know I shouldn't 'ave—"

Emma's heart dropped. She glanced back toward the front door, knowing it couldn't be Matthew in her home, even if it had been him on the street. It must be . . .

"Hart," she gasped when he stepped into the hallway. Bess's face turned red. She knew she should not have admitted a gentleman without Emma's consent. Then again, she couldn't very well turn away the duke who had saved her from her husband's fists.

"I'm sorry, ma'am," Bess offered with a nervous curtsy.

"It's fine."

Hart inclined his head with a completely remorseless smirk. There was no way to be rid of him in time to follow the man, so Emma just took the last two steps up to the first floor. "Bring tea," she sighed.

Hart's soft huff of sardonic laughter almost made her smile.

It hadn't been Matthew on the street, Emma told herself as she swept off her cloak and handed it to Bess. And she found her fear was easy to forget as Hart followed her into the parlor, his presence a warm shadow at her back. She could not have thought of anything else if she'd tried.

They were silent, studying each other until the tea tray arrived. Hart felt uncertain as he took in her pinkened cheeks and wind-mussed hair. A few strands had escaped her chignon and they curved toward her mouth, drawing his eye.

He hadn't seen her in weeks and had resented every moment he'd spent thinking of ways to run across her.

She'd shocked him with her casual dismissal of children and motherhood. She had seemed cruel and selfish, but he should not have been surprised. His own mother had had similar feelings. After three children she had declared herself quite done with the whole wretched business and had never bothered herself with her children if she could help it.

Perhaps that was why he'd reacted so strongly. He had disliked his mother in self-defense of her distaste for him. But he'd had time to think over the past three weeks. Emma's few words about her childhood had eventually filtered past her shocking statements.

Emma broke the silence. "I thought you had finally resolved to be done with me."

"So had I."

"And yet you are here." She offered him a cup of tea and dropped a sugar into her own.

"And yet I am here."

Her eyes rose to meet his. "Why?"

God, she was beautiful. He didn't know why. She shouldn't be. But the sight of her hazel eyes staring him down . . . He felt himself relax even as something inside him tightened.

"My father was a cruel man as well," he finally said.

She blinked and the certainty vanished from her gaze. "Pardon me?"

"What you said about your father, his treatment of your family . . . It is no wonder that you do not want children."

She set her tea down and creased her napkin. "It is not so dramatic as all that, I'm sure."

"But it is. There is nothing worse than being betrayed by someone who is supposed to love you."

Her eyelids fluttered. She pressed her hands flat to her thighs. "As you were?" she murmured.

His jaw tightened, but he had known that she must say

something like this. He had invited it. So he nodded. "As we all have been."

"Yes, well . . ."

"You were trying to drive me away, Emma. I let you. But time heals all wounds, even those of pride and outrage."

"Not all. You have never healed, not completely."

He inclined his head in acknowledgment. "Sometimes there are scars."

"Will you tell me the story?"

"I am sure you've heard it all."

"I have no idea what is true or false."

"It's simple, Emma. I fell in love with the wrong woman."

"But that is not the whole of it. She betrayed you, made a fool of you. I don't know how . . . I don't know why she would do that."

Her eyelids rose, and Hart saw true distress there. Even past the familiar rage he felt at the topic, he could see that her interest was not prurient, her concern bordered on pain.

And he had missed this illogical connection between them. He wanted to talk with her. So he sighed and gave in. Slightly. "Perhaps she was a bad person. Perhaps she was simply bored and I was her entertainment. I have no idea. I did not think much about it afterward."

That was the truth, at any rate. Because her betrayal had hardly been the worst of it. Her betrayal had been only the beginning.

"She had been deceiving you the whole time?"

"She had. She and her lover. Those rumors were true. He was a voyeur, it seemed. And I was the young, debauched nobleman they chose to involve in their game. The other rumors were not true. I did not know he was watching. He stayed hidden." Hart shrugged the stiffness from his shoulders. "Not that I was morally opposed to much. Regardless, all I could see were her and her considerable charms."

"But she let you fall in love with her."

"Oh, yes. She encouraged it. It gave them ample fodder for amusement."

"The letters."

"The letters." Hart waited for the faint, familiar buzzing in his ears to stop. "But I am no longer so vulnerable. And I never write love letters to women."

Emma offered a faint smile, but it quickly fell back to a serious line. Her brow furrowed and she clasped her hands together. One thumb rubbed over the other. "You became a different person. Harder."

"Yes. You understand that."

She nodded, but didn't look up from her hands. "I do."

"Emma, I have no intention of hurting you."

"Unlike your experience, Hart, there is rarely bad intention. People just happen to get hurt." She finally met his gaze. "And I am already too changed."

"Your father."

Her frown wavered for just a moment, but she smoothed it out before Hart could even think that she might cry. "Yes," she said, and left it at that.

A little horror darted through his mind, a shadow of a thought, but he refused to chase it. He did not need to know her past to know that he liked her, that he'd missed her turbulent presence in his structured life. Perhaps, in time, she would change her mind about their relationship. In fact, he was counting on it. She was far too sensual to live with an empty bed.

So he only leaned back in his chair and crossed his booted foot over his knee. "I have heard disturbing rumors about you, Lady Denmore. I came here today to chastise you for your dangerous behavior."

She relaxed at his change of topic. "Rumors are rarely true, as you know. What have you heard?"

"Betting on the change of weather. Horse races in the

park. Games of brag that go on until dawn. Less than respectable soirees put on by questionable hosts."

"Mm. I never bet on horses, Your Grace."

His loud laughter startled both of them. She pressed a hand to her chest before her surprise turned to a grin. "What?"

"You deny nothing else?" he chuckled, thoroughly delighted at the familiar frustration she inspired.

She said simply, "I have been winning," as if that were answer enough. And he supposed it was, because her shining hazel eyes crinkled with her smile and her cheeks glowed a soft and kissable pink.

"Promise me something," he said in an attempt to keep from pouncing on her in the parlor. "That day at Matherton's, on the pond, do not put yourself in that kind of danger again."

She shook her head. "That pond was—"

When Hart held up a hand, amazingly, she stopped speaking. "I have resigned myself. You will be scandalous and naughty at every turn, and I will stand by and look exasperated enough to entertain the ton. But if I think you will put yourself in true danger, I will likely go mad. So please, promise just this one thing."

She'd ceased to smile. Her eyes were wider now, but her cheeks just as pink. Her mouth looked pinker still, and soft and lonely. "Hart . . ."

His name was little more than a sigh, gentler than any word he'd ever heard her utter. Hart felt something painful blossom inside his chest, a slow explosion, dull and aching.

"I promise," she whispered. "But you mustn't say anything like that ever again."

He couldn't think past the disturbing pain. "Like what?"

"You mustn't be kind and . . . and . . ." She shook her head. "Promise *me* that. No kindness or . . ."

Hart looked into her desperate eyes just before he pushed

to his feet. He'd crossed some line that neither had expected him to cross, but he hadn't done it on purpose. He'd simply looked around and here he was.

"Don't be ridiculous," he muttered, trying to sound cruel, but Emma stood too and reached for his hand. Her fingers looked small and perfect against his.

"We flirt," she said, the words sounding strained and rushed. "We flirt and we argue and we occasionally engage in a seduction. We entertain each other, Hart."

"Yes," he said, not meaning it at all.

"But we are not kind, neither of us. Are we?"

"Surely not," he sneered.

"Please," she whispered. Her eyes glowed again, but not with laughter. They were luminous with tears. "Don't be kind to me."

"Emma, for God's sake." The pain in his chest had spread to his arms, and he knew how to make it fade. He eased his arms around her and pulled her body to his. Her hands pressed against his chest, succeeding only in becoming trapped between their bodies. She hid her face against his shoulder.

"You are so stubborn." He rubbed his mouth over her hair, mussing it further. He wanted to free it from its pins, let it fall over his hands, let it sweep across his arm, his chest. He wanted to kiss her, seduce her, work the buttons free on that ugly dress. Sex was something they could both understand. It wasn't kind or caring or painful.

And afterward she would smirk at him and comment on his successful attempt at charm. She would comfort herself with the knowledge that he was not kind, that they were not friends. And he could tell himself the same thing.

Hart let her go, stepped away from her warmth and vulnerability. "Stay out of trouble," he grumbled, and then he fled from both their fears.

Chapter 12

Emma paid the hack and hurried up her front steps. It was well after midnight, probably after one, but the night was eerily bright. Moonlight illuminated the thick fog and cast strange, shifting shadows over everything. The cold made her shiver, but an irrational fear pushed her to shove her front door open and scramble through it. She slammed it behind her and shot the lock with a satisfying click.

The whole day had conspired to make her anxious. First, Hart had lain in wait for her, armed with gentleness and caring. That had shaken her to her core, the glimpse into the secret man the duke kept well hidden from the world. She'd wanted to explore him, his soul as well as his body. She'd wanted to belong to him, to love him, and wasn't that utterly ridiculous? To love Winterhart himself?

That frightening possibility had followed her like a ghost throughout the rest of the day and night. A relentless spirit that brushed up against her with every movement, every thought. She could love him. Oh, Lord, she could. And he would never forgive her. Another woman who'd deceived him at every turn.

So she hadn't been able to think clearly, and it had been her first invitation to Chestershire's home to play against his deep-pocketed friends. But she did not have deep pockets, and luckily there had been only a few tables open for her participation. She'd only lost ninety-two quid. It could have gone much worse.

The parlor was cold, but Emma stopped there and made her way to the small door at the back. The tiny, hidden room served as Emma's office and she felt an overwhelming need to work out her numbers before she retired for the evening. She needed to see them in black and white, remind herself of what she was doing here in London.

Lifting a corner of a cheap rug, she crouched down next to the desk. She'd hidden a small safe beneath the floorboards, and it was growing increasingly full. Emma keyed the iron door and carefully counted out the coin she'd managed to hang onto throughout her disastrous play. When she was done, she sat at the desk in cloak and gloves and opened her ledger. Two thousand and sixty-seven pounds. She added another line, documenting the amount she'd just redeposited. Two thousand one hundred and twenty-two pounds.

Not bad. She'd arrived in London with just under six hundred quid, and even after the expense of renting this shabby home and outfitting herself in a closet full of secondhand dresses, she'd managed to make quite a profit.

Three thousand. That was the magic number, though she wouldn't mind reaching four. Still, with three thousand to invest in bonds, she would have an income of one hundred fifty a year. More than enough to lease her own cottage on the coast, though she would dearly love to buy one outright. Enough to provide Bess a position as long as she wanted it. A hundred and fifty a year would buy food and furniture and clothing and even books. It would see to her independence, her comfort. She could provide for herself and live however she saw fit.

Emma stared hard at the numbers, jotted a few more down, checked her figures. Yes, another month and she would be there, even with conservative play. And whatever was blooming between her and Hart, whatever that was in his eyes, it would have to be smothered. She couldn't encourage it, for her own sake as well as his. But the idea of discouraging him was a heavy yoke on her shoulders as she closed the ledger book and took the lamp in hand. She sighed with nearly every step as she made her way up the stairs to the second floor.

Even before she reached her door, Emma felt the warmth radiating from the darkness. Bess had stoked the coals before she'd gone to bed, bless her. Emma was able to swing her cloak off her shoulders without the least bit of regret. She slipped off her gloves and tossed them onto an empty chair, then reached for the small buttons that ran down the front of her dress.

She'd purchased as many front-fastening dresses as she'd been able. Bess had to be up early in the morning to start fires and begin breakfast. The woman could not stay up until two or three in the morning just to help Emma undress.

The backs of her knuckles brushed the skin of her chest, and she grimaced at the cold. The bed would be icy too, but it would warm quickly enough and Emma found herself jerking at the stubborn top button of her gown, eager to climb beneath the thick layers of linens and quilts. When she moved into her own cottage, she would be sure to buy a shiny new bed warmer. What a pleasure that would—

"Emily."

"Oh!" she screamed and whipped around toward the male voice. *Hart,* was her first thought, before she registered that he could not know that name she hated. Unless . . .

"Emily."

The room was small but the corners were deep in shadow. She backed away from the voice, searching the dark corners farthest from the door. It took an endless moment to finally separate the man's figure from the blackness. Her heart beat so hard that it seemed to do nothing more than shake until her body trembled from the force of it.

"Hart?" She pushed herself along the edge of the bed, trying to reach the little table where she'd set the lamp.

"I did not mean to frighten you."

No, no, not Hart. It wasn't him. And, oh, God, he'd said *Emily.* Only one person called her that. "I . . . I—"

"It's all right. Shh." He stepped forward, legs moving into the light, and she couldn't hold back a little scream.

Slender hands rose, trying to calm her. "I'm here to help."

And then she could see his face. Matthew. It really had been him, out on the street. Not just her fear, her imagination.

"You have gotten yourself into a world of trouble, Emily. But I'm here now."

"Don't . . . *Matthew* . . . What are you *doing* here?"

"I'm sorry." His thin mouth offered a familiar, condescending smile. "I did not want to frighten you. I snuck into your home to avoid drawing attention to you. If word got out . . ." He shook his head, the picture of sympathy.

"No, what are you doing *here*? In London?" She found that her body was sinking slowly lower. Suddenly the bed was beneath her thighs and she was sitting, staring up at her old suitor. His straight blond hair fell over his brow. His green eyes glowed with an intensity that hadn't been there when they'd first met.

"Well, I have been looking for you. I never thought a young lady like you could manage to disappear quite so thoroughly. You're distressingly devious."

"I didn't . . . I didn't disappear. I just wanted to come to London."

"Emily." That head shake again. "Your place is in Cheshire, as I've told you countless times. And now I'm here to fetch you home."

The fear and shock had formed a ball of tension in her chest that pressed against her lungs and made her ribs feel too small, but the tension began to melt. Emma clenched her fingers into fists. "Cheshire is not my home, as I've told *you* many times. And you had no right to follow me. No right to come into my house."

Matthew smiled, showing very pointed eyeteeth. "I did not follow you, Emily. Well, to be honest, I tried. But I lost your scent somewhere in Birmingham. But two weeks ago, my father received a letter from London written on fine stationary. Luckily, I intercepted it."

The tightness melted completely and left sliding, slippery liquid inside her chest. "A letter? From whom?" She pressed a hand to her heart, trying to calm the violent waves that rocked against it.

"Does it matter? Suffice it to say it was a man of importance, which does not bode well for you."

Hart. Hart had done it. He had taken up her challenge. Exposed her.

"It was a very mildly worded letter, which said nothing much at all, but it was quite strange. He seemed to be under the impression that your uncle had left a widow behind. He wondered if, perhaps, she still had family in the area."

"I don't . . ." She swallowed hard, stalling for time. "I'm sure he was mistaken. Perhaps we haven't been introduced. If you will tell me who—"

"Emily." His sigh was bursting with self-satisfied weariness. "There are two invitations on the front table addressed to Lady Denmore. You're lying to these people. Just as you've lied to me."

Emma swallowed again. And again. Nausea was rising up, choking her. "I didn't . . ." Oh, Lord, she needed time to think. "You shouldn't be in here," she blurted out, remembering his obsession with propriety. Just saying something effective gave her a little strength, and she pushed to her feet. "You shouldn't be in my room."

Matthew held up his hands, but Emma stabbed a finger at the door. "This is completely improper. You snuck in like a thief, stood there and let me begin to undress. How dare you."

His cheeks darkened. "You only removed your cloak."

"I was unbuttoning my dress!"

"I have seen—" he started, but choked on his own words. "I've touched . . ." His cheeks looked on fire now as he rubbed a hand over the back of his neck. "You have always tempted me to reckless behavior, Emily. You've always caused me to sin. You are Eve to my Adam."

"Matthew, all we did was kiss. I never meant you to think we would marry."

"But you let me touch your . . . breasts."

Oh, for God's sake. She could not believe his mind was still so twisted around a few paltry embraces. He would ruin everything with his delusions.

"I am a lady, Matthew. I am requesting that you leave my private chambers and my home."

"You are living here unchaperoned!"

"Exactly my point. You cannot be here."

"Emily," he growled and stepped toward her.

She lifted her chin and put on her haughtiest face. "You may return tomorrow between the hours of three and six if you wish to call on me, Matthew Bromley."

"I am not calling on you," he hissed. "I am here to take you home before you destroy your family's name and our entire future together."

"We will speak of it tomorrow during civilized hours."

His mouth twisted into the violent sneer she'd seen only once before. Emma stepped back, out of his reach. She was next to the table now and the lamp. She could hit him with it if he attacked her.

Matthew didn't move closer, but his hands clenched into fists. "You must think me an idiot. You will slip away like a rat scurrying from danger, but I am not blind to your deceptive nature any longer, Emily. It is something we will work on during our marriage. I've already spoken to the Reverend Whittier about it."

"I have an entire household here; I could not possibly gather everything up in a few hours time. This is my home, and I will not leave it. I will be here tomorrow during receiving hours. *You may return then.*"

His eyes glimmered with anger as he studied her. He swept his gaze down her gown. "You are dressed like a harlot," he muttered, but even he could not put much force behind it. It simply wasn't true. Her meager budget restricted her to nondescript dresses that could be taken apart and remade into more nondescript dresses. Still, Emma managed to look outraged.

"You, a man who thinks to be my husband . . . You feel free to call me a harlot? Get out of my home."

His face spasmed into tortured lines before smoothing out to appeasement. "My apologies. I did not mean that. I have simply been so worried."

"I am not going to 'scurry away like a rat.' And even if you did think me so cowardly, the banks are not open tomorrow. I do not keep my inheritance tucked away beneath the floorboards, Matthew."

"Of course not. I . . ." He clearly could think of no further arguments. Anxiety had never been his friend.

"Tomorrow, Matthew."

He opened his mouth, closed it. Finally, he gave one short nod of his head. "Fine. Tomorrow. But you may begin packing. We will leave within the week and pray to God no one ever finds you out."

"Matthew," she started, deciding to take one last chance on reason. "Please understand. I enjoy London. If my father hadn't died I would have had my Season, time to—"

"Your father did die, and his death brought you to me, and that is where you were meant to stay. I will hear no more of it. How you could even propose that I leave you here to live a life of utter falsehood . . . You insult me."

She nodded, having known what he would say before he'd

opened his mouth. She'd heard something similar many times before. "Then I will see you tomorrow."

"Good evening," he offered with a polite bow, as if he hadn't been hiding in the dark for her like a spider. "And if you try any of your tricks, do not forget that my father is a magistrate."

Emma waited until he had descended the stairs before she followed and locked the door behind him. She'd have to walk the whole house, figure out how he'd gotten in.

Bess, she thought with a rush of panic, and ran down to the basement and the little room off the kitchen that Bess used as her own. She flung open the door, but Bess was there, snoring, undisturbed even by Emma's loud entrance. She was fine. Emma eased the door shut and stood there in the dark kitchen.

She could hardly see and realized she must have run through the hallway and kitchen on blind memory. But now she felt completely helpless. Lost. The faint smell of bread and thyme expanded through the vast emptiness.

Hart had betrayed her. It must've been him. She really had managed to lose Matthew during her trip to London. He wouldn't have found her but for that damned letter. But now what to do? Run?

She should run. She should. She had made a decent amount, could live something close to her dream. She could have security, if not absolute comfort.

But her victory in sending Matthew away had kindled her natural willfulness. Determination burned inside her, a tiny ember that glowed brighter with each breath. Yes, she was alone here in the dark, in her empty kitchen in her shabby house. She was alone as she had always been, and that would not stop her.

Emma nodded and stepped into shadow. She had found her way through the dark a few minutes ago. She could do it again.

Chapter 13

Over the course of an hour, Emma found that every full circuit of her ground floor hall took fifteen seconds. The south end of her path brought her face-to-face with the wall clock. Four turns saw one minute tick by. Emma clutched her hands together and continued pacing.

Doubt writhed in her chest, and she wished that she could physically beat it down. She did not want to ask for help, but she would do whatever it took. Yes, it was a risk, but if she knew anything in this world, it was the value of risk.

She needed Matthew gone. She needed him powerless to harm her. If she had descended into the depths of blackness she knew ran through her veins, it would have been simple enough. Even a lonely stranger to London could find someone willing to kill a man for a few pounds. But she had not gone to the gutters yet. She wouldn't see Matthew harmed. The man was a threat to her, and his mind took turns that she couldn't comprehend, but she wouldn't see him hurt.

There was one person she could turn to. She did not trust him completely, but she trusted him enough.

She'd reached the wall again, and stopped to stare up at the clock. Five fifty-two. If she said it was an emergency, would his butler follow through? Would he light a lamp and wake him, put the letter into his hands? She could not know. She could only try.

Emma counted off twelve more turns of the hall before she finally lost her patience. She drew the cloak's hood up over her head and tugged on her thickest gloves and prayed that she could find a hack at this lost hour 'twixt night and day. Prayed that she encountered a servant with a heart or at least sharp eyes that could see her sincerity.

Fog crept up to Emma's ankles when she opened the door. No one could follow her path, at least; she lost track of her own body when she stepped into the mist.

If there were a hack anywhere near, she could neither see it nor hear it. In fact, nothing seemed to move in the world but Emma and the thick fog. She could only begin walking toward his neighborhood.

The fog parted for her, swallowed her, over and over again as she walked, like a giant, hungry mouth. Sounds jumped back and forth: her own footsteps and other, unidentifiable noises. She should have been afraid, but she simply walked. Her greatest threat had already appeared.

Matthew Bromley had been the closest thing to an appealing, unmarried man in her uncle's hamlet. And Emma had been a young woman with a body bursting with curiosity. He had chased her and she'd let herself be caught on several occasions. An innocent—or perhaps less than innocent—mistake. His interest in her had only grown focused and intense. He'd no longer been content with walks and kisses. He'd wanted everything, not just her body, but her soul as well. He'd wanted marriage, had demanded it, and she had refused.

Then during a beautiful Lenten moon, he'd asked her to walk with him again. She'd been bored and restless and she'd met him near the river that night though she'd shrugged off his embraces, and by the time she'd smelled smoke on the wind, they'd ventured far down the lane. Her uncle had died in the fire, alone because she'd snuck away.

Emma sighed and stopped to look around. The night was easing from black to gray. Surely the streets would begin to stir soon.

Matthew had been a friend to her at first. He'd hustled her to his father's home, had stood by her side through her grief and guilt. The Bromleys had taken care of her and provided a home, but Matthew hadn't forgotten his desire. Only short weeks after her uncle's death, he'd started tapping on her bedroom door, whispering of her duty and his love. He'd cornered her in hallways and stairwells, spoken constantly of their future and the gratitude she should feel for his devotion. Emma had been well and truly trapped.

But her uncle's will had finally been settled, and she'd received her inheritance. What a relief it had been to move out of the Bromley home. She'd let a room at the miller's rambling house, but her relief had been short-lived. Matthew had been furious and unrelenting in his pursuit.

Soon enough, she'd realized she must escape. From the rented rooms and intrusive neighbors. From the constant talk of when she would marry and who. She could not explain to Mrs. Shropshire, the miller's wife, why she had no interest in marriage. She'd grown tired of the arched looks of disapproval every time she'd turned down Matthew's offers. And she could not live her whole life on six hundred pounds.

A cart passed by her, splashing dirty water near her feet. Emma moved closer to the buildings, but it was no help. She stepped right into a deep puddle and cursed her bad luck. Another cart rolled by, a woman bundled up to her ears scurried past, and Emma realized that the fog had begun to lighten. Finally, Emma emerged onto a wide street and smiled. Three hackney coaches were lined up just one street down, seeming to float above the road, wheels vanished beneath the fog.

Ten minutes later she stepped from the straw-strewn floor of the hack and stared up at the green door before her. It was morning, finally, but the sun barely shone through the dull gray air. Emma smoothed her hair back and wiped her gloves over her face. She straightened her cloak, eased it back a little to show the fine fabric of the dress beneath. And then she walked up the steps and tapped the knocker.

A long while passed with no answer. The household must be waking, but they certainly weren't listening for a knock at the front door. If no one answered, she'd be forced to go to the back. Emma tapped harder.

Voices approached. She made very sure to straighten her spine and raise her chin to a haughty level just before the door snapped open.

The butler—a rather *young* butler—looked her over. He studied the dark blue silk of her dress and stared pointedly at her wet shoes before he nodded. "Madam?"

"I am in need of assistance. It is quite urgent. Would you take this to Lord Lancaster?" She held out the sealed note. The butler glanced at the paper, but did not take it.

"My lord will be at home this afternoon, madam."

"I am Lady Denmore, a friend of your master. He offered his support should I ever need it. I am in need of it now. Please take the letter to him."

"This is quite irregular."

"Yes. Yes, of course it is. I would not have left my own home so early if it weren't dire. *Please.* Wake him. Give him the note. I'll wait outside if you like. You can send me away if he refuses my plea."

The young, round-faced man looked from her face to the note. He was visibly torn between protecting the sanctity of a viscount's home and treating a supposed lady as she should be treated. And he had clearly not had much experience with this type of thing, if any; it occurred to Emma that this young man was the best butler that Lancaster could afford.

"Please follow me to the morning room, Lady Denmore. I'm sure Lord Lancaster would be happy if you warmed yourself with tea while you wait."

Emma let out a deep breath and felt the prick of actual tears at the thought of hot tea and a warm room. "Thank you."

The butler took the note as well as her cloak, and led her to a yellow morning room before he left to wake his master.

It would be quite a wait, and she was thankful for the time to compose herself. Lancaster would need to be awoken, he'd need time to read the note and dress. Shave. Perhaps even brace himself with a cup of tea.

The maid arrived with tea and hot rolls. Emma devoured them, suddenly starving. She barely had time to wipe the crumbs from her mouth when Lancaster strode in.

"Lady Denmore?"

Emma was struck dumb by the sight of him. The man was normally the very picture of neat elegance. Not so this morning. He was dressed in boots and buff trousers, a wrinkled white shirt and black coat, but there the modesty stopped. His shirt gaped open to mid chest. His hair was a tousled, golden mess, lighter than the brown stubble that glinted against his jaw. And she could have sworn that there was a smudge of rouge on the collar of his shirt.

"Lady Denmore, what is wrong?"

She snapped her eyes up from the triangle of naked chest that she hadn't meant to stare at. "I . . . I need your help, Lancaster."

He nodded, an impatient jerk of his head. "Of course. Are you in trouble? In danger?"

"No, I . . ." Her nerves were taut, straining, so Emma jumped to her feet. "I'm sorry to come at such an ungodly hour."

"For God's sake, Lady Denmore, will you only tell me what is wrong?"

She didn't know how to start. "Please call me Emma."

"Emma." He didn't make her name a caress as Hart did. It was more of a growl really, a threat of violent impatience.

She was staring at his chest again and noticed the strange roughness of a scar against his neck. The whole *width* of his neck. When she frowned, Lancaster's hands rose to fasten the buttons of his shirt, and he scowled when she met his eyes.

"I need help," she finally said. She paced over to the small hearth and the fire the maid had started. When she glanced back, Lancaster was standing with hands on hips, still scowling. She had no choice. "Someone . . . a man from Cheshire has followed me."

"Followed you?"

"He was . . . He developed an interest in me even before my husband's death. After Lord Denmore died, he became . . . intent. He would not leave me be, he insisted that he loved me and we must marry. He would not accept my refusal. And then he began to imagine things."

Lancaster shook his head. "I don't understand."

Emma bit the inside of her lip and called up the lies she'd created. "He began to speak as if I'd never been married. He claimed that Lord Denmore had not been my husband. I grew frightened. I decided to move to London and put him and my husband's death behind me. But he has followed me here."

"You saw him?"

"Yes." Emma did not have to feign her distress as she pressed a hand to her stomach. "I came home last night and found him in my bedroom. Waiting."

Sharp alarm sparked in his eyes. "Emma?" he asked, but she shook her head.

"I talked him into leaving. He is coming back this afternoon. He insists that we will return to Cheshire and marry, says he'll ruin me if I don't agree."

Lancaster's eyes narrowed, he cocked his head in question. "He did not hurt you? Is that the truth?"

"I'm fine. Just frightened and . . . I need some time. I will move my household, but I need days, maybe weeks, to find lodging and make arrangements . . ."

"Do you wish to stay here?"

"Oh! Well . . . I'm flattered, I'm sure."

He flashed a quick smile that made him look quite wicked. "I meant that I would decamp, of course."

"Oh, um, of course. No, I would not risk angering him or . . . anyone else."

"And why have you not called on Somerhart for help? Not that I mind at all, you understand."

Emma clasped her hands together and held on tight. "Things are not as they seem. We are no longer involved. Even if we were, he is not the most understanding of men."

"Ha. Very true. Well then, I'm relieved you are uninjured and I'll do anything I can to help." He waved her toward the settee and followed her over. "You sound as if you have some idea you'd like set in motion."

"Do I?"

He smiled again as she poured him a cup of tea. "You may be in need of help, but I seriously doubt that you are ever helpless."

"Mm. I do have a small plan. I just need him kept from me so that I can leave."

"But where will you go? He will find you again. He may hurt you."

"I don't wish harm to him or his family. They were kind to me."

"But you mean to give up your life here and run from him?"

She met his worried gaze and decided to tell the truth. "I never meant to stay here, Lancaster. I could not afford to do so even if I meant to. I only came to—"

"It is clear why you came here, Emma. You came to make your fortune." His eyes were sympathetic. Understanding.

She looked away. "It is not so much of a fortune."

"I know. But you have a right to it. More so than I will have to mine. You have worked for yours; I will simply marry."

Emma gave into a watery laugh. "Some would consider that a lifetime of work."

"Perhaps." His hand covered hers. "If I had a small fortune to spare I would give it to you and send you on your way. Or not."

She blushed as she laughed. Even in her distress she could still find him charming. Attractive. And not the least bit tempting. And she wasn't honestly sure that he was tempted by her. She was a diversion from the very real fact that he would need to find a wife in short order. Any wife, as long as she came with money.

And she was not the only diversion if the state of his shirt was any indication.

She smiled more easily and met his eyes. "I do have a plan, but I need your help. I would like to have Matthew arrested. I'd like him held for a week or two; held but not harmed. But I do not know how to find the right constable, someone willing to take bribes. Someone dishonest, but trustworthy." She laughed again, though surely it wasn't appropriate.

He grinned. "And so you thought of me?"

"Only because you're my friend, Lancaster, not because I think you a scoundrel."

"No, I may be too honest a friend for you. I'm not sure I know how to find an honorable constable who's open to bribery. But I will try my best."

"Thank you. I could never repay you for this."

"Oh, I imagine you could but, again, there is that damned nobility of mine."

"A burden, I'm sure."

"What time will he return?"

"Three o'clock. I appealed to his sense of decency. He won't return until then."

"Well, then, I will be in contact before then. Either I will deliver a likely constable or I will come and retrieve you and beat the daylights out of your spy."

Emma's throat closed. She was choking on tears of relief and shame. She needed his help and wanted his friendship, yet she lied to him at every turn. She felt guilty about what would happen to Matthew, but she could not let him control her life. And Hart . . .

She drew a shuddering breath and squeezed Lancaster's hand. "I am truly sorry."

"Nonsense. I'm relieved that you asked me for help."

She nodded, and let him think that she was apologizing only for the inconvenience and not for the betrayal of him and everyone he knew.

Chapter 14

The simple white china felt cold against Emma's hands as she leaned over the chamber pot. Her fingers trembled. A drop of sweat fell from her temple and landed on one pale knuckle. When Emma realized that she wasn't going to be sick, she sat back on her bed and wiped her brow with a sleeve.

She had done it. She'd sent Matthew off to a little stone room with barred windows. She'd locked him up. The constable had promised that he would be kept safe and comfortable. He'd have his own cell and plenty of food and special luxuries not afforded to the other inmates. Still, Emma was sick with guilt.

If only he hadn't followed her. If only he'd waited one more month.

"Stop it," she whispered, pushing her clenched hands to her forehead. "Stop it, stop it." She'd had him arrested. It was done. It would only be worth it if she moved forward with her plans.

Bess scratched at the door. "Lord Lancaster has gone, ma'am. He asked me to convey his concern and requests that you contact him tomorrow. He was very worried."

She could see that Bess was very worried as well, but the

housekeeper held her tongue. She'd been sent on an errand before three o'clock and had only just returned.

Emma forced her shoulders into a straight line. "I'll need the red dress pressed."

"Ma'am?"

"I'll be leaving at nine."

"But . . . I thought we were to begin packing."

"Yes, but slowly. We will go in a few days."

"But this trouble—"

"The trouble has been contained. We will be fine, Bess. The red gown please," she reminded. Bess left without another word, though she gave Emma one more disapproving glance as she stopped to retrieve the gown from the wardrobe. They'd never taken it out before. It was too red, too beautiful. It couldn't be worn more than once, but that wouldn't be a problem now.

Even if Matthew would simply go away, Lancaster had heard all the accusations. He'd watched her carefully as Matthew had ranted, spitting that she wasn't Lady Denmore, that she was Lord Denmore's niece. He'd sworn that Emma was a fraud, a virgin shaming herself by living as a widow. He'd raged that she belonged to him and had promised to be his wife.

Emma had watched in horror, she hadn't had to pretend at that, but she'd seen the dull glint of suspicion in Lancaster's eyes. The constable had been calm and fatherly through the entire incident, even when Matthew had begun his favorite speech. The one where Emma was Eve tempting them all with the apple. Or Jezebel. Or even Mary Magdalene, the redeemable harlot.

At those words, Lancaster's suspicion had disappeared in a blink, replaced by disgust. Emma had maintained her composure as the accusations flew. She'd maintained it as Lancaster and the kind old constable had wrestled Matthew into a police wagon. But when Lancaster had returned and reached for one of her shaking hands, Emma's composure, already frayed, had snapped, and she had turned and fled up the stairs to her room.

But she couldn't afford to indulge her fragile nerves with a long rest. Even an hour of missed play would be too much. She wanted—*needed*—one thousand more pounds, and not even her own soul could keep her from it.

Lancaster's sympathy would fade as the days passed, but suspicion had a way of holding tight. Friend or not, he could not ignore his own doubts. So Emma's stay in London was quickly nearing its end.

"Why?" Matthew wailed at the wall of his cell. "Why have You let her do this to me?"

He thought he heard a scratching beneath the bed and jerked his feet up onto the mattress. Wrapping his arms around his knees, he rocked back and forth and muttered prayer after prayer.

He was being persecuted, tortured by these sinful city people who'd lost all touch with the Lord. They could not see the devil even when she flaunted herself so gleefully in front of them.

Some rough voice shouted from far down the long hallway, and Matthew sobbed into his knees.

He could not live like this, locked into a little room like a thief. The rug that covered the stone floor was cheap and stained. The tea that had been set out was likely poisoned. The constable had insisted that Matthew tell where he'd left his possessions, but he'd told the man nothing. He knew that they meant to steal his valuables and sell his clothing on the street.

When the lock rattled, Matthew yelped and pulled the pile of blankets up to his chest. He'd likely be beaten and tortured now. Martyred for his beliefs. It occurred to him suddenly that this could all be the work of the church, those men seduced by money and power, the men who resisted glorious change. They might even have set Emily against him.

A cold gust of air foreshadowed the entrance of menace and set him trembling. "Mr. Bromley, I've brought that heating pan I promised."

Matthew peeked above the blankets. The old constable. He reminded Matthew of his father, which gave him the courage to sit up straight. "You've made a terrible mistake listening to that harlot. She is unnatural and deceptive. The snake in the garden."

The constable sighed. "You're not quite right, are you?"

"I am right and righteous! Can you not see her for the temptress she really is?"

"For the love of the Lord, boy. You've said you mean to marry her."

"I do. It is her only hope, and mine."

The man moved to leave and he would lock the door on this terrifying, horrid box. Matthew gingerly set his feet down to the cheap rug. "Listen. Please listen. You know, you must know that women are the source of all evil in this world. Set down to tempt us and lead us astray. Emily is without the guidance of a man. Her only hope is a firm hand and an iron will and I mean to provide both. Please. Help me save her from Satan. I will beat the devil out of her if I have to."

His father would have conceded by now, bowed beneath Matthew's greater wisdom. This man might look like Matthew's father, but the similarity ended there. His soft, lined face had grown stiff with anger.

"I have five daughters, Mr. Bromley. Five lovely daughters. And I pray to God that none of them ever meet a man like you."

The door slammed with an echoing boom. "My father is

a magistrate!" Matthew screamed, but the lock shot into place like the clatter of a great metal insect.

He dared to lunge for the heating pan and tugged it beneath the bedclothes before he curled into a tight ball. Despair overwhelmed him, and he collapsed into the great, heaving sobs of a man betrayed by love and a wicked world.

Chapter 15

"Where is she?"

Hart regretted the way Bess flinched at his harsh tone, but he was being as reasonable as was possible. Her rough red fingers clutched tight to the edge of the front door. "I'm sorry, Your Grace. Truly. My mistress is not at home."

"Oh, I expected that she would not be home. The play's not nearly lively enough here. Where has she gone?"

Bess shook her head. "She doesn't inform me of her plans, sir."

Hart sighed and leaned an arm against the doorway. "No, I suppose she does not."

"My apologies." Bess bowed her head, mouth drawn down in regret.

"Not your fault." No, it certainly wasn't Bess's fault. Lady Denmore was fully to blame. "What the hell has gotten into her?"

"She . . ."

He glanced up to Bess, surprised the woman would answer the mumbled question.

"She has been . . . upset, Your Grace."

Unease crept through his gut and he straightened from his slouch. "Upset by what? By whom?"

Bess shook her head, but Hart thought immediately of the most annoying of the rumors he'd heard over the past two days. "Lancaster?"

"Your Grace?" Her face turned pink.

He told himself it was completely inappropriate for him to quiz a servant for information. "Lord Lancaster? Is he the reason for her upset?"

"No, sir." But her face was red now and growing brighter by the second.

"I see." Hart spun on his heel and stalked back to his carriage. She couldn't be having an affair with Lancaster. She'd said she didn't want that, and Hart had believed her. But the rumor that she'd been seen sneaking from his home after dawn . . .

No. Perhaps Hart himself had upset her. She'd seemed nervous, almost frightened, by his honesty the other day. And now . . . now all the rumors pointed to a woman out of control. She was placing large bets on card games, engaging young men in ridiculous dares, flitting in and out of unsavory parties until the sun broke over the horizon. And she was completely ignoring Hart and his frequent notes.

His stomach had been burning with anger for forty-eight hours now, and it seemed unlikely he'd feel better any time soon. Attempts to track her down in one of her smoky lairs the night before had failed. The woman was as slippery as an eel. But tonight . . . tonight he would find her, and Lady Denmore would discover that his patience was at an end.

"He left?"

The housekeeper didn't look up when Emma stepped from her small office. "Bess? The duke has gone?"

"Yes."

She ignored Bess's clear disapproval and turned her back to her. "Finish fastening the dress then." The amber skirts reflected the flickering candlelight, beautiful as long as you didn't know that mud stains had ruined the hem. Bess had purchased it the morning before and worked two days at fitting it to Emma. She'd also added rust-colored bands of printed silk to the double flounces of the skirt and the wide sleeves. Emma had tied a ribbon of the same color around her throat.

She looked lovely and felt like the fraud she was. Hart's notes had first conveyed worry, then irritation, and finally anger. She had hurt him with her reckless disregard for him, for her reputation. And while she resented his betrayal and the disastrous events he'd set into motion, she couldn't pretend that he'd been malicious. He couldn't have known what would happen when he contacted Matthew's father.

Still, he hadn't trusted her, and that made it so much easier to do what she needed to do. She wasn't trustworthy and there was no need to pretend she was.

Realizing that Bess's tugging had stopped, Emma turned to find the woman standing with arms crossed. "Thank you, Bess. Two more days. Three, at most. Then we will be done with London, just as you wanted."

"He's been good to you."

Emma cocked her head, not bothering to pretend she didn't understand. "Yes, Somerhart has been good to me. But not exactly honorable, wouldn't you agree? He wants to be my lover, Bess, not my husband. He has no say over what I do or where I go."

"He cares for you."

"Yes, just as I'm sure he cares for his favorite hound. The duke is a rich and powerful man. I would not worry over him if I were you."

Bess gave a begrudging nod. "I suppose you're right."

"Now, how do I look?"

That finally softened her frown. "Beautiful, ma'am. I only wish we had a nicer cloak to cover that lovely gown."

"It is lovely thanks to you. Now I must be off. I'm late. I'll only get two hours of play in before my dinner engagement. Do not wait up. I expect I'll return toward dawn again."

The coach she'd hired awaited her at the end of the alley. She had meant to be in it a quarter hour before, but Hart had descended upon her door, pounding the wood as if it were her willful nature beneath his fist. The memory urged her legs to move faster. The surprised driver jumped from his perch and yanked the door open just as she arrived.

She should have canceled her dinner plans, but she was to have a late private meal with Lord and Lady Osbourne and she couldn't bear to miss it. She wouldn't see them again after tonight; she knew that even if they did not. "One last relaxing night before the Season begins to whirl," Lord Osbourne had said, and Emma was thankful they'd invited her.

But first there was this fete at Tunwitty's. Then another party to attend after her quiet meal with friends. Friends who would be hurt when they heard the truth.

But that was not her concern. Her safe was slowly filling. She'd almost reached her goal.

Emma was so lost in gloomy thoughts that she didn't notice the carriage had stopped. The door simply opened and she descended. As soon as the butler swept open the door of the house, as soon as she stepped through, Emma realized she'd made a mistake. She should not have come to this party.

Gentlemen strode by whom she'd never seen before. Ladies were everywhere. The women's heads turned as they passed her, taking in her utilitarian cloak and simple hairstyle. Emma hurried to unfasten the cloak and hand it to the butler. It seemed she had inadvertently gotten herself invited to a respectable party smack in the middle of the Little Season. More households were arriving every day, and while there would be no glittering balls for at least a few weeks, the new arrivals needed entertainment.

Emma maintained her pleasant smile and told herself not to panic. These ladies might disapprove, but none would know the truth about her. Her uncle's village was a tiny, sleepy place. Whatever squires or baronets she had known were not wealthy enough to travel early to town. Their funds simply would not stretch so far. Her plan would hold.

Checking to be sure her hair was still in place, Emma felt the hard jut of the little crystals she'd woven into her braid. She could not afford spectacular hats or expensive feathers, but she was glad for the crystals at least. Between them and the lovely gown, she probably wouldn't be mistaken for the governess.

Two women passed, arm in arm, and Emma felt the burn of two pairs of suspicious eyes, but when she nodded, they nodded stiffly back.

"Lady Denmore!"

She jumped and couldn't suppress her gasp as she scanned the large entry for a familiar face. When she caught site of Mr. Jones rushing toward her, her tension broke on a wide smile.

"Mr. Jones," she sighed and watched a flush work up to his cheeks as he bent to kiss her gloved hand.

"A great pleasure to see you, Lady Denmore. It has been at least a week. I mean to say . . ." He cleared his throat loudly. "Would you care for a refreshment? I would be happy to—"

"I'm afraid I will not be here long, but I would enjoy a tour of the rooms if you'd be so kind. I have never been to Lord Tunwitty's home."

"Of course, of course." He offered a thin arm, his eyes not quite meeting hers. Mr. Jones was young and shy, and Emma was very careful to always be kind but not encouraging. His arm jumped beneath her fingers.

"Will you be playing tonight?" he asked. "I have never . . .

I mean I wonder if you will always be keen to play so . . . ardently."

"I do not think so," Emma answered honestly. "I am simply enjoying the challenge of it."

"You are quite good, of course. Quite good. I am a great . . . a great admirer of yours. I have never mastered the intricacies of most of the card games, not well enough to bet more than pennies. You are so very clever."

"Thank you, Mr. Jones." He blushed again, and Emma scrambled for a way to change the subject. "Tunwitty's home is quite lovely." They'd toured three rooms already, but Mr. Jones had been too involved in his compliments to offer commentary.

She steered him toward the more raucous end of the hall. Before she had passed the first door, she heard a loud hoot.

"The lively Lady Denmore! I was hoping you'd make it to my table this evening, my dear."

She managed to hold onto her smile despite that it was Marsh shouting from the crowded library. In fact, her mood inched up to something close to glee. Here was a chance to fleece this disgusting man before she left town. "Marsh," she purred and let Mr. Jones lead her into the room. "I am in the mood for brag tonight. Do you play?"

"Brag?" He looked her up and down, his eyes lingering at the bodice of the dress. "I've been known to play a round of brag or two. That game is quite old-fashioned for someone so young. And quite involved for a woman. Are you certain of your feminine skills?"

"Oh, yes," she offered with a smile.

The men parted to let her make her way to an empty chair at the curved table. Emma glanced over the other players, nodding to the men she knew. There were fewer than normal and she counted that to her advantage. In general, men considered women inferior players, and, in general, those men lost to her.

"Might I get you some champagne?" Mr. Jones asked from her shoulder.

"Please."

Marsh gave a low laugh. "Careful, gentlemen. The Dowager Lady Denmore is a fearsome player, and she only gets bolder as the night goes on." The other men chuckled and accepted her demure smile at face value. Fools.

They thought Marsh was simply humoring her, and they also assumed she did not understand the less savory interpretation of his words. The man was implying that he knew something about her skills at night play, as if she would deign to let his chapped lips touch her skin. Oh, yes, she'd enjoy taking his coin.

Mr. Jones brought her the champagne, the cards were dealt and Emma placed her first bet. The game was begun.

One thousand pounds. A thousand.

One thousand pounds lay on the table in a pile of gold and notes, enough to support a laborer's family for half a lifetime or more. And Emma was about to win it. Probably.

Except that she had thrown her last quid in on the previous bet, and Marsh knew it.

Emma broke off from her worrying to look around at their audience. She and Marsh were the last ones left in this hand, and the other players had spread the word. The table was surrounded by gentlemen. The atmosphere had become too hot and fogged with smoke for the other ladies. The *real* ones.

Sweat soaked through Emma's low-quality gloves, darkening the stains the coins had already left.

You can't back down now, she told herself. *You have four hundred pounds in that pile.* Not that she wanted to call off. She had a good hand, a win was almost guaranteed. Almost.

"You have me at a disadvantage," she finally murmured.

Marsh tried to appear sympathetic. "Surely you have

property? Something that could be used as collateral. I'd be happy to offer a loan."

"I do not."

"I see." His green eyes glinted like moss beneath water. He leaned a little closer, and Emma laid her cards facedown on the table.

His eyes fell to her low neckline. "Are you quite certain you have nothing to offer?"

"Quite. Unless you would accept my word."

"The word of a woman? An unnecessary risk as, in fact, you have something of great value to wager. Something I prize very highly."

"And that is?" She didn't bother leaning forward to make his task easier. She knew exactly what he'd propose, and if he wasn't willing to make his offer in front of others, then the coward could keep his thoughts to himself. He was about to ruin her reputation, and he could damn well ruin his own as well. The sweet scent of port wafted over her as he breathed.

"I believe you know what I mean, Lady Denmore."

"I'm sure I do not."

He glanced up at the men closest to them, but his eyes darted quickly back to the tops of her breasts. "A night in your bed," he finally whispered.

Despite that she'd been expecting it, Emma still felt her body jerk with the shock of it. That wave of tension seemed to continue past her to the observers at her back. There was a small bubble of silence around them all.

Emma raised her eyebrows. "You think my virtue is worth only four hundred pounds, Lord Marsh? I'm not sure which is more insulting—the offer itself or the measly amount attached to it."

The murmurs around them grew louder.

Her opponent looked into her eyes and smiled. He could see that she was insulted but not exactly outraged. "Fine. Retrieve your previous bets from the pile. That would raise your worth to . . . what? Seven hundred? Eight hundred pounds?"

Emma simply stared at him. If she did this, her name would be ruined forever, but her name would soon be ruined at any rate. And if she did this, and won, she could leave London at dawn. All her worldly possessions were packed in trunks and crates, and not very many of them at that. She would be done. She'd have more money than she needed, and she would be free.

And if she did this and lost . . . then she would leave in the morning anyway, not quite rich enough, because she'd be damned if she'd honor a bet as dishonorable as this one.

Emma clasped her hands tight together and squeezed against the wave of dull pain that roared through her body. *You are a liar and a cheat. One more time won't make any difference.*

She didn't know why the thought of walking away from a dishonorable debt caused her stomach to knot, but perhaps she would be well served to follow through even on a loss. A night in Marsh's chambers would cool her fiery blood for good. She would be cured.

"Perhaps you wish to simply forfeit," he offered, eyes mocking her turmoil. His mouth curled up in a sneer. He'd played her often enough to know she would not back down.

She unclenched her hands, one finger at a time, and raised them both to the table. Then slowly, slowly, she reached one gloved hand out and began to count out the four hundred pounds she'd tossed out so casually moments before.

"One night," she said clearly, and the room exploded into a beehive of indistinct words. She was glad she could not make out any one conversation. She did not want to know what they said.

Marsh's lips flushed pink as they stretched into a leer. His eyes strayed back to her décolletage, and Emma could *see* his thoughts, flickering and varied, as he riffled through the things he wanted to do to her. She had never seen him at one of her father's gatherings, but he would have been entirely comfortable at the worst of them, she was sure.

Emma finished collecting her previous bets and retrieved her cards. She willed her hands to stop shaking, but Marsh saw and his eyes sparkled.

"Well, then, my dear. Let's see them."

Emma gritted her teeth. "The play is yours."

"Of course." He laid down his cards. The room dropped into silence, as if they'd all been plunged suddenly into deep, cold water.

She stared at the cards, taking in the suits, the numbers. The jack of spades and the jack of hearts were both winking at her, mocking her with knowing smiles. Throat thick with rising tears, Emma nodded. A pair, not a thrice.

Her skin burned as she carefully tilted her cards and placed them flat on the glossy wood. "A running flush," she whispered, and the cries of the gentlemen around her pierced straight through her skull.

"I say, Marsh, that was outrageous."

"Scurrilous. You should be ashamed."

"She may have won the hand, but that is the end of her."

"Disgusting."

"Unthinkable."

She ignored it all, staring into her opponent's cold eyes as she carefully opened her reticule and began dropping handfuls of coin in.

Well done, he mouthed, but his congratulations ended on a sneer. Emma smiled back and tugged the cord of her bag closed. Triumph and relief twisted through her, though they felt strangely like acid, burning her lungs, heating her skin. She took a deep breath, then another. The terrible words around her began to fade. She smiled more genuinely as she stood. No one pulled out her chair.

She turned to leave and within a few feet, found herself

face-to-face with a very pale Mr. Jones. Emma inclined her head, but he seemed frozen. Nodding to let him know that she understood, she started to pass around him and was shocked when his arm appeared, hovering just under her hand.

"You needn't do this," she murmured.

He shook his head. "I escorted you in. I shall escort you out as well."

"Thank you."

As they neared a door, Emma caught sight of two elegantly dressed ladies. They turned their backs as she passed; word had spread already. She forced herself not to care. She did not know these people and they did not know her.

"I shall take my leave," she informed Mr. Jones, and tried to walk more quickly toward the stairway, but his arm held her back.

"Do not hurry as if you are fleeing. Leave with dignity."

"With what dignity?"

He glanced toward her. "I never thought of your gaming as a shameful thing."

"Until now?"

He was too much a gentleman to answer. Another lady turned her back. A younger woman stepped back and retreated into a doorway as Emma swept past.

"Just take me to the door, Mr. Jones. Do not wait with me."

"Nonsense."

She ordered her cloak from the butler. A footman went to signal her driver. When Emma dared to turn, she found dozens of pairs of eyes focused on her. They looked down from the landing of the first floor. She offered them all a curtsy, then closed her eyes as Mr. Jones swept her cloak around her shoulders.

"I shall wait outside."

He followed her, stubborn boy.

"Why are you doing this?"

His eyes no longer met hers, his head tilted down toward the pale stone of the walk. "I had thought . . ." An icy breeze blew his hair awry and made him shiver. "I had thought perhaps your wildness would grow tempered with time. You are enjoying your first weeks in London, I know. And I . . . My income is respectable. My uncle holds an old title."

"Mr. Jones—"

"I'd even taken the step of trying to locate your family, to make inquiries . . ."

Her sympathy froze to shock. "You what?"

"I wished to make the acquaintance of your family, in order to—"

"My father is dead."

"Yes, I am sorry. Terribly sorry. But I had thought to—"

"You could have asked me. Why did you . . . ? To whom did you write?"

He looked utterly confused. "I am sorry, Lady Denmore. I wasn't sure. You are still in half mourning. I did not think it appropriate to press my suit until the summer."

"Whom did you contact?"

"The local magistrate. A Mr. Bromley."

Wheels crunched somewhere to her left. Turning, Emma watched as the hired carriage stopped a few feet away. The driver hopped down and opened the door.

Emma unlocked her jaw. "I apologize for this evening. You will excuse me? I have a private dinner to attend."

When the carriage door closed, Mr. Jones still stood there, staring down, arms crossed to hold off the cold. Emma did not know what to do, so she let the coach move on toward Osbourne's home.

When another vehicle rolled past, turning into the Tunwitty's drive, Emma glanced out in time to see the golden, outstretched wings of a solemn hawk flying through the night. The Somerhart hawk on the Somerhart crest. The duke's carriage had arrived.

Emma let her head fall to her hands. She breathed in the sharp metal scent of dirty coin and thanked God that she had left so quickly. She had shamed him, and he would never forgive her. And suddenly she felt very afraid.

Chapter 16

"Must you leave so early? It is only past twelve," Lady Osbourne insisted.

Osbourne placed a hand on his wife's arm. "Let her go to her tables. The girl has a gift. We mustn't stifle it."

"Oh, you are encouraging her to be a dreadful gambler, Osbourne. Hush."

Emma smiled at them and told herself she really must rise from the warm comfort of the fire and be gone. No gambling tonight, but there were preparations to be made. And she felt odd, not herself, but her lethargy was part of the oddness as well. She felt pulled down, heavy and weary.

The Osbournes continued their affectionate bickering. She would miss them so much. Her uncle had told her that theirs had not been a love match; in fact, they'd quite hated each other for several years. But after the birth of their first child, a daughter, something had changed for them. Animosity had been transformed to love, and it had lasted for forty years now.

Lady Osbourne could no longer travel comfortably to their country house. Three days in a carriage caused her hip to ache terribly for weeks on end, so Lord Osbourne had given up his months of hunting in the north, and they stayed in London all year. Together.

Emma sighed, knowing she could not leave with just a casual farewell. She'd come to care deeply for them.

"Actually," she started, "I will be leaving town. Tomorrow, I think."

"Oh," Lady Osbourne gasped, "but you will be back in time for our ball, won't you? It's the first ball after Easter and I intend for it to be a complete crush."

"I . . . No, I'm afraid I won't be back for the ball. In fact, I will have to miss the Season entirely. You must—" Emma paused to think how much to say. "I'm afraid I created quite a scandal earlier. You may wish to disavow my presence here this evening."

Lord Osbourne huffed. "We will disavow you entirely if it suits us, but it will not. Now what is this nonsense about quitting town for the whole Season?"

"Oh, it is your wardrobe, isn't it?" his wife cried. "Everything is so dreadfully expensive. You must stay with us, dear girl. There is no need to waste money on your own apartments; we have fifteen empty chambers here! Stay with us and we will see to your dresses."

Emma held up both hands. "No, no. I cannot. It is not my lack of funds, or not entirely. And it's not even my disgrace, though that would be enough. It's clear that my nerves cannot take the gaiety and energy of the Season. Why, even the winter rounds have me tired beyond belief. No, I will retire to the country for the summer. I'm afraid that Denmore passed his passion for gardening on to me."

Lady Osbourne did not give up. "But we have gardens here!"

Emma shook her head, and Lord Osbourne exchanged a meaningful look with his wife before he reached for Emma's hand.

"We will miss you. You have become as a daughter to us.

You must promise to return in the fall to stay here. We are old enough to delight in scandal as we no longer create any of our own."

Lady Osbourne slapped his arm and giggled like a young girl.

"Nothing public at any rate," he said with a raised brow.

Emma smiled past her tightening throat. "Thank you so much. Your friendship has meant everything to me. Everything. Please remember that."

She rose to her feet and was enveloped in the plump arms of Lady Osbourne. After long hugs and several motherly kisses, Emma was free to go, but her feet felt heavy as she descended to the drive.

She'd arrived in London already anticipating her triumphant exit, and now that it was time to leave she couldn't quite imagine it. She would be an impostor in her next life too, though she'd be pretending at respectability instead of worldliness. But the effect would be the same. She would be lonely, without real friends. But everything would be better soon. It must be.

"Where to, ma'am?" her driver asked as he handed her up. Emma tripped over her skirt and fell hard into the seat.

"I don't . . ." Where was she going? Home, she supposed, but she remembered Hart's carriage. He'd arrived at the Tunwitty's in the full force of the drama she'd created. He would have been furious. More than furious. Enraged. And he might very well have gone straight to her home, might be there still. Waiting.

"Ma'am?"

But she had nowhere to go. She could not damage Lancaster's chances of finding a wife by driving up to his front step like a whore making her rounds.

"Drive to my street, but not to my door. Turn 'round the corner and stop there."

"Ma'am." He tipped his hat and betrayed not an ounce of incredulity as he closed the door and shut her up in darkness.

Her weary body urged her to lie down on her seat, to lay her head on her arms and curl her legs beneath warm skirts. But if she gave in now, she was sure she would dissolve into a useless mass of jelly, weak and unsure of herself. So she kept her spine rigid and did not let it touch the seatback as they passed from the hulking luxury of the mansions of Regent's Park to the beautiful rows of Mayfair. Somerhart lived here, in the heart of the fashionable district. She wondered idly how many properties he owned, and which one he would bury her on, given the chance.

They turned a corner, and the bright lights of Mayfair fell behind them. St. James now, then Belgrave. And finally her street.

Her shoulders grew tighter, froze to rock when the coach leaned around a corner before rocking to a stop. Emma eased toward the window, squinting into the night. A light drizzle began to patter against the glass, obscuring her view. She could just make out her door and there was no fuming duke standing before it.

But he could be inside, he could be in his carriage watching for her, he could be careening through the streets right this moment, racing toward her home. Shivers raced from her belly outward.

It hadn't been Hart who'd betrayed her. She could no longer pretend to ease her guilt with his transgressions. He'd been unfailingly honest with her, and she had lied at every turn. But he was a rich, powerful, degenerate duke, so why should she care?

Her lonely door shone wet in the faint light of the corner lamp. How sad it looked, and censuring. She would walk out that door tomorrow and disappear. Hart would never know anything about her but her lies. She would leave him with nothing but humiliation. She wanted to leave him with more, wanted more for herself.

If he was in there, waiting, she owed him this confrontation at least. The chance to call her every foul name he could. The chance to vent his hurt. And he would be hurt.

She should go in. She should.

There was nowhere else to go.

Her hand moved toward the handle, then the carriage dipped to one side and she heard the driver yell, "Hey!"

Emma's heart stopped as the far door swung open. She cringed into the corner, not certain what Hart would do, but fearing it all the same.

Then a little face popped into view. "Stimp?"

"Get off my damn carriage, you worthless rat!" the driver yelled.

Stimp jumped inside, demanding, "And where've you been?"

The box rocked from side to side as the driver began to descend.

"It's fine," Emma called. "This rat is known to me."

Stimp's jaw edged out. "Yer in big trouble."

"Being paid to spy on me again?"

"Oh, not just that. I'm to send for him when I see you. The man's furious."

"Yes, I know."

"And he seemed quite drunk by the time he left off waiting in his shiny carriage. Murder in 'is eyes."

Somehow just knowing made Emma feel bolder. "Drunk and murderous and you mean to scurry off and bring him straight to my door?"

The stubborn chin inched up. "Can you pay me better?"

"Perhaps."

"But you'll pay me once and then not at all. I'm practically on His Grace's payroll." He shrugged, conveying his sympathy but no regret.

Emma turned away to stare again at the sad door that led to her sad little home. Hart was furious. And drunk. And determined to make her pay.

The shivers in Emma's belly intensified until she felt she couldn't breathe. She'd made her decision. She could finally afford to be foolish.

"No need to inform him, Stimp. I'll find him myself."

His little face scrunched up. "I don't believe you."

Emma pulled off her soiled gloves and tossed them onto the opposite seat. "Believe me or not, but I'll not sit here and wait to be cornered. Now out of my carriage. If the man wants a fight, he'll get it."

He could not believe it, even hours later.

Scandalous as she was—defiant and reckless and sensual— Hart could not believe she'd offered up her body in a bet.

He told himself she hadn't meant it and wouldn't have followed through with it. Hell, Hart wouldn't have *let* her. But that did not change the fact that she'd publicly offered herself to another man as she'd refused Hart even a hint of private affection.

We are not nice, she'd said. "No," Hart growled to the empty library, "we are not nice. Not anymore."

The tenderness he'd begun to feel, the dreaded caring, had been pushed down into his gut, condensed into a burning, writhing knot of hatred. He was doing his best to drown it, but liquor was flammable, after all.

Hart clenched his fingers tighter around the leaded crystal in his hands. The scrapes on his knuckles burned like fire when a little bourbon sloshed over the side of the glass and dribbled over his fingers. That bastard Marsh had had it coming. Hart wished he'd gotten more than two blows in before the other gentlemen had intervened. They'd claimed it wasn't fair to continue beating an unconscious man. Hart had loudly disagreed.

Despite that he was alone, Hart growled several heartfelt curses before he tossed back the last of the bourbon and reached for the bellpull.

He knew he'd only made the whole thing worse by confronting Marsh. He realized now that it would have been a simple thing to imply that he and Emma had severed their friendship long before. Then there would only have been nods of sympathy and a few congratulations at having the wisdom to cut Lady Denmore loose. But there had been no thinking for Hart. There had only been blind, howling fury, prodded on by unexpected pain.

"Your Grace?"

"This bottle's empty."

"Sir." His butler bowed from the room and returned within seconds. Hart was thinking that the man must be a god of anticipation, but then he noticed that his hands were empty.

"Now, Morton."

"Of course, Your Grace. But the footman informs me you have a visitor."

Hart blinked, and even he could tell that his eyelids were moving slowly. "Stimp?"

"No, sir, a Lady Denmore. Shall I see her in?"

He blinked even more slowly this time as he tried to think past the bourbon and nod at the same time. Was there some other Lady Denmore? It could not be Emma. She wouldn't be so foolish. He felt a sudden fear for what he might do to her if she walked through those doors, and then she walked through and Hart's lethargy vanished.

The liquor burned off in the heat of his rage. He pushed to his feet with no trouble at all and no hint of unsteadiness. Emma stared at him, unafraid, and Hart felt a smile twist his lips. She should be afraid. She should be terrified.

"What have we here?" He looked her over, taking in the lovely amber-gold dress that made her skin glow like cream pearl. Her breasts were pushed high, her waist cinched tight. He'd never seen her look more beautiful. "A foolish lamb."

"You are the lion, I assume?"

"Oh, I am."

Morton had closed the door behind her and she still stood only a few feet from it. She seemed surrounded by a soft gold aura against the dark wood of his library. Her hair picked up the color of her dress in streaks of lighter brown.

She took a deep breath. Her breasts rose, straining against the bodice. "I was told you sought me out, Your Grace."

"And you obliged by coming to me?"

"I did."

"Emma," he sighed in mock empathy. "Tut-tut. That was an incredibly stupid thing to do."

She crossed her arms over her stomach. "How so? I assume that you wish to chastise me for my behavior."

Hart cocked his head and strolled across the wide room, drawing closer in slow increments that inched his blood toward a boil. "Is that what you assumed?" Her arms tightened. "That I wished to chastise you? How very naive, Emma. I am not your guardian to offer wisdom and guidance. I am not your father. I don't wish to chastise you, Emma."

He drew within a foot of her, and watched her breathing grow fast and shallow. "I wish . . ." Her eyes followed his hand as he raised it to drag one finger along her collarbone. "I wish to punish you."

She inhaled. The tops of her breasts brushed his knuckles. "I've done nothing . . . You have no right."

"Oh, my sweet." He traced a path along the edge of the straining fabric. "If I did not have the right, you wouldn't have come here."

She shook her head and took one step back, throwing up her hands to hold him off. "You are drunk."

"Why did you do it?"

That shocked her into dropping her hands. "What?"

"Why did you play the whore for him?"

"I—" She shook her head again, and all the defiance leached from her eyes. "I knew I could win."

"No. Your hand wasn't that good. Any thrice would have beaten your running flush. Oh, yes, I was given all the details of your transgression. So why did you risk it?"

"I don't know. It was a stupid impulse. A mistake."

"A mistake. A mistake like taking the wrong turn on your way to the park, or perhaps leaving a glove behind after a visit?"

"A more dire mistake than—"

"*A mistake.* Like telling one man you will never take a lover, and telling another that you will spread your legs for a few hundred quid?"

"No," she whispered.

"I would have offered more. I still will, Emma, since you haven't been sullied up yet. Will two thousand be sufficient? I consider it quite generous."

"I did not mean to follow through."

Her chin trembled a little and the sight of it brought him joy. "Ah, so you are not a whore, just a cheat."

"Yes." Her trembling chin rose, trying to look proud.

"Why did you come here, straight to the lion's den?"

Emma took another step and her back was against the paneled door. He wanted to press her hard against it.

"I wanted to apologize to you, for causing you any embarrassment."

"Liar."

"I . . . I knew you would . . ."

"You think you've injured me, and you feel guilty, and you want me to make you pay."

"Ridiculous," she hissed.

"And then you will leave here feeling better, and telling yourself you owe me nothing."

"You are drunk and irrational. I needn't listen to this."

"Wonderful. I'm through talking."

She was drawing herself up to argue when Hart shot his arm out and wrapped a hand around the back of her neck.

"Oh!"

Her body stumbled into his when he tugged her forward. Hart tightened his hold and pressed his mouth to her temple. "Marsh," he growled into her ear, "a worthless piece of rubbish."

"Hart—"

"Shut that lovely mouth, Emma. Or I will shut it for you."

Her teeth clicked together.

"Good girl."

He reached behind her to open the door, then edged her out into the hallway. Morton was nowhere to be seen, but Hart knew he was close. "Have wine sent to my chambers," he snapped and was rewarded with the quick appearance of a bowing footman.

Emma jerked from his grasp, but she did not fly toward the door. Instead she followed the sweep of his hand and moved regally toward the staircase. She stepped carefully up, calmly toward the second floor. Toward his bed.

Hart's cock, already swelling, stiffened to heavy attention. She would be his now. Regardless of what she'd offered that disgusting bastard, she would belong to Hart. Only to him.

This could only make it worse, could only make her betrayal more painful, more personal, but he did not care in the least. He wanted her as he'd never wanted any woman. In his youth he'd had the women he'd wanted, had them every which way. And later . . . well, later he'd never wanted like this, because he'd never let himself.

But now the sight of her trussed waist and swaying hips moved him. His heart, that heart rumored to be made of ice, shifted with each of her steps. It lurched at the thought of her spread naked on his bed, trying to appease his anger with her body. She could not make it better, but she could damn well try.

And she wanted it like this, he knew it. She wanted him angry and demanding, so she could tell herself that she'd been overwhelmed. But Hart had no intention of absolving her of responsibility. She would ask for what she wanted, or he would not oblige.

Emma had reached the top of the staircase and now she stood, uncertain and suddenly younger. Hart took her arm and walked her to the set of carved doors that led to his chambers. The footman was close behind with the tray, so Hart simply led her through the door and stopped her in the middle of the room.

When the door closed, he offered a glass of wine, and wasn't the least bit surprised when she finished it in four gulps. "Another?"

"Yes."

"Trying to catch up? I warn you that I've three hours on you."

"I'll do my best." She sipped the second glass more slowly while Hart circled her, assessing his prey. Good Lord, she was beautiful tonight; the wine added a flush to her cheeks, or it could have been fear or arousal or both. Her eyes followed him, then darted away when he met her gaze. Her tongue peeked out to lick a drop of wine from her pink lips, and Hart knew just what he wanted.

"Turn 'round."

He took the glass from her hand as she obeyed. Her skin felt hot when he placed a hand on her shoulder and trailed it down the bare skin of one shoulder blade.

"I have never touched you here," he murmured, testing the texture of her skin over her spine. The dress dipped low in the back and he followed her spine down, and then up again, all the way to her neck. Emma shivered, but she froze when he reached for the tiny hooks of her gown and began to let them loose.

He did not hurry. There was no need. She would stay as long as he wanted.

The hooks fell open, one by one, exposing a simple ivory corset. Hart moved his hands lower until he reached the small of her back. The dress gaped; his cock began to throb as he reached to ease the straps of material from her arms. The silk fell away, crumpling into a dramatic pile on the floor. He made short work of her petticoat, and that fell too, revealing the flare of her hips beneath a transparent ivory shift. The globes of her buttocks were clearly visible, naked and rising against the thin fabric of her chemise.

He placed his palm high on her spine again and traced it down, but this time he continued over the hard brace of her stays, then down, down to the soft curve of her bottom. He cupped one warm cheek and spread his fingers out to measure that flesh.

Emma gasped as he smiled. Her flesh was yielding here, firm and tender at the same time. He followed the rise up to her hip and stepped around to enjoy the view from the front.

Ah, this was even better, and there was no pretense in the smile that showed his teeth and his hunger. Her breasts were pushed high enough to reveal the shell pink edge of her areolae. Below the corset, the linen did nothing to hide the dark shadow of her sex, and the shift itself ended above her knees. Ivory garters gripped her thighs and held up pale gold stockings.

He took her hand to help her step from the circle of her discarded clothing and was well pleased at the sight of her, almost naked, but still wearing her heeled slippers. Yes, she looked made for his indulgence.

Her eyes glittered as she watched him watching. She knew the picture she presented as she stood a little taller and arched her back the tiniest bit. A wider edge of pink showed above her stays.

"Have you wanted me to see you like this, Emma? Have you looked at yourself in the mirror and thought of me watching?"

"Yes," she said evenly.

His heart skipped. "It is a lovely sight. Beautiful." Stepping closer, he curved his hand over her jaw and kissed her gently, reverently. Her mouth opened with no urging, and he eased his tongue inside to trace her lips and teeth. The heat of her, the wetness. Her tongue met his to rub desire to other parts of his body. Other parts that wanted that slick heat and velvet tongue.

He kissed deeper and her hands rose to hold his wrists tight. She pressed her lips harder, angled her mouth to take more. When he drew back her mouth was pink and swollen, and the dozens of times he'd entertained this particular fantasy rose up to strangle him to breathlessness.

"On your knees," he whispered.

Her hands spasmed, clenching his arms tighter. Shocked knowledge flashed through her eyes.

"Your knees," he rasped, and she sank down, slow as a feather, eyes still on his face, fulfilling every picture he'd painted of this moment. She held his gaze as she let go of his wrists and reached for the buttons of his trousers, and Hart unfastened his shirt and shrugged it off.

Her fingers were a torment, pressing into him as she worked the buttons free. "Would you have done this for him?" he demanded.

She shook her head.

"Say it."

Her hands trembled against him, torture, torture. "No," she finally said.

"And will you . . ." He stopped to draw a rough breath

when she slipped her hand into the opening she'd created. "Will you do this for me?"

"Yes," she whispered as her hand closed around him, cooler than his heated flesh, and drew him free. He wanted to gasp but held it back.

Her eyes fell to his jutting erection. "Yes," she said again, with a little hiss of eager breath.

Her hand fell open, until just the tips of her fingers touched him, and those fingers drew fire as she traced a tentative exploration of his shaft. He shuddered. His knees wanted to shatter, so he locked them against that weakness and watched her slow petting.

She traced the rim of the head, skimmed her palm over the tip. Her eyes rose to meet his for just a moment, then down again to his cock. When her hand fell away to rest on his thigh, his muscles jumped beneath the thin fabric.

She pursed her lips to press a simple kiss, and Hart couldn't help the loud hiss of the air he drew through clenched teeth. Her mouth twitched up into a little smile that faded just as quickly as it appeared.

Something froze inside him. He knew he'd remember that forever: Emma smiling against his sex. Then she licked a tiny taste, quick as lightning, and Hart forgot the smile.

She licked again, a flick of her hot tongue, and then a more lingering trace of that wetness. His cock twitched and she jumped a little, eyes darting up.

A shock of pure lust shot through him, trailing some deeper pressure. A hint of a shadow, a dark wisp of suspicion.

She pressed another kiss, twirled her tongue over and around the head, and *for God's sake,* he was sure he'd die with any more teasing. Finally, she parted her lips and eased her mouth over him, just a tiny bit, an inch. He felt her tongue pressing wet and strong, then she let him go with a little *pop.*

That wisp of suspicion unfurled into a certain, stunning realization: she had never done this before. Never.

Her seventy-year-old husband had never asked her or never wanted it. She had never taken another man like this. My God.

He supposed that this should have shamed him or lessened his demand, but it only pushed his lust to a more dangerous peak. His knees shuddered.

"Emma."

She glanced up, and he was sure he saw eagerness there. Please, let it be eagerness.

He took her pliant hand in his, telling himself he should draw her to her feet, but knowing he would not. Instead he wrapped her fingers around the base of his shaft. She squeezed, a delicious amount of pressure.

Hart eased his shaking hand to her hair. His fingers found a half-dozen hairpins and tugged them free. The thick curtain of her hair fell down to brush her shoulders, her back.

"Do you want to do this?"

"Oh, yes." Her breath curled over him, a promise of ecstasy to come. "Yes, I want to. I've wanted to. I'm sorry I don't . . . I—"

"Open your mouth."

Her lush lips parted.

"More. Now, now your tongue . . ." He eased her head closer. Her tongue slid under him, her mouth took him in. Hart felt the tight grasp of her hand and the slippery pressure of her mouth as she swallowed around him. He urged her back, then guided her closer again, and when his hand fell from her hair, Emma took up the movement herself.

He watched past fading vision, body aching with stiff tension, as she found a slow rhythm and took him deeper. Her fist offered a steady pressure that held him still for her pleasure, gave her control.

She was sin and innocence twisted all together. The picture

of seduction, in her corset, on her knees, her face a study of innocent concentration, her hair a wild temptation. Hart wanted to thread his fingers through the silky length, urge her to take him deeper, faster. He wanted to control her, but this was even better: Emma learning what she liked, what he liked. Emma doing what she wanted.

Her eyes opened slowly, and she watched him through her lashes as her mouth slid down, all the way to the edge of her hand.

Hart groaned aloud. His whole body shuddered as pleasure wound tighter and tighter, suffocating all thought and rationality. Desire was a heavy, perfect weight that began to pull him toward the edge. And her mouth . . . so wet and warm and unknowing.

He could not last. And this was part of his fantasy too, Emma drinking him up as he spilled his seed. But some hesitation stopped him. He clamped down on the rushing need and cupped his hand around Emma's head to slide her back.

She was panting, her bottom lip still pressed to his cock, breath rushing over him in cold puffs of torment.

He had to slow down. He wanted more than this. He wanted everything he could take.

"Enough," he groaned, taking her hand to pull her to her feet.

She watched him, pupils wide with lust, lips bruised. Primal possessiveness crashed over him, pressing the breath from his lungs. She was almost innocent despite her lustful nature. And he wanted to keep her for himself, seduce her, teach her things that she would do with no other man.

Then the thought of what she'd meant to do with Marsh fell like a rock through his twisted, stormy thoughts.

He was losing control here, treating her as if she were different, as if she were precious when he'd meant to show her she'd become *less* to him. Meant to show her that their strange friendship had ended and she was just like every other woman he'd had.

Hart refastened his trousers and her brow crinkled.

"Let us go through the ground rules first, shall we?" He strolled over to the tray to pour himself a glass of wine. He didn't offer her any as he returned to stand in front of her tempting form; he didn't dare hold out a glass and reveal his shaking.

"You will not speak of me to anyone. You will not confirm or deny our relationship. If I hear even a hint, a whisper, some intimate knowledge that has been passed on, I will cease to know you. Not only will our interlude come to an end, I will cut you dead. Understand?"

The lust had faded from her eyes, leaving them narrowed against hurt.

"There will be no other man in your bed while I am there. And there will be no further flirtations. When the affair ends there will be no tears, no hysterics. This is purely physical. It is not love, it is not the start of love. It is only the natural end to a mutual attraction. Is that clear?"

Her mouth was tight with rage. "Is this the speech you give all your lovers?"

"It is."

Her head jerked back a tiny bit. "And how do those women react to this list of demands?"

"Some look at me as you are doing now . . ." Oh, she did not like that at all. Did not like being compared to nameless, faceless women. "And some seem cowed. But they all agree."

"Arrogant coward. Are you really so afraid?"

He shrugged and took a sip of wine. "I prefer to be in control."

"Oh, but not always." Her eyes drifted down his naked chest to rest on his lap.

Hart was quite happy with the anger that raged back to full strength at her words. "I am in control *now*, Emma, and that should be all that concerns you. Remove the rest of your clothing."

"You insult me."

"Ha. You may pretend at your outrage, but you have wanted this from the moment we met. Almost as much as I have."

Her jaw jumped at his words. "I did not want *this*."

The last of the wine quenched his dry throat, but it did nothing for the angry want that was stretching his skin tight as a drum. He only felt angrier when he tipped the glass down and met her gaze.

"You came here knowing I was a man on a razor's edge. You knew I was half drunk and damn near violent, and you came to me. You may not want this, Emma, but you *need* it.

"And I . . ." He smiled, smiled until her eyes fluttered with nervousness. "I am pushed too far. Everyone in the world is talking about me right now, my sweet. Laughing at me. Discussing me, my life, my stupid, lustful, unwise heart. They are looking at *me,* Emma. And I will damn well have tonight even if I never deign to speak your name again."

He let his rage free with one wide sweep of his hand and the fragile crystal shattered in a musical crash against the door.

Emma backed up one step.

Hart rolled his shoulders and willed his boiling blood back to a simmer. "Now. Let's start with the corset, shall we?"

Chapter 17

The corset was squeezing her, pressing her lungs too tight. She couldn't draw more than quick, useless gasps of air that did nothing to help her find reason. Instead, every shallow breath sent little bits of sparkling pleasure to her sex.

She was afraid, afraid of Hart, and that only made her body throb with more intensity. Between her fear and that arousal, Emma couldn't think what to do. So she turned, and Hart began to work on the tight lacing that held her in.

As soon as she felt the ties loosen, Emma reached to free the hooks. Suddenly, she could breathe. Blood seemed to fill with life and rush to every nook of her body. Emma had expected to feel relief, but there was no ease in those breaths. Instead, an urgency overtook her.

The final hook gave, and she let the corset drop to the floor.

"Now the shift," Hart murmured, and Emma drew it over her head, thinking of him staring at her naked backside, knowing how much he would like that.

"The shoes," he said. "The stockings."

She could not fathom how he knew her so well. Was it simple recognition on his part, like knowing like? Or was it etched on her skin, a terrible heritage writ in subtle code that

Hart had seen from the start? Or was it possible that every woman wanted this?

Rolling down her last stocking, Emma reveled in the thought of how exposed she was for his eyes. When she turned and found that Hart had undressed as well, the sight of him seized her heart. His body was lean and tightly muscled, his cock thick and rock hard. He would be inside her soon, and she felt she had waited her whole life for that.

His voice slashed like a sword. "Lie on your stomach."

Odd that she now felt powerful when he was so clearly in control. But Emma wasn't the least bit timid when she walked the few steps to his massive bed. She stood on tiptoe to brace one knee against the silken tapestry of the bedcover, then she pulled herself up and crawled toward the pillows, picturing her own body in her mind. Tormenting him with every twitch of her hips.

She thought she heard his breath hitch, and then the cool silk was against her belly, her breasts, and Hart's hand was smoothing up her calf.

"You will . . ." she started, shocked to find her voice so weak. "You are determined to treat me as you treat every woman?"

"Ha." His humorless laugh tickled the back of her knee. Emma could feel his chest brush her heels. "Yes, I mean to treat you like any other woman, but I will fail spectacularly." He spoke closer to her thigh now. His hand caressed the tender skin behind her knee before it rose to massage higher. "I mean to take you simply and savagely, but I can't imagine how. What I want is so much more. I want to have you the way I used to have women." His mouth brushed the back of her thigh, swirling darkness past Emma's vision.

"You . . . You refer to your past? You want me to be one of those women who would . . . a companion for those. . .?" She found she could not speak of it. He was arousing her with his touch, breaking her heart with his words.

"Those secret, sinful parties? Would you like that? Would it arouse you to watch strangers having sex? To know they were watching you as they clawed toward their peak?"

"I . . ." He would make her into what she'd always feared, give her over to the monsters.

His hand smoothed up, fingers curving to fit the flesh of her buttocks. "Yes, I would take you there, beast that I am. That is what you reduce me to, Emma. The selfish, sexual animal I used to be. I want to sneak you into one of those homes, watch as you watch, as you blush and grow wet with horrified arousal. I want to be that man with you, but also something more. I'd never let them touch you. Even if you wanted, I would never share."

She froze, her grief suspended in disbelief. "I would never—"

"Good, because you would not. I would not let them even gaze upon you. But I would escort you there, and I would have you. In secret, alone, against the door of a dark chamber.

"I want you like that. And I want you like this." He kissed her, lingered over her hip as his palm pressed into the small of her back. Emma could feel his shaft now, thick and heavy against her leg. She squirmed, pressing her sex harder to the bed.

"I want you like this," he went on, voice deep and mesmerizing. "And I want you on your hands and knees. I want you on your back. I want you tied to my bed with silk ribbons."

Her gasp couldn't be contained by the pillow.

Hart chuckled. "Would you like that? Helpless, limbs spread, sex naked and open? I want to be wicked and shameful with you. I want to do things I've refused to even think of for ten years. I want to lean you over a bench in Covent Gardens, have you right there while people pass by only yards away. I want to hide you behind drawn curtains at a ball, make you come while I swallow your cries with my mouth."

His kisses worked their way up to her waist, then climbed up to her spine. His knee nudged her legs apart; his arousal was heat and strength against her thigh. Emma spread her legs farther.

"You and that bedroom voice and that knowledge in your eyes. You've reminded me of who I don't want to be, Emma."

"Yes," she sobbed as his tongue traced a circle over her shoulder blade. He sucked her flesh between his teeth, bit a gentle pressure there. His thigh pressed between her legs and she opened for him, arching her back, grinding her hot sex into the coolness of his leg. The crisp hair of his thigh tickled her skin as his muscles flexed and rolled.

"You're so wet for me. I haven't even touched you."

My God, she knew that, she knew it as she wriggled against him, needing his attention. His shaft was pressed hard to her thigh, and she wanted it between them, wanted it *inside* her.

"Shh," he whispered. His tongue teased her skin until he reached her neck. He kissed her a half dozen times, his touch a confusion of lips and tongue and teeth. She groaned and arched and raised her hips like a cat in heat.

"Please. Hart."

His knee shifted and she felt a sharp hope, but then he was nudging her thighs closed, straddling her legs and raising up on his hands.

"Turn over."

Emma scrambled, twisting beneath him until she was looking up into his moon-bright eyes. Holding her breath, she waited, waited. Hart eased his knees between hers, his jaw jumped and he closed his eyes as his sex touched hers for the first time.

"Yes," she breathed, "Yes, yes." But he shook his head and offered a cruel smile.

"No, not for a long while yet, Lady Denmore."

She was going to demand an explanation, but then he was leaning down to kiss her and she ceased to care. His kisses were deep and hot and he rocked his shaft into her mons in a slow, slow rhythm.

His kisses alone were a wicked sexual act. He sucked and tasted and nibbled and licked until Emma found that she could no longer breathe. But when she turned away, gasping, he simply moved to her neck where he sucked and tasted and nibbled and licked. Then down to her collarbone, her shoulder, the rise of her breasts. When he finally reached her nipple, she was desperate and sobbing, and when he caught that hard bud between his teeth, she was horrified to hear herself cry out in a tiny scream.

Hart chuckled against her. She glanced down to find him watching her face with arrogant pleasure. "That was a lovely sound. Let's see if we can find it again."

She clamped her mouth shut and considered pushing him off her, and then his tongue worked while his mouth sucked and Emma was reduced to a panting wreck.

He tortured her, lingering until she screamed again, and when she thought he'd show mercy he only moved to lavish attention on the other breast. Emma dug her fingers into his scalp until he grunted and finally raised his head.

"Is there something I can help you with, Lady Denmore?"

"Yes, you bastard."

"That hardly smacks of contrition."

"I'm sorry!" she cried too late. Hart had already wrapped his hands around her wrists to hold them down. He bent back to his task, and Emma was helpless to resist. But something about his strength against her arms . . .

Every nerve in her body seemed to swell to tautness. Her nipples were hard peaks of sensation, her sex jumped when she rubbed against his hip. And all the while, she pushed back at his grip and found that her struggles couldn't move him an inch.

His mouth finally slid lower, trailing fire down her abdomen, then her belly. His tongue swirled around her navel, then lower. Emma held her breath until she couldn't stand it anymore, then she began to beg.

"Please, please." She felt his breath tease the skin of her belly. "Oh, please," as his chin nuzzled the dark hair of her sex.

His hands gripped harder, shooting sparks of pleasure into her blood, then finally, he kissed her *there*. Right there where she wanted him. He dragged his tongue over her wetness as Emma raised her knees and tugged against his hold.

She cried out, urging him on. She only needed a few seconds of his skilled attention . . . just a moment.

And then his hot mouth was moving on, kissing her inner thigh, biting gently at the tendon before he sucked the hurt away.

"No!" Emma screamed. "Please, Hart. *Please*."

"What are you begging for, Emma?"

"*You*."

"Mm." But he was moving lower, tugging her arms down to her hips, moving away from what she needed. His mouth touched the side of her knee before she snapped.

"I need you, Hart. Please. You inside me. *Please*. I want . . ."

She was rewarded quickly. His body moved up, his mouth dragging promises over her skin. His fingers curled tighter around her bones and she whimpered as she dug her heels into the bed.

"I'm sorry for what I did," she moaned, meaning every word. "I'm sorry." He'd moved too high now, he was rising above her instead of sinking down, but she didn't care. She'd started telling the truth and now she couldn't stop.

"You're the only one, Hart. The only one I've ever wanted. I need you. *Please*."

He let go of her wrists and lay upon her, hands framing her face for a deep, devastating kiss. Then his hand was skimming down her belly as he raised up, his fingers were stroking her. She was sobbing.

She felt the blunt head of his erection then, nudged against her sex. "Please, Hart. I feel so . . . I need you inside, filling me."

He silenced her with a kiss as he eased inside her. Her shocked cry was swallowed in his moan as her body stretched to take him. Emma sucked in a sharp breath against the pain; she dug her fingers into his shoulders and tried to hide her distress. But she was so ready for him, she wanted him so much, and she found the pain fading to a faint burn before her tears had a chance to fall.

She blinked them back as Hart eased out only to slide deeper still.

"Emma, my God. You're . . ."

Fear spiked through her, disintegrating all other feeling for a brief, lonely moment.

His words whispered over her neck. "You're so tight. So damn hot around me."

He began to move within her and her fear was gone. Everything was gone. Everything but the overwhelming knowledge that his flesh was filling her, stretching her tight, rubbing and sliding in a slow, steady motion.

It felt so good, so good, just what she'd always wanted, and Emma realized she'd breathed the words aloud and Hart was shuddering over her. She shifted and found deeper pleasure in that, and when she wrapped her legs around him and pressed her heels to his thighs, Hart rubbed against something inside her that made her groan for more.

He gave her more, and he was whispering, murmuring words that pulled her further into a deep chasm. Words of promise and threat, tender words mixed up with the wickedest things she'd ever heard. Vile, sweet predictions of what they'd do together. And Emma was floating in a dark sea, struggling, reaching for the darkest, deepest part.

All her nerves, muscles, skin—everything—pulled tight as his shaft stroked faster.

He urged, "Yes," as she threw her head back and strained toward him. Time hung, unmoving and cruel, until finally, finally, all that tension turned in on itself, twisting together until it exploded in waves of light and dark that left her screaming beneath him.

She was still sobbing when Hart moaned her name and slid from her body. His muscles turned to stone beneath her hands; she felt the hot brand of his seed spilling against her thigh.

Her body slowly settled back to its normal state, feeling normal sensations. The coolness of the room, the dampness of their mingled sweat, the sharp burn between her thighs. And tears going cold on her cheeks.

But beyond all that was his wonderful weight against her and the heavy satisfaction of her limbs. She felt decadent. And relieved. He hadn't known. She should have done this weeks before: gotten him drunk and enraged, too angry to notice the subtle resistance of her body.

Hart gave a sleepy sigh when she stroked a hand over his hair. She stroked again, memorizing the glossy texture, the faint scent of spice and vanilla that must be his soap.

His weight lessened slightly, and his lips brushed her collarbone just before he lifted himself from her body. "It's cold." The way his chest pressed against her arm made the words rumble through her.

He twisted and turned, tugging the bedcovers from beneath them so he could pull them over their bodies. Emma nearly melted with pleasure when the warmed linens floated down to her skin. And then his strong arm was reaching over to pull her tighter to him and his knee was resting on her thigh, and she felt safe and warm and even loved.

"Stay with me," he sighed. "Stay."

Emma didn't bother to answer. He was already asleep, or close enough, and it was one less lie to tell him.

By the time he woke Lady Denmore would be gone. Less than a ghost. She would, in fact, never have existed. But the same could not be said for her feelings or for his.

In the coming days Hart, at least, would have his hatred to protect him. Emma would have nothing but enough regret to last a lifetime.

"Tea, Your Grace."

The words floated over him, accompanied by a dull, warm light. Hart ignored both. He was exhausted and vaguely ill, and he could feel the crisp bite of cold air against his shoulder. In other words, there was no good reason to wake.

The scent of fresh, hot tea touched the air and grew stronger. Hart buried his head in the pillow, trying to escape, but he found another scent there. The faint citrus kiss of a woman's perfume. *Her* perfume.

The reason for his exhaustion—and his pounding head—crawled through his sticky mind. Emma. Emma was here. In his bed.

Even the alcohol that still clung to his brain couldn't stop his slow smile. She had finally surrendered. Or he had surrendered. He didn't know and didn't care. All he knew was that it had been intense and impossibly good.

Christ, if only he felt a little better, they could do it again right now. But his sour mouth and pounding head stopped him from reaching for her. Tea first. Lots of tea. And then perhaps he'd show her his Turkish bathing room.

He smiled once more into the pillow, and his body began to protest that it didn't need tea or time; it was ready to entertain his guest this very moment. Ready to ease her into hot water, lay her against the tile floor while steam billowed around them. Surely the warmth would help his head.

But first he'd have to raise himself up enough to reach the bellpull. The servants would need time to ready the bath and he'd need at least enough tea to wet his parched mouth. But he could let her sleep until then.

Plan in place, Hart managed to roll over, though it took him several minutes to force his eyes open. His valet had only cracked the curtains, but the light seemed impossibly harsh. He was too damn old to get drunk, infuriating lover or not.

Speaking of . . .

Hart reached toward her as he turned. He was still reaching to touch her when his eyes revealed the truth, the sad truth. Emma was gone. Snuck away in the night. He'd asked her to stay—he remembered that—and she'd left.

Just to be sure, he sat up to look for her scattered clothes, but the room was pristine. Even his own clothing had been retrieved and taken away to be washed and pressed. All evidence of their interlude had vanished.

He let himself fall back to the pillow; he even let himself groan out a loud, vicious curse. Had he really expected one night in his bed to transform her into a tender, obedient lover? Hart snorted at his own question. Hell, he didn't even want her tender and obedient, just here.

The bedside clock caught his eye. It was nearly one. Perhaps she'd stayed and had finally given up on him when morning ticked into afternoon.

Hell, he couldn't think.

Resigned to being awake—and alone—Hart reached for the cup of tea that steamed weakly in a narrow ray of sunlight. He didn't open his eyes again until he'd finished it, and that was only to refill the cup.

By the time someone tapped at his door, he'd finished that cup too. His head felt marginally better and his stomach showed no sign of rebelling as he called out for the servant to enter.

"Your Grace." The footman bowed and averted his eyes. "That Stimp fellow is here. He insists you'll want to see him."

Hart shook his head, then winced and rubbed it gingerly. "He's hours late. Send him on his way. I'll be in touch."

"Yes, Your Grace."

Hart reached for the cold toast and assiduously avoided the boiled egg. He was swallowing the first bite when he noticed the stain on the bedcover. Rust red stood out in smeared blotches against the gray and green weave. The toast turned to plaster in his throat and choked him until he finally forced it down with a gulp of tea.

It's nothing, he told himself as he wiped his watering eyes. *It's not* that, *for God's sake.*

But he still rose to his knees to stare down at the small spots. Nothing really, hardly even noticeable. But definitely there. Probably she'd started her menses.

Yes, of course. And that was why she'd left before he woke.

"Of course," he said aloud, relieved at the simple answer. His pounding heart began to slow. Emma was a widow, after all, not a maid. And she hadn't behaved as if . . .

His heart turned over with its eagerness to thump faster again.

He remembered the way she'd knelt before him, ready and completely unsure. Remembered the stunning tightness of her body, even as desperate and wet as she'd been. And her strangled gasp, the painful bite of her fingernails digging into his skin. The way she'd frozen beneath him for long seconds.

"No." His own voice, full of certainty, did nothing to quell the confusion. He glanced down to his cock, to the faint streak of dried blood that marked it. "No."

It simply wasn't possible, even if she had been married to

an old man. The woman had ordered him to *perform* for her; she was no innocent, blushing miss.

Hart jumped naked from the bed and snapped the bellpull tight. He was rifling through stacks of clean shirts when his valet entered and sounded as if he choked on his own spit.

"Your Grace!"

"I need to get dressed. *Now*." He needed answers, answers to so many things. And he wasn't going to find them in his own bedchambers. Although . . .

"When did Lady Denmore leave?"

"Sir?"

"What time did she leave here, and don't pretend at discretion."

"Of course, Your Grace. She departed just before three."

Three. So she'd left soon after he'd fallen asleep. Snuck away. Fled. Escaped. But surely not.

Ten minutes later he left his perspiring valet behind and raced to mount his most nimble horse. It was much quicker than his carriage in the midday traffic. And so he found himself, not an hour after waking to thoughts of her, standing inside her open door, staring at the lonely dance of dust motes floating in the sun.

He'd already raced upstairs, already torn through every room. The few paltry pieces of furniture were covered. The drawers were empty. She was gone. Gone farther than he'd even imagined.

"I tried to tell ye," a small voice said from his side. Hart glanced stupidly down to see Stimp, hands clutching a hat, face scrunched up in worry.

Hart shook his echoing head. "Pardon?"

"They left 'fore dawn. When I found out, I tried to see ye."

His mind was turning, turning . . . so slow that Hart could see every single painful, unwelcome thought. "Where have they gone?"

Stimp just shrugged. His eyes darted up to Hart and then away. "Sorry, guv."

Sorry. *I'm sorry*, she'd keened so prettily. She, who must have been lying with every damned word she'd breathed.

The painful thoughts faded beneath a welcome onslaught of rage.

"Help me search," he snapped, startling Stimp into a jump. "They must have left something behind, and I will damn well find it. And then I will find *her*."

Chapter 18

Nothing. Two weeks and there was nothing left of her. Nothing but talk of her wickedness and scandalized glee that she'd flown from town to avoid the shame of it all.

Hart clenched his jaw and glared at the pristine white of the paper laid before him.

He had returned to his club the week before, not out of a need for companionship, but because he needed to hear *something.* Anything. And he'd heard plenty, and all of it useless. Nobody knew anything about her except that she was a wild harlot with an almost primal need to gamble. Oh, also that she was a duke's mistress and an uncontrollable and disloyal one at that.

She was rumored to have taken on Hart in every dark corner, and a few others as well. Richard Jones, Marsh, Lancaster, of course. Hart felt the small relief that he did not have to wonder about those tales. And the proof was the crux of his obsession.

Any day now, he expected her to stroll through his door, offer a sly smirk and claim that he owed her marriage. Though how she could prove ruination as a widow was another riddle. But that . . . he was beginning to wonder about that as well.

There was no proof that the woman—whatever her cursed name might be—was actually the Dowager Lady Denmore. She had breezed into town, charmed an old couple, rented some rooms, and flirted her way right into society.

She could be an imposter. She could be . . . By God, she could be pregnant with his child. He hadn't used a French letter with her, hadn't wanted to. And she might very well be just a wily neighbor of Denmore, or, at most, his maid or housekeeper.

It would not be hard to determine.

The paper seemed to glow with menace in the bright afternoon sun. All he need do was write Denmore's solicitor. Drop a note to the local magistrate. He could travel to her little hamlet. She might even be there, holding court with tales of her adventures in London.

But he knew, he knew in his heart that she would not be there. Knew she had played them all false. But he did not want to *see*.

He also did not wish to feed new rumors and deepen his own humiliation. If he began investigating, word would get out. Not just that she was a fraud—as she must be—but also that Hart was broken enough to put time and energy into chasing after her.

The mighty duke, brought to his knees by another harlot. Watch how he raves and rages against his own stupidity. There is a man who refuses to learn a lesson.

And it would all be the truth, and that was the worst of it. It always was.

But just one letter. Just one. He could not live his whole life with her lies hanging over him. He needed the truth so that he could hate her with clarity.

He was reaching for the pen when the sound of a woman's voice danced faintly through the air. The hair on his neck rose. Numbness flashed over his skin, followed by a wave of heat.

Emma.

"I will inform him myself," that voice said, as Hart rose woodenly from his chair. A woman's voice. Familiar, but . . .

"Hart!" the bright and happy voice called. The doors of his library flew open, and a petite figure stepped through, black curls trailing on the breeze she created. "Hart," she said again, and tears welled in her big blue eyes as she rushed toward him.

He opened his arms automatically as his little sister rounded the desk, but his heart had dropped with a thud. "What are you doing here?"

"I love you too," she sniffled, wiping her tears all over his coat.

"Alex?"

"I wrote you a month ago, you fool. And you can't tell me you didn't know. You wrote back!"

"I . . ." Oh, Christ. Of course. He'd even considered throwing a dinner party and inviting . . . that woman. "Where is your husband?"

"He's out front ordering your servants about. They seemed quite surprised by our arrival, Hart."

"I . . ."

She leaned back to regard him with an arched brow. Her small face was damp from tears and tight with the laughter she was holding back.

"I'm sorry, Alex. I'm afraid I forgot you."

Her mouth quirked up in a mocking smile. "Well, I have been gone seven months. Memories fade."

"Minx."

"Ah, so you do remember me."

"It's starting to come back."

Her smile widened. Hart felt his own mouth twitch up. He'd forgotten this, how much light his sister added to his life. "Well, you're here now. I suppose I must act pleased to see you."

He took her by the shoulders and backed up a step to

sweep a careful glance down her body. "You look well. As always."

"Thank you."

His eyes lingered on her narrow waist. "You're not . . . You haven't. . .?"

Her smile faded a little. "No. Not yet. But in truth I think Collin is relieved. He's convinced I'm too small to carry the child of a big Scots brute like himself. Rubbish."

"Perhaps he's not doing it right. I hear those Scotsman can be—" He glanced up to find the big Scottish brute glowering from the doorway. "Hello, Blackburn."

"Somerhart," the man growled. "If you're through disparaging my manhood to my wife, I thought I would show you the mare we've brought."

Hart inclined his head and managed not to glance back toward the mocking blankness of the paper on his desk. "Of course. I'll have my stable master ready her stall."

"I've already spoken with him. But I believe your housekeeper desires a word."

Hart winced. Emma's lies had wreaked more havoc than even she could know. There was little worse than living with an angry household. Still, they'd all be so happy to have Alex back for a visit, surely their resentment would vanish before the hour was out.

And surely Hart's resentment would disappear just as quickly. He loved his sister much more than the ghost of Lady Denmore, and she'd be far better company. So why did he feel the loss of his solitude so sharply?

Alex looped her arm through his and interrupted his brooding. "Don't worry. We'll only be here a week." She looked him up and down. "You look terrible. Drawn and thin. Fallen in love, have you?"

Hart nearly groaned. He managed to hold it back, but apparently his little sister didn't need the sound to sense his dismay. She jerked to a stop, and Hart soon found himself staring down into a severe frown.

"You," she bit out, "had better tell me everything."

He was surprised by the urge to do just that. But of course he couldn't. He shook his head.

"Collin!" she shouted, her husband stopped near the front door. "The mare will have to wait an hour. My brother is sick with love."

Collin arched a look of disbelief over his shoulder.

Alexandra steered Hart back toward the library.

"I've nothing to tell," he growled. "You've gone mad. Again."

"Mm." She paused to stick her head back into the hallway. "Morton! Bring the whisky!" The sweet smile she turned on Hart had lulled many a man into tenderness, but it sent a shiver of apprehension up Hart's spine. "A toast to celebrate my arrival? How thoughtful! And lucky you, we've brought a whole crate of the Kirkland's best whisky."

Slumping into the nearest chair, Hart ignored Morton and the freshly opened bottle he delivered. He ignored the generous glass that Alex poured and shoved into his hand. He even ignored her expectant smile.

Finally, she gave an innocent little blink and raised her glass. "To notorious friends," she said.

Hart tensed.

"And to Aunt Augusta who sends the most entertaining letters."

He glared.

She sipped her whisky and made a little humming sound before turning those twinkling eyes back to him. A shiver of foreboding dripped down his spine. "But, Hart, perhaps you could clarify something for me. Who in the world is this young Dowager Lady Denmore I've heard so much about?"

Hart was refilling his glass before the last drop of whisky had burned from his throat. Alex waited patiently, innocent smile still in place. He'd never been able to resist her. Ever. In fact, he'd spoiled her rotten as a child. So it was no surprise when he broke like a cracked pitcher, and spilled his story to his baby sister in a great and glorious mess.

It's clear what you must do, Alex had said. And of course it was clear to her, who had such an inevitable sympathy for scandalous women. So he'd dashed off the letter to the solicitor and now here he was in Lancaster's morning room, hands clenched to fists as he waited for the viscount to meet him.

If anyone knew anything about her, he supposed it must be Lancaster. They'd been friends of some sort. Stimp had seen the viscount visit on more than one occasion.

"Somerhart?"

Hart stood as Lancaster entered and he shook Lancaster's hand, though he rather felt like punching him. As far as he knew the man had done nothing wrong, but the thought of breaking his nose proved immensely satisfying. Hart shook off the temptation.

Lancaster raised one tawny eyebrow. "Is there something I can do for you?"

"Perhaps. You know that Lady Denmore left town rather abruptly."

The man's expression of helpful concern shut down to immediate blankness. "Yes, I'd heard that."

Hart held his gaze, and let his eyes go cold. "Did you speak with her before she left?"

"No."

"I ask because you two seemed to have developed an association of sorts."

Lancaster tilted his blond head in cautious acknowledgment. "A friendship. Nothing more."

"Yes, I know."

His eyes betrayed a moment of surprise, and Hart supposed that it was odd for a man to be so certain of a dishonest woman's virtue. Little did he know.

Lancaster shrugged. "Lady Denmore and I took the air together on a few occasions, but I know nothing of her personal life. I gathered that was your area of expertise, Somerhart. What is it you think I might know?"

"Don't be snide with me. I'm not as susceptible to your charm as others."

Their gazes clashed and held. Ten seconds passed before the lightness faded from Lancaster's face. His eyes flashed with something icy and his face turned much harder than Hart could ever have predicted. It seemed he was more than just a careless charmer.

"What do you want?" he finally asked

"I want to know where she is."

"I have no idea."

"Did you know she was planning to disappear?" No answer, which was answer enough. "Why?"

"It has nothing to do with you. None of it did."

Hart scowled. "What the hell do you mean?"

"I mean she was in London for a specific reason, Somerhart."

"What reason?"

The charming smile flashed momentarily back to life. "Why, filthy lucre, of course. I find it easy to recognize the signs." He gestured vaguely toward himself.

"She's not a thief," Hart said with more certainty than he felt.

"No, she was honest enough to work the tables for it. Though . . . I assume you've considered the possibility that the honesty ended there?"

Who else had determined that she was a fraud? Hell, it didn't matter. The Season was set to begin. Someone would arrive in London spouting the truth before long. Despite the letter he'd sent out that morning, he found he no longer needed to see the reply.

"She was not Lady Denmore," Hart muttered, and the words pierced deep into his heart. He had exposed his soul to her, whispered things he hadn't even dared to think for so long, and she'd been nothing more than a well-crafted illusion.

"I think it likely she was not."

His fury, never well hidden these days, flowed to the surface of his skin like welling blood. "Why was it easy for you to see all this?"

Lancaster shrugged. "It wasn't easy. It wasn't obvious. Emma was no gypsy girl masquerading as a lady."

Emma. The sound of his voice around her name . . . Oh, it grated. "What else do you know?"

"Nothing. Or nothing I'd reveal to a man who's looking for revenge against a woman."

Bastard. "I could destroy you with one word, Lancaster. It's clear you're living a hairsbreadth from ruin."

"Not a difficult thing to discern." But the man's eyes didn't look scared. He looked cold as winter. "But as you said, we were friends, and I have loyalty and decency left, if little else."

Jesus, the man had to be noble as well as charming? Oddly enough, Hart found himself capitulating easily. "I will not hurt her. I swear to that. I need to know who she is, where she is, if only for my own peace of mind. She's clearly a gentlewoman, if not the one she claims to be. She's alone and running God knows where. She could be in danger. I need—" The subtle shift in Lancaster's smooth expression stopped Hart in his tracks. "What? Is she in danger? Is she under threat?"

"I'm sure she will be fine."

"You're *sure*?"

His shoulder rose in a shrug that Hart caught in a vicious

grip before the man could finish the gesture. "What are you not saying, Lancaster? You will tell me or I'll beat you to a pulp, do you understand?"

"Do you think I cannot see it in your eyes? That you mean to have revenge?" He knocked Hart's hand away. "She is only a young girl. She did not mean to hurt you."

"She didn't—"

"She was desperate. Afraid. Couldn't you see that?"

"I . . ." But of course he had seen those brief flashes of anxiety that she had never explained. He'd never pushed her to explain. And why was that? Because he'd wanted to pretend she meant nothing to him.

"Tell me." He nearly choked on the word, but he got it out. "Please."

"If you find her, and I don't know that she can be found, I want your word as a gentleman that you will not harm her and will not see her brought to harm."

"I give you my word." He did not even think about it before he spoke, though surely he'd meant to have revenge. Still, Lancaster studied him for long moments, doubt writ clearly on his features.

"All right. I believe you. And I've been worried. There was . . ."

"*What*?"

"She came here, several weeks ago. Arrived on my doorstep at dawn. She said she needed help."

A shaft of fear slid slowly through Hart's chest. When it reached his heart, he realized it was pain too—hurt that she hadn't come to him. "What was the matter?"

"A man followed her to London. Someone from her past."

Hart shook his head, but Lancaster didn't pause long enough for Hart to clarify that there *were* no men in her past.

"He was from Cheshire. She said he'd fallen in love with her and made a nuisance of himself. After her husband died he became irrational. Delusional. Claimed that she had never been married and that she was meant to be his wife. She was frightened."

Hart was still thinking over the man's so-called delusional claims. "What else did he say?"

"That was all she told me. But she was obviously frightened. Apparently the man had broken into her home and confronted her. She wanted him gone. She wanted to *be* gone."

"*That's* why she left?"

"Partly, I suppose. But she needed to make sure he didn't follow. I found a willing constable to take him to jail. Emma paid to keep him comfortable and well fed until she could leave."

"He's still there?" This man, he would know—

"He was freed last week."

"His name."

"Matthew Bromley. I was there when the constable took him. I have to admit I doubted her story, but the man was clearly disturbed. He ranted about Adam and Eve. The treachery of women."

"And what did he say about Emma?"

Lancaster flashed a humorless smile. "Why, he said she was not Lady Denmore."

His mouth went dry. "Who is she?"

"I would not claim him as a reliable source. But he said she was not the wife of Lord Denmore, but the daughter."

"The . . ." The startling feeling of truth shivered over his skin. "His daughter."

"Actually, the daughter of the *ninth* Baron Denmore, great-niece to the tenth."

"That . . ." Good God, could that be her story? Daughter to that . . . that disgusting reprobate? "The ninth Baron Denmore died six years ago. Did you know him?"

Lancaster shook his head.

"He was a selfish drunk with no apparent decency. He belonged to one of the old Hellfire clubs, if that gives you an idea. Killed himself and his heir in a riding accident. That was the last I heard of the Denmore line. Until recently. But I think perhaps he had a daughter."

A daughter, a young noblewoman, raised in that filth.

"The constable," Lancaster said without being asked. "His name is Rawley."

"All right. I'll see what I can find out from him. But you've no idea where she might have gone?"

"None. Although she once mentioned Scarborough and the seaside. She'd gone with her mother as a child."

"Scarborough?" He couldn't quite picture her there. Rather, he expected to track her to Paris or Rome or Lisbon. Scarborough would be too simple. Not enough adventure to be had. No deep pockets to be turned out. No rakish dukes to mislead.

"I'll keep that in mind and I thank you for your help. And your trust. If there's anything I can do for you in the future . . ."

"Ah, well. I'll put the bank on notice of your good opinion. But for now I'd be happy with word of her good health when you find her."

If Hart hadn't been so anxious, he would have quite enjoyed his driver's expression when he stepped to the street and gave him his new driving instructions. "The city jail. Quickly."

He'd never expected that Emma would lead him to visit the jail for the first time in his life, but somehow he couldn't muster any surprise.

Chapter 19

The silence of the church contracted around him, squeezing Matthew's heart until he began to weep. Tears spattered against his folded hands.

That mad constable had finally let him go, but Emily had disappeared again. All that searching and suffering and he had gained nothing but a terrible fear of confined spaces. He had not repaired his soul, had not brought her to God.

Reverend Whittier had welcomed him home with a sympathetic embrace and stern words. *If you still lust for her, you cannot enter the service of the church with this sin on your soul. If you cannot make it right with the young woman, you must pray for forgiveness. Pray for your very life.*

And so he had. Every day, every night. His knees had long since given up working properly. His neck ached with strain. But Matthew did not stop. Either God would remove this hunger from his body, or he would offer a miracle and return Emily to her rightful place.

"Mr. Matthew, sir?" a small voice said.

He raised his head and stared up at the statue of Christ. "You are never to disturb me during prayer."

"I'm sorry, sir," the maid stammered, voice echoing

around the chapel. "Your father bade me fetch you. Someone has arrived from London. A gentleman."

When he spun toward her, the girl backed away. "From London?"

She nodded and added in a whisper, "In a crested carriage, sir."

Matthew lurched past her, limping as fast as he could toward the doors. His miracle. His miracle was here.

The black carriage seemed an enormous beast lounging in front of his father's home. The gold crest shone in the sun, glinting danger and decadence. Matthew didn't bother studying it; he was a simple man of God. He knew nothing of great names or family crests. He only knew this man *must* have something to do with Emily.

He rushed through the door, letting it slam into the far wall. Three faces turned toward him from the parlor. His father, his sister, and some man who looked like Satan in his most beautiful disguise. That face was like a sculpture of a Greek god. Perfect and cold and frighteningly confident.

Matthew shivered.

"Matthew," his father said as the stranger rose from his seat. "This man is the Duke of Somerhart. He is here about Emily."

Emily, Emily. His mind spun, sending all his thoughts into useless disarray. "Where is she?" he finally managed to croak.

His cow of a sister gasped his name and his father paled, but Matthew only stared at them in confusion. What did they want from him? "Where is she? Shall I fetch her home? This is her home, you know. We are to be married. There's no time to waste. I—"

His father took a step forward. "Matthew, show your respect."

Propriety? This was what worried them? Matthew waved an impatient hand, but when he looked to the visitor, he realized his terrible mistake. Their worry had nothing to do with propriety and everything to do with the menacing power in those impossibly pale eyes.

Matthew dropped into a deep bow. "Your Grace," he rasped, picturing that devil gaze, wondering if he would be haunted by it in his dreams. The man looked perfectly capable of murder.

"As I was saying . . ." The duke's voice had turned away, so Matthew felt it safe to rise from the bow. They had all seated themselves, though his sister fanned herself and shot terrified glances in Matthew's direction. He limped over to join the discussion.

The duke's smooth voice held little emotion. "I do not know where she is, but I have something I wish to return to her. I am hoping you can assist."

"You mean to find her?" Matthew blurted, then swallowed his breath when the man glanced at him.

His question was ignored, but Matthew had found his miracle. This man, this duke with all the power of England behind him, he would find Emily. And he would deliver her right into her rightful husband's arms.

Hart wanted to leave this place, jump into his carriage and move on. He'd passed her uncle's home at the edge of town. The wreckage had never been razed, the pristine white "Jensen" sign at the gate stood in morbid contrast to the piles of bricks and ruined wood.

She was only nineteen, the solicitor had said. Eighteen when her uncle died and alone in the world with only a pittance for income. Eighteen when she had first arrived in London.

The ninth Baron Denmore had run the entailed estate into the ground and sold off all unattached lands. He'd killed his only heir and so the title had rescinded to his uncle, but there had been no income to funnel to maintenance, no money to pay servants. Her great-uncle had inherited an impoverished title and crumbling estate. He'd wisely chosen to stay in his own home.

Hart had felt already overwhelmed with the story of the Denmores, and now these people, the Bromley family, sitting pale and frightened before him, and the young man, Matthew. Hart gritted his teeth.

Emma had claimed to be afraid of him, and Hart believed it now. The boy was pale and far too thin, his blond hair lank and in need of washing. Sickly as he seemed, his eyes burned with life. Hate and lust and conviction. The sister seemed afraid, the father resigned. And by the solicitor's account, Emma had lived here for months after her uncle's death.

"I understand that you took her in after the fire."

"We did!" the sister, Catherine, blurted. "She had no one else and we thought . . ." She glanced toward Matthew. "Well, we thought perhaps she would remain with us."

"We were to be married," Matthew said firmly.

Hart raised an eyebrow. "There was a betrothal?"

"Ye—"

"Not a formal one," the father interrupted, "no. But Emma was like family to us."

Hart stiffened at the sound of her name. He'd thought that a lie too. All the documents had named her Emily. "Emma?" he heard himself say. "I understood her given name was Emily."

The sister nodded. "Yes, but she preferred Emma. Matthew was the only one who called her Emily."

"It is her given name," Matthew insisted, his tone making clear he had argued this point many times. "To use it is to honor her mother and father."

A weight lifted from Hart's shoulders. It made no sense, changed nothing, and yet it did. Her name was Emma, just as she'd said. Hart felt pitiful in his relief, but so much lighter as he pressed on. "But she had plans to go to London?"

"No," Matthew barked. "She had plans to marry me."

"And yet she did not."

"She was quite upset after her uncle's death. She lost her way, that is all. She only needs leading back."

Temper clenched Hart's hands into fists. "Yes," he ground out. "I understand you did your best to lead her back from London. By whatever means necessary. Mr. Bromley." He turned back to the father. "I find I would prefer speaking with you alone. Would that be possible?"

The sister sprang immediately to her feet, dropping a curtsy before she'd even managed to rise to her full height. "A pleasure, Your Grace," she chirped, then rushed from the room.

Matthew stayed seated until his father cleared his throat. Then he shuffled from the room under muttered protest.

"My apologies, Your Grace," Mr. Bromley said. "My son is . . ." He gave up with a shrug.

"As magistrate, you undoubtedly know of the trouble Matthew could face if he returns to London. Or if he continues to harass Miss Jensen. I would feel conscience-bound to turn him over to the authorities."

"Yes. Of course. I . . . They were friends once, truly. But when she refused his hand . . . He does care for her."

"As do you."

"Yes. I thought she would be my daughter, and I was glad for it. She was a quiet girl when she moved to this village. Watchful. But a good niece to her uncle. Devoted to him. Always puttering with him in his gardens.

"But after he died, she changed. Grew restless and nervous. Almost as if . . ."

Hart waited as the older man rubbed his forehead.

"I can't explain it. She would not answer sometimes when I spoke to her. It was as if she were already gone away. I knew then that she would not stay here, regardless what we all hoped."

"And one day she hopped the coach to London?"

"No, she left our home after a few months. Boarded with the miller for a time. We did not find out she'd gone from there until days later. She said she was moving back to Denmore, but Matthew found no sign of her there, and no evidence of the cousin she'd mentioned to the miller's wife.

"In truth, she'd run off and did not mean to be found."

Hart nodded and frowned. He was no closer to her now than he'd been in London. She was not here and clearly meant not to come back. "So she has no family at Denmore. And the new baron says he does not know her."

"Yes, I understand the title went to a distant cousin. He was taken by surprise."

"And you have no other ideas? No guesses? It's quite important that I find her."

The man's gaze fell away and shifted slowly about the room. Finally, with a long look of caution toward the archway that led to the hall, Mr. Bromley leaned forward. "I had thought," he whispered, "before Matthew found her in London . . . I'd thought she might have gone to the Yorkshire coast."

Sparks tingled over Hart's skin. The feel of the truth again, rare as it was. Lancaster had mentioned Scarborough and the sea. He made his voice as mild as possible. "Why Yorkshire?"

"I took Emma fishing once, in the stream behind that forest there. And she spoke of the water. How much she loved the sea. Her mother took her to Scarborough every summer when she was a girl." He looked again toward the hallway and leaned closer. "I never told Matthew," he added needlessly.

Scarborough. Yorkshire. Not the most narrow of directions, but it was better than searching the whole damned civilized world.

Chapter 20

The tilled ground was soft and unbelievably rich, and the wind from the ocean often warmer than she expected. Already, tiny sprouts were beginning to peek through the dirt, protected by the hay she'd spread the week before.

Emma felt blessed whenever she stood here in her own garden, at the side of her own home. She could see the pale blue haze of the sea, just a glimmering line above the edge of the cliffs.

She'd found exactly what she'd wanted. She'd put the land agent on notice months ago, let him know exactly what she needed and where. He'd recommended four properties; she hadn't looked farther than the second.

It was perfect. Beautiful and quiet. Everything she'd ever wanted. Until the sun set and closed her up alone in her lovely cottage.

Emma brushed a hand over the waist of her dress, still tossed between desperate relief and a strange yearning. She'd taken the precautions recommended by the herb woman, and Hart had taken his own precautions. She'd trembled with relief when she'd felt the first of her monthly cramps, but she'd also felt the distinct concussion of a door slamming shut on her past. All of it.

Emma Jensen was gone. As was Emily. And the false Lady Denmore. She was now, simply, the Widow Kern. As false as Lady Denmore, but so very, very different.

She dug her spade hard into the dirt and wondered how different she really was. Her lust for Hart hadn't faded. That night with him had unlocked all those horrid desires that she feared. And yet . . .

It wasn't exactly what she'd feared. She wanted things from him, fantasized and dreamed about the promises of future pleasure he'd made. Her body roused itself at the mere thought of him. If she'd stayed in London she'd have been lost, just as she'd worried.

But the wickedness seemed to stop there. She didn't find herself watching the men of her new village with need. In fact, she'd even tried to look upon them with something close to lust and had failed miserable. The shirtless young men splashing in the sea did not tempt her to anything even close to sin.

It was just Hart.

The salt wind snatched away her sigh, and Emma leaned her spade against the grayed wood of her cottage wall. She would have to whitewash this summer to protect it from the constant caress of the wind, but she would miss the silvery glint of the worn boards.

Emma slipped off her apron and waved to Bess in the kitchen window. Then she headed straight for the path she'd already worn in the waving grass.

Bess couldn't begin to understand the charm of the narrow cliff path and the stone-rough beach below. *You'll break your neck*, she'd warned countless times, but Emma thought the reward worth the risk.

Down on that narrow strip of sand she felt free. Strange, since she couldn't walk more than two hundred yards in either direction. But the steady breeze and the cry of the gulls and the strange green scent of the air . . . it all filled her up, pushed into all the empty places inside her and made her whole. She was young again, seven years old and happy. She was safe. Loved.

But she couldn't seem to carry that feeling back up with her. She certainly couldn't coax it inside to keep her company at night.

"This place is good," Emma whispered as she picked her way down the path. Her foot slipped on pebbles and she banged into the rough cliff face but hardly slowed at all. "My life is good," she muttered instead, determined to make it true. Soon London would be a distant memory. Hart no more than a . . . a . . .

"A footnote," she said, tasting cruelty in the word and trying to make herself believe it.

Something crawled over her neck. She brushed at the sensation, but it remained. Anxiety probably, sprung from her own guilt. She had lied and cheated and used people. Though she'd told herself that Hart was a powerful, impervious man of the world, there was no denying the burn of her shame. She'd hurt him, could only have hurt him more by her calculated disappearance.

Her hand rubbed idly at the nape of her neck, but the sensation remained, even through the hour she spent staring out to the white-capped sea.

He had started in Scarborough, certain that Emma would be naturally attracted to the crowds of the resorts. There was some money to be made there, trouble to find, though at this time of the year the crowds would be less flush than she was accustomed to in London. Still, perhaps the merchant classes were a livelier sort, and more easily swayed by her gentle manners. *If* she could manage gentle manners for any length of time.

But she hadn't been in Scarborough. His week there had

been entirely fruitless. He had found no trace of her, no evidence that she'd even passed through. Now he felt he was wandering aimlessly.

If he did find her, he no longer knew who she'd be. She was not the woman he'd thought she was. She was a girl. A daughter, a niece. A quiet young woman remembered fondly in her village.

She was not a widow or a vixen or a roving thief. She was not worldly or experienced. The sensual knowledge he'd recognized in her had been nothing more than the echo of years spent in a den of inequity. Or that was what he hoped anyway. Hoped that she had only seen and heard.

A sense of something misplaced would not stop taunting his brain. He'd been to Denmore's home once, a giant block of cold granite and crenellated towers, but he could remember little more than an impression of dark hallways and darker guests. Whatever memories he might have retained had been jarred from his brain a few days later when he'd proposed to his lover and found devastation instead of joy.

Vague memories aside, he was sure her childhood had been less than it should have been. First her mother had died, then her father and brother. Then she'd been sent to live with a stranger, a great-uncle she'd never met. At least it seemed she had been happy there, for a short time.

Hart no longer knew how to hate her; he no longer knew what to feel. He only wanted to see her and . . .

And what?

Whenever he tried to puzzle it out, his chest hurt, his lungs froze. So he moved blindly forward, tracking a woman who meant not to be found. A woman who'd torn down everything he'd built to protect himself.

"Only a mile more, Your Grace," the driver called back.

Hart nodded absently, fairly certain they'd find nothing here, as they'd found nothing in the other huts and manors and cottages. Every lead seemed like a good one, every land agent perfectly sure that he'd dealt with a woman of her description. But a week of traveling up and down the coast through every village and hamlet had turned up two widows, several harlots, and one woman old enough to be his grandmother.

She wasn't here, and if she wasn't on the Yorkshire coast, then she may as well have sailed to America.

Jesus, she probably had sailed to America. And it would take his investigators years to find her, if they ever did. A headache bloomed to life behind his left eye.

"Just coming up on it now, sir. Shall I drive past?"

"Yes." He pushed wearily off the seatback to look out at the view. Green grass, wind-shaped trees, the same vista he'd been studying for seven days. And then a cottage, worn but charming. Chickens pecked at the yard. Hart's eyes began to glaze over.

The far side of the house came into view and two women bent over the furrows and hills of a garden. One of them looked like . . . He leaned closer to the door until the breeze touched his cheek. One of them looked like *Bess*, and the other . . .

She wore a wide-brimmed hat and a stained apron tied at the waist. Her dress was simple and modest, blue muslin sprigged with little green leaves.

It couldn't be her, laboring in a garden like a drover's wife. She was a baron's daughter, a gentlewoman. Then Hart remembered the extensive plots that had surrounded the burned-out shell of her uncle's home. He remembered that Mr. Bromley had commented on her dedication to the gardens.

But the dress and the chickens and the worn hat, and then she looked up and . . . and it was Emma. Her face transformed itself in an instant, from caution to intensity. She narrowed her eyes at the carriage, clearly studying its crest.

"Stop," Hart said, and the wheels began to slow as her face settled on stark fear.

He heard her say, "Bess." His foot touched the packed dirt lane.

She'd dropped her little bucket of weeds and was moving toward the back of the house when he snapped the carriage door closed. That froze her in her tracks.

Hart's emotions were held strangely at bay. He felt every inch the impervious lord as he walked toward her. Impenetrable and heartless. "I've been looking for you for weeks, Emma. Now I get the feeling you are about to claim you're not receiving visitors."

Her shoulders heaved with her panting, pale fingers twitched against her skirts.

"I have a few questions for you. I'm sure you understand."

Her hands reached beneath her chin to untie the ribbons of the hat. "Bess, I'll need a moment," she rasped.

Hart caught the motion of Bess rushing around the back corner. A moment later, a door slammed. Emma eased off her hat and smoothed her hair down before she turned slowly to face him.

She looked . . . lovely. Rested and healthy, cheeks turned pink in the warmth of the garden, hair damp at the temples. But her eyes had gone nearly vacant, animated solely by fear.

She said nothing, just stared at a spot beyond his ear. Whatever heat had colored her cheeks was retreating now, leaving sick white behind.

"Surprised to see me?"

When her eyelids fluttered, Hart felt satisfaction rush through his limbs. He was no longer the helpless one.

He cocked his head. "Did you think I would simply shrug and count myself lucky that you had gone? Did you think I would bathe away your scent and dress for the first ball of the Season?"

Her lips trembled as she tried to form a word. "Y-yes. Why would you not?"

"Why not? Hmm." He clasped his hands behind his back

and looked her up and down until her fingers wound together in tight anxiety. "I was drunk, Emma. And angry. I was not, however, unconscious. Did you think I would not notice the blood, or remember the way you went so still beneath me?"

"I . . . I don't . . ."

"I know who you are, who you really are. Emily."

Her gaze finally snapped to his, eyes wide and swirling with dark emotions. "Please don't. Please don't tell. I am done with the kind of life I lived in London. This is all I have, all I wanted."

"And what of the deception you perpetrated in town? It is illegal to impersonate a noblewoman, you know."

"I know! I am sorry!" But her eyes were glinting with thought now, instead of regret. "I promise not to return. I've disappeared and that's all I ever wanted. I did just as you advised and bought into the funds. And I've never stolen from you or anyone else."

"Really? What of our trust and our friendship?"

"Please . . . I'll . . ." Her eyes darkened. "I'll do anything to make it up to you. *Please*."

Well, she'd gotten there quickly. Hart forced a laugh to cover his hurt. "Anything? Then invite me in. We will start with tea."

She nodded, a simple assent to the implication that he would use her body as payment for her crimes. And that cool nod finally popped the bubble that had muffled Hart's mind since he'd spied her. Everything he'd learned about her in the past month rushed into him like a tidal wave, sweeping his detachment away. By the time he'd recovered enough to think to pull her into his arms, Emma had walked past him.

Shaken, Hart turned and followed her toward the front of this new home she'd made for herself. At that moment, he felt sure he would have followed her anywhere if only she would give him some truth.

Chapter 21

The heart was surely not meant for this type of abuse. Emma's pulse beat madly, the same fluttering, useless speed that afflicted a captured bird. And like those birds, she was sure she would fall dead at any moment, that useless organ too overwhelmed to go on.

When his figure darkened the doorway, Emma jumped, though she'd been standing there waiting stupidly for him to appear. He had to duck to clear the lintel and so he looked that much larger when he straightened to his full height.

The door of Bess's private room creaked open; Emma heard her tentative footsteps as she came toward them through the kitchen.

"Bring tea, please," she said. "And then we will need privacy, Bess."

"Yes, ma'am."

"Privacy," Hart muttered as his eyes roamed the large front room.

This was all there was, this large space and the kitchen and two small bedrooms besides Bess's room in the back. She had her own entrance. She could come and go as she pleased, though she rarely budged. It was the perfect situation for Bess and for Emma, and he would ruin it all.

She hated him for gazing upon the walls, taking stock, and no doubt dismissing it as little worth losing. He could not see the tragedy he was about to unleash; it would mean nothing to him. And still he looked beautiful and tempting. Still she wasn't horrified to think that she would take him to her bed.

"How did you find me?"

He took his time finishing his perusal. By the time he looked at her again, Bess was rushing in with tea. Emma found herself trapped in his gaze for that long moment. Where there had been coolness, there was now heat. His ice blue hatred had shattered into sparkling torment.

She couldn't breathe, couldn't speak, until the sound of Bess's door slamming snapped through the room, and Hart blinked.

"How did I find you? I looked for you. I traced you back to Cheshire, spoke to everyone you've ever known. By all accounts you have always loved the ocean."

"But . . ."

He actually offered a pitying smile then, which spun her into confusion. "I am a duke, Emma. Most of our good countrymen will never meet a duke in their life. My status is a useful tool for gathering information from, say, land agents."

She snapped her jaw closed. "I see. Life unfolds its creases for you as it always does."

Hart cocked his head in agreement, surprising her. "I have never known a life like yours, that is certain." His gaze was gentling, his mouth losing its hardness.

He pitied her.

Oh, that scraped her pride in a vicious slash, even though her brain insisted his pity would prove useful. It could save her, save this life she'd carved for herself. And still she bared her teeth in a sneer.

"So you heard my story, did you? Found yourself melting

for that poor orphan girl? Let me guess the rest: you thought to yourself 'Well, here is a girl who needs a hand up. A gentle woman unused to a life of labor. She could use an income, a way to buy herself the pretty things she deserves, and I can provide that for her.'"

"Of course not—"

"Did you come here to strike a deal, Your Grace?"

The pity had vanished, along with her most likely chance of mercy. "You are as ridiculous and shocking as ever, I see. I did not come to make you my mistress."

"Do you mean to have me arrested?"

"No."

"Well, pardon my ignorance, but why have you gone to all this trouble if you don't mean to punish or take advantage? *Why are you here?*"

At least she was no longer terrified. She'd passed terror and headed straight to reckless and irrational, challenging him when she'd meant to appease. But she could either meet him as an equal or fall to her knees and beg for mercy.

She would not grovel, not yet, so she forced herself to wait quietly for his answer, sure that if he would only give his reason, she could turn it on him, talk him out of it. But she'd shocked him somehow. He only swallowed and shook his head as little furrows formed between his brows.

Emma lost her patience. "You've hunted me down like a fox. I have a right to know why. What will you do with me?"

His hands opened as if to show that he held no weapon. "I don't know."

"Come, Hart. You claim to have searched weeks for me. Don't lie about—"

"Damn you, *I do not know*. I meant to have revenge, repay you for your lies. I hated you. But I promised someone I would not see you hurt. Strange to say it was an easy vow." His voice had fallen to a husky warmth that worked through her, but she fought the pull of that sound.

"Just your coming here hurts me." Her words were too close to the truth, so Emma scrambled to cover her feelings. "Your coach is parked in my lane, ducal crest ablaze in the sun. My neighbors will think me your doxy."

He raised that arrogant brow. "Ah, yes. What would a modest young woman have to do with a bachelor lord? How could the grieving widow of a merchant even have met a duke?"

He knew everything, had ferreted out all her lies. Emma's mouth went bone dry. He was drawing this out, torturing her like a cat tortures a mouse. "What do you *want*?"

"Emma, I . . ." The words broke away on a sigh and he glanced at the chair behind him. When he dropped into it, Emma realized how very disturbed he was. He had probably never taken a seat before a lady in his whole life. This wasn't an act. He stared up at her, unaware of the emotion he'd betrayed.

He whispered, "I believed your lies in London."

"Yes."

"And I treated you as a widow."

"Yes."

"I did things I shouldn't have done. Said things to you . . ."

How strange men were. Out of everything, this was his greatest upset? As long as some other man had taken her maidenhead, Hart had felt her deserving of all manner of lust. But her virginity had transformed her into some other being, someone more worthy than who she'd really been.

"Lay your guilt aside, Hart, if that's what it is. I was a maiden, but I was no innocent . . . in case you could not tell."

"You could not have known the—"

"Of *course* I knew." She was trying to show disdain through her look, but as the seconds passed it grew more difficult. His eyes, his beautiful blue eyes, were normally so shielded. But now she could see everything in them: worry and pain and knowledge, and a dawning horror.

And then softness that wanted to pull her in and make everything better.

Emma backed a step away.

"In your father's home—" he started.

"*Don't.*"

He closed his mouth, but his eyes stayed the same, telling her things, making her *feel*.

He had wanted her body before, but now she was *different*. Now she wasn't like his other women, she was pure and vulnerable and weak. She was a damsel in distress. A little girl wandering the dark halls where monsters roamed.

In his eyes was everything she'd ever wanted as a girl, everything she'd given up on years before. Emma had grown weary of waiting for rescue. She'd had to rescue herself and she would never forget that.

"Emma—"

"I may have been a virgin, Hart, but I was not the least bit innocent, so wipe that regret from your eyes. If that's all you came to express, then you've done it. I absolve you. You may leave."

"That's hardly why I came, and *you* do not have the power to absolve me, so—"

"Why did you come? Why? Just tell me. Say what you need to say so that we may both—"

His soft voice broke through her tantrum. "I need to know."

She froze, hand caught midair in its dramatic sweep. "Know what?"

"I need to know why you did it. Why did you come to London and pretend to be Denmore's widow? Why gamble your way through London and masquerade as a scandalous woman? Why . . . why did you come to my house that night, Emma? And why did you *leave*?"

His eyes wouldn't let her go. They begged for answers and sympathy. She could give him one but not the other.

"I came to London for money, Hart, nothing else. I'd inherited a small amount from my great-uncle and I needed more. Gambling seemed the best way to get it."

"The *best* way? To become a fraud? Lie and cheat? Risk imprisonment?"

"Would you have had me become a courtesan?"

"As if that were your only option! You were a young noblewoman in need. And the Osbournes adored you. If you had only explained, asked for assistance, they would have been happy to sponsor you, give you a place to live."

"Oh, what a glorious idea from the wealthy man. To live as a supplicant, begging for scraps. Yes, they liked me well enough, I suppose they would have taken me in as a pet. And then what? A short career of obedience until they found a gentleman desperate enough to marry me? And what an ingrate I would be to turn him down."

He shook his head. "There are hundreds of noblewomen of limited means. None of them take up gambling as a form of support."

"Yes, it seems I am the only one with the correct combination of skill and gall. I'm quite proud."

"And this was your plan?" Oh, his sweeping gesture held a world of scorn. *This*. This pitiful cottage. This small life.

"Yes, *this*. This is what I want."

"I don't understand. You worked for weeks, collected hundreds of pounds, a small fortune." His eyes swept once more around the room, one last dismissive glance. He didn't notice the walnut sideboard she'd found in town and bought with her own coin. Didn't see the fine tapestry she'd hung on the wall to brighten the room with blues and greens the exact shade of the ocean. It was all nothing to him, just a life less than his own.

"Yes, Hart," she whispered. "Yes, this is what I was working for. Just this. So please have mercy on my small life. Don't call on the magistrate or expose me to my neighbors.

Don't ruin me. Just leave me be. I promise I'll never return to London."

He stood. She thought he was leaving and felt a small twinge of regret. But he only paced over to her front window and stared out at the smudge of blue that was the sea.

"You love the ocean."

She stared at his back.

"Are you happy here?" His shoulders were nearly wide enough to block all the light. He turned to her. "Emma? Are you happy?"

Her lungs were so weak, her word just a whisper. "Yes."

"Because I am not happy. You had to know how I would feel. You left a scandal in your wake and I am the undying focus of it. Me. The idiot duke once again."

"I'm sorry." She was sorry, but she could hardly force the words out. Emma cleared her throat and gathered up her courage, false as it was. "I'm sorry, Hart. I never meant that. Never."

"I hated you. Despised you. If I'd found you in those first few days I would've seen you thrown in Newgate with no regret."

"I'm sorry."

His strong shoulders rose in a shrug. "It seems it has all gone away. Perhaps because I am not in the city, but . . . I do not care about that. I only care that you are well, Emma. And out of danger. And somehow . . ."

Emma shook her head, not quite knowing what she denied. But Hart provided the answer.

"I feel responsible for you. And we have passion. There is one way to fix this. Fix the scandal as well as your future."

"No."

"Marry me." He looked confused by his own words, almost as confused as Emma was.

"No."

"There would still be talk, of course, but it would end. We are comfortable with each other, alike in more ways than not."

"That is not true." She did not want it to be true. She wanted it all to be lies. His offer, his logic, and most of all the sincerity in his eyes.

Emma's heart was twisting back to life, trying to free itself from the stone she'd built around it. It wanted the freedom to swell with hope or beat harder in despair. It wanted to feel something, but Emma held tight to it, squeezed it until it stilled. She needed him gone. Now, before she broke into a million pieces.

"No," she said again.

"I understand that this is sudden."

"Yes, it is sudden, not to mention completely unwelcome."

"Emma—"

"I am not suffering. I need nothing. Hard as it is to believe, this is exactly the life I want. I am not interested in the disgusting cruelty of the ton. I will not return to London with my tail between my legs, hoping that one day they will accept me. I do not need a vast, echoing castle and heavy, uncomfortable gowns. And I certainly do not need you as a husband."

"I've shocked you. I apologize. But whatever you think of London and the ton, I hope you will consider my proposal. Because I think it is possible . . . Emma, I think I could love you."

"Nonsense," she snapped, shocked that she could even manage that. His words were swimming toward her through dark water. She'd heard them come from his mouth, but now it seemed they were approaching again, the reality of them, the feel.

Her face tingled and went numb, then her neck and her chest. Soon her whole body was a husk, lifeless and dead. "Nonsense," she tried to whisper.

Hart was moving toward her and she could not stop him. Her limbs were paper, weak and useless.

His hot hands rose to cradle her face. Long fingers eased into her hair, spreading tingles over her scalp. "I could love you, Emma. I could. If we married, it would not be an arrangement, a means of creating heirs and legacies. It would be more. We would argue and laugh and love. You would drive me mad and I would irritate you to no end. We have so much passion. We would scandalize the ton and enjoy every minute of it."

Each word had snuck closer to her lips, until he breathed her name into her mouth. "Emma . . ." He brushed a delicate kiss, then pressed into her, his tongue offering a small, slow taste.

Her heart bloomed, the stone cracked, and pain poured deep into her soul. Emma jerked back, pushed him away. "Stop it. *Stop*."

Those damned beautiful eyes stared at her, still swimming with tender lust, soft and hot as sin. Emma wanted that softness gone before it swallowed her whole.

"You are ridiculous," she spat. "You speak of my childhood as if it were horrid, yet you would drag me back into that kind of hell. I know who you are, what you are. You are just like my father."

"No! No, I never was."

"You think I would deign to marry a man like you? How long before you would be sniffing after some other woman, or two or three for that matter?"

The softness was fading but there was no anger yet. "I would not—"

"Don't deny it. You are a rake and a reprobate. A connoisseur of women. Do not even claim that I would be your last."

"I will not deny that I have had lovers, but I have never been married, never even betrothed. I know what your father was like, but I promise—"

"You know what my father was like because you were well acquainted." She saw the ice forming over his eyes, saw the way he'd drawn straight, holding himself with rigid dignity. Emma moved in for the kill. "You are just like him, Hart. Do you know how I know? Because you showed me in your chambers. You whispered it to me in your bed."

Shutters of blue metal seemed to snap into place over his gaze. Any semblance of the man who'd just spoken of love vanished with those few words.

Emma smiled. "And in case that is not enough evidence for either of us, let me make it even simpler. I would never love you. My childhood was no childhood at all. There were far too many predatory men prowling down the halls, searching for any thrill they could find. Do you know what it is like to lie in bed in the darkest part of night and listen to a monster test the knob of your door? Do you know what it is like to pray for that lock to hold?

"And then . . ." She took a deep breath. "Then I'd wake in the morning, and those parties did not end at dawn. So sometimes I'd spy, because it seemed better than wondering. But I shouldn't have. Those men, those parties, they ruined my world, Hart, and you were part of that."

Horror and fury warred for control of his face. "I was never one of those men."

"Not at my door, perhaps, but I remember you quite clearly. In my father's home. In a dark hallway. I saw you there. I saw you. So you see, Hart, it's simple. We could never marry, because you disgust me."

Even past his shield she saw the bright, stunning shock of pain that flashed over his face. Then it was gone, locked tight away from the world. He was gone, vanished without taking a step.

"Now please leave here," she managed to say. "And if you ever cared for me, never come back again."

He stood, not even breathing. Seconds passed, dragged on

like years, until finally he inclined his head. His jaw ticked forward. "As you wish."

He took a few steps across her small home and he was gone. Out of her life. Him and his ridiculous, horrible promises. Gone.

Emma waited for the sound of his carriage pulling around in a circle. Once the wheels had crunched away into silence, she opened the door and walked slowly to the cliff path. Rocks tried to trip her. Gravel rolled beneath her shoes, but Emma stumbled on.

She did not slow at the bottom of the trail, but walked straight into the creeping tide. The water chilled her feet and legs, but she dropped to her knees and let the waves lap at her waist.

So many dangers had loomed over her for so long. She'd tempted disaster when she'd become Hart's lover, risked so many things. But she'd never anticipated the chance that someone could love her. Or that she could love him back.

Yes, they could love each other. And that would make the inevitable betrayal so much worse when it came. A man like Hart, beautiful and sexual and always given what he wanted . . . he would be the worst kind of husband. Exactly the husband she'd always feared.

So she knelt and waited for the sea to numb her breaking heart and wash her sins away.

The day had faded to the purple haze of dusk before Emma dragged herself back to the shore and up the path. The sea had offered no peace, and Emma wondered if it ever would again.

Emily.

Emma grimaced and brushed the whisper away, but it came again, that name she hated. Unwilling to wake up and face her fears and regrets, she turned to her stomach and pressed her hands to her ears. The night swallowed her back into sleep.

Emily. A touch now, tracing the edge of her jaw. Emma's eyes snapped open. Hart was here. Hart.

She gasped and turned, pushing away from him as the voice came again.

"There is a fire, but do not be afraid." A hand reached toward her, severed from its body in the dark. "I'm here to save you."

A dream. It must be a dream. She'd dreamt of fire so many times after her uncle's death. The smoke thickened suddenly, making her cough. She wanted to go back to sleep.

"Come, Emily. We must go. I will take you home."

Her eyes stung from the biting smoke. And her ears were playing tricks on her. She'd heard this before. Matthew had uttered those words after her uncle's death. *Come, I will take you home*.

"This is a dream," she said.

"The smoke will make you sick."

And it was making her sick. She couldn't think past it, so Emma scooted forward toward the voice, toward the hand and the body it was now attached to. The hand closed around her arm. She looked up.

"No!" she screamed at the sight of Matthew's face. "Where is Hart?"

"It is me, Matthew." His fingers dug deep and pulled her from the warm bed into hot air. "I've come to save you."

"No, no, no." She struggled, choked on burnt air. "This is a dream. There is no fire. Let me go. I want Hart." But he yanked her toward the hallway, toward the dancing orange light.

"Matthew!" she screamed. "Stop!" But then they were out in the hall, heat burning her skin.

When he pulled her toward the rear door, Emma got her feet beneath her and followed. She could see the dark rectangle ahead, the door that would free her from this inferno. And Bess . . .

Oh, no. "Bess! Wake up. Please wake up. There's a fire! Matthew, you must get Bess."

"I've come for you, Emily. Hurry. You don't need this place. This is not your home."

Beautiful, cold air poured over them. Emma drew a deep breath and realized they were outside. "*Bess!* I must go back."

"No." He dragged her toward the silhouette of a shying horse while Emma fought and screamed. The horse screamed too, desperate to be away. Emma strained to look over her shoulder and found that the fire illuminated the whole yard. And there, crawling on hands and knees, was Bess. She cleared the door of her room and collapsed onto the grassy yard.

Emma cried with relief, and every sob drew fresh air into her lungs. The dullness of sleep and smoke was scrubbed free. "You," she groaned. "You did this." Something squeezed her hands. She stared down at the rope as it tightened to a knot. "*You* did this."

"Get on the horse."

"I won't. You're mad. You set fire to my home."

"This is not your home. Your home is with me."

"You . . . Oh, Matthew. You burned my uncle's house too, didn't you? You killed him!"

"No," he muttered. "No, no."

"You *killed* him."

"It was an accident! If you'd only been true to me. If you'd only married me, I wouldn't have had to trick you into my home. I meant for him to get out, meant for you both to live in my father's home until you saw reason. It was your fault. All your fault."

"Oh, God, my uncle."

"Get on the horse, Emily."

"No—" His slap cut off her protest. Pain blossomed over her cheek just before he slapped her again. When she tried to lash out, the heel of his hand caught her cheekbone and she fell. All she could do was shield herself as he hit her over and over. Blood trickled down her lip and she sank into a gray, noiseless fog.

The world shifted and fell and she felt her body being carried away. There was nothing she could do to stop it.

Chapter 22

The carriage bounced over the rough road, jolting Hart's tense muscles. The crash of the waves should have been a soothing distraction, but he found himself grinding his teeth with hatred for the sound. He'd heard those damned waves all night as he'd tossed and turned in an unfamiliar bed, and he was beginning to think he'd be haunted by them for the rest of his miserable life. Haunted by the waves and this stupid decision to give up all hope for his pride and see Emma one more time.

The late morning light sparkled off the water, mocking his mood.

She'd told him she hated him, asked him never to return. And how did his heart interpret that? *Ah, yes, old man, let's try once more.* And so he was back on this road again, heading for her home.

He'd been done with her. Humiliated and abused. Cursing her for a heartless, cruel witch. She had aimed right for his heart, and her bullet had found its target with ease. Except . . .

Except that her attack hadn't made any sense. After he'd calmed down, after he'd nursed his hurt in half a bottle of whisky, he'd had an unexpected moment of clarity. Emma Jensen was a liar.

She'd said she wanted nothing to do with him, claimed he disgusted her, and that could not be true. Every move she'd made in London, every word spoken and bet placed, had helped her toward her goal. She'd calculated everything *except* the time she'd spent with Hart. He hadn't helped her plan in any way. And that night at his house—that could have ruined her completely. If he'd realized the truth that night, her deception would have crumbled around her.

Yet she'd come to him. Willingly. Recklessly.

She could not hate him.

So she was a liar. A consummate liar. A woman who lied about important things. Her life, her past, her feelings, her thoughts. And somehow that didn't matter in the least to Hart because, fool that he was, he trusted her. He understood her. He'd spent years lying to the entire world, lying to himself. He understood what it meant to keep everyone out, to hide yourself even from people you loved.

And she'd had more to protect than her heart; she'd had to protect her body when her own father had failed her. The one man who should have protected her had not, and Hart could understand that better than anything.

So she lied. But it wasn't so hard to see, as long as he could keep his temper in check. Emma lashed out, struggled against anything that might hold her. She would break his heart before she let him break hers. That's what he was risking. His heart. His pride and his soul.

If he didn't take that risk, she would never, ever believe him. And the thought of going back to London without her . . .

Hart shook his head. He couldn't stand it. Going back to that place where he kept all his desires in check. Where no one ever said anything sincere. Where the world bowed down when he neared and snickered when he left.

The thought of it burned like coal in his gut. He wanted

Emma and all the tumult she'd brought to his life. All he had to do was convince her. Perhaps he should take out a lease in Scarborough. It wouldn't take more than a year of dedicated effort, surely.

He was actually starting to smile when the carriage jerked and rattled. "Whoa," the driver called. "All right. All right."

The carriage rolled on at a slightly slower pace.

"Sorry, Your Grace. The horses are a bit spooked. There's smoke ahead."

The smell of woodsmoke had been growing steadily inside the carriage, and Hart hadn't realized how strong it was till the driver spoke. Odd. There weren't many trees around.

He was just tensing with the first hint of concern when the driver spoke more sharply. "Your Grace!"

Hart knocked open the door and stood, bracing himself between the carriage roof and the open door. They'd taken a small rise, and the lane below stretched out in clear expanse. Clear except for the haze of smoke that stretched out like a gray puddle. A steady breeze swirled the haze around and around itself, sending occasional tendrils farther inland. A small group of people milled about a structure that had collapsed. Flames still licked at the blackened wood, but there wasn't much left for the fire to consume. A small shed had been spared, but the bushes next to it were scorched.

When his eyes fell on the neat garden, Hart's mind shuddered with recognition. "No." He looked around the yard again, then farther, to the surrounding meadows, the low rock wall at the back of the property, the trail that wound through tall grass to the edge of the cliffs.

This was Emma's home.

The driver glanced back and Hart met his somber gaze. He wanted to scream for him to go faster, damn it, but the horses struggled against the reins and the lane was only a few feet from the danger of the cliffs.

Finally, when Hart could no longer take the pace, he jumped to the grass and ran the last hundred yards to her home. Three men knelt in the grass, bent over a white shape laid on the ground. Hart sprinted toward them.

"Emma!" He saw a limp arm stretched across the ground, saw the fingers twitch. "Oh, thank God," Hart groaned as he skidded to a halt and dropped to his knees. The men parted and Hart was staring down into a slack face. The lips far too pale, eyes unmoving beneath closed lids. And it wasn't her.

"This is Bess," he choked out. "Bess Smythe. Where is Emma? Where is the lady of the house?"

He twisted desperately around, straining his eyes, demanding that they find her. When he looked back up to the men, their gazes fell away, then shifted one by one to the smoldering wreckage.

"She is not in there." His voice sounded sure and calm. "She escaped. You must check the yard, the—"

"We've searched the grounds, sir. We found Mrs. Smythe in the rear yard. But Mrs. Kern . . . the other rooms were farther from the door. Did you know her, sir?"

Hart didn't bother answering, instead he picked up Bess's hand and felt for a pulse. "She needs a doctor. Have you—"

"We've already sent for Doctor Jersey, sir."

"Lark!" Hart shouted as he pushed to his feet. His driver and footman rushed forward. "We need to search every inch of these grounds. Out to the cliff and back as far as you can see. Lady . . . that is, Mrs. Kern is here somewhere."

His driver sprang into action. They searched for a full hour, walking over every inch of grass, searching every rocky crevice, every thorny bush. He refused to think of anything but finding her, refused to consider any other possibility, until he finally found himself standing only a foot from the edge of the blackened wood. The wind shifted, blowing smoke and heat into Hart's eyes, but his tears quickly washed them clear.

The house had been reduced to a tangle of pitch-black sticks and chunks of charcoal covered with pale soot. And Emma was in there, charred like the rest of it, her precious body indistinguishable from lifeless bits of wood.

"Mrs. Smythe is resting in your carriage as you requested, Your Grace." The doctor's nasal drone infuriated Hart. Why was this man alive and speaking and Emma dead?

"There's nothing more I can do for the woman, though I believe she'll wake. May I leave now? I've patients to attend. A woman close to childbirth—"

"Go."

Time passed. The sun slanted lower, glaring into his eyes from the west. Hart kept his vigil. And sometime . . . at some point as he stared into Emma's temporary grave, Hart remembered. For no reason at all, he remembered. That memory that had nagged at his mind for weeks . . . Emma's taunting words . . .

I saw you there.

That part had been the truth. She had seen him. He could picture her now. A little girl a bit younger than his sister. She'd startled the hell out of him, tiptoeing past in the dark in a place she should never have been. Eyes wide with fear, twin braids swaying against her back.

Oh, God, he remembered now. *Someone has come to my room,* she'd whispered, as if sharing secrets with a friend. And Hart, young and arrogant and so damn sure of himself, what had he done to help her? He'd flayed her father with a few choice words, threatened him with dire consequences if the girl came to harm, and then . . .

And then he'd left. And forgotten all about her.

A stray spark caught a wisp of air and danced up from the smoke, weaving a slow pattern in front of him before it rose and disappeared into the sky.

I saw you there.

She'd seen him, had watched him with gratitude in her

child's eyes. That was true. And perhaps the rest of her words had been true as well. Perhaps in the end she had hated him, been disgusted by him and everything he represented.

But he could have changed her mind. With time, he could have shown her.

The sure knowledge that any time with her was lost forever rocked Hart to his knees. Cool damp soaked through the thin fabric of his trousers and reminded him of the dirt beneath the grass. The dark earth that would keep her from him forever.

She'd been so strong. Fighting him, fighting herself. She'd carved her way through her world with reckless bravery and doubtful morals, and she'd delighted a duke's numbed heart.

Now he was left with this living, beating, feeling heart and no Emma to bring it joy.

Another spark shook free of the wreckage and danced its slow, winding way higher. Hart watched it fly up, pretty and free, as the world closed in around him. The air, sharp with smoke, pressed in, a weight on his chest.

Hart tried to draw a breath and couldn't. Tried again, but the air fought him, struggling against his throat until he threw his head back and gasped in a great breath that wheezed into his lungs. His throat had opened, but he'd freed up the tears too.

He had no idea how to cry, was frightened by it. So he knelt there, gasping, and stared up at the smoky sky and waited for it to be done.

"Your Grace?"

He dropped his head.

"Your Grace, the woman, Mrs. Smythe, is stirring."

Bess. Of course. Bess needed care and attention. Hart stumbled to his knees, grateful that his driver did not reach out to assist him.

He heard her coughing before he'd walked halfway across the yard. "Have you given her water?"

"Yes, sir."

Knowing what must be done, Hart stopped in his tracks and looked back at the site of Emma's home. He let his eyes roam over it, memorizing the scene before he continued toward the carriage. "We must go then. She'll need care and rest. A comfortable room."

"I'll see to the room, Your Grace."

Hart stepped into the coach and took the seat opposite the nest of blankets that made up Bess's bed. "Bess, can you hear me?"

He wrapped his hand around hers and felt her squeeze weakly back. "Bess, do you know what's happened?"

"Fire," she rasped, and the word tore another fit of coughing from her throat. Tears leaked from the corners of her clenched eyes.

"Yes, a fire. You're not burned though, just stunned by the smoke. I'm taking you to an inn where you can rest."

Her hand clenched his fingers harder. She tried to clear her throat, but only coughed again before subsiding into silence.

"I am sorry . . ." He should do this now. Get it over with quickly. "I'm sorry, Bess. Your mistress, she . . ."

Her eyes opened, bright with fear.

"She did not escape the fire."

No, her lips said, though she made no sound.

Hart was overwhelmed by the urge to agree, to join her denial with his own. But he owed her the truth, not stupid hope. "We searched everywhere, Bess." He swallowed back the emotion that tried to crack through his words. "She's gone. I'm so sorry."

Her fingernails dug into his skin as she squeezed, but the pain provided distraction from the sheer panic in her eyes. She shook her head and tried to rise.

"Calm down. Don't injure yourself." He leaned forward

to press her shoulders down, but she grabbed his wrist with her free hand and held him tight.

"*Listen*," she rasped. "Please. Listen."

"Yes, of course." The coach jerked forward as it moved out of the soft ground and back to the lane.

"She's not . . ." The wheels drowned out her tortured words, forcing Hart to lean close to her lips. "She's not there. A man . . ."

"What?"

She began to cough again as a strange, brittle pressure formed in Hart's chest. He forced himself not to grab her. "What are you saying?"

"Not there," Bess choked out, her face reddening with the effort. She let go of his wrist and pressed her hand to her throat as if to push the words out. "A man took her. Someone took her."

His heart stopped and held itself still, not daring to believe. "You saw this?"

"Yes. I saw him . . . pull her away."

"Who?"

"I couldn't tell, but she . . . she said 'Matthew.'"

His heart burst back to furious life as he raised his fist to the roof. He wanted to race back to Emma's home, but he could not give chase in the carriage. He'd let the whole damn day pass. They must have gone miles.

"Stop!" Hart slammed open the door and hung himself out the opening again. "Lark! We need to get back to Whitby as quickly as possible. She's not dead. Someone took her, a man named Matthew Bromley. Get me back to Whitby before sundown and let's find out if he's been seen."

"Yes, Your Grace."

"I'll need you to get me the swiftest horse you can. I have to find her."

"Of course. Hie!" He yelled to the horses before Hart had

even snapped the door shut. He was jerked back to his seat and the force slammed cold fury into his veins.

She was alive. *Alive*. And he would find her and make that bastard sorry he'd ever even spoken her name.

"Help her," Bess whispered, shocking Hart. He'd forgotten she was there.

"I will."

The woman choked on a sob. "She wronged you. I know that. But she's not a bad person. You must help her."

Pushing aside his need to do violence, Hart reached out to take her hand again. "I promise to find her and to keep her safe. I promise."

"Bless you."

Hart offered a false smile. Bless him. Or damn him to hell, for he was about to commit murder.

"I will freeze out here," Emma snapped, trying to wrap herself in the oiled skin that was supposed to keep the damp from seeping into her nightdress. It wasn't working. She was wet and cold and enraged. The ropes around her wrists and ankles had set fire to her skin.

Matthew looked little better. His red nose set off the crimson that shot through his eyes. "'Tis your fault, so shut your braying mouth."

"You're a murderous bastard." The slap that landed across her cheek was almost a relief. The cold was numbing her from the outside in. She needed reminding of her hatred before it seeped completely away into the damp ground.

"A modest woman minds her tongue," Matthew said through clenched teeth.

"Even in the face of evil?"

"I will not be judged by you. I have a higher judge—"

"Oh, and how did you explain my uncle's death to your Lord?"

The rage dropped away, leaving his face limp with regret. "That was an accident, I told you. I never meant for your uncle to die."

"You caused his death with your selfishness."

"I am sorry for that, Emily—"

"*Don't call me that.* My name is Emma. And I want to go home."

"Your place is with me."

"You killed my only family! You might have killed Bess. And now you think I will be your wife? You are even madder than I thought."

"In time you will—"

"In time I will murder you in your sleep." She kicked out at him with her bound legs and caught a solid blow to his hip. "Untie me!"

He lunged at her, grabbed her shoulders and forced her to the ground beneath him. "You want me to untie you? If I untie your legs, I will be between them, do you understand? Is that another sin you want on my head?"

"Matthew," she sobbed, afraid for the first time since he'd dragged her out of her home. His hips pushed into her. A rock dug deep into her back. "You're hurting me."

"You have hurt me for years. I love you, Emily. Despite all you've done, all your sins, I still want to honor you with marriage." His eyes closed against pleasure as he thrust himself against her. "It is . . . It is the only way I can redeem myself. By . . . redeeming you." His hands squeezed her tighter, bruising her as she wept quietly beneath him.

"Please, Matthew."

"And if I untie you, I will want to rub the marks the ropes have left. And then I'll . . . I know you have been wicked. So wicked. Men have t-touched you. Ah . . . Please Lord, I must not let her sin again. We must be married . . . Oh. Oh, Emily."

He shuddered above her, and she vowed not to mention

the ropes again. She'd already worn her fingers raw trying to work them free. She wouldn't risk worse injury at his hands.

"Emily," he was choking on her name, sobbing as he rocked back to rest on his knees. He straddled her, pinning her down; she couldn't escape the blow when it came. "Why are you so bad? A temptress worse than Eve. But I will save you. I'll save you. When we marry, my soul will be clean and I will lead you to the Lord. A man is the shepherd of his family."

Emma turned her head and stared at the grass swaying inches from her face. The pitiful fire illuminated only those blades, beyond was pure blackness. How long before he truly raped her? It would take days to get to Scotland, more than a week if she was able to slow them down. How long before he attacked her, how long before he beat her half to death for tempting him into fornication?

Bess was alive, but what could she do? There was no one to send for, no one Bess could turn to. Emma had run from everyone she'd known, and Hart . . . well, Hart was well and truly done with her.

If only she'd let him stay as she'd wanted to. If only she'd let him tempt her with the promise in his eyes. But she could not love any more. She couldn't stand the inevitable pain, the heartbreak that crouched in unexpected corners, waiting to pounce.

This was better. This she could understand. Matthew Bromley wanted her, and so he took her. And while she was afraid and her face was swollen with hot pain, at least she knew what was coming. The same kind of hatred and lust she'd witnessed her whole life. Strange that she'd ever thought she could be free of it.

Hating her surrender, she whispered to the night, "I will see you punished."

Matthew's hands took hers gently. He checked the thick

rope around her wrists. "No. You will love me, Emily. Now go to sleep." One of his hands stroked a slow line up her hip. His sigh filled the night when he reached the curve of one breast and cupped his hand around it. "I will keep you warm."

Her despair steamed instantly to rage and she knew in that moment she would fight him with every breath. "You'd best keep your hands to yourself. Every touch outside the marriage bed is an insult to your God."

His hand snapped away, and Emma rolled to her side, pushing him off her body. If she could not escape him tonight, she would escape tomorrow or the day after that. If he dared to take her to another town, she would make the same kind of scene she'd made in that village they'd passed through. She would escape him.

Matthew could find salvation for his own damned soul. She had enough trouble keeping hold of her own.

Chapter 23

Hart had started shaking with the cold about an hour ago. He'd given up trying to stop it soon thereafter. If the shivering would keep him slightly warmer, then it was welcome. A thick fog had fallen over the world around midnight, dampening everything and offering an added danger to his night. His mount had proven quick and sure-footed, but even the sturdy gelding became skittish on the misty trail. The road stayed a good ten yards from the jagged cliffs, but occasionally the sound of waves would grow loud as if a crevice had opened only feet from the horse's hooves.

The fog shrouded everything and floated strange sounds to his ears. He'd thought he'd heard a woman's cry once and had chased inland after it, but he'd found nothing. Likely it had been a gull or a crow. Then there had been a mysterious creaking, a flash of faint light. That had come from the east, a passing ship perhaps.

So he'd given up his search and simply urged the horse slowly forward, waiting for the sun to rise and burn off this muffling blindness.

Matthew Bromley had to have taken her north. It had seemed so simple the night before when he'd set out from Whitby. Between Hart and his driver they'd made quick work out of canvassing the small town. They'd found the run-down room Matthew had rented three nights before, but no one had seen hide nor hair of him since. So Hart had taken his horse and headed back toward Emma's home and the road beyond, determined to catch them. But now . . . after so many cold, dark hours in the saddle, it seemed they could be anywhere. The man could have taken her away in a sloop. Or they could have traveled inland over the fields. But he'd met Matthew Bromley, and he couldn't imagine the man sleeping anywhere but in a bed. He looked as if he might float away in a high wind.

A cow lowed somewhere ahead and Hart thought he heard a woman's voice murmur in response. His hunched shoulders straightened and he strained to see something. A new light was setting the fog aglow. Sunrise, he hoped, and good weather for hunting.

A dog barked, a light sparked to life, seeming to float above the ground. Then a figure formed like a ghost.

"Madam?"

The stout woman gasped and stepped back, fading a little. "Ye scared the wits out of me!"

"My apologies. Can you tell me if I'm nearing Rumswick Bay?"

"Why, ye're in it!" She glanced around as he did. "Or at the edge anyway. But there ain't much here. An inn at the other side of town, but he'll cheat ye if ye're not careful."

"My thanks." He started to urge the horse on, toward the sound of water slapping at boats and the faint shout of a fisherman, but pulled back on the reins after a few steps. "Have there been other travelers about this morning?"

"None, but it's early yet."

"Of course."

"But there was quite a pair last even'."

He wheeled the gelding around. "Who?"

"A man and his wayward wife, he said. She'd run away

and didn't care for being fetched back it seemed. Made quite a fuss about being slung over his old mare."

"A young woman? Dark-haired?"

"I couldn't see much under her cloak, but the man was young and fair. Aside from the scratches she'd laid on his cheek."

His heart began to thunder furiously. "When did they pass?"

"Afore dinner. Twasn't dark yet."

Hart put his heels to the horse and raced blindly into the village. The fog swirled before him, clearing the way just enough to help him avoid a lumbering cow.

A few minutes later he was shaking awake the snoring innkeeper. The man reeked of ale and sweat, but he came alert as soon as he spied a gleam of gold.

"Oh, sure, they were here. He come pounding on the door but changed his mind quick after she started in screaming."

Hart's skin prickled with gooseflesh. "Screaming."

"Screaming to wake the dead. Claimed he was a kidnapper and a murderer. He couldn't shut her up, so he just led the horse on out of town."

"And you? You let him go?"

"If a man needs to discipline his wife, it's none of my concern."

"She was screaming for *help*. He's not her husband, you imbecile. He is a kidnapper and likely a murderer as well. You may have sent a woman to her death."

The bastard actually snorted. "And if he was a murderer, what should I have done? Risked my own life?"

"Yes," Hart snarled. "Yes, you should have risked your worthless life." He was mounting his horse when the man came rushing out, shirttails flapping.

"You promised a coin!"

Hart was tempted to spit in the coward's face, but he reminded himself that he was a duke. Then he tossed the coin into the deep mud at the north side of the yard. "There's your coin. I suggest you use it to take a trip. If she's come to harm, I'll be back to teach you how it feels to cry for help and get no response."

The horse jumped beneath his heels, springing forward toward the road as the innkeeper yelled out some defense behind him.

They were close. Hart could feel it in his bones. They'd left this village near sunset, looking for a place to stop for the night. The next town was only a few miles ahead. They were either there or somewhere on the road in between. Surely they were just rising, surely they couldn't be far.

His muscles were coiled in painful bunches beneath his skin. He was crushed beneath terror and hope and violence and sorrow.

If he could just know she was well . . . She *must* be well. Matthew hadn't taken her to kill her.

Hart's brain started spitting out ideas of what she might have suffered short of death, but he shut it down with a curse. "She is all right," he whispered. "Scared, but well." He tried to swallow the fear and found that it wouldn't budge. It stayed stuck there, deep in his throat, for the next half hour.

He was nearly upon them before he realized it. It was less than a campsite; just a pile of blankets and a long-cold fire not a few feet from a crumbling edge of rock. He didn't see her, didn't see anyone, and was standing in his stirrups, searching the horizon when movement drew his eye.

A flash of billowing white at a cliff's edge, a dark band of black holding it still. His mind registered only shapes and colors for a moment, then focused with a snap on Emma and Matthew.

They stood at the edge of the rock, Matthew holding up one hand to warn Hart away, the other arm was wrapped around her neck. Emma's skin was alarmingly pale, pale except for the bruises marring her left cheek. Matthew's jaw was pressed against her darkened temple.

Hart eased his pistol from its hiding place and wondered if the roaring in his ears was the sea.

"Why are you here?" the man shouted, dragging Emma back a step. Hart's gaze fell to her feet, unshod and tied at the ankles. Then he noticed her captor's boots. They were only inches from the edge. A rock, disturbed by his shifting, clattered away and dropped from sight.

Hart slid from the saddle and strode toward them. "Let her go."

"Stop!" Matthew's boot slid farther back.

Hart skidded to a stop, heart tripping in alarm. "Let her go! Are you mad? If you get any nearer that cliff, you will both be killed."

Matthew glanced behind him, seeming unconcerned. "Why are you here?"

Hart met her hazel eyes, wild now with fear. "I've come for Emma."

"She's not your concern." His arm tightened around Emma's neck, and her bound hands rose briefly in protest.

"Of course she is. I've asked her to be my wife."

"Hart," she gasped, trying to shake her head.

"No," Matthew shouted. "No, she is mine. Meant for me!"

Hart eased forward, trying to get close enough to snatch her away. "She does not want you, Matthew."

"You know nothing. I love her and she will be my wife. She promised. Promised when she let me put my hands on her, tempted me to all kinds of sin."

Hart's pulse fluttered, but he ignored it. Instead of lashing out, he raised a calming hand. "Think about it, Matthew. What kind of life can you provide? You set fire to her uncle's home, didn't you?"

Shock sparked in the man's eyes.

Hart nodded. "You killed a man and you'll go to jail for that. How will you provide for a wife?"

"No! It was an accident! I won't go back to jail!"

"Matthew—"

"Move back!" he shouted, just as his boot slid right over the edge. Emma stiffened at the movement.

Hart lunged, trying to catch her. She was helpless against the man dragging her backward. Her heels scraped over moss and rocks as she reached out with her bound hands.

"Hart, I'm so sorry," she whispered, the words seeming to float up as she fell.

Hart dropped the pistol and dove forward, grabbing nothing but air. He fell to the ground, felt the jolt of rocks and unforgiving ground, thought of Emma's body falling even farther, too far—

But her fall had been stopped. He was staring at her, looking into her eyes, her shoulders and face still visible above the edge. She wasn't lost.

He vaulted to his feet and rushed forward, kicking rocks out into the salt wind.

"Do you want her to die?" Matthew screamed. He'd dragged them both onto a narrow ledge that trailed down at a steep angle. He wrapped an arm tight around her waist and tugged her a little farther down. "Leave us!"

"I won't. Just let her go. She's cold and she's hurt. Let me take her someplace safe."

"She will be safe enough once we're married. At least her soul will be in God's hands."

"Even in Scotland they will not marry you to an unwilling woman."

"Oh, she will be willing by then."

Struck with fury, Hart jumped down and landed with a great clatter of sliding rock and grit. Emma gasped and fell backward, tugged down by Matthew's violent jerk.

"*Please*," Hart ground out, "you are going to hurt her. Just release her. It's too steep here, you cannot drag her down the cliff face. Let her go. I won't follow you, I give you my word."

Matthew shouted, "I love her!" and pulled her along the narrow ledge. His body began to disappear around a curve as Emma's feet kicked futilely against stone and gravel. "Why can you not just go away? She is mine!"

Stay calm, Hart reminded himself, keeping his eye on Emma as she was pulled backward. *Stay calm*. If he got too close, he'd make it worse, put Emma in more danger. So instead of lunging, he crept. Instead of screaming with rage, he held his breath.

Emma's gaze locked with his. One fat tear fell, tracing a track through her dusty face. *I'm sorry*, she mouthed, and Hart was shaking his head just as she disappeared around the angled jag of rock that blocked his view.

He tried to move faster and stay quiet, but his foot slipped on loose sand and he crashed to one knee. Pain shot straight to his spine. He dug his nails into his palms and forced himself up to inch forward. *Slowly, slowly, slowly*.

"Tell him to go away," Matthew was sobbing. "He has shamed you. Do you think I don't know? Even after all that, I've offered you my name. Why can you not see me?"

"I see you, Matthew." Her voice shook in time with Hart's shattered pulse. "I see you," she repeated.

"I love you so much, Emily."

Hart moved to the very edge of the corner and eased his head around. They were stuck. Wedged into a shallow corner of broken, crumbling slag. Matthew had forced Emma into a wedge, had propped her up against the wall of stone, and stood with one hand pressed to her shoulder and the other holding something close to his thigh.

His back was to Hart, as if he'd forgotten him. And perhaps he had. He was clearly mad, obsessed with this woman he couldn't have.

Not taking his eyes off her, Hart knelt carefully down and

plucked a large stone from the ground. He tested it in his hand. He couldn't have used the pistol even if he'd retrieved it. She was so near, just behind Matthew's head. But if he could sneak close enough it would be a simple thing to slam the rock down and pull Emma into his arms.

"Why won't you love me?" Matthew groaned.

Emma was weeping, shaking her head. "I've loved you as a friend, Matthew, cared for you. And your father loves you, depends on you. Please don't do this. What will he do without you?"

He flung his hand up in frustration, and Hart froze at the flash of sunlight on metal. A knife. A long knife, surely sharper than any he'd ever seen before. "You will be mine," he gasped. "It's the only way."

Hart raised the stone, eased one foot closer, but Matthew's head snapped around at the scrape of sound. "Leave us!" He let go of Emma and swept the knife in a grand arc that stirred the air near Hart's face.

He jumped back as a strange sound reached his ears. A rumble that shook the stone beneath his feet, punctuated by tiny pings and cracks.

Emma screamed and clutched at unyielding rock as the stones beneath her feet seemed to sink. Pebbles fell like rain.

Hart yelled, "Don't move," but Matthew was shifting. He reached for an ancient arm of root that protruded from a crevice. Even as his feet wobbled against a rocking stone, Matthew was swinging the knife back toward Emma.

Hart gave up on yelling and began to beg. "Please don't. I beg you. Don't hurt her." But the knife drove toward her and Hart could do nothing. *"No."*

"No!" Emma screamed, and then the knife was on her, sawing into her belly and she gasped and threw her hands up as Hart felt his heart shatter to dust.

"Go," Matthew snapped. "Go past me."

She looked down at her belly just as Hart did. There was

no blood, and her hands were free. They both stared stupidly at the rope that curled over the tops of her feet.

Hart snapped back to sanity first. "Come, Emma. Quick and careful. Try to hang onto the wall."

She nodded and reached shaking hands up to grasp at the jagged rock near Matthew's shoulder. She eased closer to him, sobbed when a rock simply disappeared from beneath her toes. The whole floor would break and roll away any moment.

"Hurry," Matthew urged, as he wrapped an arm around her and eased her past him. The man's other hand strained against the root, but Hart could see the dead root twisting, raining bits of brittle wood down on their heads.

Just as Emma made it past Matthew, the shale beneath her sank a good six inches, throwing her to her knees. Her hands were close to solid rock now and she tried to crawl. Hart winced as he fell to his own knees and scrambled forward to grab her hands. But she slipped back. The rumble started again, freezing them all in their places.

She spread her arms wide to try to balance her weight.

"Reach for me," Hart ordered, but she shook her head.

"I can't."

They stared at each other, separated by three feet of rock that was cracking like glass beneath them. Hart tore his gaze from hers and looked up to Matthew. The man's eyes had lost the bright gleam of madness. His face was set in a sorrow that Hart recognized.

He met Hart's gaze for a long moment of understanding, then he slowly uncurled his fist from the small safety of the root. Stones shifted beneath him, rocking him as he knelt down and reached for Emma's feet. One swipe of the knife and her legs were free to help her scramble up.

Matthew nodded. "I love you, Emily. I only ever loved you." Then, as Hart reached down and grabbed one of her outstretched hands, Matthew gave her a hard push from beneath. The force threw Emma to the safety of solid ground and loosened the last of the cliff beneath Matthew's feet.

His face was set in calm grief as he slipped from sight, as the rocks fell away and set him free for a short moment. Hart heard silence and then a grotesque thud as the ground caught Matthew's body far below.

But Emma was wrapping her arms around him, her body shuddering with life, and Hart couldn't dredge up any sympathy for the man. Emma could, it seemed. Before she'd finished sobbing she pulled away and crawled toward the new edge of shale.

"Emma, don't. Don't look. It's not safe."

"But . . . Matthew." She shook off his restraining hand and eased her head closer to the precipice. He knew she'd spotted the body when she stiffened, turning to pale marble as he watched. Hart glanced over also, just to be sure. There was no doubt the man was dead. When he tugged her back she gave in and slumped into his lap.

"We need to get off this cliff. And the authorities must be informed."

The fear had left her eyes now, along with everything else. She stared straight ahead, gaze blank as death, and the sight spurred Hart to stand and carry her back to the highest point of the ledge. He eased her up, hating the way she just sat there. This wasn't his Emma; he prayed to God that she hadn't gone far, that she'd be back.

After wrapping her in a blanket, he gathered the reins of the old mare and scooped Emma up. Somehow he managed to mount the gelding without killing all of them.

"Staithes is to the north. A little farther than that last village, but larger, I believe."

She gave no answer, so Hart held her tighter and urged the horse to a run.

Chapter 24

"I didn't want to leave you alone," Hart explained, as if Emma cared that he'd taken only one room. She did not care if he was here, didn't care that he knew she was curled naked beneath the quilts. She had no clothing, no belongings, no home.

"You did not eat."

"I was bathing," she muttered as she turned away from him.

"Shall I bring you something now?"

"No."

"Emma, you must be hungry and thirsty. Please, eat something."

Well, she'd been wrong. She *did* care that he was in the room, wished he would go away. The man was hovering, showing sympathy and worry and that damned softness she'd never wanted from him.

"Have some wine at least."

She scooted up and reached a hand from beneath the blankets.

Hart muttered, "I should've known," as he pressed the goblet into her hand. Yes, he should have known. She liked wine almost as well as gaming, and both so much more than honest emotion.

She drank deep of the rich red liquid, but she lowered the glass when she caught the direction of Hart's gaze. He was staring at her arm, at the bruises left by Matthew's hands, the bloody rawness of her wrists. Emma set the wine down and curled back beneath the covers.

"I'm sorry I left you," he whispered. "I should never have left you alone."

"I didn't want you there. Didn't need you."

"Yes, you were insulting and hurtful. And I was stupid enough to fall for it, as I always do."

Emma shook her head. "There was nothing to fall for. I simply made clear how I felt. How I still feel. I do not want you."

She felt his weight dip the bed when he sat next to her. His thigh pressed against her back, and she wanted him to move, because his weight and heat only made her want more. Emma curled tighter into herself.

"Why did you come to my home that night?"

"What night?"

He sighed. Loudly. But his fingers stroked over her hair, rubbed her scalp. "You've only been to my home once, Emma."

She snuck deeper into her nest, "I don't want to talk. Please leave me alone."

"No, I won't. I need to know why you came to my house that night. If I disgust you, if you think I'm no different from your father's friends . . . I need to know."

Her eyes, wide open, focused on a fold of cream linen, but she could see Hart clearly: his beautiful face, full of fear for her, full of caring and passion. He hadn't looked like a duke today, with his two days' worth of stubble and tired eyes; today he looked like a man.

Emma swallowed. "Why?"

His thumb touched her temple, traced her hairline. "You came to me when you didn't have to, made love to me when you had every reason not to. Emma . . ."

The linen blurred to nothing before her eyes.

"I was falling in love with you. Did you know it then?"

"No," she whispered. No, because it was impossible. He was Winterhart and she was . . . she was as empty as a shell.

"And I need to know about that night, because I think you were falling in love too."

"No."

"If I'd realized, if I hadn't been so soused, you would have ruined all your grand plans by coming to my bed. I would've realized you were a virgin. And yet you came. Why?"

"Please go away. Go away, *go away*. My head hurts and I don't want you here."

His weight shifted and she thought he would leave, but he only pressed a kiss to her hair. "Better?"

"*No*. I won't be better until you're gone."

"You are not disgusted by me. You don't hate me. You may even be in love with me as I am with you. I love you, Emma. I want to marry you, have children, build a life. Will you—"

"No!" she cried out, and fought the tight cocoon of the covers. She pushed away from him and twisted around, flinging her fists at him in a blind rage. "No, no, no! I will not have you, do you hear me? You disgust me. You and the way you make me feel. And *children*. They are worthless and weak and, and . . ."

"You're lying again. You had a little brother. You must have loved him. Didn't you—"

"Stop!" Her throat ached with her cries. "Stop! Do not speak of him." She gulped in air, but it did nothing to stop the wild sobs that burst from her throat. He tried to reach for her and she struck out, slapping him away. "You have no idea. None!"

"Tell me."

"Of course I loved him. I loved him and he died, just like everyone else. My mother. My father. My uncle. Matthew. And all of it my fault. *My* fault."

"Emma," his voice was a soothing lull. He didn't understand. "You didn't cause those deaths."

"You have no idea. My mother, she was ill after I was born. She should never have had another child. We killed her, Will and I. And my uncle . . . If I'd left Matthew alone, if I'd told him I couldn't meet him that night . . . I was bored, you see. Flirting with him was my only excitement. I didn't care if he loved me. I didn't care that I would drive him mad, push him to kill my uncle and himself."

"That man hunted you like an animal. He set fire to both your homes!"

"*Because of me.* There is something inside me. Something wicked that pushed him to madness. I am terrible and sinful just like my father."

"You are nothing like your father. You are a sensitive woman with healthy passions."

"And Will . . ." Emma sat slowly back on her haunches and pulled the linens tight around her. She stared into the hearth, at the jumping flames that looked like life, but brought pain and death. "My father was drunk. He was drunk and laughing in that way he has after a long night of drinking and wenching. He wanted to take Will for a ride in a phaeton he'd won in some game the night before.

"I told him no. I did. But Will was so excited. My father never paid attention to us. He began whining that he wanted to go, and my father told me to shut my mouth or I'd discover the taste of a real whip. And I was scared. I'd seen women whipped in my home before, and I was scared, so I backed away and watched him lift Will up into that carriage and I knew. I knew he was drunk and reckless. I *knew*. I saw it in my head in that moment, the horses, the road, the crash. And I did nothing."

"You were just a girl. He was your father."

She began to cry. Soft, high sounds leaked from her throat as her tears fell against the sheets. Hart reached for her and she let him, hating her weakness and overwhelmed by need.

"He was so small, just a baby. And when they told me, I didn't believe them. I couldn't. I told the nurse that she was a stupid cow and I ran, ran all the way up to the attic to hide. I must've stayed for hours. By the time I came down it was dark. And . . . and they were all gone. All of them. My father hadn't paid most of them for months. They took silver and rugs and crystal. It was cold and pitch-black."

"You must have been terrified."

"I just . . . I didn't know what to do."

"Of course not." He'd slipped beneath the quilts and held her tight to his body. His hands stroked her naked back, a touch that took nothing and had naught to do with sex. She wanted to climb into him in that moment. Disappear into his warmth and strength. But she couldn't disappear, no matter how much she wanted.

"I found a candle on the floor, just laying there. I lit it and walked around, looking for someone, sure that my brother was in his bed or in the schoolroom. I remember the wax dripping on my hand, but I didn't dare put it down. And then I found him."

His breath shuddered from his chest. She realized her ear was pressed just above his heart and his blood beat so strong and sure.

"They'd been laid out on the dining room table. Their . . . the servants laid them out, but that was all. They knew I was there, knew I would find them. I don't know why . . . They didn't clean them up or even wipe the blood away."

"I'm so sorry."

"And my brother . . . my little baby. He never had a mother. I took care of him and loved him. I picked him up when he fell, made it better. And he was crushed beneath the carriage when it turned, caught under the wheel. In pain."

"I'm sure he didn't feel it."

"But he did. He did. They brought him home covered in dirt and dried blood. Filthy and cold. But there were clean streaks on his face. I know he cried, because those were the paths the tears had traced through the blood, where he'd lain on that hard road and cried. For me."

"Emma. No."

"I know just what he sounded like. I can hear it. He wanted me to make it better, Hart, as I always had before. And I don't know how long he cried, and sometimes I want to die too."

"Shh," he murmured, as she sobbed into his heart. "Shh. You loved him. You gave him something good in his life. It wasn't your fault."

"I knew what would happen."

"You were a child. Oh, Emma, you were just a child. I'm so sorry."

She cried for her brother, for all of her family who'd died. Even for Matthew. And Hart held her and stroked her back and whispered wordless murmurs into her hair.

When she finally quieted, he pressed a kiss to her forehead. "I remember you, you know. In that hallway, in your nightdress and long braids. You were very brave and bright, and you did not deserve to be in that home. I'm sorry I did nothing about it."

She breathed a watery sigh, so relieved that he recalled that night, as if he made that little girl real. That child who'd thought she could save them all if only she could take enough care. That girl who hadn't yet lost everything dear to her heart. "There was nothing you could've done. He was my father, if by blood alone."

His hand rubbed soft circles, over and over. "I had another sister. Before Alex."

Emma nodded, rubbing her cheek against his wet shirt.

"She died just after her first birthday. Nobody told me what happened. One day she was there, toddling around, laughing at me, chewing all my toys. Two days later the nursery was empty. I thought maybe a monster had come and stolen her away. The silence was the worst thing, sitting in my bedroom on the third floor, listening for her cry in the morning."

"I'm sorry," she whispered, tearing up again. Was the world like this for everyone?

"You're afraid to have a child."

She didn't answer. Couldn't.

"When Alex was born I wouldn't go near her. I hurried past the nursery, ignoring all the toys and laughter. I was terrified of her, angry every time she smiled at me."

"What happened?"

His soft huff of laughter vibrated against her ear. "Alex happened. She started walking, then running. Whenever I was home from school, she'd chase me to my room. Then she learned how to turn the knob. I was cornered, trapped. And that was the end of me. I fell under her spell."

"But she lived. She was fine."

"Oh, yes, she lived. And she continually scared the hell out of me. Broke my heart a couple of times. Drove me mad. Infuriated me." He paused. "You two would get along splendidly."

Emma was surprised at her hiccup of laughter. Just a few minutes ago, she'd felt as if she'd never laugh again. Now she felt only tired. Exhausted actually. And Hart was twirling her hair around his fingers, the feeling so strange and lovely that she closed her eyes.

"I don't want you to love me," she whispered. "I don't know how to love you. Especially you."

"I know." He kissed her head again. Wound his finger round and round. "But you'll learn. We'll both learn."

"I don't think we should. You will destroy me."

"Emma, you made my worst fears come true. Do you understand that? No, you couldn't."

"I embarrassed you, just like that woman."

His pulse sped a little, but he shook his head. "That woman, as you say, embarrassed me and broke my heart. She made a fool of me. Just as you have."

"I'm sorry."

"I thought I loved her, but I didn't. I would have recovered. She was just an illusion."

"Like me."

"No, not like you. She was malicious and degenerate. And her betrayal stung like mad and then it was done."

"But—"

"*But*," he interrupted, "then there was my father. My damned father. So cold and perfect. And so disgusted by his passionate, unwise son. He was determined to see me become a man worthy of the dukedom, and he found his chance. There were those letters, you see. Not an uncommon problem in broken affairs. My father paid a lot of money to retrieve them from her. He showed them to me, let me stammer out my grateful thanks, my apologies, my shame for having loved her in the first place. He let me grovel at his feet. And then he chose one particularly sordid letter and sent it to a friend, who sent it to another friend."

"*Why?*"

"He wanted to build me into a man, and he had to break me completely to do that. He engineered my utter humiliation. My own father. Gave his tacit approval for society to mock me. Made it acceptable to laugh at me, point.

"But I rescinded that approval two years later when I became duke. It was no easy struggle, Emma. I built a fortress around myself, and you have destroyed it."

"Hart . . . I'm sorry. I never meant—"

"But that is my point, Emma. I do not care. Don't you see? I simply don't give a damn. I just keep wanting you."

"You can't. I don't want you to."

"He made me into someone different, but you have brought me back to myself. You can't leave me now. Come to Somerhart. Stay as my guest." He swallowed hard. "I'll keep my hands to myself. Show you there is more between us than lust." His hand stilled. "Though I will leave my bedroom door unlocked, just in case."

She smiled as sleep pulled hard at her melting mind. "I won't marry you," she murmured. "I won't." Then she let his heartbeat lull her into dreams. Dreams of a man who could not love her, but did.

Chapter 25

"Emma," he whispered into her ear. Emma shooed him away with her hand. She was warm and so tired . . . and Hart was shaking her awake.

"What is it?" she cried in a hoarse voice.

"It is dawn. Time to go back to your room."

She waved her hand in his direction and clenched her eyes shut. "As if your servants don't know. The maids have begun leaving sconces burning in the hallway all night. They don't want me to trip." She curled tighter and her hip nudged a very interesting part of his body.

He took that as an invitation to pull her tight against him. "Then marry me. Make me respectable again in my household's eyes."

"I don't want to talk about this now."

"You never want to talk about it. You've been here a month and you avoid the subject at every turn."

"Yes."

"And yet you sneak into my bed every night."

"I'd hardly call it sneaking. I simply stroll down and knock."

"You don't knock."

"All right, I'm going to my room now. I won't get any more sleep here."

Hart's arm held her tight when she tried to move. She struggled and got nothing for her efforts but a body that throbbed to excited life. One of his hands was clamped around her upper thigh. His strength sizzled through her. His arousal was a hard brand against her bottom.

She arched, trying to get away and knowing the struggle would press her more firmly into that length. His grip tightened for a moment, then he wrapped his leg over hers to hold her in place. His long fingers slid between her thighs and snuck higher.

The edge of his hand slipped easily along her wet sex, shaking her toward complete arousal. Emma inhaled on a moan. She pushed against him with her feet and he pressed more weight against her legs. She felt helpless . . . and somehow he knew how much she liked it.

"Don't," she moaned, even as she eased her thighs open.

He ignored her, thank God, and plunged two fingers deep. "Hart," she cried.

"Marry me, Emma." His fingers stroked a slow, hard rhythm. "No other man can know you like this."

"I don't . . . I don't want *anyone* to know me like this."

"Little liar. I know very well what you want." He pressed his body against her, rolling her to her stomach.

When his fingers slid out of her, she sobbed. But he quickly made it better. He pulled her to her knees and was sliding deep inside her before she could even think to ask for it.

He did know her, knew her so well he could bring her to climax within a few heartbeats or keep her on the edge for a full hour. This morning he was clearly taking advantage of this knowledge; her body was flying fast toward its peak, pushed by his brutal strokes and powerful grip. Within minutes they'd both collapsed to the bed, sweat-slick and gasping.

Emma cleared her throat, knowing she'd be hoarse again today. She blushed to think of the servants who must have heard her.

"I'm done humoring you," Hart gasped. "We'll marry in one month. I'll post the banns tomorrow."

She laughed in disbelief. "Post banns? Surely you can afford a special license. Not that I'll marry you."

"I'll post them in all the London papers. I'm proud of you and I'll not have anyone think otherwise. No special license."

"Hart, nothing has changed."

"Everything has changed. You're in my home, in my bed every night. Careful as we are, you could be carrying our child right now. And I love you. I love you."

She shook her head, pressing her lips tight together.

"You're afraid, Emma. Just afraid. But I am a risk worth taking. You claim to think I will be spectacularly unfaithful, but put that gambler's brain to use. I'm a man of strong physical needs, but I'm clearly a romantic at heart. For God's sake, I proposed to someone else's mistress in a fit of irrepressible love!"

Emma held back an unwilling smile.

"Yes, I've been with many women, but . . . Emma?" He touched her chin and gently turned her face toward his, caught her in that sky blue gaze. "I was never really *with* them. I was not there. There is so much more pleasure in trust. I am myself with you and I'd rather die than lose that."

Her eyes burned with tears. She seemed to be constantly close to weeping these days, and surely that was a bad sign. "I am myself with you and it terrifies me."

"Why?"

"I don't—" She choked on the words and had to start again. "I don't want to be him."

His thumb stroked her cheek.

"I'm afraid I'll be like him," she said again, relieved to have said it, finally.

"You won't."

She turned away from his touch and buried her face in his shoulder. "I am wicked with you."

"Yes, you are."

She shook her head hard.

"Just as you should be. I will be your husband. How sad if you could not be wicked with me."

"Other wives are not—"

"Other husbands are not me. And everyone, Emma . . . everyone wants to be tied up with silk ribbons on occasion."

"You!" she gasped and reared back to hit him. He'd promised never to even mention it. His hands caught hers in an easy grip.

"Everyone," he whispered and kissed her closed lips. His eyes sparkled down at her, inviting her to laugh, and Emma's outrage slowly floated away. Wicked man.

"Even you?" she asked and was rewarded with a slow, wide smile that called to mind fallen angels. His eyes fell to her mouth.

"Even me."

Oh, that might be worth any risk at all. Hart's eyes sparked with triumph. The man could see everything about her.

"And children?" she blurted out.

"We will do our best to wait until you're ready. That will be your decision. It is a gamble, but . . . Make this your last, great gamble, Emma." He kissed the knuckles of her left hand. "The best bet you've ever placed. Risk everything on me. Be afraid if you must, Emma, but love me."

"I . . ." Her stupid heart was doing happy flips in her chest. "I . . ." Oh, she could not do it.

But Hart knew her far too well. He tossed one more wager on the table. "Ten thousand a year in pin money to sweeten the pot."

Her mouth trembled into a smile. She did not care about

the money, but it was so much easier to pretend greed while she bared her tender soul. "Done," she whispered.

"Done?"

"I mean, yes. Yes, I will marry you. And I will . . . I . . ." His eyes shone with joy. "I will love you and be very afraid while I'm doing it."

But when he sighed and kissed her, Emma felt not a stitch of fear. Instead she felt hopeful and strong and very, very lucky. But she was not above hedging her bets. "If you ever betray me, I will move Stimp from your London household to Somerhart."

Hart's jaw dropped in mock horror.

"He has expressed an interest in training to be your driver. Perhaps even your valet."

Real horror replaced his acting. "Well, there is your insurance then, Emma. Trust me to be completely devoted."

"I will." And strangely enough, she knew that she would.

Please turn the page for an exciting sneak peek at
Victoria Dahl's next historical romance,
coming soon from Zebra Books!

Chapter 1

Nicholas Cantry, Viscount Lancaster—known by friends, family, and every single person in the ton for his unerring charm and constant good humor—was furious. His vision blurred faintly at the edges, and his teeth ached from the pressure of being clenched together, but as he made his way through the crowd of the waning dinner party, people still offered him smiles. If they thought anything at all, perhaps they wondered if he had a touch of dyspepsia. Certainly, they didn't suspect him of anger.

He was, after all, an ornament. A pleasant way to pass the time. A fairly harmless fortune hunter. And that was the way he liked it, because no one ever looked past his humor and goodwill. No one looked deeper. He could hardly regret a reputation he'd taken pains to cultivate.

But finding his fiancée spreading her legs for another man had ruffled even Lancaster's carefully sculpted facade. The hateful things she'd screamed at him hadn't helped his temper. Neither had the knowledge that he could not simply turn and walk away.

"My good Viscount Lancaster!" a voice trilled from his left. Lancaster stopped in his tracks, spun toward the petite matron and bowed in one fluid motion.

"Lady Avalon," he murmured over her offered hand. "A light in my dismal evening."

"Oh, pah," she giggled, and smacked him in the shoulder with her oversized fan.

"I had no idea you'd returned from the country so early. Fleeing an ill-thought affair, are you?"

"Lancaster, you are *scandalous.*"

"Only occasionally. You are acquainted with Mr. Brandiss?" He gestured toward their host and resisted an urge to massage the tight pain from the back of his neck.

"Oh, yes. Mr. Brandiss may be a merchant, but he's as much a gentleman as any peer of the realm." She leaned a little closer. "I've also met *Miss* Brandiss. What a beautiful bride you've chosen, Lancaster."

Beautiful, yes. And treacherous. And surprisingly loud when backed into a corner.

But he only inclined his head in modest agreement.

"Lovely," Lady Avalon continued, "and a very smart alliance. I told everyone you would do quite well, and you have."

"Yes, Miss Brandiss was willing to overlook my fearsome face and thread-worn title for a chance to get her delicate hands on my apple orchards. They're quite profitable."

"Ha! If you'd had a fortune, young man, you'd have reigned as the bachelor king for a decade. It takes a barrel of charm to be seen as a decent catch even in your straits. Very impressive, Viscount. Mr. Brandiss is a stickler when it comes to his little Imogene."

"Quite," Lancaster managed to grind out past a smile. "Now if you'd be kind enough to excuse me . . ."

"Oh, yes! I'm sure you'd like to get back to that darling fiancée of yours."

He turned, but not quickly enough to avoid another whack of her fan. The whalebone cracked against his arm, and Lancaster imagined his nerves as taut wires, popping with just that sound as they snapped apart. Darling fiancée indeed. He'd thought her darling enough until a few moments ago. Had thought her demure and shy and as pretty as she was intelligent.

"Demure," he growled, as he moved out of the crowded hall and closer to the front door. He'd made it past the densest of the crowd, but he wasn't free yet. Mr. Brandiss himself stood near the door, bidding farewell to the first of his guests to leave.

He'd not be as easy to fool as the rest of these people, and he was the last man Lancaster wished to speak with right now. Martin Brandiss was shrewd, smart, and almost preternaturally astute. Though perhaps not where his daughter was involved.

He made it past the cluster of Brandiss and his guests without notice, but there was no way to escape completely. He had to request his greatcoat and hat, had to wait for his driver to be summoned. Lancaster hardly even winced when he felt a hand slap his shoulder.

"Off so early, sir?"

Lancaster made himself chuckle as he turned to shake his future father-in-law's hand. "I've an appointment at my club, I'm afraid, but it was a truly delightful evening. Your wife is an estimable hostess."

"Never worry. She insisted that Imogene participate in all the planning. She'll make a fine viscountess."

"I've no doubt." She'd managed to pretend affection for a suitor she hated; Imogene would play the part of the Lady Lancaster with aplomb. A sudden idea sparked. If she backed out, he would have no choice. The decision would be beyond his control. The wedding could not go forward. "Mr. Brandiss, are you certain she is eager for this match?"

Brandiss's bushy white brows slowly lowered until Lancaster could hardly see his eyes. "What do you mean?"

"I mean . . ." His neck burned with strain, but he managed

to look merely concerned. "Your daughter has been quiet these past weeks. Since the betrothal dinner."

"Imogene is an obedient girl," Brandiss answered, his voice hardening to steel. "She is happy with this betrothal, my lord. She knows her duty."

Her duty. Yes, she had screamed something about duty while her lover tried to shut her up.

Duty. Despite the circumstances he'd still hoped for something more.

Instead of shouting at the man that his daughter was nothing close to happy, Lancaster inclined his head. "Of course. Please convey my farewells to your wife and daughter. As always, it's been a pleasure."

"My lord," Brandiss replied with a cursory bow. Yes, as Lady Avalon had said, Brandiss was every inch the gentleman despite that he was a glorified merchant. Lancaster had been disappointed at that, actually. He'd hoped he was marrying into a warmer, more relaxed family. But they couldn't afford to relax. They were a family on the rise; eccentricities, scandals, and even pleasure in life could not enter into the equation. Lancaster was merely a factor in the mathematics of society and wealth. His feelings did not come into play at all. He'd been foolish to imagine they should.

The springs of his carriage were in serious need of repair. Lancaster wondered how much longer they'd last as he stepped onto the street and heard the low groan of protest echoing from the underside of the box. The ride was uncomfortable, but at least it was no longer embarrassing. His groom had solved the problem of the peeling crest by scraping it off entirely and repainting the door. An obvious sign of poverty gone in a few strokes of a brush. If only the rest of the problem could be solved so easily.

"My lord," his butler murmured as he bowed Lancaster

inside. The young man's face was unlined, his brown hair unmarred by even a hint of gray. In other words, he was far too young to be a viscount's butler, but his services came cheap and he was eager and intelligent.

"Beeks," he offered as he swept out of the dark and into the hall. "Having a pleasant evening, I hope."

"Yes, sir. Very pleasant. Lord Gainsborough has arrived, sir. I've placed him in the White Room."

Gainsborough. Damnation. He wasn't in any position to cheer the old man up tonight.

"Sir? Shall I tell him you've arrived home?"

"No," Lancaster snapped, then immediately softened his voice. "No, I . . ." Hell. However unhappy he might be, he couldn't bring himself to send the lonely widower away. "Just give me a moment, Beeks. Trials of pleasant society and all that. Quite exhausting." He tossed his hat and coat to Beeks and strode down the hall toward the library. The brandy snifter awaited him on the small table next to his desk. Lancaster poured a glassful before he even took a seat.

The small stack of correspondence tipped from its pile when he collapsed into the chair. Lancaster picked idly through it as he made quick work of the glass of brandy. A short, friendly letter from a woman who'd once been his lover. A scrawled note from the Duke of Somerhart, curtly confirming that he and his new bride would attend the up-coming nuptials, though it was implied that only the duchess was actually *pleased* to attend. He managed a ghost of a smile at the thought.

Two creditors' notes, of course, though they'd gotten friendlier since his betrothal to the daughter of London's richest silk importer. Still, he dropped them immediately in the waste bin, then thought better of it and retrieved them to sit on the corner of his great-grandfather's desk as a re-minder. He was not free, and he could not afford to forget.

His father had inherited an estate teetering on the edge of

ruin and had quickly tipped it straight over the chasm. Not that he'd bothered to inform his heir of the matter. Lancaster poured himself another glass of brandy and picked up the last letter.

It was from the housekeeper of Cantry Manor, the smallest of his estates and the only self-sustaining one. God, he hoped it wasn't bad news about the sheep. Cantry Manor was the one estate he didn't worry over; he'd never even visited in the past decade. Lancaster downed another gulp of brandy and slit open the letter.

Throat burning with liquor, he read the words, his brain not quite understanding the meaning of them. They didn't make sense. But he read the letter again, and his heart sank as reality reared its ugly head.

I regret to inform you . . . I know you were once close to her . . .

Miss Cynthia Merrithorpe was dead.

Sad news. Very Sad. She could not have been more than two-and-twenty. What had killed her? An accident, a fever?

A sigh broke free of his throat. She'd been only eleven the last time he'd seen her, waving farewell as he left Cantry Manor behind. He hadn't seen his young neighbor since, so why did his guts feel suddenly knotted up with grief?

His fingers dug into the mess of his dark blond hair and pressed into his scalp. Perhaps it wasn't memories of Cynthia twisting his gut. Perhaps it was more that the letter was a sign that his world was on the descent and likely to continue in that direction.

You thought it could get no worse, foolish mortal, some wicked god was chuckling from above. Or actually . . . perhaps, *Your troubles cannot be compared to poor Cynthia Merrithorpe's, selfish man.* Lancaster felt chastened at the thought.

She'd never married. Never left Yorkshire. A short and lonely life.

He'd thought she would have grown into an attractive young woman. Thought her wise gaze and stubborn chin would fit a woman's face better than a child's. He must have been wrong. She'd died a spinster. But she'd been so lively in her youth. Honest and open, country-free and peaceful. Nothing, for instance, like Imogene Brandiss.

He grimaced at the thought and tossed back the last inch of liquid in the glass.

No, Miss Imogene Brandiss knew nothing of honesty, though the terrible things she'd shrieked had seemed honest enough. *A real man doesn't look to a woman for money! A real man works for it! Have you ever worked a day in your sorry life?*

Some weight inside him, some weight that had been slowly adding to itself over the past months, finally made its presence known. It pulled at his bones and tendons, threatening to collapse his body in upon him. Threatening to collapse his whole world.

Too much had gone into this, the plans were too far forward. His family's creditors had retreated to await the bounty brought by his marriage to an heiress. If he called off now . . .

He pictured crows picking at his eyes and knew he had no choice.

Something dark and overwhelming breached the surface calm he always displayed to the world. Something black and trembling with strength. Lancaster recognized it. He'd been well acquainted with it all those years ago. Rage. Fury. And fear. All of it coiled so tightly together that it seemed to have formed some heretofore unknown emotion. There was only one way to deal with it.

Rubbing a hand over his numb face, Lancaster took a deep breath. He ignored the harsh buzzing in his ears and tried to summon his customary smile. It didn't take hold the first time, nor the second, but eventually it felt in place on his lips, and he tugged the bellpull next to the desk.

A few minutes passed, though the buzzing stayed.

"Milord?"

"Please have a light supper sent to the White Room for Lord Gainsborough and inform him I shall be in for our chess match momentarily."

"Of course," the young man answered with a bow.

He would pretend good cheer, offer a happy evening for a man still grieving his dead wife, and pretend not to notice the darkness writhing inside his own soul. His smile slipped as Beeks turned away. The buzzing was only growing louder. "Wait."

"Milord?"

"I believe . . ." Lancaster started, the idea forming as he spoke. "I've received word . . ." The buzzing began to recede, so he rushed on. "A neighbor has died. I'll need to travel to Yorkshire to pay respects. It's only right."

Beeks nodded.

"You'll need to pack, of course, and make my excuses to Miss Brandiss's family." Eager as he was, Beeks was not predictably knowledgeable.

"How long do you expect to be gone, milord?"

The sound rushed back into his ears, louder than before. He shook his head, looked at the letter. The weight pulled him down, pressing him into his seat. The beast writhed against the pressure. How long? He'd say his wedding vows to an unwanted wife in only two months.

"Six weeks, I'd think."

"As you say, sir. And you'll leave . . . ?"

Now, he wanted to bark, but he didn't, of course. He only squinted thoughtfully and tried to tamp down the need to flee. "Tomorrow morning, I suppose."

"Yes, milord." Once Beeks had departed to start the frantic packing, Lancaster gave the letter one last glance, allow-ing himself the luxury of a few more deep breaths. He only needed a little time. Marriage would not be the worst thing he'd ever done for his family, after all. Not by far.

Once the surface of his soul was calm, Lancaster walked from the library and stepped into the White Room with a grin. The broad-faced man standing in front of the fireplace raised his head and his sad face broke into a smile. "Lancaster! It's bloody good to see you."

"And you as well, of course. Have you prepared for our match?"

"Prepared?" the older man snorted. "By dulling my wits with whisky? 'Tis the only preparation I need for a chess match with you."

Lancaster inclined his head. "Then I have you exactly where I want you, Gainsborough. I shall strike when you least expect it, pounce upon you like a doxy on a drunkard. Or a debutante on a duke, I suppose."

"Oh!" the old widower chortled, holding his gut against the laughter. "Oh, by God. You do cheer me up, young man. Every single time."

Lancaster chuckled and glanced toward the mantel clock. Twelve hours more and he would make his brief escape.

Chapter 2

Spring may have begun its arrival in London, but it hadn't yet touched the coast of Yorkshire. Freezing rain drummed against the carriage roof and tinged the air with ice, despite the brazier hidden beneath the seat. Lancaster watched his breath form mist before him, and marveled that he'd planned to stay here for six weeks.

His family had abandoned their smallest estate when Lancaster's father ascended to the title nearly ten years before. He'd never returned, had never even thought much about it, despite all the years spent here during his adolescence. It was cared for by Mrs. Pell, the housekeeper, and the rents were just enough to support the nominal upkeep. No thought required.

But, of course, it was deeper than that. He did not like to think about his time here, specifically the last two months. It was a testimony to just how desperate he'd been to escape London that he'd given no thought to the memories that might be exhumed here.

I am a man now, he told himself as he shifted in the hard seat. *Not a boy to run from nightmares.*

Just as anger began to rise like bile in his throat, the driver shouted something and the carriage began to slow. They'd arrived. Old Mrs. Pell would be out to greet him in a matter of moments.

For the first time since he'd departed, it occurred to him that Mrs. Pell would be grieving. Cynthia Merrithorpe had spent hours in her kitchen every day. Sometimes it had seemed as if she'd spent more time in his family's home than her own; if she hadn't been following Lancaster around the estate, then she'd been in the servants' quarters, trailing after Mrs. Pell like a shadow. Poor woman probably felt as if she'd lost a daughter.

The carriage slowed to a stop, sliding a little before the driver controlled it. Within seconds, the door opened to a blast of rain; clearly his driver didn't want to remain in the sleet any longer than necessary.

"Looks dark, milord. No one about."

"Lovely. Well, I'll let myself in, Jackson. You get the horses settled, then come 'round the kitchen for something hot."

"Yes, sir. My thanks, sir."

Lancaster steeled himself against the shock of the frozen rain before he stepped to the ground and dashed toward the wide front doors. He made it to the faint shelter of the doorway, but Jackson was pulling away before he realized the doors were bolted tight against him.

"Christ." A niggling suspicion that had begun to bounce around his head suddenly became solid and real. Beeks had neglected to inform Mrs. Pell that the viscount would soon be in residence. He could only hope that the housekeeper hadn't decided to take this week to visit her sister in Leeds.

"Well, there's no help for it," he muttered, and stepped back out into the deluge. By the time he made it around the square bulk of the manor, he was soaked through and half numb with cold. But the knob of the kitchen door turned easily in his hand, and then he was rushing into warmth and glowing light.

"Adam," a familiar voice called from the darkness of a short hallway, "if you're dripping rain all over my floor, you'd best be planning to clean it up. I'll not—"

When Mrs. Pell stepped into the kitchen, she looked up and gasped in surprise. Her shock did not turn to horror until Lancaster spoke.

"Good evening, Mrs. Pell. It seems my man in London has neglected to inform you of my imminent arrival. But here I am, all the same."

"Nick?" she whispered, causing a little shock to course through his veins. No one had called him Nick in years.

"Yes, it's me. Returned from the—" He caught himself just in time, and cleared his throat. "I apologize for catching you unawares, Mrs. Pell. I know the past two weeks must have been difficult for you, and now I have come to add to it."

She'd yet to recover; her lips were still parted in shock, her skin pale, and he'd begun to fear she'd simply fall over, though she looked as sturdy as ever. The laugh lines around her eyes had deepened certainly, her hair had gone grayer, but she wasn't as old as he'd remembered. Youth had a way of inflating age, it seemed. "Mrs. Pell?"

Her eyes blinked, and that finally seemed to release her from her trance. "My lord," she gasped, and fell into a slow curtsy. "My lord, I apologize. Please forgive me. I— Let me put the water on for tea, and then I'll open the parlor for you, if that will do for a few moments. I'll need to make up your bed and . . ."

"I'm sure the parlor sofa would be just lovely for the night, if—"

"Never say so!" she gasped. "A bare hour, sir. That's all I need." She snapped into motion, and the teapot was on the stove and warming before he could form another sentence. A blur of calico and white cambric flashed by, but Lancaster managed to snag one trailing end of an apron tie and tugged hard enough to distract her.

"Mrs. Pell." She'd stopped, but she hadn't turned toward him. She stood frozen, hands clasped tight in front of her, wisps of gray hair drifting from her coiled braid. Her shoulders rose and fell in deep, rapid breaths.

"Mrs. Pell, I want to offer my condolences. I know how close you were to Cynthia. Her death must have been a terrible shock."

Her breathing hitched, and he was sure that she would cry. He was reaching out to wrap a comforting arm around her when she nodded and stepped away. "Yes, sir. Thank you." A brief glance over her shoulder showed eyes bright with tears, but she blinked them away. "You are as kind now as you always were, milord." She brushed her hands over the apron as if she were dusting off flour. "Come now. Let's get you settled in the parlor so I can brew the tea."

"Hm. You wouldn't happen to have any of my father's special Irish whisky about, would you?"

Her face creased into a familiar smile. "Only for medicinal purposes, sir. But you're clearly on the verge of catching your death. I wouldn't want that on my conscience."

"You're an angel sent from heaven, Mrs. Pell. The best housekeeper a man could hope for."

The smile that had taken over her face fell away, and she dropped her clutched skirt and turned away. Lancaster had no choice but to follow. Any questions he had would wait until the morning.

A half-filled cup of tea. An empty glass tumbler. The crumbs of a vanished bit of bread and cheese. These things were scattered over the long table.

She drifted closer.

A man was stretched out along the dark green fabric of

the sofa, his feet crossed at the ankle, hands folded over his flat stomach. A strange visitor. A stranded traveler. Or . . .

No.

The cool air of the room pressed her white gown to her legs when she stopped in shock before him. It could not be. Not now, not when he could no longer help her.

But the golden waves of his hair were undeniably familiar in the flickering light of the fire, as were the fine straight line of his nose and the gentle curve of his mouth. She did not need to see the color of his eyes to know it was him.

"Nick," she whispered, the word falling from her unwilling mouth and stirring his eyelids.

She backed away, but not before his eyes opened, just for a moment, then lowered again in sleep.

Cynthia Merrithorpe turned and ran, disappearing into a dark shadow in the wall. If the man woke behind her, she did not know and did not care.

Nicholas had returned, the answer to her girlhood prayer . . . and she could not allow him to stay.

"What have you done?" Cynthia whispered as soon as Mrs. Pell stepped foot into the attic.

Mrs. Pell jumped, already shaking her head. "Nothing!"

Cyn clutched her arm. "You wrote to him, asked his help!"

"I did no such thing, missy. And how did you know of the viscount's arrival?"

"*Viscount,*" she muttered, irritated as ever by his new status in life. He'd been no more than a tall, humble boy when she'd known him. A tall, humble, handsome boy with impossibly sweet brown eyes. "I saw him," she finally admitted.

Mrs. Pell looked doubtfully toward the tiny gabled attic window.

"No, I was worried when you did not bring supper. I

feared you'd fallen ill. I had no idea I'd stumble over a grand lord asleep in the parlor."

"Tell me you didn't!"

"What?" Cynthia chewed thoughtfully on her thumbnail.

"*Stumble* over him!"

"No, of course not. He didn't see me." Hopefully.

"Well, for the love of God, no more sneaking about. Stay in the attic. Surely he'll leave soon. If he finds you here, he'll toss me out on my rump without a reference."

"He would not."

"And stop biting your nails. It's not ladylike."

Cynthia snorted at the woman's priorities. "You just told me to stay in the attic. I'm hidden away like a leprous mistress. Hardly ladylike."

Mrs. Pell nodded in distraction, but then her eyes focused on Cynthia's woolen socks and thick robe. "It's not fair, what's happened to you," she said, as she'd said every day since Cynthia's bloody arrival on her doorstep.

Cynthia stepped forward to take her hands and clasp them between her own. "I know I shouldn't have asked you to take me in. I'm sorry. Did you . . . Did you write to Nicholas and ask for his help?"

"I wrote, but only to inform him of your death." She crossed her arms, only succeeding in making herself look more guilty. "It would've seemed strange otherwise! And he's not Nicholas, anymore, sweeting. He's Viscount Lancaster."

"Yes," she agreed quickly, and met Mrs. Pell's eyes straight on. "He's not Nicholas anymore. And we'd do well to remember that. We must get rid of him as quickly as possible, or he'll ruin us both."

"Cynthia, you're plan is mad, child. And he doesn't seem so changed. Perhaps he'd—"

"No. Even if he didn't turn me over to my stepfather, there's nothing he can do to help me. I need him gone."

Mrs. Pell didn't nod, but she pressed her lips together and
didn't voice whatever objection she had.

"Promise you won't tell him. If he sent me back to my
family . . ."

The old housekeeper, more a mother to her than her own
mother had ever been, finally gave a curt nod. "I'll not tell him.
But we will discuss this again, missy. Don't you doubt it."

Cynthia held her tongue, implying consent, but she had
no intention of discussing Viscount Lancaster and his imag-
inary usefulness. If she had anything to do with it, he
wouldn't be around long enough to unpack.